LITTLE MAN'S DREAM

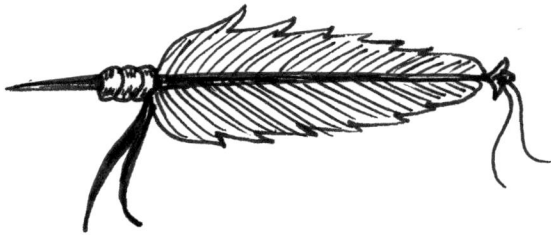

Enjoy "THE DREAM"

Lonnie Magee
'08

LITTLE MAN'S DREAM

❀

A Novel

Lonnie Magee

iUniverse, Inc.
New York Lincoln Shanghai

Little Man's Dream

iUniverse books may be ordered through booksellers or by contacting:

iUniverse
2021 Pine Lake Road, Suite 100
Lincoln, NE 68512
www.iuniverse.com
1-800-Authors (1-800-288-4677)

Because of the dynamic nature of the Internet, any Web addresses or links contained in this book may have changed since publication and may no longer be valid.

This is a work of fiction. All of the characters, names, incidents, organizations, and dialogue in this novel are either the products of the author's imagination or are used fictitiously.

ISBN: 978-0-595-48537-6 (pbk)
ISBN: 978-0-595-60632-0 (ebk)

Printed in the United States of America

Acknowledgements

❀

Thanks to everyone who helped me get this book to the publisher.

Special thanks:

To my wife Lynne, who helped with the proof reading and put up with me while I did the rewrites

To Christy "Nevada Slick" Sheppler, without her computer skills this and my other three books, would have been a much larger challenge.

To friends, both new and old who have become fans of my books.

Last, but certainly not least, my dear departed friend
Jeannie Sutton Hogue.
Jeannie, author of the "Jesse Statham Mystery Series" will be missed. The late night calls and laughs are something I'll not forget. Friends such as Jeannie are Treasures.

Introduction

❀

This book is dedicated to all the little "Mom and Pop" racehorse breeders who spend a lifetime dreaming of breeding that one great horse.

My late wife Joan and I were fortunate enough to have raised an Oklahoma State Champion Thoroughbred. He was our first thoroughbred.

The stallion "Accomplished Lover" may have not been the derby champion on that first Saturday in May. But, to us, was a champion in every sense of the word.

In 1985, Lover gave us the "Little Man's Dream".

In eleven starts as a three year old he had eleven wins, four of which were stakes. He also set four track records.

One day soon, I plan on telling the whole story of Lover. The true story will read like fiction but will be the truth.

So reader, remember Little Man's Dreams do come true.

Lonnie Magee
"07"

CHAPTER 1

※

I walked down the side of the dusty gravel road in the early morning sun. My run-over boot heels threw small puffs of dust as I took each long determined step.

I was leaving the ranch, as my father called it. The eight hundred and fifty acres of sand and mesquite wasn't anything to brag about. Everything about the place was run down. I'd tried to keep things together as best I could, but with my father drinking up everything I made breaking horses, it had been hopeless.

A customer would come pick up a horse and my father would collect the training fee. He would leave and wouldn't show up again until the money ran out. Sometimes he was gone for a week or more.

Last night he'd come home broke and not near drunk enough. He'd hit me while I was asleep in bed with a cast iron skillet because his supper wasn't ready. Never mind it was one o'clock in the morning. He'd hit me several times before I was awake enough to try and defend myself.

I had somehow managed to get out of my bed and get out of the room. My father in his drunken state tried to catch me. He had stumbled over a stool and fell to the floor unconscious.

I had taken a look to see if my father was breathing then walked to the closet and took a duffel bag the army had sent my brother's things home in after he'd been killed in an training accident. I began throwing everything I owned into the bag, which wasn't much. I grabbed my worn out hat and went outside where I sat down and made my decision. I was leaving this time for good. I'd wait for daylight and maybe be able to catch a ride with one of the oil field trucks going north. I figured my father would sleep late like he did after every one of his drinking bouts. I'd caught rides before when I was trying to get to horse sales where I made money riding horses in the sale ring. I had a reputation for making a bad horse look good in the sale ring. This was money I used to buy food and the few clothes I had. I did my own laundry and tried to look as neat as possible when I went to school. I might have been poor but I was always clean.

My brother and I did all the work with the horses and our father made sure we did it. He was always pushing us to get the job done faster. Finally my older brother had had all he could take and run off and joined the army. He had lied about his age and was gone when our father got home from one of his drinking trips. When our father had returned and found out what had happened he had refused to go after his son. He said the army would make a man of him.

Nine months later we got word that my brother had been killed in a training accident.

They wanted to know where my father wanted the body shipped. He had told the Army they could bury the boy wherever they wanted. He didn't have any money to do it. The boy had run off and it wasn't his problem.

That had been almost four years ago. I had worked even harder, not wanting to get beaten by my father. Last night had been the last straw. My father had been gone for more than a week. The day before one of the owners had shown up and watched me work his horse. He had been pleased and had paid me the bill and taken his horse home. I had the four hundred dollars in my jeans pocket. I had no idea where I was headed and didn't care. I would be called a thief by my father but didn't care. I had wages coming and my father had never paid me more than a few dollars at a time. With the money I'd be able to eat until I found myself a job, a job that would pay. I had to finish my schooling. I'd managed to maintain a solid B average while riding horses every evening. School activities had been out of the question. I had horses to ride even if it meant riding after dark.

I was known around the area sale barns as "The Kid" and had almost forgotten my real name William Dale Patton. William, as my mother called me. I felt the money in my pocket and kept walking. When I reached the road I sat the bag down and took the money from my pocket and put all but twenty dollars in my boot top. I picked up the bag as I saw a truck coming from Amarillo and stuck out my thumb.

The truck turned out to be a milk truck and slowed as it approached me.

"Where you headed youngster?"

"North right now sir, how far are you going?"

"I can take you as far as Dumas. You might be able to catch a grain truck from there. I know a few of the boys."

"That would be great. I crawled up into the truck and the adventure began. I never once took a backward glance.

I listened to the man talk and before we reached Dumas I knew all about the man. He had two twin boys who played football and a daughter who rode race-horses. She had left the week before to go to the track in Raton New Mexico. That was when the idea struck me. I might find a job at the track. If there was one thing I knew it was horses.

When we pulled into Dumas the driver, Art pulled into the parking lot of a small café. I saw several large grain trucks in the parking lot. Art went inside the café and a few moments later came out with a gentleman he introduced to me.

"Bill, this is Fred Bennett. He can give you a ride as far as Clayton New Mexico. If you're planning on going to Raton you can probably find a ride from there."

"Thanks Art, I really appreciate your help. Mr. Bennett, I'm ready when you are."

Before we reached Clayton I knew everything there was to know about Fred. His wife, their three kids, what they ate, and what sports they played. I even knew what T.V. programs they watched. I had to admit his talk made the trip go by quickly. When we pulled into Clayton he took me to a café where several horse trailer rigs were parked.

"Bill, you come with me. I think I know one of those boys who drives one of those rigs. I'll see if he can give you a ride up to the track."

I followed Fred into the café and waited while he talked to a gentleman sitting at a booth. Fred waved for me to come over.

"Bill, this feller is Spunky Davis. He's going to the track in Raton. Spunky is a trainer and may be able to help you find a job."

"You looking for work son?"

"Yes sir, are you needing any help?"

"You know anything about Thoroughbred horses?"

"No sir, but I know horses. I've been breaking and training horses most of my life."

"You can ride a rank horse?"

"Yes sir, been doing just that for a lot of folks. That's one reason I'm looking for a job. I got tired of riding bad horses, thought I'd like to work with a few good ones."

"You know how to wrap legs?"

"No sir, but I'm willing to learn if someone will teach me."

"Bill, I'm going to make you an offer. I'll let you stay in my tack room for a couple of days. If you work out I'll get you a groom's license. Does that sound fair to you?"

"Sounds fair to me sir."

"Do you have a drivers license and social security card?"

"I do sir, but I don't have a car. Is there anything else I need?"

"How much do you weigh Bill?"

"About one thirty sir. Maybe a little less."

"That's light enough to be an exercise rider. I may be able to get you a few rides so that you can make some extra money. Are you still in school?"

"Yes sir, I'll be a senior this fall."

"You're planning on finishing your schooling?"

"Yes sir I am. I know I have to have an education. I won't be able to ride rank horses all my life nor do I want to."

"That's good, a feller needs an education to get along in this world. Have you had lunch?"

"No sir, I've been traveling since daylight this morning."

Spunky waved the waitress over and ordered me the special of the day.

"You better eat up Bill. It may be late before we get a chance to eat again."

While I waited for my meal I found out that Spunky was from Oklahoma. He had a small string of claiming horses along with a couple of two year olds. The two year olds were colts he and his wife had bred and raised. I finished my meal and thanked him.

"Thank you for the meal sir."

"Call me Spunky, Bill. If we're going to be working together we don't need any formality."

"Spunky it is. When do we leave?"

"Right now, you got your things in that bag?"

"Yes sir."

"Throw it in the back of the truck while I check on the horses."

I threw my bag in the back of the truck then walked around the trailer to see what the horses looked like. The vents were all open to let in what breeze there was to cool the horses while the trailer was parked. Spunky began calling out the names of the horses as he checked on each one.

"This one in front is a colt we call Gray Light. He's by Fly Away Bob and out of an own daughter of Zip Stream. He's not near ready to run yet but needs to get that way. I sent him to a feller to break and I think it worked out to be a draw. He has a mind of his own and sure enough needs work. Think you can do anything with him?"

"I'll give it my best Spunky. He's sure enough a good looking horse."

"That he is, but he has to earn his way or someone else will own him. My horses have to work. They don't work and I go hungry."

"I can understand that Spunky. I had a nice mare a year or so ago. She was a good looking thing but had a bad habit. She would get mad and lay down. It took me a month or so to figure out what her problem was. Once I figured out what was wrong she made a wonderful horse."

"What happened to her Bill?"

"My father sold her."

"The mare really belonged to him?"

"No sir, I had broke a sure enough bad horse and took her as payment. My father said we needed the money and I sure enough couldn't argue with him."

"I guess we'd better get moving. We're a good two hours out of Raton and it's all up hill from here on."

We got in the truck and pulled out of the parking lot onto the highway. Spunky had been right, we did seem to be going uphill. Half way to Raton Spunky shut off the air conditioning and rolled his window down. I was shocked to feel the cool air that streamed into the cab of the big truck.

"It gets a lot cooler up here at night. I've seen it snow on opening day a time or two since I've been coming up here."

"How long have you been coming up here Spunky?"

"This will make the eleventh year Bill."

The high plains desert fascinated me. I saw cattle along with herds of antelope on both sides of the road. The black lava rock jutted out of the soil in various spots. Spunky had pointed out an old volcano off the east side of the highway as we rolled north. I got a glimpse of the snow-covered mountains far ahead of us. Spunky explained to me that the track sat at the base of the mountains I was seeing in the distance. He told me his wife Patty would be up in a couple of days in their motor home. They had a space rented in a trailer park for the length of the summer meet. As we traveled north I noticed that there was a brown paper sack sitting in the floorboard. It was filled with candy wrappers and such. It showed Spunky didn't like things messy around him. I figured we'd get along fine.

He explained that the meet didn't start for another three and a half weeks. He told me the horses needed the time to adjust to the thin mountain air. He told me about learning this the hard way. He had shown up the first year and not allowed for the thin air. His horses had run the first part of the races like he figured but just fell back towards the end. Another trainer told him what was happening, it had taken him another three weeks to get his colts adjusted to the thin air. After they became accustomed to the thin air he had had a good meet and won his share of the races.

"I know what you mean Spunky, a couple of boys brought me a couple of horses they were going to take elk hunting. They wanted me to get the horses in shape. They later told me the horses did fine but when they had to walk they wore out in a hurry."

"It sure makes a difference, I'm considered a flatlander up here."

"Where is your place in Oklahoma?'

"My place is just west of the town called Elk City."

"I've heard of it, they raise some fine Quarter horses over that way."

"They sure do, a couple of the boys just west have made quite a reputation for themselves."

"They sure have, they always seem to have some fine horses running in all the big races."

"You'll like Raton, Bill it's small but it's a pretty little town. The folks are all nice and welcome us every year. We bring in a lot of money for the town. Patty and I look forward to coming back here every year. The purse money is decent and if a man knows his string and where to put them he can make a decent living. We don't have the quality of horses to go to the big tracks. We raise a couple of colts every year and try them when they get to be two year olds. A friend of mine foals my mares out over near Clayton, that way they are New Mexico bred. They have a good breeders program here and if you run New Mexico bred colts you can pick up some real good money when you win a race."

We were nearing the outskirts of Raton and it had my attention.

"First time up this way Bill?"

"Yes sir it is. My father did all the traveling. He kept me pretty busy at home."

Spunky had let the subject drop. He somehow felt I didn't want to talk about my home life. He figured he'd give me some time and if I wanted to talk he'd listen. Otherwise it wasn't his business. All he wanted was for me to make a hand and be a help for the upcoming meet. Somehow, I think he felt I just might end up being a good hand.

As we pulled into Raton I noticed the way Spunky handled the big trailer on the city streets. He turned the corners slowly and was careful not to sling the horses around inside the trailer. He turned off the main road and pointed out the track grandstands that sat at the end of the street. We approached a gate that had a uniformed guard. Spunky spoke to the guard who welcomed him back and asked about his horses. They visited for a minute and then we drove through the gate and parked the truck beside a large barn. A sign said "No Parking".

"Don't worry about the sign, Bill. We can park here until we get unloaded. Now let's go inside and see what we have to work with."

I looked at my watch and saw it was close to four o'clock. I figured we had a lot of work to do and followed Spunky into the barn. People seemed to be running everywhere but things seemed to get done. Spunky had signed our names on a clipboard at the gate and now I understood why. With all these people running around someone had to know who was here.

"Folks are trying to get their chores done up for the day, Bill. We feed at four in the morning and work the first of our string at daylight. We have to be off the track by ten so the track crew can get the track worked for the races in the afternoon. It will be a little confusing to you at first but you'll get the hang of things soon enough."

There was a bale of straw outside the stalls that had Spunky's name on them.

"Bill, start spreading the straw in the stalls. I'll get the gate and bucket hardware out of the trailer and get them put in while you're bedding the stalls. We'll get the buckets and feed tubs out of the trailer when we're through."

I took my pocket knife out and after I threw the bale of straw into the stall I cut the strings on the bale and began to spread the straw around. I finished the last stall as Spunky was screwing the last of the eyebolts into place on the sides of the stalls. The water and feed tubs would be hung on them with double ended snaps. When Spunky finished we went to the trailer and got the water buckets and feed tubs. We quickly hung them in place and again went to the trailer for the web gates that would go across the front of the stalls of the mares and geldings. Spunky had a full steel gate for the gray stud. Too many folks were around and too many mares not to have a steel gate on his stall. I helped Spunky hang the gate and waited for instructions.

"Bill, let's get them off the trailer and get them settled and fed."

"I followed Spunky out to the trailer and took the first horse to the stall Spunky had pointed out. Soon all the horses were in the stalls except the stud. I opened the side door on the trailer and threaded a lead chain through the stud's halter. When I had it adjusted to my satisfaction I asked Spunky to release the panel that kept the stud in place. I began backing the stud out of the trailer, but when he had all four feet on the ground he tried to rear. With a short jerk on the chain I quickly had him under control and led him into the barn and put him into his stall. I removed the lead strap from his halter and left him in his stall. I closed and locked the steel gate and put the latch in place. Spunky stood by and was watching me.

"That's not the first stud you've ever handled is it Bill?"

"No it isn't Spunky. I've broke and handled a bunch of them over the last few years."

"I'm beginning to believe I may have hired a good hand back down the highway. Let's get them fed Bill. I for one could eat a bite myself."

Spunky and I began carrying the feed he had brought up with him into the feed room which joined the tack room that Spunky and I would sleep in together until his wife Patty came up with their motor home. Spunky began to measure out the feed for the various horses. He told me he would make a list in case he was gone and I had to feed without him. We took the feed to the horses and watched as they each began to eat their ration. I took the last bucket to the stud and after opening his door I walked to his feed tub and dumped his grain into it. My back was turned to him for only a split second but that was all he was waiting for. He laid back his ears and charged. I side stepped at the last moment and hit the young stud square between his ears with the side of my hand. The young stud suddenly stopped and shook his dazed head. I took his halter in one hand and his ear with the other. I backed him into the corner of his stall and said whoa in a soft voice. The colt was confused and stood still. I put my hand under his jaw and led him up to his feed tub then walked out of his stall. I still had water buckets to fill.

"Bill, where in the world did you learn that trick?"

"A neighbor of mine spent a bunch of time in China and picked up the trick while he was there. He taught me a few things a few years ago."

"Seems as though you've not forgotten anything he taught you. That was the neatest thing I ever saw."

"It worked but he still has a lesson or two to learn. I'll work with him tomorrow after we finish chores if it's all right with you?"

"Bill, you have full charge of him. I think he may have just met his match. Now let's get them watered."

"I can handle the watering Spunky. Why don't you go get us a couple of burgers? It's my time to buy."

"I'll unhook the trailer and get gone. Keep your money in your pocket. I always feed my help the first day. By the way Bill you're hired.

"I'm hired? You mean I'm hired to work for you?"

"That's what I mean. I think it will be worth the pay just to see you and the stud reach an understanding."

Spunky left to park the trailer and get us something to eat. He sat my duffle bag and his suitcase down by the door before he left. I took the water hose and watered all the horses. When I got to the stud's stall he backed up into the corner and watched me. He wasn't sure what I had done or how I had done it but he was going to watch me. At least I had his attention. I coiled and hung up the hose after draining it and went to carry our bags into the tack room. Spunky had left two canvas cots and a couple of blankets by the door with our bags while I was watering the horses. I took the cots to the tack room and set them up. I carried our bags and the blankets in and sat them down. Spunky could pick whatever cot he wanted. I had a job and I was happy. I felt better than I had felt in a long time.

When Spunky returned, we ate a burger and fries and washed it down with a soda as Spunky called it. When we finished we walked out to the trailer and began unloading the tack we would need for the rest of the race meet. It took two trips but when we finished, the bridles, blankets, saddles and such were all in their places in the tack room. Spunky took a blanket and threw it on one of the cots then took two of horse blankets and laid them on the cots.

"These things will feel real good before daylight Bill. The nights get a little bit cool about daylight."

"From the chill in the air now I'm thinking you may be right. I'll probably be needing my sweatshirt in the morning."

"A light jacket will feel good if you have one Bill."

"I've got a light windbreaker in my bag. I'll dig it out first thing in the morning."

The alarm went off at four the next morning. We quickly dressed and I did dig out the sweatshirt and windbreaker. Spunky began to dish up the feed for the horses. I went outside and began to empty and wash out the water buckets. When they were all cleaned I hung them in their stalls and after hooking up the hose began to refill them. I had just finished when Spunky handed me the stud's feed and took the hose. I took the feed and after unlocking the stall door walked in. I pointed my finger at the stud who backed up and waited in the corner of his stall. I poured his grain into his feed tub then walked over and put my hand under his jaw and led him to his feed. He'd learned something the day before but I still didn't trust him. He and I would try and reach an understanding later this morning. I left the stall and locked the stall door.

"Bill, he's not sure about you. You got the better of him and he just hasn't figured things out yet."

"That's true Spunky. That's why I want to work him in the round pen this morning. I've got him on the ropes and don't want him to get set."

"I can see what you mean. We better get started mucking the stalls. We'll get ourselves some breakfast when we're through. The racing office will be open by then and we can get you your license. You'll have to have it to work here on the track."

"Where do we eat here at the track?"

"At the track kitchen. Every track has one Bill. The food is good and it is usually cheaper than eating in town. They do a good business with the folks on the backside and it's handy for everyone.

"Normally I work my horses first and then eat, but after traveling all day on the trailer I'm going to give them the day off."

"Don't change your schedule because of me Spunky. I can wait."

"I'm not changing a thing Bill. I simply think the colts need a day off."

"Good enough then. Let's get the stalls mucked. That burger we had last night is wearing mighty thin."

I mucked stalls while Spunky checked the horses' legs. When he finished he went to work helping me. We were finished a short time later. We washed up in cold water before going to the track kitchen. It was located in a small building near the barns. I was shocked to find it neat and clean. Better yet, the food was good and there was plenty of it. Spunky introduced me to several folks while we ate our meal. When we were finished we walked around the grandstands and watched the horses being worked on the track. At first I was confused but Spunky explained to me how things worked. Horses that were being jogged stayed on the outside rail. Horses that were being given a light work stayed in the middle of the track. Horses that were being given a fast work were down on the inside rail. What had looked like total confusion suddenly made sense. It was really a very organized operation. With this system thirty horses or more could be on the track at once.

A short time later I followed Spunky to the track office where I filled out the necessary paperwork, and then was fingerprinted and photographed. The folks in the racing office all seemed to like Spunky and told me I'd hired on with a good trainer. I had thanked them and said I also thought I'd done well. Spunky had some paper work to fill out so I told him I'd go back to the barn and keep an eye on things.

I walked into the barn and decided to take a good look at all the horses in Spunky's string. I'd fed and cared for them but hadn't had a chance to look them over the way I wanted to. The first was a three year old filly who had had a fair year for Spunky the year before. She had made a little over twenty thousand. She was a good looking filly with a good long shoulder and hip. She was well balanced and had a beautiful head. I wish she had a little bigger eye but not knowing that much about Thoroughbreds I figured I'd better wait and make a decision on that after I had a chance to learn more about them.

The second horse was a brown gelding that Spunky had said was a four year old he had claimed at the end of the meet. I had no idea what a claimer was and had told Spunky so. He had explained the rating system to me. Claimers were horses that most of the time were beyond their prime racing years or had never shown enough racing talent for their owners to keep them in training. A horse that couldn't win cost too much money for an owner to keep. They would put them in claiming races where any other trainer on the track could put a claim tag in the box before the race and regardless of whether the horse won or lost the horse belonged to him for the claiming price of the race. Some trainers would gamble they could help the horse and improve his performance. If it worked they made money. If it didn't they had wasted a lot of time and money. Spunky had explained to me it was the claimers who really made up most of the races. There were several divisions of claiming horses, everything from five thousand to one hundred thousand. Spunky's gelding had been running for five thousand when he had claimed him. He had an injury to an ankle and Spunky had had it operated on. He felt the gelding was almost ready to go and should improve a lot from the previous year. He called the horse Habit. It was not the horse's registered name but few trainers used their horse's real name.

The next division was called allowance horses. These horses could not be claimed and were of a better quality and had more racing ability. However, there were fewer of them and therefore the races they entered were for bigger purses. Spunky had said he'd had two allowance horses in his ten years of coming up here to the track.

The last division was stakes horses. Less than one percent of the horses born in a year would ever be good enough to become a stakes horse. Every track had a few stakes races but there were not that many of them. Some of the stakes horses would enter an allowance race to try and steal a pot as Spunky put it.

The third horse in the string was a bay mare that had been in Spunky's string for a couple of years. She was a good solid claiming mare and as Spunky had put it, she gave a hundred percent every time you put her in a race. I liked the mare because she had a big, kind, sort of an eye. She was a sprint mare and had a lot of muscle and reminded me of the Quarter horses I had grown up around.

The fourth horse was a two year old gelding that Spunky had bred and raised but had not shown that much talent as of yet. Spunky was rather upset with the colt but hoped he would make a turnaround when he was put in a racing situation. He explained to me that some of the horses he'd had in the past were lazy until race day. They didn't like to work but they loved to run in a race. I looked the horse over and liked what I saw. I hoped for Spunky's sake that he did compete when race time came. He was called Slinker.

The fifth horse was another mare that Spunky had in training for a friend. The mare was a three year old and had only had a few races the year before but had shown some promise. Spunky had hopes for her this year. The mare was a nice looking mare but just didn't have that look in her eye that I looked for in a horse.

We had an empty stall between the stud and the mare. I'd ask Spunky about shifting the gelding and mare around. Keeping a mare next to a stud was not a good idea as far as I was concerned. Besides I'd like to have a gelding next to the stud for company.

I walked to the stud's stall and looked him over carefully. I liked everything about him. He had a good long shoulder and hip. He had enough muscle in his hindquarters to power him along. His head was a thing of beauty with a big eye that seemed to demand you to look at him.

"Big man, you and I are going to get along. We'll go to the round pen and get better acquainted this morning. You're way too fine a horse to just run as a claimer."

"I think so too, Bill. You ready to go to work on him?"

I'd not heard Spunky walk up behind me.

"I'm not crazy Spunky. I just talk to all my horses. I believe the stud is something special and I've just got to figure out how to get him going in the right direction."

"Well let's get started then. After that little trick you used on him the other day, I want to see what else you have up your sleeve."

I got the stud's halter from the tack room and put it on him. Spunky held the stall door open for me to take him out. The stud was full of himself but gave me no trouble on the way out to the round pen. I waited for Spunky to close the gate behind me then turned the stud loose.

He spun away and began to trot around the pen. I walked to the center of the pen and watched as he seemed to float across the ground. I noticed that Spunky had a friend outside the round pen who was watching what was going on. I forgot about them and went to work on the stud. I took the lead rope I had used to lead the stud to the round pen and began to swing it around my head. The stud seemed to explode and began to run around the pen. I watched until he began to settle down to a canter then stepped across the pen and made him reverse direction. I swung the rope and the stud again exploded into a run. I watched as he worked around the pen and began to slow down. I slowly swung the rope and kept him moving. The horse was beginning to work up a light sweat on his neck. I again cut him off and made him reverse his direction. I began talking to him and noticed he was starting to listen to me. After another round I coiled the rope in my hand and stood still. I was waiting for the stud to stop. When he did stop I turned my back and took a couple of steps away from him and stopped.

I waited a moment then turned to face him and again uncoiled the rope and swung it above my head. Again the stud ran around the sandy pen but this time he was more in control of himself. He had worked the edge off and was now having to work. I could almost hear him thinking as he cantered around the round pen. Again I cut him off and made him go in the opposite direction. Sweat was now showing on his neck and shoulders. I slowly swung the rope and asked him to keep moving. Once again I coiled the rope and waited for the stud to stop. A round or so later the stud stopped and turned to look at me. I again turned my back and walked a few steps away from him. I waited a moment and was rewarded when the stud pushed my back with his nose. He was mine!

I took the lead rope and snapped it on his halter then put the loose rope over his neck and tied the loose end into his halter for a loop rein. I stepped around to the side of the stud and crawled up on his back. I pulled his head around and rode him around the pen for a round or two then turned him towards the gate. I slid off his back and asked Spunky to open the gate.

"Bill, I don't know how, even after watching you, but I know I just watched something special. Another week around you and the stud will be drinking coffee and reading the paper."

"We'll see about that Spunky, he just needed to be shown he wasn't the boss of everything. Now that we have his attention I think he's ready to start galloping. You might want to put someone on him who knows more about it than I do though."

"I'll do just that. We need to start getting him in condition so we can give him a try. Bill, I want to introduce you to a friend of mine. This is Dick Sheppler. I've known him for about thirty years. He is the person who talked me into coming up here the first year.

"Pleased to meet you sir. Any friend of Spunky's is a friend of mine."

"Bill, just call me Dick. All of my friends do. I've got a gelding I'd like you to look at and see if you have any ideas about how to cure him. I claimed him last year and I still haven't been able to get him into the gates. Would you take a look at him?"

"I'd be glad to Dick, just as soon as I have the stud bathed and put away. That is if Spunky doesn't mind."

"Mind, Bill I'm going to go with you. This might be something fun to watch. Besides when we finish with the stud all we have to do is hang the other horses on the walker for and hour or so. Dick, we'll be up to your barn in an hour or so."

"I'll have a few cold sodas on ice when you all get there."

Spunky led the way back to the barn where we cross tied the stud and gave him a cool bath. As I sponged his back he began to try and nuzzle me with his nose. I rubbed his ears and watched as he slowly began to close his eyes. I'd just found another way to get along with the stud. It might be what turned things around sometime in the future. When I finished washing him I began walking him around the barn like I had seen the other people in the barn do. Thirty minutes or so later the stud was dry and ready to be put back into his stall. Spunky came out of the tack room with some liniment, cotton and bandages. When I had the stud in his stall, Spunky began to rub the stud's legs with the liniment, while explaining to me how it was to be done. Later he took the wide roll of cotton and began wrapping it around the stud's legs. When he had the proper thickness he tore it off the roll and then took the elastic bandage and wrapped it over the cotton. He tied the strings at the end of the bandage and stood up.

"Your turn Bill. You rub and wrap the other leg. I'll help you if you need it."

I went to work on my first leg wrap and found that I liked the smell of the liniment and enjoyed putting the leg wraps on. I remembered what Spunky had told me and made sure I put the leg wraps on correctly and didn't have them too tight. When I finished I looked at Spunky for his approval.

"You did a fine job Bill. Let's hang the other horses on the walker then we'll go over to Dick's barn and see what you can come up with for him to try."

We led the horses out to the walker and snapped them on. Spunky turned the walker switch on and we watched the horses being led around in a circle. When it appeared everything was settled down we quickly mucked out their stalls and made sure their hay nets were full. When we finished we went to the walker and returned the horses to their stalls.

"If you're ready Bill we'll wander over to Dick's barn and see what can be done with his gelding. I remember when he claimed the horse everyone in his barn laughed at him. Now if we can figure the little feller out maybe folks won't be laughing quite as hard."

We walked up past four of the track barns that I saw were mostly full and then walked into Dick's barn. He was sitting on a straw bale outside his tack room reading a paperback western.

"Reading a bang, bang, shoot'em up Dick?"

"You bet. I just love these things. Makes me want to go back in time."

"When you're finished I'd like to read it Dick. I have a couple of books in my bag. When I'm finished with them I'll swap with you."

"Sounds good to me Bill. There is a store in town where we can swap them after we have read them. By the end of summer we'll have read about everything he'll have in his store."

"Sounds like a plan Dick. I'll bring them up after I'm finished with them. Now where is this gelding and what does he do?"

"I'll put a halter on him and show you Bill."

Dick got a halter and led a nice looking bay horse out of a stall. We followed him as he led the gelding out of the barn and down the side of the track to the starting gates. When he got close to the gates the bay horse began to throw a fit. It was plain to see he wanted no part of the starting gates.

"Dick, do you have any idea why he hates the gates so much?"

"Feller who had him touched him with a hot shot. He's been a nut case ever since."

"I can't say I would blame him."

I looked further down the track and saw an old set of starting gates parked off to one side of the track. I had an idea.

"Dick, does anyone use those starting gates?"

"Haven't been used in three or four years Bill. Why?"

"Well if you can find a half dozen panels or so I'd build a small lot and connect it to the gates. I'd put his feed and water inside the gate, maybe half way. If he wants a drink and wants to eat he'll have to go in them. After a week or so he should be over his problem. It's just an idea. I don't know if it will work or not."

"Spunky, Jim has a half dozen panels on the side of his trailer. Let's go see if we can borrow them."

A short time later we had the small lot completed. It took the three of us another half hour to get the gelding into the lot. It was near lunch time and Dick informed us he was buying us lunch. We followed him to the track kitchen. Afterwards I got to thinking. I was really enjoying my work and I sure enough was eating better.

When Spunky and I got back to our barn we found the straw truck parked outside. Spunky paid the man for the straw bales we would need for the next couple of days. I began stacking the bales in the empty stall and understood why the stall had been left empty next to the stud. Spunky said the hay man would be around the next morning so the stall would be full and the stud wouldn't be able to see the mare anyway.

"Bill, we've got everything done up so I think I'm going to take myself a nap. We'll clean and oil the bridles and such this evening. You can take a nap or just do whatever you want for a couple of hours."

"I think I'll just wander around and look at everything Spunky. I've not had a chance to see much of anything. I'll be back in a while.

Spunky went into the tack room and closed the door. I began to walk around and look at things. I was amazed at how things were getting done. People were running everywhere but things were getting done. I watched as folks began setting out flowers. Others were painting fences and washing the seats in the grandstand. The barns were beginning to fill up just like Spunky had said. When I got back to our barn I found a bunch of new folks moving in across the aisle from us. I helped lead horses off the trailer and put them in their stalls.

The folks who were from Texas thanked me for my help. I went over to our tack room just as Spunky opened the door. I went into the tack room and gathered the bridles that needed to be cleaned and went to work.

"Bill, you're making a fine hand. I'm glad I hired you. By tomorrow a half dozen trainers will be offering you a job."

"Why would they do that Spunky? I've got a lot to learn about the race horse business. I don't think anyone will be asking me to go to work. Besides, you hired me and you'll have to fire me first."

"That's not likely Bill. You've shown me you have a good head on your shoulders and you know a lot about horses. You've made more progress with the stud in two days than the trainer I had working him did in three months. Bill, I don't know anything about you but I know I like you and one day when you want to talk about it I'll be here."

"Spunky, right now I'm just trying to get things straightened out myself. All I do know about is horses. I've broke several hundred head and I've learned the trade the hard way. What I will tell you is that I don't smoke, drink, steal, or cheat and I'll never lie to you."

"A man can't ask for more Bill, but if you need help getting things sorted out I'd be glad to listen. If you're about finished with those bridles we'll do chores. Do you happen to like Mexican food?"

"You bet I do. There is a Mexican place back home that is great. Some of my clients have taken me to eat there a few times."

"Well tonight we're going to eat Mexican at a place up here that I think is pretty good. I think we deserve a good meal tonight. Our breakfast will be a little small in the morning. We'll have coffee and doughnuts while the horses eat. I want to work the whole string and see how they react to the track and all the other horses. The two year olds are the only ones I'm worried about. I hired a boy to ride them for a day or two or until you learn how to ride an exercise saddle. Ever ridden an exercise saddle Bill?"

"No I haven't. I've never had the chance to try one. I've watched the jockeys at the exercise track ride but could not figure out how in the world they rode those little saddles like they do."

"It's something anyone can do Bill. All it takes is some time and some athletic ability. I've watched you and I think we'll get you started real soon. If the boy doesn't get along with the stud you may have to work him until he is ready for a jockey to ride him."

"I'll try, Spunky, if you've got the patience to teach me."

We went to the Mexican place Spunky had talked about and were treated like family. The owner and Spunky were old friends. He asked about Spunky's wife and called her by name. Spunky introduced me to the gentleman and told him I was his new assistant trainer. The gentleman asked about his string of horses and wanted to know about Patty's gray colt. Spunky told him the colt was at the track and that I was in charge of him. He explained about how the colt had a mind of his own and that I had adjusted it this morning and went on to explain how I had worked the stud and how things had worked out.

"You must be the young man who helped Dick with his bay horse?"

"I made a suggestion as to how he might get the colt to load into the gates."

"Well it must have worked. He was in here a while ago to get some tacos and was telling me all about it. He said the horse was eating his feed in the gates this evening."

"Well at least it's a start. We'll see what happens later this week when he tries him in the gates on the track."

"He doesn't seem worried about it. Said he'd leave the colt for a couple of days and then try to load him."

"Like I said Bill, people will be talking to you before too long."

"It won't make any difference Spunky, you're stuck with me."

"Good enough, lets get back to the track. I have to call Patty and tell her what has happened today. She should be here day after tomorrow so you'll only have to listen to my snoring for another couple of nights."

"Spunky, if you have snored I've not noticed. When I've laid down at night I've gone straight to sleep."

We returned to the track and I checked on the horses while Spunky called and talked to his wife. The stud came to the front of his stall. I opened the gate and rubbed his ears. He seemed to be in heaven. The longer I rubbed the lower his head got. I couldn't help but laugh about what a big baby he was becoming now that we knew who was boss. I remembered Spunky saying I was his assistant trainer. I'd have to ask him about that later.

Early the next morning after we had fed, watered and mucked the stalls we had a cup of coffee and some doughnuts. When we finished we began getting the horses ready for their works. Spunky put what he called track bandages on the horses and was ready when the exercise boy showed up at our barn. All of the horses worked well until we got to the stud. He went well on the track but I could tell he didn't like the boy riding him. The boy was too heavy handed and from everything I could see the colt had a tender mouth. I'd mention that to Spunky. I'd not say anything about the boy because I still didn't know enough about the thoroughbred horses.

Spunky was quiet as we went back to the barn. I mentioned to him we might try a lighter bit on the stud.

"You saw it too, Bill. The boy is a little rough handed but can ride a rank horse if they get that way. I don't want the stud to get spoiled so we'll change the bits until you learn to ride the exercise saddle."

We bathed and walked the horses. The stud was not as happy as he had been but after his bath and a little ear rubbing he was happy again. Spunky was going to go to the trailer park and be sure their spot was ready. I told him to go on. I was going to walk over to a western store and look at boots. Mine were getting to the point they needed to be replaced.

"You need any money, Bill?"

"No Spunky. I've got money. I had traveling money and didn't spend any on the way up here. You've fed me since I've been up here so I still have it all."

"If you need anything let me know. You've shown me I sure don't want you leaving."

I watched Spunky walk out to his truck and leave the track. I put on a fresh shirt and walked the two or so blocks to the western store where I began to look at boots. A gentleman came over and asked if he could help.

"I'm looking for a pair of boots that is suitable for riding morning works sir."

"Well I have the regular riding boots but all you really need is a light weight boot with a thin sole. I think I have a pair over here that will work for you."

The gentleman looked at my feet then went to the rack and pulled out two boxes and brought them back for me to try. I was glad I had remembered to put on clean socks. I'd have to ask Spunky where I could do my laundry soon. I didn't have that many clothes to start with.

"Try this pair. They have a thin sole but are well made and should last you the summer. Who are you riding for son?

"I'm working for Mr. Davis sir."

"Spunky, he's a fine fellow. Been coming up here for a number of years now. Did he bring his wife's gray colt?

"Yes sir, I'm working with the colt right now."

"Wait a minute. Are you the young man who worked with Dick's horse?"

"I don't remember the gentleman's last name but I did make a suggestion on how to cure a problem his horse had."

"Well son you might want to watch the gate works tomorrow morning. He's going to try and get his gate approval. The colt is riding through the gates just fine. Dick said he stops to see if his feed bucket is in there each time he starts through though. Now how do the boots feel?"

"Fine sir, they may be just a little bit snug. May I try the other pair?"

The gentleman handed me the other box and I tried the second pair on and found they fit me fine. I walked around the chairs and was sold. The boots were soft and would fit the iron stirrups on the exercise saddle. I looked at the price on the box and figured I'd have enough cash left to make it to my first pay check. Besides I had to have the boots if I wanted to ride the stud.

"I'll take them sir."

"Fine son, you do have a license don't you?"

"Yes sir, Mr. Davis got it for me yesterday."

"You get a ten percent discount on anything you buy in the store. We try and help the track folks all we can."

He wrapped the boots up for me and wished me luck as I walked out the door. Now all I had to do was learn to ride the exercise saddle. Deep down something told me that it was not going to be easy. When I got back to the barn I put the boots in the tack room and went to check on the horses. Everything seemed to be fine. I had just closed the stud's stall when Spunky came back into the barn. He was carrying a sack that smelled wonderful.

"Think you can eat a burger Bill?"

"You bet I can Spunky, I was just thinking about going over to the kitchen and getting something."

"We'll go over there tonight Bill. Did you get your boots?"

"They are under my bunk Spunky, the feller over at the store even gave me a discount."

"He gives everyone from the track a discount. He been in business a long time and has made a darn good living off the folks from the track. He sells to the local ranchers and such in the off-season. Now get us a couple of sodas out of the cooler and let's eat. It's almost my nap time."

We ate the burgers and fries and drank the cold sodas. The mountain air had made me hungry like I'd never been before. Everything I ate tasted good to me. The regular hours and hard work had made my body demand food. Later while Spunky took his nap I again wandered around the track and looked at things. It was amazing how things had gotten done in such short time. Everything was freshly painted and all of the trash had been picked up. As far as I could see the track was ready to open. I walked up into the grandstands and sat down. I looked at the freshly worked track and thought that maybe in a few days I'd have a chance to ride the stud around it. I could just imagine the wind in my face as he raced around the track. I couldn't wait for that first ride. I thought of home and figured Pa had discovered that I'd taken the money for the training of the horse. He'd not be looking for me but would have to either go to work himself or try and find someone to ride for him. Either way I simply didn't care. I was gone and I wouldn't be going back.

Spunky had just gotten up from his nap when I returned. He got the exercise saddle out of the tack room and adjusted the stirrup leathers to what he thought would fit me. I cleaned and oiled the saddle when he was through.

"Bill, we'll start you on the pony horse I use when I'm up here. You'll need some coaching and I know someone who will be just right. I'll have them stop by tomorrow after works."

"I'm ready, Spunky. I want to learn everything I can. I like working for you and I want to be a help to you."

"Don't worry about it Bill. You've already taken to things a lot faster than anyone I've ever had here before. Everyone except my son of course."

"You have a son? Where is he now?"

"He's dead Bill. He was killed in Viet Nam two days before he was to come home."

"I'm sorry Spunky. I'm always putting my foot in my mouth."

"It's alright Bill. I'd have told you about him before but we have been rather busy these last few days. He was a good boy and felt he should do his part for his country. He enlisted and was decorated twice. It about killed Patty when we were notified but bless her heart, she has managed to go on. It was really hard on her. He was our only son."

"Sounds like she is a fine woman, Spunky. I only hope I can find someone someday who will be a partner to me."

"Bill, you know a lot about horses and if you put that knowledge to work you'll probably make more money than I have ever dreamed of making."

"But Spunky, you're happy doing what you're doing. You know this business and sooner or later you'll get the horse that will make your name in the business."

"Bill, the wife and I had a nice little horse about six years ago. Not a stakes horse but a real good allowance horse. We had to sell him. We know how a horse can break down and be worth nothing. We had the boy in school and couldn't afford not to take the offer. That is the problem Bill. Little folks come up with a good horse and the rich folks offer so much money the little folks can't afford to not sell."

"I can understand but it still doesn't seem right. I'm afraid if I got a good one I'd just have give it a try. A man may only get one chance and if he doesn't take it he'll wonder the rest of his life what might have happened."

"You're right about that Bill, the little horse we sold made a pile of money before he finally broke down. I called the man who owned him and asked to buy him back. He gave the horse to me, said he wasn't any good to him anymore. Bill, the man didn't care about the horse at all. He even had him delivered to me just to get rid of him."

"Spunky, what about the stud? He may just be the one you've been looking for."

"Bill, I'd like to think so but it's a one in a million chance."

"It's a dream Spunky, it's what keeps folks going. The best part is sometimes dreams do come true. I'm new to your business but not new to the horse business. I think you may have the horse you've been looking for in the stud. His conformation is great and I like his attitude."

"I'm glad you like him Bill but right now he's got a long way to go before we can even begin to think about him really being a race horse. Folks from Kentucky bought a yearling full brother to a Derby winner for over two million. He couldn't outrun the pony horse that they had leading him. They figured they would stand him at stud and maybe get part of their money back. That's when they discovered he was sterile."

"Good lord, I'd die if something like that happened to me. It won't because I don't have two million to buy that kind of horse to start with."

"The boys that bought him are still trying to pay the money back. When you try and play in the big leagues you'd better get set to take a fall or two. Are things here starting to make sense to you around here now Bill?"

"Yes they are, it's been an experience but I have begun to adjust and understand why things are done the way they are. I admit things were a little confusing at first."

"They will line out for you son just relax and go with the flow. I guess we'd better start our chores. I like to feed at the same time every day."

Spunky began mixing the various mixtures for the horses. I started washing and refilling water buckets. I helped Spunky feed the string and then began mucking their stalls and adding straw where it was needed. When I finished we washed up and walked over to the track kitchen and had supper. The special was meat loaf and that was what I ordered. My mother made the best meatloaf when I was young. When our food arrived I found it to be good and was happy I'd ordered the meatloaf. I'd have to remember what night it was the special.

"Well Bill, tomorrow night you will have the tack room all to yourself. Patty will be here tomorrow afternoon. I'll not get any hamburgers after she gets here. She makes me eat my veggies and such."

"I'll keep an eye on things Spunky, I'll check on them the same way you do."

"Bill, I'm **not** worried about it at all."

I was worried but I wasn't about to let Spunky know my fears. I didn't like the exercise boy and sure enough didn't want him ruining the stud. I was going to keep an eye on him the next morning. It was true. Spunky did snore. I lay back on my cot and went to sleep, I was full and tired which made for a very good night's sleep.

CHAPTER 2

❀

The next morning we fed and watered as usual. I mucked stalls while Spunky went to get us a snack while the horses were finishing their feed. He brought orange juice with sausage and egg biscuits. They were delicious and nothing was left a few minutes later. We began to wrap the horses legs and get them ready. The exercise boy came to the stalls and he and Spunky took the first two of the horses to the track. They came back later and took two more. I put the track bandages on the stud and put his bridle on. I wanted him ready when they got back. Spunky had a lady bathing the horses when they came back. Two men who looked as if they were down on their luck walked them dry. It was what was called walking hots. The men got a set fee for walking the horses dry. They went from barn to barn and at day's end made enough to keep themselves going. It was a boring job and I was glad that Spunky had hired them. When Spunky and the exercise boy returned I led the stud out of his stall and had him ready to go. The jock, as he wanted to be called, noticed we had changed the bit on the stud.

"Kid, you have screwed up, you've put the wrong bridle on the stud."

"I don't think so, the horse has a soft mouth and you had him all upset when he came back from his work yesterday."

"Kid, who do you think you're talking to. I've rode more horses than you've ever seen. The stud can't be held with a rubber bit."

"Fred, I put the bit on the horse and he won't give you any trouble. This young man is my assistant trainer and has extensive experience with horses. If you don't want to ride the horse, just say so."

"I'll ride him Spunky, but don't blame me if he runs off."

I hadn't liked the jock before and now I sure didn't. I followed Spunky and the horse out of the barn and watched as the jock took the stud backwards or in the opposite way from what all the other horses were working.

"It's called back tracking Bill, he'll jog the horse to loosen him up before he goes to work. He'll turn him in a moment and move him out into the middle of the track and give him a slow three quarter work."

The jock took the horse half way around the turn then turned him and began to work him in the middle of the track. The stud wanted to go but the jock kept him in check until he relaxed and held a steady pace. After working the stud for the three quarter of a mile the jock stood up and began to slow him down. He took the horse to the outside rail and stopped him. He turned the colt and brought him back around the track. A hundred yards or so from where we stood, a couple of horses who were working down on the inside rail went by the stud. He wanted to go after them and began to turn. The jock hit the stud over the head with his stick for no reason. The stud blew up! He dropped his head and threw the jock onto the track rail then wheeled and took off after the other horses.

One of the things that was feared on the track was a loose horse with all the other horses working. Suddenly the cry "Loose Horse" was being heard all over the track. Exercise riders began to pull their horses to a stop and get them out of the way. The stud was now down on the rail at the far end of the track and was running full out.

"Oh my god, he'll cripple himself or kill someone."

I jumped the rail and ran to the rail near the finish line in the mid stretch. I uncoiled the lead rope and watched as the stud came around the turn and started down the stretch towards me. I spun the rope around my head and began to call to the stud as he got close enough to hear me. I could only pray he would remember the work in the round pen. When only a hundred yards or so was between us, the stud's head suddenly came up and he began to slow. I kept swinging the rope and he slowed some more. When he slowed to a trot and came to me and stopped it was the greatest thing that had ever happened to me. I spoke to him and snapped the lead rope into his bridle. I started to lead him back to Spunky when I saw Spunky come running to me.

"Thank god you got him Bill, I'll bring him to the barn. Get one of the clean muck tubs and get it filled with ice then run water over it. We've got to try and cool his legs down. Hurry Bill, we've got to get his legs cooled."

I left the track on the run and when I reached the tack room it took me three tries to get the key in the lock. I grabbed one of the clean muck buckets and quickly took it to the ice machine and began filling it as fast as I could. As I carried the bucket back I heard Spunky tell me to put it in his stall. I sat the tub down inside the stall and rushed to get the water hose. I added water as Spunky led the stud into the stall.

"That's enough water Bill, we've got to get his front legs into the tub."

I quickly removed the leg wraps and then lifted the stud's front leg and placed it into the tub of ice water. I removed the last leg wrap and put the leg in the tub also. The stud stood still and didn't appear to have any problem standing in the tub as long as I stood at his head.

"Bill, stay right where you are. He wants you close, so stay close."

I began to rub the stud's ears and he relaxed. I thought he had gone to sleep so I quit rubbing. The stud raised his head and touched my hand. Spunky began to laugh.

"He wants his newspaper, Bill. Next he'll want his pipe and slippers."

"Just as long as he hasn't crippled himself is all I care about, Spunky."

"We might get lucky, Bill. He wasn't carrying a rider and the track was real soft. All we can do now is pray. Stay where you are Bill. I'll get you a soda."

I was rubbing the stud's neck when I heard someone say.

"That was either the bravest or the dumbest thing I've ever seen out there today."

"Probably the latter, I've been working with him in the round pen and only hoped he'd remember me. I had to try and stop him before he crippled himself."

"But he was running scared."

"No he wasn't, he was running mad. The jock hit him with his stick after his work for no reason. The stud simply threw him and ran off."

"Was the jock's name Fred?"

"That's right, why?"

"He's what we call stick happy, he likes to have his horses afraid of him."

"Well I guess he's figured out the stud wasn't afraid of him."

The young lady standing outside the stall laughed. I looked at her for the first time and saw she maybe five feet tall and would weigh about a hundred pounds. She had medium length sandy red hair that showed out from under her riding helmet. She had just enough freckles across her nose to set off her vivid green eyes. She was cute and had a sense of humor. I noticed she was wearing the soft black flat heeled boots all of the exercise boys wore.

"Are you by chance an exercise rider?"

"Yes I am, I work for one of Spunky's old friends. He sent me over to see how the gray was doing."

"That was nice of him. Spunky's the finest boss I ever had."

"Pardon me for asking but just who are you?"

"I'm sorry. My name is Patton. Bill Patton."

"Well Bill Patton, I'm Cassie Morgan. Glad to meet you."

"You wouldn't happen to be related to Art Morgan would you?"

"He's my father. How did you know?"

"He gave me a ride from just north of Amarillo to Dumas, then got me a ride to Clayton on a grain truck. I met Spunky at a café there and he's giving me a chance to work for him."

"Wait a minute Bill. Are you related to Frank Patton the horse trader?"

"He's my father but I don't brag about it much."

"I've heard about you. You're the one they call "The Kid." I know several folks who have horses that you have broke for them. One was a sure enough outlaw. You've got quite a reputation for working bad horses Bill."

"I don't know about that. The only reason I broke them was to eat and I did darn little of that."

"Your father has a drinking problem doesn't he Bill"

"That's why I'm here, I got tired of working for free and getting beat when he came home drunk."

"Now I know why you ran out on the track and stopped the stud. You expected him to stop didn't you?"

"Well I certainly hoped he would. I didn't want him to get hurt. He is far too nice a horse for that."

"Well I'm glad it worked. The colt belongs to Patty and she would be heart broke if he crippled himself before he even got to race."

"That's what Spunky said. She must be quite a lady."

"She is that Bill. She mothers all the kids who work the summer here. You'll love her."

"Cassie girl, how are you?"

"I'm fine, Spunky. Randall sent me over to see how your stud was doing."

"I see you've already met my new assistant Bill."

"Oh yes, you've hired a local celebrity Spunky."

"What do you mean Cassie?"

"Bill here is known as "The Kid" back home. He had a reputation for breaking bad horses. You've got yourself a fine hand. You should have him riding your string this year."

"I'm glad you said that Cassie, I was going to ask you to teach him how to ride an exercise saddle."

"When do you want me to start?"

"Today if you can work it into your schedule."

"I'll be down after we get the morning chores done. It will be fun teaching him to ride a flat saddle."

"Thanks Cassie, after this morning works I want him up on my string as soon as possible. By the way girl, you want another job until Bill here gets lined out?"

"Sure Spunky, you know dad won't let me ride for anyone he doesn't know."

"That's being smart Cassie, there are a bunch of horses here that aren't that well broke and might hurt you. Your father is using good sense."

"I know Spunky, he doesn't want me to get hurt. I've had a bunch of folks wanting me to ride but I promised dad and I'll stick to my promise. I'll see you all in a little while. I'll bring Randall's pony horse, he's quiet and it will make it easier for me to teach Bill here to ride exercise."

"Thanks Cassie we'll see you in a little while."

I was shocked to think that Cassie knew so much about me. The thought of being known as someone who could break a bad horse had never entered my mind. I'd been too busy trying to earn enough money to eat on. I was looking forward to my first lesson on the flat saddle as Cassie had called it.

"Bill, we may have got lucky, I'll put cold wraps on the stud and keep them on all day. It will mean we'll have to keep them soaked all day but it may be what we need to do to keep him from shin bucking."

"Spunky, what is a shin buck?"

"A lot of colts do it Bill, the cannon bones develop hair line fractures from the stress put on them by the work they do. When the fractures become numerous the shins develop swelling and the horse gets sore. A trainer has a choice, he can turn the horse out for ninety days and wait for the fractures to heal or fire him. I don't believe in pen firing as it's called so I just turn my colts out and let them heal up."

"I'll learn Spunky, but if I don't ask I'll never learn and I want to know everything I can about this game."

"I know you do Bill and I'm going to teach you. This may turn out to be a fun summer. By the way son, thanks for stopping the stud today. He'd have crippled himself for sure if you hadn't stepped in and got him to stop."

"It's just part of my job Spunky, I'm just glad I could help."

We took the stud out of the ice water and I watched as Spunky put on new bandages on the stud's front legs. When he had finished he took a can and filled it with ice water from the tub. He poured the cold water onto the bandages. When he had them soaked he explained to me how we would have to keep them soaked for the next few hours. We'd have to check them every hour or so, the dry mountain air would dry them out in a hurry.

A short time later Spunky went to get us something to eat. I kept an eye on the stud and finished mucking the stalls. The muck truck would be by in an hour or so and I wanted to have our stalls clean. The muck truck came by every morning and emptied the container outside the barn, they hauled the waste off to a plant where it was processed and sold to stores so folks could buy it to put it on their gardens and such.

I had just finished cleaning the stalls when Fred "the jock" came walking up. He was walking slowly and had a mad expression on his face.

"Hey boy, where is Spunky?"

"Mr. Davis has gone to get us something to eat. He should be back in a few minutes."

"Mr. Davis is it, I'm glad to see you know your place."

"My place is anywhere I choose. You hit the stud with your stick this morning. Don't ever do that again."

"Or what boy?"

"I'll wear your stick out over your head for starters, then give you the whipping you deserve. You may push the younger kids around here Fred but you'd better leave me alone."

"Boy, you'd better be careful. I just might get upset and kick your tail."

"I'm right here Fred, you can start anytime."

Fred reached out to slap me and suddenly found himself laying on his back in the barn aisle. My neighbor who had taught me the trick I'd used on the stud had taught me a whole lot more. Fred got to his feet and stared at me. Hate was in his eyes.

"Fred, like I said, leave me alone.

"Wait until you get out on the track, I'll get even with you."

"That would be your second mistake, the first would be thinking about it. Now get away from here before I get mad."

Fred limped off down the barn aisle. I had made myself an enemy for sure but I didn't care. I didn't like the man and I had no intention of putting up with his trash."

"You'd better watch your back Bill, Fred has the reputation of being a bad person to mess with here on the backside."

"Cassie, where did you come from?"

"I was just coming in the side door of the barn when I overheard Fred threaten you. The next thing I knew he was laying on his back in the barn aisle. Bill, where did you learn that throw?"

"A friend of mine back home was a prison guard during the second world war. It was a Japanese camp and he learned from one of the men he befriended. The man was a graduate of UCLA and had gone back to Japan to visit. They had put him in the army. All the man wanted was to see the war end and get back here to the states. My friend is older now but I'd seen him do a couple of things that I thought were great so I asked him to teach me. I'd rather ride a rank horse than suffer through the things he taught me."

"That explains it then, I brought you this crash helmet as we call them here. The chin strap needs some repair but I figured you could fix it up enough until you can afford to buy your own."

"Thanks Cassie, I'll get to work on it just as soon as I check Light's bandages. We have to keep them soaked in cold water for a while yet."

"Light, is that his name?"

"Gray Light, is what Spunky told me but I've just been calling him Light."

"Mr. Bill Patton, you are something else. I'm going to enjoy teaching you about the flat saddle. I'll be back in about thirty minutes with the horse and we'll get started."

"I'll be looking forward to it Cassie."

I had put more ice water on Light's bandages and had started to go to work on the helmet when Spunky returned with a sack of tacos. We sat down and ate. We had just finished when Cassie came walking down the aisle leading a big brown gelding.

"School is about to start Bill, ready for your first lesson?"

"I'll be ready as soon as I change my boots."

I quickly changed into the light boots and walked back to where Spunky and Cassie waited. I followed them with my crash helmet in hand to the round pen. Cassie led the gelding inside and waited while Spunky put the exercise saddle on the gelding.

"Hop up on him Bill, we need to get you started."

I had to jump and crawl up on the gelding. Once I was on I leaned over and put my foot in the iron stirrups. I found that my legs were bent far more than I was used to.

"Relax Bill, I know they feel strange. When you ask the horse to move you push behind you and stand up in the irons. Keep your knees as close together as possible, they will help keep your balance."

The next half hour was the most miserable time I'd ever spent on a horse. Cassie had laughed and I had done the same. My legs were burning something awful when I finally began to get the hang of things. When I started to get off I had leg cramps and could hardly stand.

"Legs burning Bill? I'd be surprised if they weren't."

"They sure are Cassie, I thought I was in good shape."

"You are in good shape, it's your legs you're going to have to work on. I run a mile every morning and evening until I get them built back up. You're using muscles you haven't used before."

"I guess I'll have to start running then."

"You'll need to get yourself a pair of tennis shoes. You don't want to try and run in your boots. You can get a decent pair over at the discount store."

"Where is the discount store Cassie, remember I just got to town and only know a few places out here by the track."

"Spunky, if it's alright with you I'll take the gelding back then come pick up Bill in my truck. I'll take him over and get him a pair of running shoes."

"Fine with me, he was just getting the hang of things when you all quit. I want him on Light as soon as possible. Cassie he will need the running shoes but you take him to Bradleys and get him a pair of riding boots. I'm going to help him study and get him his assistant trainers license. I can't have him running around the track looking like a beginner."

"Assistant trainer? Spunky do you think I'm ready for something like that?"

"More than ready Bill, you already know more about horses than half the trainers here."

"Thank you Spunky, that means a lot to me."

"You've earned it Bill, you may have saved my wife's colt this morning and besides I just happen to like you."

I didn't know what to say, it was all I could do to keep from crying. No one had ever treated me so nice before.

Cassie took the gelding back to her barn while I began mucking stalls and filling water buckets. Spunky was mixing the feed and when he was finished I was ready to help him. I fed Light first and rubbed his ears while he ate. He quit long enough to rub his head against me to let me know he liked what I was doing.

"You've started feeding him first Bill."

"I figure he deserves it Spunky. Did you see how he ran today. His stride was tremendous and he gathered up so quickly. Even after running all the way around the track he didn't hardly take a deep breath."

"I hadn't thought about it but you're right Bill. Most colts his age would be blowing like a freight train. He led back to the barn and was still on his toes. Bill, you may be right. The colt could be something special. Now all we have to do is sweat out the night and pray he is sound tomorrow morning. When you and Cassie get back from your shopping trip we'll take the cold bandages off and I'll put the liniment on to tighten his legs. If he walks out fine in the morning I'm buying you the biggest breakfast the track kitchen has to offer."

"Spunky you don't have to do that."

"I don't have to do anything Bill, but if I don't my wife will buy you the best steak in town. Lets face it Bill, breakfast is cheaper."

We were still having a good laugh when Cassie walked into the barn. Spunky had to explain to her what was so funny. She had a good laugh too. We went out and got in her truck and drove into town. As we drove through town Cassie pointed out the different stores that sold things I might need. She pulled into a parking spot in front of a huge tack store. We got out of the truck and walked inside. Several of the folks who worked there called her. by name.

"You must shop here a lot."

"They are the only place in town who handles the jockey pants. I have to have at least three pair each spring. I also have to have a new pair of riding boots."

"Why do you need so many pairs of pants?"

"If it rains you get mud on them and it's not fun to ride in wet muddy pants. I've seen jocks spray each other with the water hose before going into the jock room."

"Then you actually ride in races."

"Of course I do. I ride for a friend of my dad's. I ride works for several folks and when the summer ends I've made a fair amount of money. That's how I bought my truck."

"I just hope I can make enough money to make it through the winter. I'm going to have to find a place to break and train horses. I've got one more year of school and I intend to graduate. I only need two more courses so I should be able to ride horses and go to school without a problem.'

"What about your father."

"Cassie, I really don't care. He's not going to control me any longer. I've taken the last beating from him I will ever take."

"I can't even imagine how you survived as long as you did."

"I'm not looking for sympathy, it's just the way things were. The last time was one time to many. I just up and left it to him. I'm happier now than I've ever been."

The gentleman who ran the store took my shoe size and brought a pair of boots for me to try on. I'd never felt anything on my feet that felt so good. The boots were as soft as a good pair of gloves. They felt strange to me because they had no high heels. I really looked forward to trying them out this evening.

"Young man, I'd not wear them except to ride. You're used to the high heels on your boots and your legs will get sore if you wear them too much."

"'I'll only wear them to ride in sir, I sure can't afford to be buying this kind of boot but once a year."

"They are rather expensive but you'll find they are worth every penny. Tell Spunky I look forward to seeing him and his lovely wife soon."

"I'll do that sir, Mrs. Davis is due in tomorrow."

Cassie and I walked out of the store and went to her truck. I asked if she liked Mexican food and she had answered 'yes' quickly. I told her where Spunky and I had gone to eat and she knew exactly where the restaurant was located. It seemed it was everyone's favorite place to eat. We found a place to park and went inside. The owner greeted Cassie and showed us to a table. Cassie introduced me to him and asked what was the special of the day.

"We'll have the special then."

The owner smiled and took our order into the kitchen. We sat and visited about her family. She had twin younger brothers. They were stars on the football team at home.

"Stars on the football team, you have to be kidding."

"I'm not kidding, one is defensive end and the other is the running back. I'm quite proud of them."

"How in the world did you end up so small and they are so big?"

"My mothers is a little bitty thing but my grandfather was six foot four and weighed two forty."

"That is a big man, you're lucky to be small so you can ride the horses. I can't imagine how it will feel to take a horse around the track for the first time. I'm looking forward to doing it but I have to admit, it is a little scary."

"You'll do fine Bill. You've got the ability to ride and all you have to do is relax and get the feel of the saddle. The boots are going to make a lot of difference, you'll be able to feel the horse move.

"I sure hope so, I felt like a complete dummy earlier. To be truthful I don't really want to look dumb. I like to ride but the flat saddle is something new and I'll just have to learn."

Our meal arrived and we began to eat. The food was wonderful and with Cassie setting across from me the meal seemed even better. I looked at Cassie and thought what a wonderful friend she was making. I was indeed a very lucky fellow.

When we arrived back at the track I changed into my new riding boots while Cassie went to get the gelding. I had just stepped out of the tack room when she came down the aisle leading the horse. I quickly put the exercise saddle on him and we headed to the round pen. Cassie had been right, with the new boots I seemed to be able to feel the horse's every move. I could feel his muscles working as we went around the pen. I wasn't out of balance and I had to admit I was enjoying the ride.

"Bill, stop the horse, we need to talk to Spunky."

I stopped the horse and jumped off. I had no idea as to what I had done to displease Cassie. I had been enjoying myself. I followed Cassie into the barn where we found Spunky sitting outside the tack room.

"Spunky, have they worked the track yet?"

"Not yet Cassie, the boys are all working on the electric switches at the gates. Why do you ask?"

"We need Bill here to take the gelding around the track, he can learn more with one turn around the track than he can in a week in the round pen."

"You think he's ready Cassie?"

"Yes I do Spunky, and with the track empty he'll be able to think about what he needs to be doing and not worry about the other riders and horses."

"Sounds like a plan Cassie. You ready to take a turn around the track Bill?"

"You bet Spunky, I can hardly wait."

I would remember this day for the rest of my life. I had never had a feeling like this. Spunky gave me a leg up on the gelding when we reached the opening onto the track. Cassie removed the top rail and I rode the gelding out onto the track surface. I rode him through the opening and turned him to the left just the way I'd watched Cassie work the other horses. Cassie had warned me about the gelding being an ex race horse himself. She had told me to be ready when I turned him onto the track. It happened just like she had said. When I turned the gelding he went into a fast trot and then into a canter. I was up in the irons without thinking and had a good hold of the reins. It seemed to me that I could feel every nerve and muscle as the gelding went around the first turn. As we reached the backstretch I released my hold on the gelding and let him work a little. I had never felt anything like this in my life. The wind was causing tears to stream back over my cheeks but I didn't mind at all, I was having the time of my life. When the gelding reached the final turn and began entering the stretch I sat down and asked him to run. His stride lengthened and I felt a sudden increase in the horse's speed.

I had my head down next to the gelding's neck and watched as we neared the finish wire. I stood up on the gelding and slowly brought him back into a canter, then a slow trot. When I stopped him I patted his neck and told him what a great friend he was. I turned him and slowly trotted him back to where Spunky and Cassie were waiting. Both of them had big smiles on their faces.

"My lord, it was wonderful!"

"Spunky, I think you just got yourself one fine gallop boy."

"You could be right Cassie, now Bill tell me about your ride."

"Well he wheeled around and started to work like Cassie said. I took a firm hold of him and kept him in check. When I felt him relax I loosened my hold and let him go to work. I released my hold on the backstretch and let him work a little more. When we reached the stretch I got down on him and turned him loose. He began to run and it was the greatest feeling in the world."

"Bill, you just told me everything I saw here at the rail. When you started into the stretch and got down low on the horse Cassie was jumping up and down and shouting. You just rode a beautiful work."

"Bill, you did a lot of things I hadn't taught you and you did them at all the right times. There are boys here at the track who couldn't do half as well as you did today and they've been riding for several years. I'm proud of you Bill Patton."

"Thank you Cassie, that means a lot to me."

We took the gelding back to the barn and gave him a bath and a couple of hands full of grain to let him know we appreciated his help. Spunky hired a walker to walk him dry. I had just moved up in the race world and wouldn't miss walking the horses dry at all. After Cassie had left, Spunky and I sat down with a couple of his sodas."

"Bill, I've got a few questions I have to ask you. Is the law looking for you?"

"No sir, the law isn't looking for me. I'm sure my father isn't looking either."

"I've got some friends down that way I'll get in touch with. I sure don't want to get things lined out here and have the law show up and take you away, especially now that you've become my exercise rider and assistant trainer. I want you and Cassie to work Light and Slinger together tomorrow morning."

"You think I'm ready for that Spunky?"

"Yes I do Bill, the horse and you seem to have bonded and I think you may be the only one he won't buck off for a while. Once he gets lined out we'll have to find a jockey that fits him. I'll be wanting your opinion so be watching the jocks to figure out who will fit him."

I told Spunky about why I had left home and what had happened after my mother had left. I told him the whole story. I really wanted him to know. After I finished my story he shook his head.

"Bill, I understand why you left and I can't say that I blame you. I'll contact my friends and see how things are down that way. We sure don't want any surprises."

"Go ahead Spunky I don't have any objections. All I know for sure is that I'm sure enough not going home to my father."

CHAPTER 3

The next morning Cassie and I saddled the two horses and, with Spunky leading Light to the track, put them to work. I'll admit I was nervous and Light seemed to know it. He was nervous, too.

"Relax Bill, you've got to keep him calm. Spunky wants us to give them a long gallop. We'll be in the middle of the track so you stay to my right side. That way when someone goes by on the rail he'll not see them. Spunky said to let them work up the stretch but to keep a hold on them."

I did relax and felt Light do the same. When we turned them to begin our work I suddenly had my hands full. Light was ready to go, he shook his head and wanted me to know he was ready to run. I kept my hold on him and began talking to him. Slowly he began to relax, I saw that Cassie had a smile on her face next to me. We worked around the turn and let the two horses work at a little faster speed. When we rounded the turn into the home stretch we sat down on the two horses and let them begin to really work. The stud suddenly seemed to explode under me. The muscles in his body seemed to be working like a well oiled machine. I was pushed back in my stirrup irons and got lower on the stud's back while keeping a snug hold on him. We didn't want him going full out and crippling himself this close to his first race. The man who had broke the stud to ride had put a lot of miles on him even though he not taught him any manners. Both Spunky and I had been shocked after the runaway that he was in better shape and closer to be ready than we had thought. Tears streamed back over my cheeks and I loved every minute of it. When we reached the finish line I stood up in my irons and began to slow him down. I had finished a good three lengths in front of Cassie and was holding my horse.

Spunky stood at the track opening, called the gap by the racing people waiting for us. The smile on his face told me he was happy with the work. He caught the stud and I jumped off. I caught the gelding for Cassie and watched as she jumped off smiling.

"They went just like you wanted Spunky. They went to work and both of them were wanting to go. Bill got control of Light and got him to settle down before we reached the first turn, it was wonderful to see, Spunky. He talked to him and he just settled down like Bill wanted him to do. When we reached the stretch he moved away from me and I thought I had the jump on him."

"Alright Bill, let's hear what you have to say."

"Its pretty much like Cassie said. Light was ready to go to work. I got a good hold on him and began talking to him. He settled down and went to work. When we reached the stretch and I released my hold on him and he almost jumped out from under me. Spunky, he just seemed to gather himself and explode. I've never felt anything like this in my life. I had a lot of horse left when we reached the wire."

"You really think so Bill?"

"I really do Spunky, the horse is like nothing I ever rode before. I know I don't have a lot of experience but this horse would scare a lot of people. I have a suggestion for you by the way."

"Speak up son, it's what I pay you for."

"Let Cassie work him, she has a good set of hands and with my help she'll have him eating out of her hand in no time."

"That's your honest opinion, Bill?"

"That's what I think Spunky."

"Cassie the job is yours if you want it."

"Oh yes, I'd love to ride him."

"Spunky, you only understood half of what I meant. I think she should be your jockey on the horse as well. I think it would give you a big advantage over all the others."

"Cassie, what do you think?"

"I think I can't hardly wait until I get a chance to ride him. Bill, thank you for giving me the opportunity to have the ride. I'll try and do my best for you all."

The next few days seemed to fly by. Cassie had begun to ride Light in his works. I rode the gelding Slinker along with her and could tell her if she needed to do anything different. The two of them seemed to bond at once. Light was getting fitter by the day and would be ready for a maiden race the third week of the racing season. Spunky had already entered the two-year-old filly in a race for the first week. She was showing a lot of promise and we all hoped she would win. I was cleaning the tack when Spunky walked into the barn. He had a strange look on his face.

"Bill, I've got some bad news."

"What sort of news Spunky?"

"Bill, I called my friend and he told me your father was killed in a car accident a couple of weeks ago."

"Was anyone else hurt Spunky?"

"No they weren't Bill. My friend said your dad had been drinking and must have gone to sleep on his way home. He crashed his pick-up into a dry creek bed."

"Thank god he didn't hit a family."

"Bill, you'll have to call the sheriff down there and tell him where you are. They have been looking for you for a while."

"I'll go get some change and call him. I've broke a couple of colts for him over the last few years and know him pretty well. Thanks for telling me Spunky."

I walked over to the track kitchen and got several dollars worth of quarters then went out to the public pay phone and called the Sheriff.

"Bill, where have you been? We've been looking everywhere for you.?"

"I'm working at the race track in Raton Sheriff. I've been here ever since I left home."

"We thought maybe your father had done something to you. I even talked to him about where you were."

"I didn't want him to know where I was Sheriff. The gentleman I work for found out about the wreck and just told me. Now what do I need to do Sheriff?"

"Well first thing is pick up your dad's things, then I've got some papers for you to sign. It shouldn't take over a couple of hours' time Bill. By the way, does your father own the place?"

"No sir, the place belongs to my mother. It was my grandfather's place and he willed it to her. It's free and clear, dad wanted mom to deed it over to him but she wouldn't do it. Of course I have no idea where she is."

"Bill, get down here and sign these papers, I promise it won't take over a couple of hours. You going to have time this fall to work a colt for me?"

"I'll have time Sheriff, I'll be able to take four if you know anyone wanting them broke."

"You'll have four and more if you want them Bill. It seems folks have missed you around here. The sale barn boys have been crying the blues because they haven't had you to ride their horses."

"I'll see you in a day or so Sheriff. I'll have to make arrangements with my boss. The meet hasn't opened yet so I should be able to get a day off."

I hung the phone up and walked back to the barn. I told Spunky about the conversation.

"You want to go in the morning?"

"I thought I'd get a bus ticket and leave tonight if I can. I'd like to be home in the morning and then get back up here."

"It sounds like a plan Bill. The quicker you get things lined out the better you'll feel."

I was putting what few things I thought I would need into a small bag and was just getting ready to leave when Cassie came down the barn aisle.

"Bill, Spunky just told me about your father. Is there anything I can do for you?"

"Give me a ride down to the bus station. I need to see if I can make a connection to get out of here and home early tomorrow morning. The Sheriff said it would only take a couple of hours to wrap up what business had to be taken care of."

"Bill, I can do better than that. I need to run home and pick up some things. If you want we'll leave in a few minutes. You can drop me off at my house, take my truck and go on down and take care of your business. When you're through you can come pick me up and we'll hustle back here."

"Cassie, I can't take your truck."

"Why not Bill? If it was one of my folks and you had a truck would you loan it to me?"

"Of course I would."

"Then I guess we don't have a problem do we? I'll be back in ten minutes and we'll hit the road for home. We should be in Dumas by ten this evening."

I thanked Cassie and waved as she pulled out of the racetrack parking lot. I was thinking if we were in Dumas by ten I'd be at my place by eleven easy. I could give the Sheriff a call along the way and meet him early at his office. I knew he was usually at the office by seven in the morning. I saw Spunky coming down the aisle and told him I'd be catching a ride with Cassie home.

"Bill, if you need anything you just call me. I want you back here as soon as you can get back. You're a very important part of this operation, besides I've gotten used to having you around. There comes Cassie, you get gone now and, Bill?"

"Yes sir."

"Be careful on your way home and back."

"We'll be careful Spunky, look after Light for me."

CHAPTER 4

I had Cassie stop at a gas station on the edge of town and filled her tank. I bought us a drink each and we got on our way. I was uneasy about what was going to happen at home but the Sheriff had assured me there wouldn't be any problems. Cassie and I visited as we went along and really got to know each other better. We arrived in Dumas at nine thirty and Cassie drove to her folks home which was just east of town.

Her mother had a snack ready for us when we arrived. Nothing would do but I had to stay long enough to eat before leaving. The food, which was great, hit the spot. I got to visit with Cassie's dad about things down home. When he asked me about what I was going to do with the place I told him I was going to try and fix it up. With my father gone I'd be able to spend my money on a new barn and maybe paint the house. He had told me to let him know when I was going to start. He and his two boys, who he said were good with a hammer and saw would come down and help me.

"Sir, there's no need for you to do that."

"Bill, you've been looking out for my girl and it's something I want to do. It's sort of our way of saying thanks. Now you'd better get on your way. You'll need your rest. The Sheriff will be at his office at six thirty."

"You know the Sheriff?"

"He and I went to school together until my folks moved up here. We've been friends for years."

"But you didn't tell him where I was."

"I didn't know he was looking for you until yesterday. He told me while we were having coffee at the truck stop. He thinks a lot of you Bill. He didn't care much for your father but told me you were a fine young man and a great hand with a young horse. You should be honored to have him as a friend."

"I am sir, he's always been good to me."

"Now get out of here and get your business taken care of. You'll be wanting to get back to the track."

"I sure do. It's almost like Christmas up there. You never know what you're going to get until the package is opened."

I pulled out of the driveway and stopped in town long enough to top the tank off with gas then made the left turn onto the highway and headed home, something a couple of weeks ago I thought would not happen. When I reached the driveway to the house I opened the sagging wooden gate and thought it was one of the first things I'd replace. I drove up the drive and parked Cassie's truck just outside the now overgrown yard gate. I walked to the back door and found it unlocked. It didn't worry me because there sure enough wasn't anything in the house that anyone would want to steal. I expected the worst and that was exactly what I got. Both of the kitchen sinks were full of dirty dishes and one corner of the kitchen was a piled high with carry out cartons. It looked as if my father had cooked everything in the kitchen then went to buying all his meals out. Cans of half empty food and such sat on the table. The smell inside the house was terrible.

I began to open windows to try and air the place out. I walked to my room and found all the drawers in my dresser had been jerked out and emptied on my bed. My father must have been looking for the money I had taken with me. I put the drawers back in the dresser and put what few things there were back into them. I walked to my father's bedroom and found it to be in the same condition as the kitchen. Empty bottles and cans littered the floor. It was a shock even to me. I didn't have time to start cleaning the mess up so I simply closed the door and went back to my room. I set the clock for five the next morning and simply stretched out and went to sleep.

The next morning I got up and had myself a bath. I'd have to check with the power company to keep the lights on. I'd have to do the same with the gas company. After my bath I got in the truck and drove to the truck stop café and had breakfast. Several folks spoke to me and asked where I'd been. A couple wanted to know if I'd be riding any horses this fall when I came home. I explained I would and got on with my breakfast. I wanted to be waiting on the Sheriff when he got to his office. I had just parked the truck when I saw the Sheriff drive into the parking lot and get out. I got out of the truck and waved to him.

"Morning Bill, I'm glad to see you, you got here before I expected."

"Is it going to cause a problem Sheriff?"

"No problem at all Bill, I've got all the paperwork in my desk ready for you to sign. We should be through in an hour or less."

"That's great Sheriff. I need to get back up to the track. The meet starts this weekend and we've got horses to run."

"You're enjoying yourself aren't you Bill?"

"I sure am Sheriff. It's nice to work for someone who respects you and doesn't beat you if things don't go just right."

"Bill, if you'd have come to me and told me about the beatings I'd have had a talk with your dad."

"It wouldn't have made any difference, Sheriff. First time he took off and got drunk he'd have come home and done it all over again."

"Well you don't have to worry about it now Bill. Come on into my office and we'll get started."

I followed the Sheriff into his office and took a seat in front of his desk. He sat down and opened a drawer. He took out a large brown envelope and handed it to me.

"You dad's billfold and everything he had on him when we found him."

I opened the envelope and found dad's wallet. There was twelve dollars in it which was ten more than I expected to find. His keys, pocketknife and a few other things were all that was there. I thought to myself what little he had left behind. The Sheriff explained to me how the county had paid for dad's burial. I needed to pay the small fee if I had the money. I paid the bill and got a receipt from the Sheriff. I'll contact the insurance company agent and tell him you'll be home for an hour or so, Bill. He has a check for you, your father had full coverage on the truck and the check now belongs to you."

"I can use it Sheriff, I'm going to have to buy a truck to use around the farm. I plan on cleaning the place up and making something out of it."

"Bill, I'll help you every way I can. I'll keep an eye on the place while you're gone. The state folks shouldn't give you any trouble as long as you stay out of trouble and don't attract too much attention."

"Is that all I have to do Sheriff?"

"That's all I can think of Bill, you could contact the Social Security folks and probably get a small check until you're eighteen."

"I'd rather not Sheriff, I'm making enough to live on and I'd rather not attract too much attention as you put it."

"Good thinking Bill, I'll call the insurance man right now and get him out your way."

"Thanks Sheriff, I really appreciate all you've done for me. I'll make it right with you when I break your colt."

"No you won't Bill, you're going to need all the money you can get if you're planning on fixing your place up. Your dad really let things go."

"Sheriff, if I could afford it I'd burn the house down rather than try and clean it up. I've never seen so much trash in my life."

"Your dad had been drinking down south at some club the night he ran off the road. My deputies said the folks down there had said he'd been drinking for a couple of days while he was hanging out at a horse sale. They said he hadn't bought anything they could find out about."

"Probably because he was out of money. I'd not be surprised if he was trying to get some folks to bring horses for me to break. He probably figured I'd come home when the money I'd taken ran out."

"He figured wrong didn't he?"

"He sure did. I've got a great job and I'm learning so much I never knew before. It's almost like I'm getting paid for getting an education. I guess I'd better call my school principal and see about getting my classes adjusted for this fall. I only have two classes to complete so that I can graduate."

"You're going to finish your schooling?"

"You bet I am, I know it's something I've got to do. I've got an idea about what I'm going to do but just haven't got it all figured out yet."

I thanked the Sheriff again and left for the house. The Sheriff was talking to the insurance man when I left his office. When I got to the house I did a quick walk through and figured it would take me the best part of two days to get the place cleaned up. I began making a list of the things I would need. Trash bags, cleaner, soap, mop and plenty of elbow grease. I had just closed and locked the door when the insurance man drove up and parked.

"Bill, sorry about your dad and all. I have a check here that the Sheriff said now belongs to you. He said you'd be needing it to buy yourself a truck. I guess you plan on coming back here."

"That's what I have planned sir, I'm going to clean things up and try and get the place looking decent. I've got colts to break this fall and I'll be needing things fixed up."

The gentleman handed me the check and asked me to sign a paper stating I had received payment. I looked at the check and smiled, I'd be able to buy a fairly good pick-up. Nothing fancy, just a good solid truck. I thanked the gentleman and watched as he drove down and out of the driveway. I got into Cassie's truck and headed north, I was looking forward to getting back to the track.

I stopped at a station and filled the truck up before I drove to Cassie's place. She was waiting for me and came out the door carrying a box. I took the box and sat it in the truck bed up next to the cab. We waved to Cassie's mother as we backed out of the driveway.

"Did you get everything done Bill?"

"Everything is taken care of Cassie. I'm not looking forward to coming home and cleaning up the mess my father left, however."

I told her about the house and how he had messed everything up.

"How can anyone live like that?"

"I really don't know Cassie, I guess when the bottle takes control nothing else matters."

"I guess you're right. I'd never thought of it before."

"I've been exposed to enough of it that I know I'll never drink. It's a terrible thing to see what it has done to so many people."

We visited on the rest of the trip, stopping once at a roadside park. We arrived back at the track in time for me to help Spunky with chores. Patty had arrived and wanted to meet me. She was nothing like I expected. When she showed up a short time later I was surprised to say the least. She was barely five feet tall, had short gray hair and looked almost like a cute little doll.

"You've got to be Bill. I've heard so much about you. My husband is so happy to have you helping us this year. I also want to thank you for getting my colt lined out. I guess I had spoiled him as a baby."

"He wasn't that bad. He just had to have a small attitude adjustment."

"I know. Spunky told me how you'd made the adjustment. He was very impressed. I've been after him to find us some help but we could never find anyone who suited us."

"I'm just thrilled to be here and learn all I can. I'm looking forward to watching Light run in his first race."

"We all are Bill. We've raised him from a colt and I'm ready to see if he is as good as I hope."

"Mrs. Davis, the colt is a fine horse. I don't know a lot about these race horses but I rode a bunch and I know when one feels right. The colt seems to float across the track and we've not asked him for a thing yet."

"We'll know pretty soon, I think Spunky is planning to let you give him a timed work soon. By the way Bill, will you call me Patty? Everyone of my friends do."

"Yes ma'am. I'll be proud too."

"Patty!"

"Cassie, how are you. Oh my goodness. How you've grown."

"It's great to have you here, Spunky was lost without you."

"I think the two of you kept him entertained. When he called of an evening it was the kids this and the kids that. You all have been a tremendous help to him. I don't believe I've ever seen him this excited about a season."

"It has been rather exciting. Bill here is a big help and a good horseman to boot. He's made things a lot easier on Spunky this year. They have worked so well together. Like you say, Spunky is really looking forward to the upcoming season."

I saw Spunky coming back down the aisle and saw him smile.

"Hey kids. It's good to see you back. Bill, did everything go alright?"

"Things went fine Spunky. The Sheriff had everything ready for me to sign when I got there."

"That's good, ready to go to work in the morning?"

"You bet. Which of the horses are we going to go to work?"

"I think we'll work the two year olds in the morning. The filly is in Friday and the gelding is in Sunday. I'd like to give them both a light gallop and just keep them loose. I think it will do both of them good. You and Cassie can work them together. I'd like Cassie to give Light a half mile work. I think he's ready and I'd like to see what he does."

"Sounds like a plan Spunky, it will be interesting to see what he will do. I've got an idea but it will have to be proven."

"You think he's good don't you Bill?"

"Yes I do Spunky. I think when you look at your watch after the work you're going to have to look twice. I think he's the one you've been looking for your whole life, Spunky."

"I guess we'll find out. Won't we Bill?"

"Yes sir I think we will.

The next morning after chores I helped Spunky wrap the legs of the two year olds. We put the exercise saddle on the gelding and waited for Cassie to arrive. She came into the barn carrying her exercise saddle. She had a big smile on her face.

"Why are you so happy Cassie?"

"Today I'm going to work Light and show you all what he can do."

Spunky had the leg wraps on Light and we quickly put Cassie's saddle on him. The sun was just beginning to turn the eastern sky pink when I led her and Light onto the track.

"You know what Spunky wants, Cass. Let him work as usual until the last half mile. Don't push him at all, just let him know you want him to go."

"When we reached the track gap, Spunky held it open for Cassie and Light.

We watched as Cassie took Light backwards on the track. Spunky and I walked quickly in front of the stands and took a place towards the finish line. We watched as she stopped Light then turned and started to let him work. They came by the finish line and went around the first turn going smoothly. Light was flipping his ears as Cassie talked to him. Light was moving well within himself just waiting for Cassie to tell him to run. As they were approaching the half mile pole we saw Cassie suddenly get low on his back. She released a little of her hold on Light and he suddenly seemed to shoot forward. He did it with so much ease it was unreal. Cassie sat still on him as he seemed to roll around the far turn and as they entered the stretch she shook her reins and got lower on his back. Once again he seemed to suddenly shoot forward. Each stride of the big gray colt seemed to get longer and faster. Cassie was not pushing him. She was simply letting him do what he wanted to do, run. As they crossed the finish line I heard Spunky stop the stopwatch he was holding.

I saw the smile on his face and then ran to the gate and out onto the track to catch Light when he came back. The smile on Cassie's said it all. She was thrilled. Spunky was suddenly beside me as I snapped the lead shank on Light.

"How good was it Spunky?"

"I'll tell you when we get him back to the barn Bill. Cassie and I will go through the grandstands back to the barn. You take him back to the barn. I'd rather noone knew we had worked him if we can."

I led the stud back towards the barn and no one seemed to notice. He was just another horse getting led before he would be worked. When I reached the barn Spunky was waiting for me at the wash rack. Cassie held Light while I removed the saddle and took off his leg wraps. I removed his bridle and put his halter on then led him to the wash rack. Spunky was smiling as we led him up.

"Bill, it looks like you were right again. He just may be the one I've been looking for all these years. Let's get him bathed and then we'll talk."

I held Light while spunky ran cold water on his legs then took the bucket of warm water and gave him a bath. When we were finished we turned him over to a girl who walked the horses for Spunky and went to the tack room. Once inside he picked up the phone and dialed.

"Patty, the kids are here in the tack room with me. We just worked Light a half mile like we talked about. I wanted you to know your colt just worked a half mile in forty three flat without any urging from Cassie. Patty, we may just have ourselves a race horse."

Cassie was jumping up and down with glee. I had been studying the form sheets and knew that Light's time was something special. Cassie was on the phone talking to Patty and was trying to keep from talking too loud.

"Bill, I think we need to get something on the track so folks don't begin to wonder what we're doing in here."

Cassie got off the phone and we took the two young fillies out of their stalls and rode to the track. We rode through the opening in the track while Spunky held it open. We backtracked the two fillies a short distance then turned them and then began to gallop them. We eased the horses around the track and let them work at half speed up the stretch. We took them back to where Spunky stood waiting.

"Great work kids. I think it was just what they needed to sharpen them up. Let's get back to the barn and turn them over to the hot walkers."

We turned the two horses over to the hot walkers and removed the bridles and exercise saddles. While we were doing this Spunky was busy rubbing Light's legs with liniment and then wrapped Light's front legs. We were waiting when he finished.

"Spunky, I'll take the mare and give her a light work. If anyone wants to know why we're not working the stud I'll say we're just going to walk him today."

"Good enough Bill. Go ahead and do it."

I took the mare to the track and jogged her around the track. No one was curious and when I finished, a friend of Spunky's asked me to ride a colt for him. I took the mare back to the barn and put her away. I told Spunky where I was going and went to the man's barn and started to work his colt. The colt was working well until we reached the backstretch when something went wrong. I stopped the colt and jumped off. His trainer came running across the infield of the track and ran up to where I stood holding the colt.

"What's wrong Bill?"

"I'm not sure, he was working great when he suddenly went wrong."

The man quickly checked the colt and found the problem. The colt had torn a shoe loose and it was turned crossway of his foot. One of the nails in the shoe was imbedded in his hoof.

"Thank goodness you got him stopped Bill. I'll pull the shoe and have the vet come take a look at him."

I walked back through the gap with him and went back to our barn. Spunky saw me coming and got me a chair and soda.

"Bill, we're going to finish paying the stud up in the futurity at the middle of the meet. I think we have a real good chance of winning it, that is if we can keep the colt from hurting himself."

"We'll do our best Spunky, he's listening to Cassie and working great."

"We'll have to find a jock to ride him in the race."

"Why not let Cassie ride him, Spunky. The horse loves her and will relax for her. I think it will give us an advantage over the other horses."

"Bill, she's only ridden in a couple of races. Those boys can get rough out there on the track."

"Spunky, all the jocks know her and wouldn't do anything to get her hurt. I think with a little work she and the stud will be ready for the race."

"Bill, I know it's crazy but the two of you have got Patty and I here so why not go all the way. Go get Cassie and tell her I want to talk to her."

I walked to the barn where Cassie worked and caught her just as she was ready to go to her apartment

"Cassie, Spunky wants to talk to you down at the barn if you have time."

"I was just getting ready to head home, I'll walk back with you. Any idea why he wants to talk to me Bill? He's probably going to tell me who he will get to ride Light in the futurity."

"He said to come and get you and I **did**. I work here just like you do, Cass."

Spunky sat outside the tack room **door** waiting for us, he pointed to a couple of empty chairs. We sat down and I **waited** for Spunky to ask Cass if she would ride.

"Cassie, you know we're going to **run Light in** the futurity. This means that we're going to have to be extremely **careful** with him these next few weeks. I want you to ride his works and not let **him** get away from you. That would let everyone know what kind of a horse he is. I'm going to enter him in a race week after next and I'd like you to ride him."

The look of shock and disbelief on Cassie's face was something to see. For a moment she didn't know what to say. Suddenly she recovered.

"Spunky, I'd love to ride him but are you sure? There are several boys up here that are veterans and would ride him in a minute if you asked."

"Cassie, do they know the horse?"

"No they don't, but Spunky."

"Cassie, if I wanted someone else to ride him it would be Bill but he can't. Now I want you to ride for me. Will you do it?"

"I'll have to call dad and get his okay first. I promised him I'd not ride any one's horse except Randal's. I'll go get my purse and call him. I may need to get several quarters."

"Wait a minute Cassie."

I went into the tack room and brought out my coin jar. I took out three dollars worth of quarters and went back out and handed them to Cassie.

"I got a few extra in case you had to beg."

"Thanks Bill. I'll be right back."

Spunky and I watched as Cassie ran out of the barn. We both got a good laugh out of the way she had reacted when she'd been asked to ride Light in the upcoming race.

"Think she'll get her dad's approval, Bill?"

"I'd almost bet money on it Spunky. Her dad thinks the world of her. She'll talk him into it, I'm sure."

A few moments later I was proven right. Cassie came into the barn and was flying. I'd never seen her so excited.

"I'm going to be a jock, a full fledged jock. Thank you Spunky. Thank you so much."

"Thank Bill. He's the one who told me to use you as a jock. He pointed out that you and Light have a relationship that a new jock wouldn't have. I thought about it and decided he was right. If we get beat it won't be because you weren't trying to win. I'm going to enter Light in a maiden race like I told you. I want you to get him around the track but I want you to keep him out of any trouble. We just want him to have a race and get the experience he needs.

"Spunky, I'll do my very best. I'll keep him out of trouble. It is alright if we win isn't it?"

"You bet, if he gets clear and wants to run, let him go. Not full out but let him roll and find out what it's like to run with other horses."

"Good. That will make it easy for me. We'll get out of the gate and win."

"The stage was set. Cassie would ride Light. Now all I had to do was keep him happy and in the best shape I could. Spunky and Patty had shown up in the afternoon for chores and Patty had handed me a check. I could not believe how much money I was getting paid.

"Patty, this is too much. I was even gone for a day."

"Bill, Spunky and I have talked it over and decided this is more than fair to us. My husband trusts you with everything. He said he never had to go back and check your work. You don't know how long we've looked for someone to help him. We've tried a dozen people over the last few years and none of them have worked out. You've more than earned your wages. Keeping Light from hurting himself is something I'll never be able to pay you for."

"Patty, you don't owe me a thing for Light. I love him almost as much as you do. Spunky has been my teacher and more important my friend. He's sort of the father I never had. You all have given me a chance and you'll never know what that means to me."

"Cash the check Bill. You'll be needing it for the upcoming school year. Spunky says you have been riding a few works for other trainers."

"Yes ma'am, but not until we have everything taken care of here."

"I know. Spunky has told me. He and I talked about you exercise riding. He's afraid someone will try and hire you away from us."

"Patty, no one has tried or can hire me away from you all. I'm happy and I want to be a part of the team that took Gray Light to the top, so don't worry. You're stuck with me."

"You're planning on coming back next year, Bill?"

"If you all will have me."

"Bill, we'll be looking forward to it. Now tell me how good you think Light really is. My husband is so afraid I'll get my hopes up and get my heart broken."

"Patty, I don't know a lot about thoroughbred horses but I do know a good horse when I see and ride one. Light as we all call him is truly something special. I think he will prove it in his maiden race."

"Thank you Bill. That's what I wanted to know. Now I guess we'd both better get back to work. Oh by the way, you and Cassie are invited over to the motor home tomorrow night. We're having grilled hamburgers."

"I don't know about Cassie, but I'll sure be there Patty. What time?"

"I'll have Spunky tell you tomorrow morning."

I told Patty "fine" and went on with my work. I'd be looking forward to a home cooked meal. Later that evening when Spunky and I were finishing up the evening chores he asked me about my place.

"How big is your place Bill?"

"Eight hundred and fifty acres, Spunky."

"Does it lay pretty flat?"

"Yes it does, all except the extreme backside. There is a dry creek bed where I ride a lot of the colts I start. There's a lot of sand and you can wear them out in a short while."

"Think you could work yourself up a small track there? I've got two colts I'll need broke this fall. If you had a small track I'd send them to you. You know what we need done and we'd be way ahead of everyone when we get here next spring."

"I know a gentleman who has an old horse drawn grader. I could lay out a track and work it up. My friend has a big tractor with a front-end loader. I could haul sand from the creek and work up a good soft cushion on the track. We'd want it soft so we wouldn't hurt the young horses' legs."

"That's exactly what I mean Bill. You'll not only break the colts to ride, you'll be looking after them as well."

"I'll get started as soon as I get home Spunky. I'll try and have it done before I have to start to school. I'll keep in touch with you and let you know."

"Sounds good to me, Bill. I'll let you know a few weeks ahead so you can be ready."

Things were looking up. I'd have the colts to break, which would give me money to pay bills and eat on. I'd borrow the grader and my friend's tractor and work a track. It wouldn't be fancy but I could make it work. It would be a nice place to ride the other colts I'd be breaking this fall.

The following week saw changes in the town and at the track. The town suddenly came alive. The stores all had bunting hanging across their fronts. Banners hung across the streets welcoming the racing fans. You could feel the electricity in the air. Spunky had the older mare in a ten thousand dollar claiming race the second day of the meet. It would be Cassie's first race as a full fledged jockey. She was nervous and it was all we could do to keep her calm. The first day of racing was something I'd never forget.

Folks who had horses in for the first day were at the barn early to do their chores. The hay bags were taken out of the stalls of the horses the night before they were going to run that day. The horses that were going to run seemed to know that this was their day to run. As race time came closer folks who worked every day at the track had changed their clothes and were looking nice. The horses had been brushed until their coats gleamed. As chores were finished and the horses gotten ready, I found myself looking forward to seeing my first horse race at a track.

Spunky had gone to the motor home for lunch and his afternoon nap. I went into the tack room and changed my clothes, too. I was going to go watch a couple of the races and didn't want to look out of place.

When I walked around the front of the grandstands I couldn't believe how large the crowd was. The box seats down near the finish line were all filled. The grand stand seats were filled with people as well. It was wonderful to see all the colors the people were wearing. I was busy looking around at everything when I heard Cassie's voice.

"Know anyone who might buy a struggling jockey a coke?"

"Hi Cassie, I'll get us a coke. Do you want anything else?"

"No, just a coke, I'm trying to watch my weight."

I went to the concession stand and waited in line to get us a coke. I began to see why the track was so important to the town. People were in a good mood and were spending money. I got our cokes and went back to where Cassie stood. I gave Cassie her coke and followed her to the rail down near the finish line.

"This is what's called being a railbird. Most of the folks who work here on the track stand down here to watch the races, first off, to see the race up close. Second because they don't have to pay for a seat. I usually wait until the first couple of races are over and then find a seat up high in the grandstands. You can see the gates and the whole track from up there."

"Sounds like a plan Cassie, you all don't have anything in today?"

"No, we have two in tomorrow. Is this the first time you've been to the races?"

"Sure enough is Cassie. My dad had been up here a number of times but I was home taking care of business."

"Bill, how did you manage to survive living like that?"

"If my father was gone I only had to fight with the spoiled horses. I didn't have to worry about getting cussed and beat. I really looked forward to him leaving for a few days."

"I can see why you would, Bill. Now that your father is gone what are your plans?"

"I plan on building an exercise track. Spunky wants to send me a couple of colts to break and condition this fall. I figure I'll be running through myself to get things fixed before school starts."

"You think you can get it done, Bill?"

"I don't have a choice Cassie, it will make my life a lot easier and will let me finish my last year of school. It's a chance for me to make something out myself and maybe do something worthwhile with my life. I sure don't want to be remembered as the son of a drunken horse trader."

"I understand Bill. Is there anything I can do?"

"Do you by chance have a bulldozer you'll loan me?"

"Heavens no, Bill."

"Then I don't figure there is much you can do for now. I appreciate your asking though. I've got a friend or two I can ask to help."

The track announcer welcomed everyone to the season of racing and a few moments later the track bugler sounded the "Call To The Post." I would remember this for the rest of my life. The sound of the bugle made chills run up my back. It was race day.

Cassie and I watched a couple of races then went back to the barn and brushed Light. I checked his shoes, which had been set two days before and found them to be in good shape. The mare would run tomorrow, the stud the next day. We went to the mare's stall and began to brush and give her some attention. The mare was an old pro at the racing game and was ready. She would be retired after this year of racing. Spunky hoped she would make a fine brood mare.

"Tomorrow girl, we're going to go to the track and run a race. I know you like to lay just off the pace so that's just what we'll do. It's your race, lady. I'm just along for the ride."

"Cassie, that's not exactly true. Even though she an old hand at this racing business you are the one to let her know when to run. You've got a job to do and I have faith in you."

"Thank you Bill. By the way, I want to thank you for telling Spunky you thought I should ride Light."

"It was the truth, Cassie. You all get along and I think it's to our advantage to get him off of on the right foot."

A short time later Spunky walked in the barn and we began to do our evening chores. The races were still going on but it made no difference to us. We had horses to get ready for tomorrow and the day after. After we had done our chores and Spunky had left I walked over to the track kitchen and had my supper. When I got back to the barn I checked all the horses and then went to the tack room and got my book. Tonight I was going to get that last chapter finished. I had just sat down when the phone rang.

"Davis Stable, Bill Patton speaking."

"Bill, this is Cass, is everything alright?"

"Everything is fine Cass. The mare is relaxed. I'll take her hay away before I turn in. Light is working on his hay and Slinker is upset because he can't start napping. The two year olds are just busy watching everything. The races ended about an hour ago so everything is beginning to settle down. What can I do for you?"

"I guess I'm just nervous about tomorrow, Bill."

"You don't need to be, Cass. I've studied the form and the mare should win easy. She is really working well and is on her toes. Relax and get some rest. I've a feeling that tomorrow is going to be the start of a good season."

"I sure hope so, Bill. I guess I'll get a hot bath and go to bed."

"That sounds like a good idea Cass. Get a good night's rest. I'll see you in the saddling paddock."

I picked up my book and began to read. The barn settled down and the horses began to sleep. I finished the book and went to the showers and got a hot shower myself. When I got back to the barn I checked on the horses and went to bed.

The next morning I was up and dressed when Spunky arrived. We quickly got all the horses fed and their stalls mucked. I went to the track kitchen and ate breakfast. When I returned Spunky left for his place. He told me he and Patty would be back in time for me to get a bite of lunch before we had to get the mare ready. She was in the third race, which was a six furlong sprint. I got my chair and sat down with my last book and began to read. I knew I'd be busy for most of the afternoon, so I'd better rest now.

Just before noon, Patty and Spunky returned. I got a quick bite to eat and then went to work on the mare. I had her mane braided and was just beginning to brush her when Spunky came to her stall and put her front leg wraps on. When he finished he told me to make sure everything was ready to go to the saddling paddock. He would put the race bridle on her just before we left. I checked everything and put it all in a bucket that I would take with us.

The first race was on the track and I could feel myself get nervous. There was nothing I could do now but my mind was whirling. I saw Spunky grin at me.

"Getting nervous, Bill?"

"Yes I am Spunky. I'm trying to think of anything I might have forgotten."

"Bill, if a race comes along and you don't get nervous, go home."

"I think I understand Spunky. If it gets boring I'd better find another line of work."

"I've been doing this my whole life Bill and it's always the same. I'm nervous now but it's all up to the mare and Cassie now. We've done our best to get her ready."

CHAPTER 5

A short time later we heard the racing steward call the third race to the saddling paddock. I put the mare's racing bridle on her and led her out of the stall. The mare looked great. Her coat gleamed in the afternoon sun as Spunky and I took her from our barn to the saddling paddock. Our hot walker had taken our equipment bucket to the saddling paddock a short time earlier.

I led the mare around the saddling ring a couple of times when I saw Cassie walk over to the stall where the mare would be saddled. She and Spunky discussed how he wanted her to ride the mare. A track assistant showed up carrying Cassie's saddle and the track's numbered blanket. Spunky waved to me to bring the mare over. I led her into the stall and held her while Spunky and the track's groom sat the saddle in place. I led the mare out of the saddling stall and around the walking ring until I heard the racing steward make the call "Riders Up." I held the mare as Spunky gave Cassie a leg up onto the mare. I led the mare and Cassie over towards the gap and handed the lead rope to the lead horse rider.

"See you at the winner's circle, Cassie."

"The mare and I will be there, Bill"

As I turned away I saw our hot walker Donna walking towards me.

"What do you think, Bill"

"The mare is ready. I think she will win but this is my first horse race so what do I know?"

"You're kidding. This is your first race? That's hard to believe, Bill. You ride exercise horses and I've heard trainers say that you're great with them."

"That may be, but I'd never ridden a race horse until a few weeks ago."

"Well I'm going to make a bet. Want me to make a bet for you?"

"What are the odds?"

"The mare is six to one, Bill."

"Take this ten dollar bill and put it on the mare to win. I like the looks of the seven horse, too. Take this five and get me an exacta."

"You just may be right Bill. I've watched that mare work and I think she may be the one we have to outrun. I'll place your bets. Where will you be Bill?"

I pointed up in the corner of the grandstands. Donna left to make the bets for me. I went up into the grandstands where I could see the whole track. The horses were being led past the grandstand when I finally got to where I could see. Cassie was wearing Spunky and Patty's racing silks. The dove gray and black silks would be easy to pick out when the race started. My heart was racing as I watched the horses being led back around the track to be warmed up. I was watching the mare to see if everything was alright when I heard Donna walk up to where I stood.

"She looks good Bill. I've got your tickets."

"Hang on to them Donna. I'm not old enough to cash them anyway."

"I'd not thought about that. The odds are good on the mare. She is nine to one now. The two and the ten are the favorites. The seven is twenty to one. If our two horses come in we're going to make a mint on our bets."

"You made the same bet as I did?"

"Yes I did, Bill. I didn't wager as much as you, but I think you may just be right about the seven horse. Any way we'll know soon. They are starting to load the horses into the gates."

"I watched as Cassie and the mare were led into the gates. The mare went in and the gate was closed behind her. Soon all ten horses were loaded into the gates. The track announcer said "The horses are all in line and the flag is up."

Donna and I watched as gates suddenly flew open.

"They're off" the announcer said.

It was a good clean start. All of the horses began to extend themselves. The number two and the number ten began their battle for the lead. I watched as Cassie and the mare settled into third place a length and a half behind the two front running horses. The seven horse another length behind our mare. The rest of the horses were bunched up five or six lengths behind. Cassie had the mare down on the rail and had her well in hand. The two frontrunners were going way too fast to be able to last the distance. Cassie was waiting for the two of them to begin to tire. As they rounded the turn and headed for home I saw Cassie suddenly get down lower on the mare's back and ask her to run. The two front running horses were beginning to tire and drifted away from the inside rail.

Cassie asked the mare for her all and shot through the opening on the rail and quickly was in the lead. The seven horse had followed her through the opening and was going to make our mare have to work to stay in front. Cassie tapped the mare on the hip with her stick and got lower on her back. The two mares battled up the stretch, neither giving an inch. As they neared the wire I heard both jockeys shouting to their horses. Neither Donna nor I had any idea about who had won. The photo sign went up on the infield tote board. We rushed down out of the stands and went through the track gate where I waited with the lead rope to catch the mare when Cassie brought her back. As Cassie brought the mare close I could see the concern on her face. She wasn't sure if she had won or lost the race.

The track announcer asked that both the three and seven horse were to be held on the track. I snapped the lead rope or shank, as they were called here, on the track and began to lead Cassie and the mare around in a big circle while watching the tote board that still flashed "Photo".

"I don't know if we won or not Bill, but I'm proud of the mare. She gave me everything she had up the stretch. Oh Bill, I hope we won!"

"So do I Cassie. That was the most exciting thing I've ever seen. Neither one of the mares would give an inch."

Spunky came over to the mare and had Cassie dismount long enough to take the elastic overgirth off the mare. He took the sponge from the bucket Donna held and washed the face of the mare. He gave Cassie a leg up on the mare and told her she had ridden a great race.

Suddenly the crowd roared and the number three was posted as the winner of the race.

"We won Bill, we won!"

I tried to remain calm and led the mare over to the winner's circle where I got a kiss on the cheek from Patty. I held the mare in place until the picture was taken. Spunky came over to me smiling and shook my hand.

"Follow the track steward over there, Bill. The mare will have to go to the test barn. I'll have Donna follow you with the water bucket."

"I'll take care of her Spunky."

Suddenly Cassie had her arms around my neck.

"Thank you Bill Patton. Thank you for giving me a chance to ride."

"You can thank me later, Cass. I've got to get the mare to the test barn. Besides, you've got to weigh out."

She left at a run as I followed the trackman up the track and into the test barn area. I took the bucket of water from Donna and let the mare have a small drink. I led her around the test barn area a couple of times then gave her another sip of water. The test barn crew came out and took the mare into the test barn. Donna and I waited a few minutes and when the crew brought the mare out of the test barn I took the lead shank and we took the mare back to our barn.

I was floating as I led the tired mare back to the barn. Spunky and Patty were waiting at the tack room when we led her up to them.

I held the mare while Spunky took the wraps off her legs. I led her to the wash rack where we began running cold water on her legs. After a few moments Donna brought a bucket of warm water and began to give the mare a bath. When she was bathed I handed the lead shank to Donna who began walking her around the barn. I finally had a chance to talk to Spunky.

"Spunky, the mare ran a great race. My knees were so weak when she reached the wire, I could hardly stand. I felt like I rode every inch of the race with Cassie."

"I know what you men Bill. The other mare ran a good race herself. It will be talked about for a while, that's for sure. What would you have done different if you'd been riding the mare instead of Cassie?"

"Spunky, like I said I felt like I rode every inch of the race with Cassie. Every time I thought she should do something, she did. I'd not have done a thing different."

"It's the same with me Bill, I talked her through the race myself. It seemed that every time I wanted her to move the mare she did. We may have ourselves a great young jockey Bill."

"Spunky, this race was bad enough but I can't even begin to think about what tomorrow's race will be like. I've already figured out that this business is not one for anyone with a bad heart."

"Lord, no. A man wouldn't last a week with races like we just watched. Let's have a soda, Bill. I feel like celebrating."

We were drinking our sodas when Cassie came down the barn aisle skipping along like a little girl. The smile on her face was something to see.

"Well folks, what did I do wrong? I can tell you two have been going over everything."

"Well Cassie, Bill and I have discussed it and we figure with a little help you just might make one heck of a jock. You rode a beautiful race, Cassie."

"Oh thank you Spunky, thank you! Bill Patton, I want to thank you, too. I never would have gotten this chance had it not been for you and I'll never forget it"

"Cassie, like I've told you before, you earned the ride. I still feel like I'm the outsider of the group."

"Bill Patton, don't you ever let me hear you say something like that again. You're one of the most important members of this barn and don't you ever forget it. Spunky and I think you're a fine young man and will make a fine trainer in a year or so. Now, we're all going to supper tonight and celebrate."

I'd never seen Patty upset before and I didn't think I wanted to see her upset again.

"Patty that sounds great but I think I'd better stay here and keep an eye on Light."

"Why Bill, it's his first race and everyone still thinks he's a rogue. Spunky and I have commented to several folks about what a handful he is and how this race is just a schooling race for him. No one is going to bother him. Now if we start keeping stall watch folks are going to start wondering and I'll not make near as much money tomorrow."

"She's right Bill. We can hire Donna to keep an eye on the mare. After the hard race today no one will think anything about us having someone looking after her. We might just as well go eat a good dinner and enjoy the evening."

"Sounds good to me. What time do we leave?"

"We'll leave as soon as we get the mare cooled and get her wraps put on. If we wait until the races are over we'll never get into a place to eat."

"Sounds good to me, Spunky. I've already got clean clothes on."

A short time later Donna brought the mare to Spunky for him to check. After he looked her legs over Spunky told me to put her into her stall. He would bring the leg rub and wrap her legs for the night. I took the mare to her stall and began to unbraid her mane while I waited for Spunky to begin bracing her legs and putting the wraps on her.

Spunky began putting the leg brace on the mare and rubbing it into her legs. She never minded so I continued to unbraid her mane. I had just finished when Donna came over to the stall wearing a big smile. She handed me my money, smiling all the time.

"Bill, we did well today. The exacta paid off great. The family and I will eat well next week. Thanks for the tip Bill."

"Bill did you have the exacta in the race?"

"I had a five dollar exacta, Spunky."

"Good lord, that exacta paid over six hundred dollars."

"Six hundred and twelve to be exact Spunky. Bill gave me the tip and it paid off."

"I'm glad you all had it. We made a little money but nothing like you two."

I counted my money and had to smile. This, along with my insurance money, would buy me a good used truck. It had been a very good day indeed. We loaded in Spunky's truck and went to one of the local steak houses and had a wonderful meal. Cassie sat beside me and to be truthful I really enjoyed it. When we got back to the barn everyone was full and after our evening chores would probably go to bed early. One thing about the track, I was getting plenty of sleep. Getting up at four and working all day long, a fellow was more than glad to hit his bed early every evening. Add to that that I was eating regularly and I was feeling great. After doing our chores we again checked the mare and then put the leg wraps on Light.

"Bill, we've done all we can do. I guess it's up to him and Cassie from here on out."

"Spunky, everything we've done is just to get him ready. From this point on I figure it's all up to him. If he wants to be a racehorse he will be. It's just going to depend on how much heart he has. That's the one thing no horseman can measure."

"Don't worry about the heart, boys. He'll give me his all when I ask him for it. He wants to run and he seems to know that something is up. Bill, why don't you go rub his ears so he'll know everything is alright. He seems to depend on you to let him know everything is alright. We want him to have a good night's rest."

"I'll do that Cassie. He always likes to have his ears rubbed. I'll make sure he gets all the ear rubbing he wants this evening."

"Good, I want him as sharp as can be tomorrow. I want to keep my win streak alive."

"Yes ma'am, I'll do my very best. Now go home and get some rest. The horse will be ready if I have to sleep with him myself."

"Spunky, I think I just got dismissed."

"Well he is my assistant trainer, so I think I'll just go home and rest, myself, Cassie."

They were both laughing when they went out of the barn. Patty came over and gave me a hug and told me goodnight. I gave the stud a good ear rubbing and he seemed to relax. I got the brush from the tack room and gave him a good brushing. When I left the stall he was settled and was going to sleep. I walked back to the tack room and got my book. I'd read until everything in the barn settled down. I might have a short night but I'd know the stud was ready. I was just thinking about going to bed a couple of hours later when I heard Cassie's voice.

"You couldn't sleep either."

"I was just thinking about it Cass, Light's been asleep for an hour or so. I gave him a ear rubbing session and then brushed him for a good half hour. He seemed to relax and went to sleep."

"If that's the case, then I'm going to go back to my apartment and get some rest."

"That would be best Cass, you need to be sharp in the morning."

I got a kiss on the cheek and Cassie was gone. I touched my cheek and smiled. I woke up a couple of hours later leaning back in my chair against the tack room wall. I rubbed my stiff neck and walked slowly down and checked on Light. He stood in the corner of his stall and was asleep. I went back to the tack room and went to bed. When the alarm went off at four I was up and dressed before Spunky arrived. I had the feed measured up and ready to go. I gave him a report on Light as we began feeding the horses. We mucked the stalls and put Light out on the walker with Slinker who didn't want to work. It would keep Light from expending any excess energy.

We later put the rest of the horses on the walker after we had Light and Slinker put back in their stalls. Spunky had brought sausage and egg biscuits for our breakfast. We ate them while we drank our coffee. When we finished with our breakfast I went to Light's stall and began braiding his mane. I wanted him to be looking great when Cassie showed up in the saddling paddock. I brushed him and then rubbed him down with a soft oiled cloth that made his gray dappled coat shine even under the dim lights of the barn.

"Bill, he looks great. We may not know how he will run but we'll have the best looking bugger in the race."

"He is a handsome thing isn't he Spunky? He knows something is up but he's not sure what it is yet. I figure he may be a little bit harder to handle after he gets a taste of racing. Then again he may not. He's so doggone smart."

'We'll find out in a couple of hours, Bill. We're in the second race today."

"I know. I got a racing sheet yesterday evening. One of the boys across the aisle was going to get a form. He picked up one for me while he was there. I figure we have to outrun the one and the eight horse."

"That's the way I see it too, Bill. Those colts have been working somewhat longer than he has and have recorded some good work times. He'll have to work to win the race. The two horses come from two of the top barns here at the track."

"Well I guess we'll see what happens."

CHAPTER 6

A couple of hours later we heard the call for the first race. I was busy cleaning the racing gear for the third time. The stud was fine but I was having a hard time controlling my nerves. I knew I had to so that the stud would be calm and not wash out as it was called at the track. A nervous horse never ran a good race according to the old timers at the track. Never bet on a horse that was sweating in the post parade. I'd do my best to keep Light as calm as possible.

When the call was announced for the horses in the second race to come to the track we were ready. I put the lead shank on Light and led him out of the stall. Spunky had a light stable sheet to put on him. As soon as the stable sheet was on, I started for the saddling paddock. When we got to the saddling paddock I began to check out the other horses in our race. Over the last few weeks I'd come to know most of the horses that worked on the track every day. Light was on his toes. He was stepping along with me but was not upset like several of the other horses in our race were. One of the colts was rearing and striking out with his front feet. The ring steward finally scratched the colt before we were ordered to saddle. Spunky came over to where I was leading Light and took the stable sheet off him. He seemed to glow in the afternoon sunshine. A few moments later the stewards who helped saddle the horses came to their numbered stalls. Spunky waved to me. I took Light over to the enclosure and held him while Spunky and the steward put Cassie's small saddle on Light and then put the over girt in place. I saw Cassie and the rest of the jockeys walk to the horses they would ride in the race. Each trainer would give the jockey instructions on how they wanted the race ridden.

I led Light out of the saddling enclosure and began to walk him around the walking ring. A few minutes later I heard the ring steward call "Riders Up."

Spunky and Cassie walked over to where I now held Light and Spunky gave her a leg up on Light. Things were about out of our hands. I led Light and Cassie over to the track entrance and handed the lead shank to the lead pony rider.

"See you in the winner's circle, Cassie."

"You bet, Bill. The ice cream is on you tonight if I win."

"Done deal, Cassie. Now go show folks what a race horse looks like."

I walked over to where Spunky watched Light and Cassie being led off. He waved to me and began walking to the grandstand where I knew Patty was waiting for him. I went to the grand stand and again went up to the top row where I could see the entire track and yet be off to myself. My stomach was doing somersaults. I'd never experienced anything like this before. I saw Donna come up the steps to where I stood.

"What do you want to do Bill?"

I took out my billfold and took out the money I wanted her to bet.

"Twenty to win, ten to place and ten to show, and I want a twenty dollar exacta five and the eight."

"The eight, Bill. Why in the world would you want to bet the eight?"

"I saw him work the other morning and he is fast, real fast. This is a five furlong sprint and I think he is the horse we'll have to catch. I don't believe he can run six furlongs but he can sure enough run five."

"Well, I'll go make your bets and be back. I don't want to miss this race."

I watched as Cassie warmed up Light on the backside of the track. He was not fighting his head but you could see he was ready to run when Cassie asked him to. Donna came back a few minutes later and showed me my tickets. I checked the tote board and saw that Light was seven to one and the eight was forty five to one.

"Bill, if you win the exacta today you may have to pay the IRS the taxes. Lord, it will pay off better than a slot machine."

"I don't know about that Donna. I've never played a slot machine but it's the way I see the race going. I think Light will have to run to catch the little bay horse in this short of a race. If he wins this one we're home free as far as I'm concerned."

We watched as the horses were loaded into the starting gates. I saw Cassie pull her goggles down as she and Light were led into their number five gate. A moment later the track announcer said the horses were all in line.

The bell rang and the gates flew open. We watched as Cassie and Light got out smoothly. I saw the eight horse was suddenly in the lead and was going away by four lengths. Cassie must have seen it too. She released her short hold on Light and began to let him roll. Roll he did. The four lengths were suddenly one with Cassie sitting directly behind the eight and his jockey. The jockey on the eight might hear her but he couldn't see her without raising up to look back under his arm. Cassie was riding a beautiful race. As the eight horse came around the turn and headed into the stretch his jockey went to the whip, urging him on. Cassie sat behind him another twenty or so yards then moved Light over to the right and asked him to run. He lay his ears back flat on his neck and in two tremendous strides overtook the other horse and seemed to simply fly by the still hard running eight horse as if he were wearing lead shoes.

Donna's statement summed it all up.

"Oh, Lord."

We watched as Cassie and Light went past the finish wire a good three lengths in front of the eight horse who had run a strong second. Donna and I went down out of the grandstands as fast as we possibly could. We went through the gate and out onto the track to catch Gray Light and Cassie when they came back. A roar went up from the crowd when the New Track Record sign was suddenly flashing on the tote board. I was thrilled but scared at the same time. I remembered what Spunky had said about a little man can't afford to own a great horse.

Spunky was suddenly beside me as I snapped the lead shank on Light. Cassie jumped off Light so Spunky could remove the over girt then got a leg up on Light just as the crowd again cheered. I felt like cheering, too as I took a quick look at the tote board and saw what the exacta had paid. I noticed Donna was smiling as I led Light into the winner's circle. People seemed to be everywhere all at once. I saw Cassie's folks who I know she didn't know were coming. I knew Cassie hadn't seen them when the picture was taken. I waited for Spunky to remove the saddle from Light and then followed the man from the test barn up the track. Donna again had the water bucket ready when I arrived with Light. I gave Light a small drink and began leading him around the small lot until the test barn folks came out and took Light into the test barn. Donna and I stood outside and waited until the test barn man led Light back out of the barn and turned the horse over to me. I took the lead shank and led Light back to our barn. Folks were telling us what a horse he was as we went along. We arrived at the barn and were surprised that Patty and Spunky weren't waiting for us. I gave the lead shank to Donna and removed the leg wraps from Light's front legs.

We took Light to the wash rack and began to cool his legs and were almost finished with his bath when Patty came into the barn. The smile on her face was great to see. She watched as we finished with Light's bath and then patted his neck before Donna began walking him. Patty gave me a hug and told me how much she appreciated all the work I had done with Light.

"Patty, it's almost as exciting for me as it is for you. When Cassie moved Light and asked him to run, all the hard work was worth the results."

"I know what you mean Bill. I've never seen a horse with the stride and the speed he seems to have. My husband was crying when he went across the finish line. He told me his two kids had just given us the horse we'd been looking for all these years. I had to agree with him Bill, you and Cassie have done wonders with our problem child. He's still tied up with the news people. A television station was here to get some film clips of the races to show on their news station tonight. They seem to think they got a lot more than they had planned."

"Have you seen Cassie?"

"She is with Spunky or was when I left. The news folks were busy asking her all sorts of questions."

"Well at least when Light is walked dry I know what brace to put on his legs and how to wrap him. The next couple of days are most likely going to be a little bit busy around here. You did make the last payment into the futurity here later in the meet?"

"I made the last payment last week Bill. There are forty eight horses paid up. There were over three hundred colts nominated, but like always most dropped out for one cause or another. The racing secretary told me there was over a hundred thousand dollars in the race and that does not include the twenty five thousand the track is adding."

"Good lord. That's a lot of money, Patty. You and Spunky could almost retire if Light wins."

"It would help Bill. We could build a new mare barn and do a few things to the house. I would like to win Bill, but if we don't win the world won't end. I've seen folks get their hopes up before and get their heart broken when something went wrong with their horse. I'll not let that happen Bill. I've been around this business too long to let it happen to me. I'll enjoy the time and enjoy Gray Light all a person can."

"I understand Patty, but don't get in a hurry about making any decisions. Gray Light just might be the thing that will make a lot of changes in your and Spunky's lives."

Cassie came running into the barn all excited.

"We won! Wasn't he wonderful? Did you ever see anything like the way he moved when I asked him to? Patty, he's something I will never forget. Bill, you're wonderful."

Cassie gave me a kiss on the cheek and continued talking about the race. All Patty and I could do was listen to her and smile. A few moments later Donna brought Light into the barn for me to check. He was dry and ready to have his leg wraps put on. I went to the tack room and got the leg brace and the things I would need to take care of Light. Cassie held Light while I rubbed and wrapped his legs. We had just finished when Spunky came into the barn. A bunch of folks were following him.

"Bill, would you bring Grey Light out so these gentlemen can take some pictures of him, please?"

I brought Light out of his stall and stood him up for all the folks to see. Pictures were taken and I put Gray Light back in his stall. I hung his hay net for him to nibble on until we did our evening chores. As I turned to leave one of the men asked if I was Bill Patton from down by Amarillo. I told him yes and wanted to know why.

"Mr. Patton, you broke a colt for my father-in-law a year or so ago that my daughter is running barrels on now. She's leading the state high school circuit right now."

"Your father-in-law's name was what sir?"

"Jim Melton."

"Jim is an old friend of mine. The horse is a bald faced sorrel?"

"That's the horse. You did a fine job on him."

"Thank you sir, but Jim had him well mannered when I got him. He was easy to break and was fun to work with."

"I'll tell Jim I visited with you this weekend. I think he has a filly he wants to send you this fall."

"Tell him to give me a call."

Spunky and Patty finally got free of all the people who were wishing them well. I saw them coming over to the stall where I was rubbing Light's ears.

"Keeping him happy Bill?"

"I'm trying Spunky. I think after what he showed us today he deserves a little extra attention."

"Yes he does. I've never seen anything like what I saw today. I've been at this business some twenty years and I still don't believe the move he made when Cassie asked him to move."

"He's the horse you've dreamed of Spunky, you said something about the big stakes race in Albuquerque. The one that is for only state bred colts."

"Yes I did Bill, but it was only a thought. I never dreamed I'd have a colt good enough to even enter the trials."

"Well Spunky, there's a lot of folks who think Light is good enough to not only run in the trials but good enough to maybe just win the whole thing. If I were you I'd be thinking about entering Light in the race, Spunky. I'm willing to give up my salary for the rest of the summer if you need the money to enter the race. I'm doing well riding exercise horses every morning thanks to you."

"Bill, the reason I've suggested you ride some of my friend's horses is because I believe in your ability to see and feel what a horse is doing out on the track. It's a God given gift and you've put it to work for you. As for using your salary to nominate the stud for the race, we've got plenty of money to do that. Patty has been putting money back for several years now just in case we got lucky."

"Spunky, I'm just a lucky girl jockey and don't have that much experience, but if there is a horse around here that can run with Light, I've never seen him. If you decide to enter Light in the big state race and want a more experienced jockey it won't hurt my feelings. I just want to see how far he can go."

"Cassie, you and Bill here have brought us this far and Patty and I have discussed it. We figure it's sort of like the old saying "You take a girl to the dance you bring her home." We feel we've leaned on you two kids for your input and your abilities too. We think we'll wait until we see how we do in the futurity in three weeks. If we win, we'll pay the late fee and run Light in the state race. Bill, you're my assistant trainer and Cassie you're our jockey. Let's see just how far we can take this gray bugger."

Cassie let out a yell and jumped in the air. She hugged Spunky and Patty's neck and thanked them for letting her ride Light. I shook Spunky's hand and told him I'd do my best to have Light ready for the upcoming futurity. I'll walk him tomorrow and start filling his tank for the race. Filling his tank meant we'd walk him tomorrow and then give him a few light gallops in the days to come. We'd increase the speed of his works as we got closer to the race and then back off so the colt was ready to give us his all when needed. We certainly didn't want a tired horse going into the race. In the meantime, we'd scratch his ears, brush and generally spoil him.

That evening Spunky and Patty took Cassie and I to one of the nicer steak houses in town. Patty had called and made a reservation earlier in the day. Spunky had hired Donna to keep an eye on things while we were gone. Donna had gotten me aside and handed me my money. I wasn't shocked but very pleasantly pleased. I now had enough to buy a good used truck, but I needed to open a bank account. I had far too much money in the jar in the tack room. I needed the money for the truck and the things I would need for setting up my training center. I knew it was dream but I was ready to go to work and get started building it.

Cassie picked me up at the barn and stopped at the local bank long enough for me to open an account, then drove us to the steak house. We met Spunky and Patty outside, and then walked into the steak house. We were shown to a small private room where we enjoyed a great meal. Spunky and Patty had a glass of wine with their meal. Cassie and I had cherry cokes.

We had just finished our meal when a gentleman came to the doorway. He was nicely dressed and asked Spunky if he could speak to him in private. Spunky looked at Patty then got up and left the room. No one in the room said anything. We each knew what the man wanted, Light.

When Spunky came back he could see we all knew what the man had wanted. He sat down then told us what we already knew.

"Folks, it's started. That gentleman was from Texas and saw the race today. He just offered me thirty thousand for the colt. I told him I'd have to talk to the rest of the team before I made a decision. I took his card and told him I'd give him a call tomorrow."

"Spunky, the horse belongs to you and Patty. Today he made you thirty five hundred, but if he wins the futurity in three weeks you'll pick up a very nice check as well as you'll still own the horse and have the opportunity to go for the big money in the state race. I'd not get in any hurry about selling the colt. If he wins the next race, he'll be worth far more than the thirty thousand you were just offered."

"Bill is right Spunky, if you all are not strapped for cash I'd be for keeping the colt and just watch his price go up."

"Kids, the horse belongs to Patty. It's her decision. We'll do whatever she thinks."

"I'm glad my husband remembered who the owner of Gray Light actually happens to be. I'm not interested in selling at this time. I'm having way too much fun. We've worked for years to have a horse like this and I for one am not anxious to see it end."

"Patty, you could have the brood mare barn you've always wanted."

"I could, but I'd always wonder what might have been. I just don't think I could stand to see someone else standing in the winner's circle with Gray

Light. He's ours Spunky. Let's let him take us for a ride. It may never happen again."

"Bill, you hang Gray Light on the walker first thing in the morning after feeding him. We'll start filling his tank. I want to win his trial race and win the futurity. The folks at the state race just might discount the late fee if he does what I think he going to do."

I bought a very happy Cassie an ice cream cone on the way back to the barn. I told her I was looking for a good used truck if she came across one.

"I'll keep my eyes open Bill, there is always someone who gets in a bind and has a truck for sale. That's how I got mine last year. You've got enough to buy a truck now?"

"I do after today. I had twenty across the board on Light to win and a twenty dollar exacta."

"You had a twenty dollar exacta? My lord, Bill how much did you win?"

I told her and she smiled.

"You can afford a good used truck. You'll not get those kind of odds again Bill."

"I know Cass, but I got them once and that's what matters to me now."

I got out at the race track gate so Cassie could go on home and get some rest. Spunky had two horses in the next day. The two year old gelding was in the third race and the older gelding was in the fifth race. We'd have our hands full getting everything ready.

I walked into the barn and found Donna sitting in front of Light's stall. His head was hanging over his steel gate and lay partly on her shoulder as she sat reading a book. I had to laugh.

"Teaching him to read Donna?"

"He told me this western of yours was pretty good so I just picked it up and started reading."

"Things been quiet while we were gone?"

"Not really, there were two different bunches by to look at Light. I wouldn't take him out of his stall but did let them look him over from outside. They gave me these cards and wanted Spunky to give them a call tomorrow."

I took the cards and put them in my shirt pocket. I told Donna thanks and sent her home. She would be back tomorrow morning early to help us with the two geldings. I put the cards next to the phone and went back to check on Light. I rubbed his ears and told him to go to bed. I closed his top door and walked back to the tack room. I turned out the light and went to bed.

The next morning I put Light out on the walker and watched as he kicked up his heels and played as the walker led him around.

"It doesn't look like he needs much gas, Bill."

"Spunky, the race yesterday was like one of the works we give him. He doesn't even realize he was in a race."

"We'll sure enough not tell anyone that. We'll jog him tomorrow and maybe the next day. We'll give him a couple of long gallops later in the week. No need to get him too high too quick. We want him ready but not too ready."

"That shouldn't be a problem, we can work him with one of the geldings when we do the long works. He's used to working with them and will only work hard enough to win. Cassie can ride Light and I'll ride the gelding. You can be sure the gelding won't go too fast."

"Sounds good Bill. Now let's get started on the two geldings. I'd like to notch another win."

The young gelding, Slinker, was not my favorite horse. He was lazy and I had to really make him work in his work races. I had told Spunky about it and he had told me not to worry. The colt was just like his mother. I still had no idea about what Spunky meant.

I braided Slinker's mane while Spunky put the leg wraps on him. We had just finished when the track announcer called the first race. I began to get everything ready. I had cleaned all of the equipment we would need this morning while Light was on the walker. Donna arrived and said she was ready to go to work. She would bathe Slinker when I brought him back to the barn. Patty showed up long enough to say hello and give Spunky a kiss before going to her seat in the grandstands. Finally the track announcer called the third race to the saddling paddock. I put the lead shank on Slinker and followed Spunky to the saddling paddock. I led him around the saddling paddock and looked at the other horses in the race. There were a few I didn't know.

Spunky had explained to me about what some of the boys called "shippers". They were horses that were brought in for special races and were not kept here on the track. I looked the strange horses over and did not see anything that impressed me. Spunky waved to me to bring Slinker over to be saddled. I took the gelding over to the saddling area and held him while Spunky and the track attendant saddled the gelding. Cassie showed up and listened as Spunky gave her instructions. When they were finished I led Slinker around the saddling ring until the paddock judge called "Jockey up". Spunky and Cassie walked over and Spunky gave Cassie a leg up onto the gelding. I led her through the gap and handed the lead shank to the pony rider.

"Good luck, Cassie"

"See you in the winner's circle, Bill."

"I'll see you there."

I watched as Slinker suddenly seemed to begin to wake up and come to life. I remembered what Spunky had said about the young gelding's mother. I walked to the grand stand and climbed the stairs to the top. I was studying the horses when Donna showed up.

"Want me to make a bet for you Bill?

I had looked at the tote board and found Slinker was eight to one. We had gate four, next to the favorite the number three. I made my decision. I handed my money to Donna, twenty to win on Slinker and an exacta with the three.

"I'll get it for you, Bill."

A few minutes later she was back with our tickets. We watched Cassie warm Slinker up. He seemed to be on his toes so to speak. He had woken up and just might come through for me. We watched as they loaded the horses, then I remembered something else. Cassie had been wearing several pairs of goggles. She was planning on running Slinker back in the pack. I'd have to watch the race and see how she and Spunky had planned the race. The track announcer said the horses were all in line.

The gates broke and the bell sounded. The horses all jumped from the gates as one. I saw Cassie take Slinker back and set him in fifth place low down on the rail. The race was five furlongs and the frontrunners were four lengths ahead of them. I watched as Cassie dropped one pair of her goggles. As they neared the only turn Cassie had moved Slinker into a closer fourth but still behind the leaders. Slinker was getting a lot of dirt thrown in his face. I saw him shake his head as the leaders rounded the stretch and headed to the finish line. Suddenly Cassie took him to the outside and asked him to run. The young horse was mad and began to run his race. He was third, second and was then head and head with the favorite, the three horse. It was exciting to watch, but I felt I was riding the race myself.

The jockey on the three horse went to his whip. Cassie got lower on the young Slinker's neck and shouted to him. Suddenly he had a head in front and then a short neck as the two horses reached the finish wire. Cassie had ridden another fantastic race.

Donna and I raced down out of the stands and reached the track opening before Cassie brought the now tired Slinker back. I snapped the lead shank on when Cassie rode up to where Donna and I stood. She waved her stick in the air and then jumped off Slinker. Spunky had come onto the track and removed the overgirt and given Cassie a leg back up on Slinker to have her picture made. As he walked past he made a statement to me.

"Just like his mother."

I'd been correct in making my bet. Slinker's mother must have been the same way to train. She must have been lazy, too.

I led the young gelding into the winner's circle and set him up for the picture. The flash went off and Spunky removed the saddle as soon as Cassie was off. I followed the track steward to the test barn. As soon as the gelding was returned to me in the test barn area I led him as quickly as possible back to the barn where Donna stood waiting. We removed the bandages from the young gelding's legs and removed his race bridle. I put his halter on and watched as Donna led him to the wash rack. A friend of hers was waiting and helped her give the young gelding his bath. I helped Spunky get the older gelding ready.

"I hope we can run as good as third in this race, Bill. There are a couple of horses in the race that are taking a big drop in class. They have been running in allowance races and made a good deal of money. Now they are running for twenty thousand claim."

"Is there something wrong with them, Spunky?"

"I don't think so Bill, I think they are gambling that folks will think so and not place a claim on either one of them."

"I guess they know what they are doing, but it sounds like someone can get burned in a deal like this. I'm glad I'm not the trainer."

Spunky had been right, our gelding ran a good race. He had run third by less than a length. The horse that won had been claimed. The trainer was upset but he had gambled and lost.

I later discovered Donna had talked to Spunky and had bet ten dollars on our gelding to place. I'd won a little money on him and didn't even know it. Donna had also given me my money I'd won on the first race. This week had been a very good week for me. I was happy though that we didn't have anything in tomorrow. It would take me some time to get things back in order and get the horses worked that needed working. The young filly would race on Sunday.

Later Cassie came to the barn and, after rubbing Light's ears, went to Slinker's stall and patted his neck. He had shown courage and fought all the way through the stretch. Spunky and I had talked and I found out he was like his mother who had made Spunky and Patty a little over a hundred thousand dollars in three years' time. They had retired her and made a brood mare out of her. Slinker was her first colt to run.

"Spunky, I wonder how she would cross on Light?"

"That would be an interesting cross Bill. She has a lot of foreign blood and it just might work. Patty and I will have to think about that. Of course Light has to prove himself first."

Spunky and Patty went out with friends, leaving Cassie, Donna and me alone.

"If you ladies will keep an eye on things I'll run over to the kitchen and get me a burger and fries to go. I shouldn't be gone long."

"Bill, sit down and relax. Donna and I ordered pizza a while ago. You don't need to be eating so many burgers. I know they are quick, but you need something healthy every now and then."

She and Donna got a good laugh about our diet program.

"I'll try and remember that Cass. Have you heard anything about a truck yet?"

"I may have a line on one but won't know until tomorrow. I'll let you know when I hear something. Donna says you made a nice bet today. Did you have the exacta again?"

"I did in our first race, because I thought of something Spunky had said. Besides, I saw the gelding seem to come alive when he went out onto the track."

"He did Bill. I've watched you work him and you have to drive him."

"I've got an idea Cassie. I'm going to ask Spunky if we can work him with Light."

"But Bill, he can't run with Light."

"I think he may be better than we think he is. True, he's not the horse that Light is, but few are. I'm hoping we can teach him to compete even better. If we can get him to work and get in even better shape he might make an allowance horse."

Bill Patton, you never cease to amaze me. You just might make a first class trainer after all."

The pizza arrived and we ate as only hungry people do.

"Who do I owe for my share of the pizza?"

"Donna bought the pizza Bill."

I reached for my billfold to pay Donna.

"Hold on Bill, you don't owe me a thing. I've been making the same bets you have this week and I'm way ahead of the track because of you. I didn't bet as much money but I still got a couple of super pay offs. Now put your money away."

I thanked Donna and shut up. When the women left I got out the racing equipment and began cleaning it. I was so wound up I was wide-awake and needed to keep myself busy. I'd talk to Spunky about my idea of working Light and Slinker together my way. I hoped he would accept my idea and let me see what I could do.

On Sunday we had ran the two-year-old filly and were pleased when she had run a good second. She had been bumped hard just outside the gate by another horse who was disqualified later. She had a cut on her front leg but had come back and was running well at the wire. We took care of the cut, which wasn't anything serious but would require us to rest her for a few days. We began to look forward to the trial races a couple of weeks off.

The next day or two we walked the string of horses and slowly began the process of getting Light ready. Spunky had listened to my idea about Slinker and Cassie and I had gone to work with his blessings.

The first time we worked the two together using my idea was something to see. Light would move ahead of Slinker and throw dirt in his face. I would release my hold on Slinker and go past Light. We would stay in front until Cassie would let Light go. Then we'd start the process all over again. After three days of the training Slinker began to want to run in front and didn't want Light in front of him.

Three days before the trial I told Spunky we needed a work for Light. I told him we'd try Light and Slinker together and see if my plan had worked. My idea was to let Slinker work a fast three eighths in front of Light and when we reached the finish line I'd start stopping Slinker. Cassie would pass us on Light and let him work another eighth of a mile. My plan was that both horses would think they had won.

Spunky had watched the works and was pleased with the results.

"Bill, I think your plan is working, I've noticed that Slinker is becoming a little more on edge. He's finally figured out that if he's in front he doesn't get dirt thrown in his face. He is working better everyday and is looking forward to his works with Light. Things are working out great. We get the works we want for Light and are moving Slinker forward at the same time.

The trial races were set for Saturday. We watched as Light began to show signs he needed a race. He was full of himself. He jumped and kicked on the walker and wanted more attention from me.

"Bill, the trials are tomorrow. I believe everyone is honest but not that honest. I think we should move Light's water bucket and feed tub to the back of his stall. I want it away from the barn aisle. I don't want someone putting something into either one of them."

I moved the water bucket and feed tub. I'd be staying up with Light tonight. Spunky had told me to get a nap so I'd be rested for the night. I went to the tack room and got a good nap. When I got up from my nap I helped Spunky do chores. When we were through and everything was settled, I got a chair and sat it just outside the tack room.

I had just come out of the tack room with a soda when Cassie came walking down the barn aisle. She was carrying a sack in her hand.

"Evening Bill. Thought I'd better bring you something to keep you awake tonight."

She handed me the sack that had two brand new Western paperback novels. The night would be gone before I knew it.

"Thanks Cass. These bang, bang, shoot'em ups will make the night go by in a hurry."

"I somehow doubt you'll have any trouble staying awake Bill. You're as wound up as tight as I am. You just don't show it."

"That's true Cass, I don't want to get Light upset. If I'm calm, so is he. I'll give him a good ear scratching this evening and brush him down. He'll go to sleep and be fresh as a daisy tomorrow. We'll be the favorite in the race so you'll have to watch the other jockeys and be sure they don't trap you on the rail."

"Spunky and I have talked about it Bill. I'm going to keep him out of trouble."

"I should have known you all would have talked about what you were going to do. I want to wish you luck, Cassie."

"Thanks Bill, but I came down here to tell you about a pickup that you may be able to buy this weekend. A fellow in our barn has family problems. His wife ran off with another trainer and left him with a bunch of bills. He wants to pay them off if he can. He may sell the truck so he can go on racing his small string. I'll know tomorrow or the next day about it."

"That's great, Cass. I hate to take advantage of a man's misfortune but I guess I'd be doing him a favor."

"You would be, Bill. He's a nice fellow who just made a mistake and married the wrong woman. I'll see you in the saddling paddock, Bill."

Cassie gave me a kiss on the cheek and walked out of the barn. I sat there in my chair and was more confused than ever. The kiss on the cheek was something I hadn't expected but I'd have to admit, I really liked it.

The night went quickly by. Spunky showed up an hour early and told me to get some rest. I went into the tack room and lay down. How I managed to go to sleep I don't know, but I did.

Spunky and Donna had Light ready when I woke up. I couldn't believe I slept like I did.

"I'm sorry Spunky."

"Don't worry about it Bill, we wanted you to rest. Donna braided his mane while I put his wraps on. Patty brought me a change of clothes so I'll be looking neat when our picture is taken. She said for you to change your clothes, too. She said the family had to look nice for the picture."

"I'll change as soon as you're through, Spunky. How is Light?"

"Coming out of his skin Bill, he's ready to run."

CHAPTER 7

❋

The racing steward called us to the paddock a short time later. I led Light to the saddling paddock and led him around the walking ring. There were forty eight horses in the trials. Four of the trial races would go with ten horses each. The last race would have eight. The first and second place horses in each race would qualify for the finals ten days from today. I had never been anymore confident in my life. Light was ready and I knew it. Only and act of god could keep him from winning.

Spunky waved to me from the saddling enclosure where the track steward and Cassie stood waiting. I led Light over to the enclosure and held him while Spunky and the steward put Cassie's saddle in place. When they were finished I took Light out of the enclosure and led him around with the other horses. He was walking lightly and was ready to run. The steward called "Jockeys up". I held Light as Spunky gave Cassie a leg up on him. I led him to the gap and turned him over to the pony rider who took the lead shank and led Light and Cassie onto the track. I had told Cassie good luck as she rode off. I watched as Spunky waved to me and headed to his seat with Patty. I headed to the grand-stands and found my place high up.

Donna came up into the stands and sat down as we watched the horses warm up on the backside.

"What do you think Bill?"

"I think we'll not make any money on the stud. He's two to one and won't pay anything. I think I'll wager on a long shot to run second."

"Which long shot Bill?"

"I think I'll bet on the five horse. He is a shipper but he looks fit and ready. The man who has him had done a lot of work with him and it shows. I'd like to place a ten dollar bet on him."

"You do some of the strangest things Bill, but you just may be right. I know the man who owns the horse, Bill. He's a good man who has a little place west of town. My husband used to ride a few horses for him. They were all well mannered and ran well. I don't know how you do it Bill, but you do have a gift. I think I'll make the same bet. Want to try for the exacta?"

"I guess I might as well. It's the only way we'll make any money."

I gave her two ten dollar bills and watched as she went to make our bets. She returned a few minutes later with our tickets. We watched as the horses began to load. I watched as Cassie and Light were led into the seven gate. A moment later the track announcer said the horses were all in line.

The bell rang and the gates flew open. That was when things went wrong. As Light broke from the gates the ground seemed to give out from under his front feet and suddenly his nose was on the ground. Cassie was thrown up on his neck and I was sure she was going to fall off. Light suddenly regained his footing and began to run. Cassie was still on his back and trying to regain her seat.

We watched as Light began to gain his stride but was a full five lengths behind the last place horse. The race was over for us. It was far too short a race for Light to make up the distance he'd lost when he'd gone down at the gate.

I watched as Cassie suddenly got down on Light and he began to move past some of the slower horses. As the horses began to come around the turn I saw that Cassie was asking Light for his all. Suddenly, when the horses reached the stretch of home, Light was three lengths behind the front-runners. The front-runner on the rail began to weaken and dropped back. Light and the five horse were suddenly head and head with twenty yards to go. We held our breath as Cassie got lower on Light's back and shouted to him. He seemed to stretch his neck and give an extra burst of speed. He crossed the wire a neck ahead of the five horse. He had won, won the most thrilling race I had ever seen. It seemed I had not breathed from the time Light and the five horse had begun their stretch duel.

Donna and I raced down out of the stands and ran through the gate and out onto the track. I saw Cassie bringing Light back towards us at a slow trot. From where I stood, I could tell he was a tired horse and had every right to be. As Cassie got close I could see her smile as she patted Light's neck.

"Bill, did you see him make the last move? It was wonderful!"

Spunky came out onto the track and Cassie jumped into his arms. They were both laughing and crying at the same time. Spunky patted Light's neck and removed the over-girth then gave Cassie a leg up onto Light's back to have their picture taken. The crowd cheered as our number was put up on the tote board as the winner. The five horse had run a fine race never giving an inch. I was glad he had qualified for the finals.

I led Light into the winner's circle and set him up in front of a large crowd. I set him up and waited for the flash. I waited for Spunky to take the saddle off Light then followed the track man to the test barn. I gave Light a small drink then walked him slowly around the test barn walking area. I gave him another drink from the bucket Donna had waiting for us when we had arrived. The test crew came to the door and took Light into the test barn. Donna and I waited until the crew brought Light out and handed the lead shank to me. Donna and I led Light past several people who wished us well in the finals. We thanked them and went back to our barn. The barn aisle was full of well-wishers and people who only wanted to see Light up close.

Spunky broke away from some of the people and took the leg wraps off Light as quickly as possible.

"How is he acting Bill?"

"Tired but he doesn't seem to have any problems Spunky."

"Lets get him bathed and cooled out, we'll rub his legs and put the wraps on him as soon as he's cool. Bill, did you ever see anything like it? I've been training for more time than I want to admit and I've never seen anything like it. Bill, you were right, he is something special."

"He is that Spunky. He not only has the speed he has the heart. That's the one thing you can't measure. The five horse never gave an inch."

"He sure didn't. I know the fellow who owns him and I couldn't be happier for him. He's like Patty and me. He raises his own horses and trains them as well."

Donna came to where Spunky and I stood and handed me my winnings. She was all smiles.

"He did it again Spunky, picked the long shot to run second and put him with Light in the exacta."

"Bill, I'm thrilled for you but I want to know why you picked the five. We'll talk about it later. Let's get this horse bathed and walked dry."

"We bathed Light and Donna began to walk him. Spunky and Patty were busy so I began to clean Light's bridle. I was working on the bridle when Cassie came down the barn aisle. Someone began to applaud as she got close to them.

I could see her blushing from where I sat. Patty came to her rescue and gave her a hug and a kiss on the cheek. I was thrilled she was getting the attention she so justly deserved. She had made a wonderful ride. I had just put the bridle in the tack room when she stepped inside.

"Bill, he was wonderful. You and Spunky had him at his peak. I had lost my stirrup and didn't find it until halfway down the back stretch. That was when I asked him to run."

"Well he did that, Cassie. I've never seen anything like that before. I can't wait to see the race on Spunky's tape machine."

"He'll have it tomorrow, Bill. I know the man who makes the tapes and he promised me he'd have one for me by noon."

"I sure want to get a look at it Cassie. It showed how much courage he has and that he's a fighter."

"Bill, I hope he is alright tomorrow. If he hurt himself I don't know what I would do. I want him to be alright for Patty's sake."

"We all want that Cassie, but in this business things happen. I think he's fine, though. The track just gave out from under him when he broke so hard. By the way, Spunky knew the man you outran at the wire. It seems they are old friends. They have been running horses against each other for years. I'm glad that the man got his horse in the finals. It looks as if Patty and Spunky are busy entertaining everyone."

"Oh my, Bill I forgot to tell you. The gentleman up in our barn is going to sell his truck. He said that if you wanted to look it over tomorrow he'd be available after works."

"I'll come up after we have everything taken care of in the morning. I really do need a truck. I'm tired of having to bum rides. Thanks, Cassie. You've been a big help."

"Bill, it's my pleasure. After all, what are friends for?"

CHAPTER 8

❀

The next day Spunky and I went over every inch of Light. We couldn't find a thing wrong with him. We had Donna hand walk him and he seemed fine. We both were thrilled. We didn't have anything entered until late the next week so we would have time to keep a close eye on him. After we had everything worked and put back in their stall I told Spunky about the truck and asked if it would be ok to go take a look at it.

"Take your time Bill. I've got some phone calls to make and Patty has gone shopping with a friend."

I walked up to the barn where Cassie worked and found she had just finished her last ride. She told me she would change into her street clothes and we would go look at the truck. I visited with several of the boys who worked in the barn until she came out of the tack room in her street clothes. We walked up the barn aisle where she introduced me to a gentleman who was wrapping a young horse's legs.

"Frank, this is my friend Bill Patton. He'd like to look at your truck if you have time."

"Let me finish wrapping this horse's legs and I'll be glad to show you the truck. Here, you all take the keys and go look the truck over. Take it for a test drive if you are interested. I'll be here when you all get back."

I followed Cassie out into the parking lot and was surprised when she stopped at a rather new Ford three quarter ton pickup. It was black with dark tinted windows. I walked around the truck and found it to be clean. The tires were almost new and there was a fifth wheel hook-up in the back of the bed. Cassie unlocked the truck door and opened it so I could look inside. I was surprised to find it had a light tan leather interior. I checked the mileage and found it had less than thirty thousand. The interior was spotless and I began to think I couldn't afford the truck. I pulled the hood release and then raised the hood. The engine was spotless. I pulled the oil dipstick and found it to be full and clean. The large engine would pull any trailer I needed to pull. I was sold if the price was right.

"Cass, I love the truck but I'm afraid it's out of my price range."

"I don't think so, Bill. He has some bills he needs to pay to continue running his horses. His ex wife left him in a bind. She had made a bunch of bills he didn't know anything about. Let's go talk to him and see what he says."

"Let me start the engine first, Cass. I want to hear the engine run."

Cassie handed me the keys to the truck. I started the truck and had to admit I was pleased. I wanted the truck if I could only make the deal.

We walked back to the barn and found the man had just finished working on the horse. He seemed to be a pleasant fellow and was smiling when we walked up.

"The truck suit you, Bill?"

"The truck looks great. I'm just afraid it's out of my price range."

"Bill, as Cassie knows, I'm in a bind. I know something about horses but nothing about women."

He quoted me a price he would take if I could close the deal in a hurry. I told him sold and told him I'd go get my checkbook and write him a check. I went to our tack room and got my checkbook. When I got back he and Cassie were talking about how Light's race had gone. We walked over to the racing office and found a lady who would notarize the title. I paid the lady a small fee and handed him his check. I now owned my own truck. I was thrilled to say the least. Cassie walked back down to the barn and checked on Light.

Spunky was thrilled when he heard I'd been able to make the deal on the truck. He knew how badly I had been wanting one. He told us he and Patty wanted to take us out to supper tonight after all our chores were finished.

"Cassie, I can come by and pick you up if you don't mind?"

"Oh boy, I get to ride in Mr. Patton's new truck Spunky."

"You should feel honored Cassie. He's not offered to take me for a ride."

"Spunky, you know I'll take you for a ride anytime you want."

"Bill, I'm just jerking your chain. I think it's great that you got the truck, now I won't have to worry about picking you up in Clayton next spring."

"That, and I'll not have to bum a ride from Cassie's dad."

"If we're going to go to supper I think I'll go back to my apartment and get a nap. I don't have to help with evening chores tonight. Since I'm riding in the races my boss hired a man to muck the stalls. I'm helping him sort of like you help Spunky, Bill."

"I may get a nap myself. It took forever for me to go to sleep last night. I think I ran the race over in my mind a dozen times before I finally went to sleep."

"You might as well, Bill. Everything here is fine and I'm going to take a nap when I get back to the motor home. I think I'll enter Slinker in a twenty thousand claimer the last of the week."

"Spunky, that might be a mistake. There are lots of folks who saw how he won his last race. Why not put him in an allowance race instead?"

"You think he's improved that much?"

"There's one way to find out, if our plan has worked we all might be surprised."

"Cassie, do you agree with Bill?"

"Yes I do, Spunky. We're having a very good year and people are looking at your string of horses. I think if you put Slinker in a claiming race you might just lose him."

"Well I guess we'll just give him a try against some of the allowance horses and see if our friend Bill's idea has worked."

Spunky and Cassie left the barn and headed home. I checked on the horses again and then went into the cool tack room and got a nap myself.

I had most of the evening chores done when Spunky got back to the barn later that evening. He told me he had another offer for Light. Some gentleman from Texas had heard about Light's last race and wanted to buy him.

"What did he offer Spunky?"

"Nothing, I told him the horse wasn't for sale. Patty and I have talked and decided we'll keep him and see just how far we can go. We've thought about what you and Cassie have said, we may never have another like him. Bill, it may all fall apart tomorrow but we don't care. We're going to live for the moment."

"You only go around once in this life Spunky so you'd better enjoy the first trip. Or at least that's what my good friend down home says."

"He could be right, Bill. Patty and I plan on enjoying every day. Since we have you two kids around we both seem to be laughing a lot more. Patty calls you two her kids and in a sense, I guess I feel the same way. Since we lost our son things have just never been exactly the same. I was going to turn the string over to him in a few years."

"I can't even begin to know how you feel Spunky. To lose a child is something I hope I never have to go through. I guess I should feel bad about losing my dad but I'm having trouble doing that. I guess I'll go talk to our pastor when I get back home. I know you're supposed to forgive and forget but I'm having a hard time doing that."

"Don't be to hard on yourself Bill. If you had a dog that bit you every day you'd get rid of him. You'd not have any bad feelings about that would you?"

"Of course not."

"Same thing as the beatings you took. You don't miss them either. Give it time Bill it will all work itself out. I, for one, would feel the same way as you do."

Spunky left to go home and change before we went out to eat. I went over to the track showers and cleaned myself up. I looked at myself in the mirror and decided it was time for me to get another hair cut. I could use a couple of new shirts and a pair of pants, too. I'd buy a few things along and would not have to buy so many clothes before school started.

I checked everything one more time and then went to my new truck and got inside. When I started the engine it was great. I backed it out of its parking space and drove through the back gate. I waved at the guard who waved back at me. I took the shortcut to Cassie's apartment. I pulled into her parking lot and got out. I saw one of her friends at the door and knew that she wasn't ready. I was surprised when she came out the door of her apartment and met me at the bottom of the stairs.

She looked great. Her sandy red hair was styled and I was shocked to see she was wearing a pretty spring dress and makeup. It suddenly dawned on me that she was a very beautiful young lady.

"You can close your mouth now Bill."

"Cassie I'm sorry. I've just never seen you in a dress before."

"I do wear them Bill. I'm not always riding horses you know."

I felt like a complete dummy. I hurried around and opened her door to the pickup. I'd made enough mistakes for one day.

"Thank you sir. I'm glad to see your mother taught you some manners before she left."

"Me too. I don't like to be embarrassed much. You look so fine and I look like a field hand."

"Bill, you look fine. If you're wanting to get some clothes there is a store in town that gives all the track folks a discount. I'd be happy to go with you and show you where it is located."

"That would be great. Maybe one day next week we can run in and do some shopping. I'm going to need a suit for graduation. I don't have any intension of walking across that stage in a pair of jeans."

"We'll go Tuesday after works. We can find you a nice suit that won't break the bank I'm sure. You have a white shirt and tie?"

"No, and I'll need a pair of dress shoes too."

"Oh boy, this will be neat. I'll be the first person to see you in a suit and tie."

"It won't be anything special Cass. I'm sure it won't be that impressive."

"Bill Patton, you're a nice looking young man so hush that sort of talk. You came up here a few weeks ago to clean stalls and walk horses. In that short time you've become and assistant trainer and just happen to be working for one of the best barns at the track. Besides, Spunky has told everyone how you got Light straightened out and what a success you've made out of several of his other horses. I'm quite proud to be seen with you."

I didn't know what to say. I'd never had that much experience with girls and sure enough not any as pretty as Cassie. All I could do was ask her where the next turn was.

We pulled into the steak house parking lot and found a place next to Spunky and Patty's truck. I opened Cassie's door and helped her out of the truck. I was surprised when I suddenly discovered her hand in mine as we walked from the parking lot towards the steak house. I loved the feel of her hand in mine. In fact, I had never felt better.

Spunky and Patty were seated at a table in the corner of the room. I noticed Patty's eyebrow raise when we walked into the room. It seemed I wasn't the only one shocked tonight. I held Cassie's chair and then took a chair myself. Spunky told Cassie how nice she looked and wanted to know how my truck was running. We all got a giggle out of that and it seemed the evening afterwards was a complete success. After our meal we discussed Slinker's upcoming race and how we thought it should be run. We discussed what we thought we should do in the coming week to get Light ready for the upcoming stakes race. We were celebrating but it seemed we never got too far away from the horses.

After thanking Spunky and Patty for our meal I took Cassie to the ice cream shop for a cone and then drove her to her apartment. I walked her to the door of her apartment and got a kiss goodnight, not a kiss on the cheek, either.

"Bill, you're shocked."

"Yes but I'd like to try that again."

I did and lay in bed for an hour afterwards thinking about it. I had a girlfriend. Me, Bill Patton.

We started on Slinker the next morning. His allowance race was on Sunday and we wanted him ready. We worked him with the older mare and discovered he wanted to work harder than she did. Light was feeling good and Spunky said it was time to give him a short gallop. We worked the two of them together the rest of the week. It looked as if Slinker was wanting to become a race horse. The next morning we gave Slinker and Light a light three eights of a mile work. I was surprised that Light had come back from his hard race so quickly. Cassie had her hands full trying to keep him from going full out. I, at the same time had my hands full trying to keep Slinker under control.

When we pulled the two horses up they both were still full of run. We rode them back to where Spunky was standing. He had a big grin on his face.

"You kids had your hands full this morning."

"We sure did Spunky. Slinker will be ready for his race Saturday. He's pulling like a freight train on my arms."

"I saw that Bill. It looked as if you had your hands full too, Cassie."

"You bet I did Spunky. I had to do some serious talking to keep Light in check. He wanted to run."

"He's come back a lot quicker than I expected, we'll have to adjust his works so he doesn't peak too quick. Right now we need to concentrate on Slinker. I just hope there is a gray horse in the race."

We were laughing as we took the two horses back to the barn. I was living a life I hadn't even dreamed of before. It was like living a dream.

After we had bathed the horses and worked the rest of the string, Spunky said he was going home for lunch and a nap. I asked if it would be all right to go to town and buy myself some clothes.

"Bill, ask Donna to watch the horses until you get back. I know you're needing some clothes."

"Thanks Spunky, I'll not be gone long."

"Take as long as you need Bill. Is Cassie going with you?"

"Yes, sir. She told me she knows of a place where they give track folks a discount."

"I'm sure she does, Bill. You kids have a good time. I'll see you for chores this evening."

I told Donna what Spunky had said and she was happy to get the extra work. She had to make all the money she could before the track closed. She told me she waited tables in a local diner the rest of the year.

I went into the tack room and got clean clothes and went to the track shower room. I wanted clean clothes before Cassie and I went shopping. I called Cassie from the tack room and told her I'd be over in a few minutes. She said she would be ready. I checked on the horses and waved to Donna as I headed out to my truck.

Cassie came down the stairs as I was pulling into the parking lot. She got into the truck as soon as I had it stopped. I got a kiss on the cheek and was told which way to head. She sat in the middle of the seat next to me and I felt great. I followed her directions and pulled into a parking lot outside a store that advertised discount prices. We got out of the truck and I followed her inside.

An older gentleman came over to us and asked if he could help us.

"My friend here needs a dark suit, white shirt, tie and a pair of shoes. Think you can fix him up?"

"He'll be needing socks, too I assume?"

"Yes he will."

"Come this way. I think I have just what you want."

We followed the gentleman over to another area of the store and waited until he sorted through a rack of suits. He took a black medium weight suit off of the rack and held it up for me to inspect. Cassie felt the material and nodded her head.

"This will be fine sir,"

"Try the coat on young man. We'll want to see that it fits you."

I tried the coat on and found it to fit perfectly. Even Cassie was smiling. He handed me the pants and showed me the dressing room. The pants I discovered were not hemmed and were four inches too long. I stepped out to tell him, but before I could say anything he was rolling the pant legs up and directing us to the shoe department where he began showing us several pairs of shoes. I saw a loafer with tassels on the toe and nodded towards them. Cassie nodded her head in approval. The gentleman had me slip the shoes on and then marked the pants with pins. He told us he'd have the suit ready in an hour or so, along with the socks. We left the shop after paying a lot less than I had planned on.

"Any place you want to go Cass? We've got an hour to kill."

"How about we get a coke? There is a café right down the street."

"Sounds good to me. My treat. It's the least I can do after all the help you're giving me."

"Bill, I want you to look nice, I figure you're going to need the suit before graduation."

"For what Cassie?"

"I figure Light is going to win the futurity and we've going to have to go to a big dinner. I have a new dress that I'm going to wear and I want you looking knockout nice, too. After all, you're the assistant trainer of Gray Light. You should look nice. If you're going to build the training track you've talked about you want to show a good image to the people who just may want to send you horses. It's all about appearance Bill. If you look good folks feel good about sending you their horses."

"I've got a lot to learn about running my own business Cassie. I really appreciate all the help you've given me."

"I know that Bill. You're a heck of a trainer and a fine hand with a horse but you've not had a chance to learn about the business world. You might think about taking a business course at school this fall."

"I've got one already scheduled. I've got an accounting course to take, too."

"That's great Bill. You'll enjoy them."

As we walked down the street we passed a jewelry store. Cassie stopped and pointed to a pair of gold cuff links. They were beautiful little race horses, I saw the price tag and backed up a step.

"Good Lord, Cassie. I'd need to hit another exacta before I could afford to buy something like that."

"Bill, you need a pair of cuff links for the white shirt. We can find a lot less expensive pair before you need them. I just saw them and thought they were neat."

"They are neat, Cassie. I don't think I've ever seen anything as pretty as they are but I'm going to need every dollar I can lay my hands on this fall."

We walked down the street to the small café and had our coke. Cassie said her folks wouldn't be able to come to the futurity race because her father had to work. One of his men was going to have surgery.

"That's too bad Cassie. They would have enjoyed it. Maybe they can come up another time before the meet ends."

"I hope so, Bill. I'd like them to see me ride Light this year."

"I know what you mean. It's something they would never forget. You think my suit and things are ready?"

"I'm sure they are. You have to get back to the barn."

My suit was ready. The owner of the store had put my suit in a nice plastic zipper bag, along with my white shirt. My new shoes and socks were wrapped separately. We went back to the truck and I took Cassie back to her apartment. As we pulled into the parking lot one of her friends pulled in beside us. She admired my truck and asked Cassie to go with her to pick up some things at the store. I got a quick kiss and waved as the girls pulled out of the parking lot behind them.

Donna was sitting in front of the tack room when I got back. She asked to see my suit and shoes. She was impressed with my choice and said I would look great. I thanked her and hung my suit up in the corner of the tack room.

I was dishing up the feed when Spunky arrived back at the barn. We went to work and soon had everything done. We sat down and talked about Slinker's upcoming race. We figured to let Cassie take him to the front if he broke well. We'd see if he could do as well as we thought.

"Bill, what's your thoughts on Light's training this next ten days?"

"Keep him happy and keep our works short. I think we should give him some long gallops and not take anything out of the tank."

"Good thinking, Bill. I'm glad we are thinking the same thing. If we are able to win the futurity, Patty and I will have had the biggest year we've ever had."

"What about the State Stakes race Spunky? You're not giving up on that are you?"

"No, but we have to win the next race first."

We'll work on it Spunky, I'll do my best to have him ready."

CHAPTER 9

❁

The next few days were something to see. We worked with Slinker and used him to work Light at the same time. Both horses began to look forward to the morning works. When Saturday came we had Slinker ready as we could make him. I had braided his mane and had him ready for Spunky to put the leg wraps on. When Spunky had him ready we heard the track announcer call our race to the paddock.

"Bill, we may get outrun but we sure won't have gotten outworked. Let's go see if your little idea has worked. If it has I'm going to give you a raise. I'll have to if I don't want to lose you to one of the big barns."

"Forget losing me Spunky. I'm here to stay like I've told you. Like you say, let's see if my idea has worked before we get excited about things."

We took Slinker to the saddling paddock. I led him around the walking ring until Spunky waved to me. He and the track steward saddled Slinker while Cassie stood nearby in her racing silks. When they were finished I led Slinker around the walking ring until the call "Riders Up" was called. When Cassie was mounted I led her to the pony rider and turned Slinker over to him.

"Go get them, Cassie. I'd like to get my picture taken."

"See you for the picture, Bill. I think we may just surprise some folks today."

I shook hands with Spunky and went up into the stand to watch the race. I had studied the form and knew we had to run a great race if we wanted to win. Donna came up and sat down.

"Bill, what do you think? Do we really have a chance?"

"Donna, if Slinker and Cassie get out in good shape this could turn out to be a big day for us."

"I hoped you'd say something like that. Look at the odds."

The tote board read thirty to one on Slinker. I knew we were moving him up in class but these odds were great. Great for us. I began to think about the gold cuff links.

"Donna, put me twenty dollars across the board on Slinker. I don't want an exacta. The horses have all outrun one another."

"I know what you mean Bill. They are an even matched bunch. I'll be back in a moment with your bet."

I watched Cassie and Slinker warm up on the back side. Slinker seemed to be on his toes and was ready. Donna returned just as the horses were loading into the gates. I heard Donna take a deep breath just ahead of me.

The track announcer suddenly said, "The horses are all in line." The bell rang and the gates flew open. I was shocked to see Slinker seem to explode out of the gates. He suddenly had a two length lead on all of the other horses. I watched as Cassie moved him across the track and settled him down at the rail. He seemed to like being out in front and was running easy. He didn't have to catch the gray horse who was usually in front of him throwing dirt in his face.

As Slinker and Cassie entered the turn they had a solid three length lead over the track favorite. Suddenly the second place horse seemed to stumble and went down. The group of horses behind him suddenly had nowhere to go. Horses and jockeys were going down in a heap.

Jockeys were thrown through the air and landed hard on the track. Of the nine horses to start the race four were down on the track and the rest were scattered all over the track. Two of them were without their jockeys. Cassie, in the mean time, was half way around the turn before she could see what had happened behind her. She started to raise up on Slinker then got down and asked him to run. Slinker won the race but it was a hollow victory. Two of the four horses that went down had to be destroyed.

Two of the jockeys had to be taken to the hospital. One returned to the track before the day's racing was over. We had won the race and gotten our picture taken but everyone was worried about the jockeys and horses. No one wanted to see the horses put down. The horses made a living for the folks on the back side as well as their trainers and owners. I'd lost a couple of horses over the years and from an owner's standpoint it was never an easy thing. Horses were like good friends and some were like family.

The barn area was quiet the rest of the day. Everyone was waiting on news from the hospital about how the one jockey was doing. Everyone was wondering what had happened to the horse that had gone down and caused the other horses to fall. It was something that would never be figured out. I had watched the horse work a few days before and saw no problems. He had warmed up fine with no sign of lameness or stress.

Spunky and I had taken care of Slinker and were in agreement that we were thrilled that Cassie had been on the lead and had not been involved in the wreck that had taken place. The fall was the first time I had ever seen a fall take place on a race track and, as Spunky had said, it was part of racing. Sometimes things happened that were heartbreaking but couldn't be explained.

Monday and Tuesday were called dark days at the track. There was no racing and it gave everyone time to get things shaped up from the busy weekend. I had won on my bet on Slinker's race and had gone to the store downtown to buy the gold cuff links Cassie had pointed out to me. When I got there I found out they had been sold. I was upset but figured some tourist had bought them over the weekend. I'd gone back to the barn and done my laundry. I washed my truck and waxed it the next day. I was nervous and didn't want the string of horses knowing it. Working on the truck seemed to help. When Spunky came into the barn for evening chores I had worked my problems out.

"Bill, we're going into the final days before the race. I believe that everyone is honest but there are some folks that aren't. Any suggestion on what we should do about keeping an eye on Light these last few days?"

"I've been thinking about it a lot Spunky. I don't know what other horses will come in but we're bound to be one of the favorites. There is a lot of money in the race Spunky, and there are folks who will be tempted to do something to keep us from running. Keep us from running or keep us from running the way we should. I think we should move the mare to Light's stall and put him in hers. That will put him next to the tack room and I'm a light sleeper. We've already moved his water and feed buckets to the back of his stall but that won't keep someone from trying to get to him. I think I should go on night watch until after the race. It's not that long and I'd feel a lot better about things.

"We could do that Bill, but I need your help with getting him to the very top of his game. I think moving his stall is a good idea, but I think I'll talk to Donna and see if she wants to act as night watchman for us."

"That sounds like a plan Spunky. I know she can use the money and will be glad to get the work."

"That's what I figure Bill, I'll call her this evening and have her start tomorrow night. We need to start getting him in peak form these next few days. Slinker seems to be coming back and even if we use him a little before we should he can have some extra rest after the race."

"Spunky, Cassie didn't use him that hard in the race. He was on cruise control down the backside and she just let him run the way he wanted up the lane. No one was pushing him and if I know anything about Slinker he never did anything he didn't want to. I think he'll be ready to work against Light day after tomorrow."

"You might be right, Bill. The race for him was like a good work. Cassie never had to ask him for a thing. We'll work the two of them day after tomorrow."

As Spunky had said, he hired Donna to be our night watchman. I was glad to get my sleep. Cassie and I continued to work the string and they came along nicely. We began to work Light and Slinker together and gave them a long gallop with a three eighths of a mile work at the end. When we got back to the barn Cassie told Spunky what she thought about Light's condition.

"Spunky, Light is pulling hard. He feels great and I think he is ready to run. Bill and I have discussed it and we think if we give him slow gallops, just enough to keep him happy and wanting more he will be ready for Saturday's race."

"You both think he's ready for the race?"

"Yes we do, Spunky."

"Kids, you could be right about the long slow works but I think we need one more work just to keep him tightened up. We'll give him a good work just as soon as it's light enough to see tomorrow morning. If we're lucky and are there early enough maybe a bunch of folks won't be around. We'll give him some slow long works for the next few days and he should be ready."

"Sounds like a plan Spunky. Do you want me or Cassie to work him?"

"How about you give him the work, Bill. That way if anyone says something to Cassie about us just giving him slow works she won't have to lie. You have a problem with Bill giving him the work Cassie?"

"None at all, Spunky. I'll show up at our barn and work the string as usual. No one will think anything about me not being here until later in the morning. I doubt if anyone will notice that we didn't work Light one morning."

It sounded like a plan but things didn't work out the way we expected. Just when it was light enough to see, Spunky and I had Light on the track and warmed up. Spunky waved and I began to let Light work. He seemed to float across the ground and I had forgotten how easy he went along. I let him work almost half a mile then slowed him and returned to where Spunky stood waiting. I jumped off and Spunky took the exercise saddle off him. I led him back to the barn and bathed him just as everyone else was showing up to begin morning works. I hand walked him cool and then hung him on the walker while I mucked his stall. I noticed several folks who noticed Light on the walker but thought nothing of it.

Later that morning Cassie and I worked the rest of the string. Spunky was happy with Light's work and told Cassie about how he had worked. We discussed how everything was going to be handled the rest of the week. Spunky braced Light's legs and put on extra thick stall wraps. I went to bed that night thinking of how easy Light had moved and the speed he had stored up in his beautiful gray body.

The next morning I walked Light by hand and then put him back into his stall. Spunky and I were discussing the young two year old filly when we saw Donna come running into the barn.

"How badly crippled is Gray Light?"

"Crippled, Donna what are you talking about?"

"I just got a call from a friend of mine. She said Light was crippled and wouldn't run in the stakes on Saturday.

"Sit down, Donna and relax. There is nothing wrong with Light. Bill just walked him a couple of hours ago. He's fine, Donna. Where in the world did your friend hear that he was crippled?"

"My friend at the café I work for in the winter heard a couple of the trainers talking about it this morning. They were discussing how word had gotten around the track that Light was crippled."

I looked at Spunky and saw he was smiling. I could see that Spunky already had a plan. I was about to ask what it was when Cassie came running into the barn. Tears were streaming down her cheeks.

"Spunky, I'm sorry, so sorry!"

"About what Cassie?"

"About Light being crippled."

"Sit down, Cassie. First off, what makes you think he is crippled?"

"I just got a call from one of the owners of another horse entered in the race wanting me to ride his horse. He told me he had just got a call telling him Light was crippled and he wanted me to ride his horse."

"Cassie, there is nothing wrong with Light. Bill hand walked him this morning after the work yesterday. We hadn't taken the heavy leg wraps off him from the night before. That must have been how the rumor got started. Someone must have figured out we didn't work him yesterday."

"Oh my lord, what a relief. I just couldn't believe you all would not have called to let me know. Now I know why."

"Well I guess if everyone thinks he's crippled there is no need of us having a night watchman for tomorrow night. Donna, you'll work tonight but I want you to bring a sad book to read. I want everyone to look a little sad and down in the mouth. Tomorrow night Donna you can stay home. If everyone wants him crippled let's let them think he's crippled. Donna, you'll still get paid so don't worry."

"Spunky, you're not going to say anything?"

"Why should I say anything? I didn't start the rumor. Besides, if they think he's crippled they won't be coming down here and disturb him. Looks like we just got a bonus. We can go on about our business. We need to start getting Slinker ready for his next race. I still want to know if Bill's idea is going to work. Besides we need to go along with folks if they want to be unhappy."

It was all we could do not to burst out laughing.

"Cassie, maybe we should go check on Light. I think Spunky is going to put new leg wraps on him and may need help. Donna, maybe you should hold him while you look your unhappy best."

It seemed there were several pairs of eyes on us as we went to Light's stall. Spunky came out of the tack room with leg wraps and all sorts of bottles in his pockets. He was not smiling at all. Donna held Light's halter while I helped Spunky put fresh new bandages on Light's front legs. He used a double amount of cotton before he began putting the leg wraps on. He smiled at us as he poured some of the liquid out of the bottles onto the front of the stall wall. It could be smelled when anyone walked down the barn aisle.

"Spunky, you are a sneaky old rascal."

"Why thank you, Cassie. I take that as a compliment."

"Bill, I think you should take me to lunch, somewhere off the track."

"How about we get some chicken and go up to the mountain park for the afternoon?"

"That sounds great. When do you want to leave?"

"Right now if Spunky doesn't have any objection."

"I think you kids need some time to yourselves. Besides, if everyone leaves the barn, then everyone will know the rumor is true. If someone wants to come take a look at Light, we want them to have plenty of time. You kids go on and have a good time."

"I'll be back in time to do chores this evening."

"I'll see you then, Bill."

CHAPTER 10

❀

Cassie and I drove to a store and bought roasted chicken and all the trimmings. We drove up to a park on the side of the mountain where Cassie suddenly let out a yell. It caught me by surprise and I almost ran off the road. Cassie began to laugh and suddenly we were both laughing.

"Mr. Patton, there are going to be some very upset folks around the track come Saturday afternoon. Some folks may not speak to us the rest of the meet."

"Well, I guess we'll have to suffer with it. There are not that many folks who talk to me anyway. Most of the trainers do, but the folks that work like I do don't have much to say."

"That's because you might just go to work and take their jobs Bill. I know of four trainers who would hire you in a minute if you were to quit Spunky."

"Well I'm not going to quit him so they need not worry."

We had a wonderful lunch and talked about the training center I was planning on building. Cassie offered a few suggestions I hadn't thought of that wouldn't cost me a fortune to put in that might make me some more money. We took a long walk along the side of the mountain and laughed at the long eared deer that grazed in the mountain meadows. When it got time to leave I wasn't ready but we got into the truck and began to look sad. I didn't have to work at it. I didn't want our afternoon to end.

When we arrived back at the track I got a kiss goodbye from Cassie and went into the barn to go to work. Spunky sat outside the tack room reading one of my books.

"Have a good time Bill?"

"You bet, Spunky. I didn't want the day to end."

"It was like that when I met Patty. When we were together the time just seemed to fly. It's been forty three years and the time still seems to fly by. I don't know why she puts up with me."

"Love, Spunky. She just loves you."

We began to do up the evening chores. Donna would show up at eight so I'd get my rest tonight. Tomorrow night would be another thing. There was no way I was going to leave Light unattended the night before the race. Rumor or no rumor.

Spunky called shortly after Donna came on duty. I could tell he was in a good mood.

"Bill, I just got a call from the track vet. He was curious about a rumor he had heard and was wanting to know why I'd not called him after all these years of doing business together. It seemed his feelings were really hurt that we might be using someone else. I told him to go to the barn and see you. He should be there in a few minutes. Let him look at Light. Patty and I will be down in a few minutes ourselves."

I hung up the phone and went out to where Donna sat. I told her what was going on and to get ready for company.

"It was just a matter of time, Bill. The track is getting ready to do their press releases and want to know if they will have Light in the race. They know they will have a lot larger crowd if Light is running."

"I hadn't thought of that, Donna. I can see why they would want to do all the write ups they could. He's become a very popular horse. Folks seem to love him."

"They do, Bill. Folks know he belongs to a small trainer and they can relate to him. They all like to see a little man get a chance at grabbing the brass ring."

We were visiting when we heard the track veterinarian's truck pull up just outside the barn door. He came through the door carrying his bag.

"Evening, folks. I talked to Spunky a short while ago and he said I could come check out Gray Light."

"Yes sir, he called to let me know you were coming. I'll get his halter."

I got the halter from the tack room and walked to Light's stall. I put the halter on Light and waited.

"Would you bring him out of the stall, Bill?"

"Sir, if its alright with you I'd rather you do your examination inside the stall. I think it will look better for the folks who just happen to be watching."

"Watching? Bill I don't understand."

"You will when we take the leg wraps off sir."

As the vet walked into the stall I saw him stop and sniff the air.

"What in the world is that smell?"

"Some of Spunky's special leg brace. He sort of spilled some of it in the front of the stall day before yesterday."

"Sort of spilled it? I'll bet he did. Let me get these leg wraps off so I can get a good look for myself."

A moment later the vet had the leg wraps off Light and was running his hands over the horse's front legs. After a moment he stopped and looked up at me.

"Any reason I should go on with my examination Bill?"

"None that I know of sir. I think he's in pretty good shape. I don't know what all the fuss is about."

The vet began to smile.

"I'll bet you don't. You haven't heard he might be crippled?"

"I could have heard something like that but I just figured it was something that would pass in a day or so. No one ever asked us if he was crippled."

"And you didn't bother to tell them they were wrong?"

"Why should I? We've gone the last few days without a bunch of folks coming and going from the barn and upsetting the horse. If they wanted to believe he was crippled it didn't bother me. It didn't seem to bother Mr. Davis either. We were planning on sending Donna here home after tonight but I guess now she'll have to work tomorrow night too."

Spunky and Patty walked into the barn. They saw us standing in Light's stall and walked over to where Patty could get a better look at Light.

"Evening, folks. Everything here all right Bill?"

"Everything is fine, Spunky. The vet here was just looking over Light. It seems some folks in the track office thought he might be crippled."

"Why didn't they call me? I'd have told them there wasn't anything wrong with him. I'll bet that's the reason none of the boys have been around visit this week."

"Spunky, this is going to cause one big mess. Folks are going to be making last minute scratches. Oh my, this is going to be something to see."

"Doc, we heard the rumor but thought nothing of it."

"And when you just sort of spilled the leg brace in the stall it didn't hurt anything either?"

"Now, Doc. People will think what they want to think. They can't blame me for having an accident and spilling some of my leg brace in the stall can they?"

"Not really, but they will be upset. The stud's legs are as cool as can be, and that is all the track paid me to find out."

"When will you turn in your report Doc?"

"First thing tomorrow morning, Spunky. I don't have a choice."

"Folks, I think we'd better get some rest. We won't get much tomorrow that's for sure."

"Spunky, you're one sneaky son of a gun. I can't wait to see some of the folk's faces that were happy your horse was out of the race. I want you to know I'm not one of them. You and Patty have worked your tails off all these years and deserve this horse. I hope you win it all. Call me if you need anything."

Spunky and Patty walked the Doc out to his truck and came back a short time later.

"Well kids, it looks like we'll be having company tomorrow. Bill, you'd better get some rest. There's going to be a bunch of folks here tomorrow. Donna, you're still on the payroll and I don't want anyone getting close to Light. You have any trouble just holler for Bill."

"I'll do exactly that, Spunky. We've come too far now to let some hot head tear things up. I'm honored that you trust me to watch him."

"Thank Bill, Donna. He's the one who suggested we hire you."

"Thanks, Bill. I'll not let you down."

"The thought never crossed my mind, Donna. I'll get a good night's sleep tonight and be ready for the rush tomorrow. I have a feeling we're going to have a lot of company starting early tomorrow morning."

"You are probably right, Bill. Maybe we'd better have you sitting outside his stall."

"I'll not have any problem with that, Spunky. I figure the vet will turn in his report about nine. By ten the word should be out. That's when our visitors will begin to arrive. They will have to see for themselves."

"That's about what I have figured. I'm sure the vet was caught up with not long after he left the barn by the local newspaper. The doc has to tell them the truth. It may be in the morning paper. If it is, folks, we'll be having company not long after daylight."

Spunky had been right, the headline in the sports section had a picture of Light taken just before his last race. The headline read "Gray Light to run in futurity". Spunky was smiling as he watched me read the paper. I had to admit it was a very satisfying headline.

"Bill, why don't you tack up Light and give him a light gallop. He'll feel better and maybe the folks coming around won't bother him as much."

I put the exercise saddle on Light and after Spunky gave me a leg up I started Light towards the track. I nodded my head to several folks on the way to the track and watched as others shook their head in disgust. I backtracked Light then turned him and let him go into a gallop. I kept him in the middle of the track and made sure no one else got too close to him. He really wanted to work but I talked to him and managed to keep him well in hand. As I walked him back towards the gap I heard one of the trainers comment, 'Best looking cripple I ever saw'. I couldn't help but smile, whoever started the rumor was going to have a long day. I gave Light a bath and was about to walk him when an old friend of Spunky's showed up.

"Spunky, some folks are pretty upset with you."

"Why Ben, I never told a soul the horse was crippled. I don't know where the rumor was started but all Bill and I did was use it to our advantage. You can't blame me for that."

"No I don't reckon I can. If they had come and asked, you'd have told them the truth."

"Of course I would have. Ben, we've been treated like we had the plague or something."

"I know, when I heard the news I didn't want to come down. I didn't want to see you all when you were down. All the old hands cussed when they heard the news. A couple of the big outfits shipped in late entries. It will be interesting to see if they scratch before tomorrow's race."

"I guess we'll just have to wait and see, Ben."

CHAPTER 11

❁

The rest of the day was much the same. Folks came by to say hello to Spunky and wish him luck. There was a steady stream of folks until lunch time. Spunky went to a hamburger joint and brought back burgers and fries. We ate them in front of the tack room where we could keep an eye on Light. Cassie came walking down the aisle, a big smile on her face.

"Afternoon, gentlemen. I see you're keeping an eye on our star pupil."

"You bet we are, Cass. Ater the article in the paper this morning it seems all of Spunky's friends have had to come by and wish him luck tomorrow."

"I know. The gentleman who offered me the ride scratched his horse this morning. There will only be seven horses in the race. The racing steward told me that when I came past the office a moment ago."

"That's fine with us Cassie. That means we only have to outrun six horses. Want to discuss how to ride the race?"

"If you've got time."

"Time is something we have plenty of, Cassie. Sit down and I'll get you a soda."

"I'll pass on the soda, Spunky. I'm watching my riding weight."

Spunky and Cassie began discuss racing tactics. I went to Light's stall and gave him a good ear scratching. He pushed me with his head to let me know he was happy to have me do the scratching. I gave him a good brushing and left him to eat his hay and take a nap. Cassie was just getting ready to leave.

"Bill how about walking me out to my truck?"

"Go ahead, Bill. I'll keep an eye on things."

I followed Cassie out to her truck.

"I figured you might just need these books tonight. I found them in a used book store."

"You are a women after my heart. I'll read them tonight."

"I knew you wouldn't sleep even if Donna is here."

"I can't, Cassie. There is too much riding on this race. I can't let Spunky and Patty down. They have given me a chance and I feel I owe them."

"I know, Bill. Now give me a kiss. I'm going to go to the apartment and get a bath and a good nap. Tomorrow could be the biggest day in our lives."

I gave Cassie a kiss and watched as she drove through the gate. When I walked back into the barn I noticed that Spunky was smiling. I pitched him a book and went to get my chair. I'd sit down the aisle in front of Light's stall. I had a job to do and I was going to do it. I was tired of being called "The Kid" by folks down home. I wanted to be respected and make something of myself. I'd been working on a list of things I thought I would need and would begin trying to get some of them before the meet was over.

Spunky went home at about seven that evening. Donna had shown up an hour later. I went into the tack room and went to bed. Three hours later I awoke and went out to see how things were going. Donna was sitting in front of Light's stall reading.

"Take a break Donna, I'm awake and I'll take over until Spunky gets here. He'll be here by four. You'll need some rest so that you can help after the race."

"But Bill, Spunky is paying me to watch Light."

"Go in and get some rest. We may have a very long day and we'll want you fresh."

Donna went into the tack room and lay down. I walked the few steps to Light's stall and found him standing in the corner of his stall asleep, just the way we wanted him. I walked back to my chair and opened a soda then sat down and began to read one of the books Cassie had brought me. I was well into the book when Spunky showed up at four to do chores.

"Morning, Bill. Everything quiet?"

"Very quiet, Spunky. Just the way we like it. Are you ready to do chores?"

"I figured we'd better get busy. We need to work the two year olds this morning. The rest of the string can go out on the walker. I'll help you get them tacked up. You can take one out and I'll clean the stalls until you get back and are ready for the last one. That will give us all the time we need to get Light ready. He's in the ninth race so we will have time to spare."

We fed and watered the horses. Spunky was very quiet when he got the feed ready. He didn't want to wake Donna who was sleeping.

We tacked up the first of the two year olds and I took one to the track. The sunlight was just beginning to peek over the trees onto the track when we got there. The young horse was feeling good and I had my hands full for a while. I finally got him settled and gave him a little extra work to take the excess energy off. He didn't have a race for a couple of weeks. When I had him worked I went back and got the filly. She was beginning to figure things out and Spunky had hopes she would make a nice horse. She was easier to handle than the gelding and went to work like an old pro. When I got her back to the barn I found Spunky had company. The folks turned out to be reporters from the local papers and were interviewing him. I took care of the filly and turned her over to Donna who was now up and looked rested.

"Thanks for letting me get some sleep Bill. I didn't get much rest yesterday. One of my kids was sick."

"You're more than welcome, Donna. I wasn't going to sleep anymore anyway. There was no use for both of us to lose sleep. I'll go get a nap now and will be ready to go this afternoon."

"That sound's good, Bill. Get yourself some sleep. I'll keep Spunky company and keep an eye on Light."

I went into the tack room and lay down. I slept hard for two hours. When I woke up I found that Donna had braided Light's mane and Spunky already had Light's leg wraps on. Spunky had gone home to change and pick up Patty. The track announcer was calling the horses for the first race to the track.

"Why didn't you wake me?"

"You were up almost all night, Bill. We felt you deserved a little rest."

I went to Light's stall and scratched his ears. Today would be his big test. If he gave his best we had a good chance of winning. There were no guarantee but I somehow felt he was going to win and do so in style. I went back to the tack room and changed clothes. When I was finished I sent Donna home to change. She only lived a short distance from the track.

She was back a short time later when Spunky and Patty returned. As Patty put it she was dressed to the nines. She was ready to have her picture taken. Spunky had a suit and tie on, too. They both looked great. I had never seen them so happy. They were ready to live the dream every horse owner dreamed of, winning the big one.

I took the grooming kit from the tack room and worked on Light. He loved the attention and seemed to relax. I knew he was ready to run and wanted to keep the edge off of him until we went to the saddling paddock. Folks came by to wish Spunky and Patty well.

As our race time came near, I made sure that Light's halter and lead shank were clean and polished. Spunky put a light blanket on Light just before we heard the call to the paddock. Patty walked with Spunky as we walked to the saddling paddock. I led Light around the saddling paddock walking ring and was careful to keep a good hold on him. I talked to him as I led him around the walking ring. Finally I saw Spunky wave to me and led Light over to the saddling enclosure. I held his bridle while Cassie's saddle was put in place. Cassie came to the enclosure and got a hug from Patty. I led Light out of the enclosure and walked him around the walking ring. The track announcer called "Riders Up". I held Light as Spunky gave Cassie a leg up onto him.

"Cassie, have a good trip."

"I'll do my best, Spunky."

I led Cassie and Light over to the gap and handed the lead shank to the pony rider.

"See you in the winner's circle, Cassie."

"See you there, Bill."

I walked towards the grandstand where I saw Donna was waiting. We walked up the steps of the grandstand and found us a spot up high where we could see the whole track. The horses were being paraded past the grandstands for the crowd to see. As each horse passed the finish wire the track announcer gave the horse's name, number, jockey and the owner of the horse. We had drawn the number five gate and with the late scratches would only have two horses to our outside. Spunky's friend, whose horse had run such a close race to Light in the trials, had drawn the number one gate. We all figured he would be the race pace setter because of all of his early speed.

Donna loaned me her binoculars so that I could watch the horses being loaded. We didn't talk as we watched the horses warm up on the back side. Light seemed to be in good control of himself and was not giving Cassie any problems. My heart began to quicken as the pony riders started leading the horses behind the gate. This was the moment we'd been waiting for. The months of work, sweat and tears were now completely out of our control. From this point it was all up to Light and Cassie.

I watched as Cassie pulled a set of her goggles down and was led into the starting gate. The last two horses went into the gate. The track announcer said "The horses are all in line".

The bell rang and the gates flew open, letting the horses explode out onto the track. I saw Light and Cassie suddenly have a length lead on the rest of the field. The length was suddenly three and Cassie began to take Light across the track and position him just off the rail. Light had the lead all to himself. He was floating along over the track surface with Cassie still high in her irons. She had a firm hold on Light whose ears were flipping back and forth as he and Cassie reached the turn. They were now six lengths in front and going just the way we wanted.

The time for the first quarter was twenty one and three fifths, the half mile time was forty five and two fifths. I knew then that the race was ours. Cassie had not asked Light for a thing. As they rounded the turn and started into the home stretch I thought "Now Cassie, now". It was as if she had heard me. She suddenly got down on Light's back and asked him to run. The other jockeys were using their whips and shouting to their horses. Cassie was simply letting Light do what he did best, run. She and Light were pulling away from the rest of the horses when they reached the wire. The crowd was cheering and shouting with joy as they saw Cassie stand up in her irons and wave her whip in victory.

Donna and I raced down out of the stands and through the gate so we could catch Light when Cassie brought him back. The noise around the track was like nothing I had ever heard. I looked at Donna and had to shout to her to be heard. Spunky was suddenly standing next to me. The smile he wore was something I'd remember for the rest of my life. It was the look of a man who had struggled for years and had finally won.

Cassie brought Light back up the track at a slow trot and pulled him up when she reached us. She jumped off Light's back and into Spunky's outstretched arms. The crowd cheered again as Spunky swung her around in joy. He sat Cassie down and quickly removed the overgirth. He then gave Cassie a leg up on Light and I led them into the winner's circle.

I had never seen so many people in the winner's circle. It seemed as though half the track was standing there smiling. I led Light and Cassie in and set them up for the picture. As soon as the flash went off, Cassie jumped off of Light and waited for Spunky to remove her saddle so she could go to the scales and weigh out.

I had just started to lead Light out of the winner's circle when I heard the crowd roar again. The race was official and Light had equaled his own track record and had not been touched with a stick. I, like everyone else, knew that he could have broken it and not even tried. As I followed the trackman towards the test barn people were shouting to me. It felt great to be a part of something so special. I led Light into the test barn area and found Donna waiting with his water bucket. I gave Light a small drink and began leading him around the test barn holding lot. We gave him another drink and a short time later the test barn man came and led him into the test facility. Donna and I waited for the test people to bring Light out of the barn.

A short time later they led Light out of the barn and handed him over to me. Donna and I started towards our barn. Folks, folks who just wanted us to know how happy they were for Spunky and Patty, congratulated us. When we finally reached the barn we found the barn aisle full of people. Donna took charge, "Horse coming through. Clear the aisle".

I led Light into his stall long enough to remove his leg wraps. I led him out of his stall and straight to the wash rack where Donna held him while I began to give him his bath after running cold water on his legs. Spunky and Patty were not in the crowd in front of our tack room. I had to ask several folks to move back as I gave Light his bath. Finally, I accidentally let the water spray in their direction and they moved back. I saw Donna smile at the way I had handled things. When we had Light washed Donna took the lead shank and began to walk him.

"Bill, you're the assistant trainer. Now you go play nice with all the folks over there. Remember, they may want you to take some of their colts this fall. Remember, business before pleasure."

"Yes, ma'am. Now get the horse walked."

She was laughing as she led Light away.

I walked back to the stall and to wipe Light's racing bridle down. Folks were asking me questions that were Spunky's business and I simply said the decision was up to Mr. Davis. I sure didn't want some reporter saying I was in charge of things. I was relieved a short time later when I saw Spunky and Patty come down the barn aisle.

Spunky shook my hand after Patty gave me a hug and a kiss.

"Everything all right, Bill?"

"Everything is fine, Spunky. Light is walking great and doesn't seem to know he was even in a race."

"We caught them napping, Bill. They thought we'd lay off the pace and make a late run. I told Cassie if she could get the lead take it. We all know what he can do if we ask him."

"Spunky, all I knew for sure was that when he got the half in forty five and change no one was going to catch us. Cassie stole the race. Who ran second? I never even looked. I was too busy watching Cassie and Light. I wanted to see if Light pulled up all right."

"My friend who ran second to us in the trials. I was really thrilled that he did so well. He told Patty if he couldn't win the race he was tickled we did."

"Spunky, who are all these people?"

"Some are friends, but I have no idea who most of them are, Bill."

A moment later I saw Cassie coming down the barn aisle. Folks were hugging her and telling her what a great race she had ridden. When she finally managed to get loose she came over to where I stood and took my hand.

"Bill, we did it. Isn't it the greatest thing?"

"It sure is, Cass. I don't know when I've ever felt better."

"Say, young feller. Are you getting fresh with my daughter?"

"Dad, Mom, I thought you couldn't come."

"We didn't want you to be nervous, so we told you a little white lie. It looks like you have someone looking after you anyway."

"Yes I do, and I'm quite proud of him. He's proved to everyone who knows anything about racing that he is a force to be reckoned with. He's proved to me and everyone else just how special he really is."

I didn't know what to say. No one had ever said so many good things about me before. Art reached out and took my hand and shook it. Cassie's mom gave me a hug. I was flying to say the least. Things couldn't get any better.

"William, I'm proud of you."

"Mom! How did you know where I was? Where have you been?"

"The Sheriff contacted me, William. I'm living in Oklahoma City. I work for a large hotel chain there. I wanted to take you with me, William but your father wouldn't let me."

"I've always wondered Mom. I understand why you left. Dad was hard to live with and as time went on and his drinking got worse he didn't improve. Mom, this is Cassie."

"I know, I saw her kiss you in the winner's circle. Cassie, I'm proud to meet you and see that my son has such good taste."

"Thank you, Mrs. Patton. I have to admit he is sort of special."

"Mom, come with me. I want you to meet Mr. and Mrs. Davis. They are the ones who gave me my chance to learn how to be a trainer."

I introduced Mom to Spunky and Patty. She and Patty seemed to have a lot to talk about so Cassie and I got a soda out of Spunky's cooler and stood back watching all the folks who were busy talking about the race.

"Bill, I may never have a moment like this again but at least I can say I've had this one. No one can take it away from us. We stuck together and got the job done. In style, as my brothers would say. Bill, we're two lucky people."

Donna brought Light into the barn for me to check. He was dry and cool. I rubbed his ears and told Donna to take him to his stall. I'd get the leg brace and wraps and be right there. I was wrapping his legs when Spunky walked into the stall. He looked over my wraps and to my surprise gave me a hug.

"Fine job, Bill. Thanks for all your help. Patty and I are taking you, your mom, Cassie her folks and Donna and her husband to supper tonight. We want to take our family to supper. Bill, we consider you, Cassie and Donna as family so please tell me you'll come."

"Of course I'll come, Spunky. I'll be honored. As to being considered a part of your family, I am proud and I'll try and make you proud of me. But what about Light?"

"Bill, relax and enjoy the moment. It's time to have some fun and by gum we're going to have it. I've hired two boys that I've known for a long time. They will keep an eye on things while we go to supper. Patty has made the reservations and we're ready to go. You get Cassie. Your mom is going to ride with Patty and me. Get moving, Bill. I'm hungry and I want to eat."

"Cassie was ready when I found her standing in front of the tack room. Her folks would follow us to the steak house. We went out to my truck and waited for her folks to get behind us. We pulled out of the parking lot and headed downtown. When we reached the steak house Art was asking about the training center I was planning on building. He had a lot of questions and I did my best to answer them as we walked across the parking lot. When we walked into the steak house, folks began clapping. Spunky and Patty were enjoying it to the utmost. We were shown to our table. Mom sat on my right side and Cassie sat on my left. The food and service was great. Mom and Cassie visited all evening. When the meal was over we followed Mom out to the motel where she was staying. She promised to call me and made me promise to call her at least once a week and let her know what was going on. Cassie assured her I'd call. That seemed to make her feel better.

Cassie and I each got a kiss goodnight. I took Cassie back to her apartment after we stopped and got an ice cream cone. It was indeed a great evening. I kissed Cassie goodnight and went back to the track. I wanted to check on Light.

When I arrived at the barn I told the men Spunky had hired that they could go. I checked on Light and found him asleep. I got a book and was about to sit down when the phone rang.

"Davis Stable, this is Bill. How may I help you?"

"Mr. Davis isn't in?"

"Mr. Davis has gone home sir, can I take a message?"

"This is Dave Luther. I'm in charge of taking entries for the State race next month. I was wondering if Mr. Davis had any intentions of entering his horse in the State race."

"He has talked about it sir but I'm not sure, considering the late fee and all."

"We might be able to give him a break on the late fees if he'd consider bringing his horse to our race."

"Sir, I'll give him the message first thing in the morning. I'm sure he will return your call. What is you number, sir?"

The gentleman gave me his number. I repeated the number back to him and hung up. Little did I know it was only the beginning of the phone calls I would receive. When Spunky arrived the next morning I handed him a list of nine calls for him to return.

"The ones on top are the ones I figured you'd want to talk to first."

As I turned to go empty water buckets the phone rang in the tack room.

"Your turn, Spunky. You can play office operator."

I was laughing as I walked off down the aisle. I heard him say something about a wise something kid. I think I figured what he had said a step or so later. Cassie and I worked the horses and later went to lunch at the track kitchen. Cassie had brought all the papers with her for me to read the stories about the race. They were great reading until I read the part about how I was the best assistant trainer Spunky had ever seen.

"Bill, you're blushing."

"Did you read this one, the one where Spunky said I was the best assistant trainer he'd ever seen?"

"Of course I did. What about it Bill. He meant what he said. Don't be surprised if you start getting calls about breaking horses this fall. Spunky is very well thought of in this area."

"I have to get my place fixed up first. Oh, Lord. I have so much to do and so little time to do it."

"You'll get it done Bill, my brothers and I will help you on weekends."

We went back to the barn where we found Spunky looking rather confused.

"Bill, so far I've been offered six different horses to train, and had two offers to sell Light. You were right, Bill. The offers are getting better all the time. I talked to the folks who are in charge of the big State race. We'll only have to pay half the late fee if we'll take Light there."

"I think they will do even better than that Spunky, but it still is a good deal. What have you and Patty decided?"

"We're going to go, Bill. Cassie, I've already talked to your boss and as of now you're on my payroll. That is, if you want to go and ride Light in the race."

Cassie jumped up and hollered.

"Will I go? You bet I'll go. Thanks, Spunky."

"Thank you, Cassie. We've come this far and I don't see any reason to change things. Patty and I have discussed it and think you and the colt have something going. He relaxes in his works and runs for you when you ask. Besides I'll not worry about someone paying you off to lose the race. Bill, you and Donna will be in charge here. I've got the condition book marked up so you can enter the horses where I think they have a good chance of winning."

"Sounds good to me, Spunky. When do you plan on leaving?"

"The girls will leave tomorrow morning early. I'll leave as soon as we have chores done."

"Spunky, Donna and I will take care of the chores. If we go to work now we can have the trailer packed before we do chores. That way you can leave about daylight. It will be a lot cooler on the stud for most of the trip."

"I thought you might be tired from yesterday, Bill."

"Spunky let's get started. It shouldn't take us anytime at all. Hook up the trailer Spunky. You can take my truck home tonight. That way all you'll have to do is load the horse when you get here. You'll be a hundred miles down the highway before the sun comes up. It will be a lot easier on Light and you'll have him in a stall by lunchtime."

"Let's do it, Bill. I'll go hook up the trailer while you sort Light's things out."

"Spunky, I'll call Patty and see what time she wants to leave. Would you like me to go to the office and get the silks?"

"I'll call them and tell them to let you have them. I'll need them to get Light's papers for me, too."

"I'm going to miss you, Bill."

"You'll be too busy to worry about me, Cassie."

"No I won't. I'll only have one horse to work and have the rest of the day off. You just don't let some sweet young thing cut in on my homestead."

"You don't have a thing to worry about, Cass. Not many young ladies would think the tack room is exactly a fancy place to hang out."

"Bill Patton, you just remember what I said."

"Yes ma'am. I'll remember. Call me when you get a chance. I'm going to miss you, too"

I got a kiss and watched as Cassie left the barn at a trot. I walked into the tack room and began to put the things together that Spunky would need for

Light the next week and a half. By the time he had the trailer hooked up and ready I began to carry out the equipment so he could hang everything up where he wanted it. I went back and got the leg brace and wraps. I put them in a box and carried them out to the trailer. When Spunky had everything in place he came back into the tack room and began to figure out how much feed he would need for Light while he was gone. When he had finished we began to carry the feed out to the trailer. We were finished an hour before evening chores. Donna came by to see how we were doing.

"Fine, Donna. Spunky is all ready to leave early tomorrow. Are you busy?"

"No I'm not. I was going to go by the store on the way home. The kids are at my folks this week and my husband is gone for a job interview at the state capital. If you need help I'm here."

"Good. Spunky, go home and do your packing. We'll handle things here."

"Bill, I think I'll do just that. I can get packed and get a good night's rest. I'll see you in the morning."

I gave him my truck keys and waved as he left the barn.

"Well, Donna. I guess we are in charge. Let's get the chores done and we'll go over the condition book and figure out how we'll work the horses."

We finished the chores and studied the condition book. The two year old filly was entered in a race in two days. She had had a three eighths work day before yesterday and had worked well. I'd give her a light gallop tomorrow and walk her the next.

There was even a race circled for Slinker two days before the State race. I had plenty of time to get him ready. Everything was laid out and we had plenty of time to get things done.

CHAPTER 12

❀

I was up at four and had the horses fed and watered when Spunky arrived. He pitched me my keys and said thanks. I told him I had fed Light a half ration of feed.

"Thanks, Bill. He'll travel better that way. He'll get his regular ration tonight. Let's get him ready to travel."

We put thick leg wraps on Light and then led him out to the trailer. Spunky put him into the trailer and made sure his hay net was properly tied. We shut the trailer door and walked thru the tack room to be sure we hadn't missed anything.

"Bill, I think we have everything. I should be at the other track by one or two this afternoon. I'll call you and let you know when I have him settled into his stall."

"Have a good trip Spunky, and I hope you win it all."

"Thanks, Bill. We're going to give it a try. We'll never have a better chance as far as I'm concerned. We've come this far and I figure he deserves the chance. If we don't do a thing Patty and I have had so much fun it won't matter."

"Spunky, I'm going to have Donna in the tack room after the race. I have a feeling the phone will be ringing off the hook. Now get on the road and go win the race."

I watched as Spunky pulled out of the parking lot and headed down towards the interstate. He was excited and yet was nervous about the upcoming race. I only hoped that maybe one day I could experience the same feeling.

Donna showed up and we began our morning routine. I wrapped the legs of the horses we would work and took them to the track. Everything went well. We bathed and walked dry. I sent Donna home after I had gone to the track kitchen and had breakfast. With Light gone there wasn't any reason to be so constantly on guard. I cleaned the tack and got myself a nap.

Spunky called at two thirty and told me the trip had gone well. Light was in the Stakes barn, which had twenty four hour security guards. Spunky would be able to get a good night's sleep.

He told me Patty and Cassie had called from a service station on the interstate and would arrive at the track about five that evening.

After talking to Spunky I checked on the horses and then went back to the tack room and went to work on my list of things I'd do first when I finally got home. I was working on my list when the phone rang.

"Davis Stable, how may I help you?"

"Bill, Patty and I are just a few miles from the track. It's beautiful Bill."

"You can see the track, Cass?"

"Yes, Bill. It's so big."

"Cass, the track is still dirt and has rails. Forget about how big it is and just keep Light relaxed like you always do. Don't forget to scratch his ears, it lets him know that everything is all right."

"I'll scratch them, Bill. You're right about the track, too. Thanks for your help."

"Cassie, remember to not eat too much of Patty's cooking. Look at what has happened to Spunky."

"Bill Patton, you're awful. I'll tell Spunky what you said."

"It's what he told me Cass. I'm just repeating what he told me."

"I'll call you tomorrow after works Bill."

"Let me know how they go, Cass. We'll be waiting to hear if Light seems to like the track."

After Cassie's call my mind began to wander. I walked outside the barn and looked at the nearby mountains. Only a week or so ago Cassie and I had walked along their tree-lined trails. We had enjoyed that day. It was fun to think about it.

Donna came into the barn carrying a basket. I didn't know what was in it but it sure smelled good.

"I cooked up a roast today and thought you just might want a home cooked meal so I brought you a plate. You do like home made rolls don't you?"

"Let's get chores done up. I don't want the roast to get cold!"

We did the chores in record time.

Two days later I started my first horse in a race. The older mare was entered in a six furlong sprint. She won her race by two lengths and came out of the race in fine shape. It was a thrill to saddle the mare and see her win. We would start Slinker Saturday in another sprint at seven furlong. I had talked to Spunky who had made arrangements with an old friend who was riding his last year to ride Slinker. The gentleman had come to the barn and asked for instructions on how to ride Slinker. He was a nice fellow and listened to my race plan.

When Spunky called that evening he told me that Light had had his first gallop over the track and seemed to like the track. He told me Cassie was helping him take care of Light. There seemed to be a never-ending stream of reporters and such who wanted to see Light and write an article for their papers. Patty was in charge of the phone, so Spunky had time to visit with the reporter and such. Folks were surprised to find Cassie was helping take care of Light. Most of the jockeys didn't do any work on the back side.

"She has handled the situation well, Bill. She makes the reporters take turns in their questions and thinks before she answers any of their questions. She has become quite a celebrity on the back side. When she goes to the track folks are taking pictures of her and Light from the start of the work until they are back at the stall."

Spunky and I discussed the horses in the race and had sorted out the various ones we thought Light would have to outrun to win the race. There would be ten horses in the race and all ten were nice horses. Cassie got on the phone and told me about the track and what she thought about it. She had discussed the surface with some of the jockeys who had ridden over it for the season. They had told her about the conditions along the rail and the outside. They had been very helpful and made her feel at home. She had a mount in one of the early races on the day of the big race. The horse she had wasn't a favorite but it would give her a race over the track and give her a feel of the track.

Saturday finally came and Slinker was as ready as I could make him. He was on his toes when the pony rider took him onto the track. He was nine to one on the tote board and I had bet twenty dollars across the board on him. Even though he had won his last race he was not favored to win. Everyone knew about the fall of the horses in his last race. That and the fact he was moving up in class.

Our jockey did everything just like I told him. Get Slinker out front if he could and not ask him for anything until the stretch. Slinker broke on top and the jock moved him over to the rail, never asking him for anything until they had rounded the second turn and headed for the finish wire. The two length lead they had gave him time to relax and get his mind on his business. When the late running horses began to make their move Slinker seemed to dig down deep within himself and run. He didn't want to get dirt thrown in his face. It was an exciting race. He won by a full length but a photo was required to see who ran second. Three horses were all head and head at the wire. I was thrilled to see he had run only a second off of the track record.

I was interviewed in the winner's circle by one of the local reporters. Donna took Slinker to the test barn for me. Everyone wanted to know how Mr. Davis was keeping his string of horses in such fine condition. His wins were something everyone was talking about. I had told the reporter that Mr. Davis was a good trainer who knew how to condition a horse and an excellent handicapper. He placed his horses where he thought they could win. It helped that he and Patty had raised all of the horses in their string. I hadn't thought anything about my remarks at the time but the next day when I saw them in print they looked different.

"Bill, have you read the morning paper?"

"No I haven't, Donna. I'll read it after we finish works, why?"

"The interview you did yesterday after Slinker's race was something special. It told the world what a fine trainer Spunky really is, and how he has raised almost all of the horses he runs."

"But Donna it's true, he and Patty have raised all the horses. What's the big deal?"

"It's not a big deal except we've won more than our share of races this year and folks are wondering why. When you were interviewed you told everyone that Spunky was not only a trainer but a breeder as well. He and Patty will have buyers for their colts this fall for sure."

"I'm glad. They deserve to make a good living from their work. They have worked hard and never got the respect they deserve. The wins are because we have been lucky and not had any horses get crippled. As long as we can keep everything healthy we'll be fine."

"I know Bill, but after Spunky found you and you all went to work everything has turned around. You could go to work for any one of a dozen barns. I know you won't but you could."

When I finally got time to read the article I still didn't see what all the fuss was about.

Finally it was the week of the big race. I talked to Spunky every morning and got a report on how things were going. All of the ten horses were finally in the stakes barn and the tension was beginning to build. Spunky said the track had put extra security on the stakes barn and he was glad they had. He told me that there were so many folks running around doing interviews and such you never knew who was around.

I could tell from his voice that Spunky was beginning to get nervous. When I talked to Cassie later I told her to be sure to rub Light's ears and tell Spunky to do the same. The next day she told me Spunky had rubbed Light's ears and he as well as the horse seemed to relax. Patty was keeping everyone fed and making sure they looked nice before they went to the track. Her neatness thing seemed to keep everyone relaxed and laughing.

"Bill, would it be alright with you if I brought my small portable television Saturday? We could set it up in front of the tack room and watch the race."

"You bet, we'll set it up and watch the race. I'll give you some cash and you can get us some snacks to munch on while we watch."

"That will be great, we don't have a horse in a race that day so we can get our work done and actually relax for the day."

CHAPTER 13

❀

Race day finally came. Donna and I got the string worked and everything cleaned and in good shape. I followed her out to her car and carried in a cooler. I later found it was filled with snacks and a lunch she had prepared for us. I carried the television into the barn and sat it on a small folding table we used in the tack room. Donna ran an extension cord from the tack room and plugged the small set in. After a few moments she had the picture adjusted. We were set. We would be able to watch the race without having to go out into the grandstands to watch.

I took a couple of chairs from the tack room and sat them beside the television. We sat down and had our lunch. Folks in our barn came over and asked if they could watch the race with us. Before we realized what was happening we had chairs sitting everywhere. As one of the older trainers said, it was a day for the little feller to have a chance to do something they all had only dreamed of.

An hour before race time a young man who worked for another trainer in our barn walked in carrying a much larger television. Needless to say it was hooked up in a short time. It looked as if the gathering in our barn was going to grow.

And grow it did, twenty minutes before race time the whole aisle was filled with people. There were chairs, buckets and every sort of thing that folks could think of to sit on to watch the race. Money had been taken up and pizza and fried chicken were now throughout the crowd and everyone was talking. When the pre race commentary came on it suddenly got quiet. Someone with the remote turned the volume up. For the next few minutes we watched as the track showed a film clip on every horse entered in the race. A cheer went up when Light and Cassie were shown galloping on the track in a morning work.

The folks at the track said some nice things about him but didn't figure he had much of a chance against two of the favorites in the race. Boos were heard from those amongst our now not so small crowd.

A short time later Donna, who was setting next to me, asked if I wanted to make a bet. The odds on Light were six to one. I went into the tack room and got into my money jar.

When I came out I handed Donna an envelope.

"Put half of this on his nose and split the—No, on second thought put half on his nose and get me an exacta on him and the ten."

"Bill, how much is here?"

"Two hundred dollars Donna. I'm playing with my winnings from the races and I think we can win."

"I'll be right back, Bill. Don't let anyone get my seat."

A couple of late comers wanted to know if anyone was sitting in Donna's chair but no one sat down. When Donna returned she quickly showed me the tickets.

"Bill, I hope you're right. The odds went from six to one to ten to one while I was waiting in line."

"Can you make another bet Donna?"

"Yes, Bill. There's still time. Why?"

I ran into the tack room and got the last hundred dollar bill from my jar. I handed it to Donna who took off at a run. When she returned we each opened a soda and were prepared for the race. We watched and cheered when the track cameras showed Spunky and Patty lead Light into the saddling paddock. Light was walking as if he was floating on the ground. His coat glistened in the late afternoon sun. The track announcer was talking about the two favorites in he race and seemed to forget all about Light. The favorites were the two and ten horse. They were both owned by large racing stables with ties to big Kentucky farms.

"Bill, how long a rope will Cassie need to drag those two around the track?"

"I hope a long one, Tom. A long rope would be just fine."

Everyone had laughed and was in good spirits. We watched as the horses were saddled and then led out and walked around the walking ring. Another cheer went up when Cassie and the other jocks walked into the saddling pad-dock. Cassie looked great in the dove gray and black silks. I sure wished I were there to lead her and Light up to the track and wish her luck.

We heard the track announcer say "Riders Up" and watched as Spunky gave Cassie a leg up on Light. He then led her to the waiting pony rider. I saw Cassie give him a thumbs up as she and Light were led away. The tension in our barn was now intense. Everyone was quiet as the horses were being shown in the post parade. My heart rate was going up with every passing minute.

We watched the horses being warmed up on the backside. I overheard some folks say we didn't stand much of a chance against the favorites. The horses were led behind the starting gates. They were quickly loaded and the announcer said, "The horses are all in line".

Suddenly the bell rang and the gate flew open. I was thrilled to see Light's gray head seem to explode from the gate. In two jumps he had a half length on the other horses. Another twenty yards or so he had a good two length lead. Cassie moved him over from his position on the track and set him just off the rail. Everyone in the barn was shouting and screaming for Cassie to go on and win. I noticed that Light's ears were flipping back and forth and knew Cassie was talking to him. When they reached the quarter pole the time came up across the bottom of the television screen. Twenty one and one fifth seconds. It was a quick first quarter but I knew that Cassie had Light on as she called it "cruise control". Light was running his own race. The two horse was trying to stay with him but even I could see he was beginning to labor as they started around the turn. I watched as Cassie looked back under her arm to see if anyone was mounting a charge at her and Light. Some of the jockeys were already going to their whips trying to catch the big gray horse who was running away from them. Just as Cassie and Light came around the turn I said "Now, Cassie. Ask him for everything he has". As if she had heard me, she suddenly got down low on Light's back and shook her reins. It was the signal that Light had been waiting for. He seemed to jump forward, his stride getting longer with every movement of his beautiful body. He now seemed to float across the top of the ground and was putting more distance between himself and the rest of the horses. The ten horse and the favorite in the race had made his move a moment after Cassie had moved Light. He had come from in back of the pack into second place but was getting left further behind as Light neared the wire.

When Cassie and Light crossed the finish wire a good five or six lengths ahead our barn and the grandstands above us went crazy. Folks were jumping up and down and shouting. Cups and plates went flying in the air. The little man had won the big one. I took the remote from the young man who had it in his hand and turned the volume up so I could hear the announcer's comments. The tote board was flashing "new track record" and I wanted to hear what he had to say. In fact, I was looking forward to it.

I watched Cassie pull Light up and pat his neck before she turned him around and started back for the winner's circle. A close up shot on the television showed she was crying as the track outrider led her and Light back to where Spunky stood waiting.

It was wonderful to see Cassie jump off Light's back and be hugged by Spunky and then Patty who had come out onto the track also. Spunky managed to get the overgirth off Light and give Cassie a leg back up on him. He led them into the winner's circle and set them up in front of a bunch of people. The picture was taken and a trophy presented. Patty accepted the trophy because Spunky had already taken Light towards the test barn. Patty told the reporters that if they wanted to interview Spunky they could catch him at the test barn or back at the stakes barn. He had a horse to take care of. She asked if she could say something and the announcer had said certainly.

"Bill, we got it done. Thanks to you my problem child is now a champion. I want you to know Spunky and I love you."

"Mrs. Davis, who is Bill?"

"Well, as my husband will tell you, he's the best assistant trainer and horseman we've ever been associated with."

I didn't know what to do.

Cassie was brought over to the camera and was asked about her ride. She was prepared and told the man that she and Mr. Davis had discussed the race beforehand and had planned to run it exactly the way it had gone.

"You never used your stick the entire race."

"Why should I? We were walking away from the field. My horse was on cruise control the whole race. When I asked him to run, he ran."

"What do you think his chances are of going a mile?"

"Sir, as our assistant trainer Bill Patton said, this horse can go a mile and a half. Bill has taught him to rate and he runs when you ask."

"Then you think he will be a better three year old than he is now?"

"Oh yes, he'll be more mature and will have more experience, but we're not through with racing this year yet. I'm sure Mr. Davis will find another race or two before the year is over with."

"Then you'll go on to another track with Mr. Davis?"

"No sir, I have to back to school."

"What college are you attending Miss Morgan."

"None sir, I'll be a senior at Dumas High School in Dumas, Texas."

"You mean you are a high school student?"

"Yes, sir. Bill and I both will be finishing our senior year of high school."

"But Mr. Davis said Mr. Patton was the finest assistant trainer he'd ever had, and an expert horseman."

"Sir, where does it say you have to be gray headed to be a good horseman? Bill has been breaking and training horses since he was very small. He has a way with horses that other folks can't get along with. It's amazing what he can do with a horse."

The interview ended and we turned the television off. People were thanking me for letting them come watch the race. Others were just happy that Spunky had won the race and thanked me for helping him. When things settled down, Donna looked at me and laughed.

"Now what's so funny?"

"You are, Bill. You don't have a clue what happened today do you?

"Sure I do. Light won the race."

"No, Bill. Not the race. Spunky gave you the best compliment he could. Then Cassie says you are a wonder when it comes to working with horses. Bill, that training center you've been talking about had better get done in a hurry. You're going to have more horses to work with than you ever thought possible. People are going to be calling you from all over to start their two year olds."

"I wish that were true, Donna but I just don't see it happening. Have you cashed our tickets yet?"

"No, but I'll go do it right now. Did you happen to see what the payoff was?"

"No. With everyone jumping up and down I never had a chance to see it."

"I'll go cash our tickets and see how much we made. I had a couple of dollars on Light myself. I didn't think we'd ever get those kind of odds again after his last race here. I couldn't pass up the chance to make a bet on him. When you made your exacta bet I made a small one myself. I'll be right back."

I began washing water buckets and was just finishing when the phone in the tack room rang.

"Davis Stable. How may I help you?"

"I'd like to speak to a Mr. Bill Patton please."

"This is Bill, sir. How may I help you?"

"Bill, this is Jade Ludley. I own the Ludley Ranch in Colorado Springs. Spunky Davis said to call you and see if you could take a couple of colts for me this fall. That is, if you're not full up."

"Sir, I had three openings left. When do you want your colts started?"

"I'd like to get them started in say early November."

"I usually like to start the colts in early October. It gives me a month of good cool weather to get the colts started. I'll start your colts in November though, if that's what you want."

"Mr. Patton, I'll have my colts at your place in October. I want you to break all my colts from now on if you can work me into your schedule. I usually have six or eight a year."

"Mr. Ludley, I'm just starting my training center and I am going to have to go to school. I'll be finishing my senior year and I don't want to get overloaded. I want to give every colt a chance to be as good as he can be."

"Bill, Spunky said you were honest and now I know what he meant. Let me give you my number and you can call me when you want me to ship the colts to you."

I took Mr. Ludley's telephone number and told him I'd be in touch. I hung up the phone and found Donna standing behind me smiling.

"How many colts does he want broke?"

"I told him I'd take three. He has six or eight if I had room."

"Do you know Mr. Ludley?"

"No, I don't. Spunky recommended me to him."

"Bill a few years ago he had a colt run forth in the Derby. The gentleman has good horses and has his pick of trainers and folks who can break them. You've just gone big time, young man. Now, let's see how much money you won."

She counted out the win money and I was happy, very happy indeed. It was then she smiled and handed me my exacta money. I had to sit down.

"How much money did the exacta pay Donna?"

"Two hundred and ninety dollars, Bill. Uncle Sam took his part before you got yours. I had to sign my name to the paper work but it is no problem. I don't make enough for it to cause me any problems. I did well myself by the way. I've made enough extra money this meet to buy my kids' school clothes and put new tires on my car. Thanks to you Bill my family is doing alright."

"I'm glad it's worked out, Donna. You and I both know we've been lucky. We probably will never get odds on Light like that again. He's proved he doesn't have to take his track with him. He's the real thing Donna. He's a race horse and a darn good one. After today everyone knows it and Spunky and Patty will be getting offers that would scare you and me to death. I don't know what they will do about Light but whatever they decide will be all right with me. Let's get these horses fed and you can go home. I'll want you here early tomorrow morning. Bring a pencil and a pad. I figure the telephone will be ringing off the wall and I don't have time to answer it. I've got horses to work."

"I'll play secretary for the day Bill, but I've got a feeling you'd better get set. Part of the calls are going to be for you."

We fed the horses and got all the stalls mucked. I sent Donna home and was about to go get a burger from the track kitchen when the phone rang again.

"Davis Stable. This is Bill."

"Bill, he did it. By dang, he did it."

"He sure did, Spunky. He made everyone a believer today. You've got a big time race horse. You'll be getting offers that will scare you to death. You've got phone calls to return when you get back. I told Donna to bring a pencil and paper in the morning. I'm going to let her answer the phone while I work horses."

"Bill, did a Mr. Ludley call you?"

"He sure did, Spunky. I'm going to take three of his colts. I think he wanted me to take more but I won't have time to work more than six and do it right."

"He's a good man Bill, you do him a good job and he'll spread the word to folks who will make you a very wealthy man. Your days of working with sour horses are over son."

"It sure won't hurt my feelings, Spunky. Thanks for recommending me. Now, how is Light?"

"He's fine, Bill. Ate his feed and is munching on his hay. To look at him you'd think he never had a race. Bill, he beat some very nice horses today and did it easy. When Cassie sat down and asked him to run he just seemed to explode. Did you get to watch the race?"

I told him about the party we had had in the barn aisle.

"How's Patty doing, Spunky?"

"I don't think she will sleep much tonight. She and Cassie will start back early tomorrow. I'm going to walk Light and then I'll be on my way. I should be into the track about three or four."

"I'll have the stall cleaned and ready when you get here, Spunky.

"Good, Bill. I'd better let Cassie talk to you Bill. She's standing here jumping up and down."

"Bill, you saw the race. Wasn't he wonderful? He's great. I'm so glad you got him lined out. This is a summer I'll never forget. Patty and I will be home about one tomorrow afternoon, will you be at the barn?"

"Yes, I'm glad too. I understand what you mean and yes I'll be here when you show up. Where else would I be? And most important, I've missed you."

"I've missed you too, Bill. I'll see you tomorrow."

I hung up the phone and went to the track kitchen for a burger. Tomorrow would be a very busy day and I planned on getting a good night's rest.

CHAPTER 14

❀

I was up early and had most of the morning chores done when Donna showed up. She had a pen and pad. She was ready for the day. We finished chores and had a cup of coffee. I began saddling the horses and took the older mare to the track first. I brought her back and took the two year old filly. I worked her a good three eighths and then let her gallop out. She was doing well but I thought she could do better if I could just figure out what the problem was. I'd do some thinking on her problem and talk to Spunky when we got time. I worked the rest of the string and was happy with their progress. When I was finally finished with the works I saw that Donna was on the phone.

I went to the track kitchen and ordered two breakfasts to go. When the owner of the kitchen brought the meals to me he refused to let me pay.

"Bill, take the meals and go. I made a bundle on the race yesterday. I was behind Donna when she made the bets. I knew she didn't have that kind of money herself and figured maybe you did. I made the same bet. It may have not been exactly fair but I was going to bet on Light anyway. The exacta was a bonus. Now go on and eat your meal before it gets cold."

I left the kitchen and couldn't help but smile. The man was honest and I liked him. Donna and I sat down and ate our meal. I told her about how we were eating free. She got a laugh and said she would have to change windows and look behind her from now on.

I went to work on Light's stall and had just finished when a gentleman came walking down the aisle. I was just putting my tools away when he spoke to me.

"Excuse me, young man. Can you tell me where I can find Mr. Patton?"

"You're talking to him sir. How may I help you?"

"You're the young man who helped prepare Gray Light for his racing career?"

"Well I helped Mr. Davis with him when I first got here, sir. He didn't have any big problems. He just needed a little gentle guidance."

"Excuse me, Mr. Patton but you're cleaning stalls."

"Yes sir, I'm cleaning stalls. I do that every day. I've not been able to train the horses how to use a potty."

The gentleman laughed and then introduced himself.

"Mr. Patton, I'm a reporter and I'd like to sit down with you and do an interview for the sport magazine that I work for. I've interviewed Mr. Davis and Miss Morgan. They both spoke highly of you and I felt I needed an interview with you to finish my story. Could I buy you a cup of coffee or a coke while I interview you?"

"I don't know what you need, sir but if you want, we can get a cup of coffee in the tack room. I've got a few minutes before I have some things that need to be done."

I got two chairs out of the tack room and sat down with the gentleman and answered his questions. I'd never done an interview like this but I answered the questions as truthfully as I could. Donna added a few things to a couple of my answers. When we finished the interview the gentleman thanked me and told me he'd send me a free copy of the magazine when it came out. When he asked my address I pointed to the tack room.

"Mr. Patton, you're joking aren't you?"

"No, sir. I live here at the track. Is there a problem with that? A lot of folks stay in the barns with their horses. It's convenient for me and doesn't cost me anything. The track has a shower room and a pay laundry. The track kitchen serves good meals and is right here. It works well for a lot of folks."

"Bill, you just blew the man's mind. He never dreamed you cleaned stalls and slept in the tack room. You just gave him a million dollars' worth of education. I can't wait to see the article when it comes out. It just might get a bunch of folks' attention."

"I don't know how it will affect anyone, Donna. But I'm sure some folks think that everyone who works at the track wears suits and ties. How many phone calls do you have?"

"Eight for Spunky and five for you."

"Five for me! Who has called Donna?"

"Three gentlemen who wanted to know if you were going to be training for yourself next year. One from the Sheriff. He said you'd have his number. And your mother called to say she was proud of you."

"I'll call the Sheriff first and then my mom. I'll get some quarters out of my jar and go make the calls if you don't mind hanging around for a little longer."

"Bill, I'm here for the day. I wouldn't miss what is going to go on here for anything. When Spunky shows up with Light it's going to get real busy around here. Go make your calls. I'll handle the phone chores here."

I went to the pay phones outside the track kitchen and first called the Sheriff. He answered on the second ring.

"Sheriff, this is Bill Patton. Is there a problem at home?"

"No problem, Bill. There were just a bunch of folks who watched the race on the T.V. at the truck stop. They wanted you to know they were happy for you. I told them you were planning on putting a track in out at your place. It seems everyone is in favor of your doing that. There are a few of the old time horse traders who aren't too thrilled because you won't have time to break their horses."

"Sheriff, I've got all the horses I can handle this fall. Good horses, Sheriff. Folks are calling the barn from all over wanting me to start their colts. I've got to borrow a tractor and get started as soon as I get home. I've got to get the track done in a hurry."

"When will you be home, Bill?"

"I'll be home the first part of August, Sheriff."

"I'll tell your friends, Bill. I'm sure they will all want to help. I'll see you then, Bill."

I hung up the phone and called my mother. She was happy that I had called her back. The reason she had called was to tell me she had found the deed to the farm and was going to mail it to me. She told me the place now belonged to me. I started to argue with her but she told me to hush. I'd need the deed if I needed to borrow money to start my training center. I'd not even thought of that. I was going to build a center on land that I didn't even own. I thanked her and told her I'd try and get over to the city before winter set in. She told me not to worry about it. She would come see how things were going. I was going to be far too busy to be running around visiting folks. I told her I loved her and was about to hang up the phone when she asked about Cassie. I told her Cass would be back shortly and that Light would be back this afternoon. She said to give Cassie her love.

I walked back to the barn feeling great until Donna handed me two more phone numbers to call.

An hour or so later we heard Spunky's motor home pull into the parking lot. We met Patty and Cassie at the barn door. I got hugs and kisses from both. Cassie handed Donna and I both a sack.

"It's a little something Patty and I had made for you all the other day."

We both opened the sack and found a new black and gray ball cap. Across the front was the lettering "Davis Stables Home of Gray Light". It was indeed a fine looking cap. I quickly rolled the brim and put it on.

"It looks great, Bill. It adds a little class to our little stable."

"I think so too, Patty. It let's everyone know we're a member of the team."

"Bill, you and Donna are the team. Without your help we'd not have been able to take Light to the race. I want you to know how much Spunky and I think of you two."

"Now I'd better get over to our trailer lot and get things settled. My husband will be wanting a hot shower when he gets home."

"Bill, will you give me a ride home?"

"Sure, Cassie. Spunky won't be in here for a couple of hours. I'm sure Donna can keep an eye on things here."

I took Cassie to her apartment. She told me about the race and how thrilled she was to have had the experience. I got a kiss and then drove back to the barn. Spunky would be back in a short time and would want to get Light settled.

CHAPTER 15

When we heard Spunky pull into the parking lot we met him at the barn door. I shook his hand and we began to unload Light. Before we could get him unloaded, a small crowd had arrived just to get a look at the new champion. I led Light into his stall and removed his halter. He quickly made a turn around his stall and lay down and rolled. He was glad to be home. After his roll he came up to me and got his ears scratched. He was a happy horse. I closed his stall doors and went back to the tack room. Donna was smiling when I got there.

"Spunky is entertaining all of the folks outside the barn. You think we should go start unloading all the tack from the trailer? We might just be able to rescue him from all his fans."

"Give him five more minutes. He's worked long and hard for this moment and I don't want to disturb him."

We waited a while then went out and began unloading the trailer. Spunky managed to get away from the crowd and helped us carry everything into the tack room.

"Bill, it's sure nice to be back. Maybe everything will settle down now."

Donna handed Spunky the list of calls that he needed to return.

"Spunky, why don't you and I unhook the trailer and you go home. Get you a shower and some rest. You can return the calls from your place. Maybe you can take care of your business without being interrupted."

"Bill, you've got a good idea. Let's get the trailer unhooked. We've already had two offers for the horse and I know two to of these gentlemen on the list. All I want to do now is get some rest."

Donna and I watched as Spunky pulled out of the parking lot and headed home. I got a book and sat down to read. I was going to get some rest myself.

The next morning Donna and Spunky arrived together, I was up and ready to go to work. I fed Light, rubbed his ears and began getting the tack ready for the morning works. When the horses were all worked and Donna was walking the last one dry Spunky called me into the tack room.

"Bill, this is Monday and we don't have anything in until Sunday. Patty and I have talked these last couple of days and we want to help you get your training center started. We've made more money this year than we ever dreamed of and we'd like to help you get things lined out down home. Besides, having you start our colts this fall will give us a big jump on folks come springtime."

"We know you've made some money this spring but not near enough to finance everything you're going to need to get done. Now, take the week off and go home and start getting things lined out. You're going to need a new barn with at least eight stalls. Eight good stalls, Bill. Folks aren't going to send you horses unless you have a good safe place to take care of their colts. You know a lot of folks down there so do a little horse trading so to speak and get the barn built while you're up here.

"Spunky, I want to thank you and Patty for all you've done for me. Like you say, I've made and saved some money since I got here. I'll go down home and see what I can get done. If I need any help, I'll holler at you. I'd rather get things done on my own if I can. But I know to get things done right, I may need to take you up on your offer."

"Don't hesitate to ask, Bill. You've done so much for Patty and me we'd like to help. Now get your things and get gone. I want you back here Friday evening about chore time. Patty and I are having a party and we darn sure want you here."

"I'll be here, Spunky. I've got a date with Cassie and I don't intend to miss it. I'll go call the Sheriff and let him know I'm heading home. He may know someone who can do me a good job and save me some money at the same time. I'll leave as soon as I talk to him. I'll see you Friday afternoon."

I went to the pay phone and called the Sheriff's office. I got him on the line and told him I was headed home and wanted to talk to him about having a new barn built. He said I could catch him at the truck stop about six that evening. I told him I'd see him there and after hanging up the phone walked towards my truck. Cassie pulled into the parking lot and hollered at me.

"Bill, I heard you were leaving and hoped I could catch you before you got away."

She handed me a small narrow box. I opened the box and found it filled with business cards. The cards were done in gold leaf and read "Running P Training Center" Owner Bill Patton. My phone number and address. They were a little fancy for my taste but I had to admit they did get your attention.

"Thanks, Cassie. Now I've got to get down home and get things rolling. I've got to make something to live up to these cards."

"You'll do fine, Bill. Just look things over and go with your feelings."

"I'll do that, Cass. I'll see you Friday evening."

I got a kiss and ran to my truck. I didn't want the Sheriff waiting on me. I had filled the tanks on my truck the evening before so all I had to do was head south for home. I drove out of Raton and headed south for Clayton. I put my truck on cruise control and enjoyed the drive. I saw antelope and even a few deer on the high desert plain. I pulled into Clayton and noticed a few new shops had opened to handle the trade of folks on vacation out into the area. I cleared town and headed towards Dumas, the place where my dream had really started. I stopped long enough to get a Pepsi and top off one of my tanks. I left Dumas and headed towards home. Home, the place I hadn't figured on going back to for some time. I did take a look at the place as I drove past on my way to the truck stop. It was just like Cassie had said. I'd take it one step at a time and build on it from there.

As I pulled into the truck stop I saw the Sheriff's car parked up next to the building. I found a parking spot and parked. I walked into the café and found the Sheriff talking to a couple of men sitting at the counter. I spoke to both men who I had either broke or ridden horses for over the past years.

"Bill, come sit down. You're right on time."

"I try to be, Sheriff. I don't like to be kept waiting, myself. Have you come up with any ideas about who might be able to build me a barn?"

"I have, Bill. I contacted the Parker brothers. They have worked for a half dozen builders over the last ten years and finally set out on their own. I'm sure you can deal with them. They will want to do a good job because you may build something everyone will be seeing. They will be out to your place about eleven tomorrow morning."

"That will be great. I've got to stop at the store and pick up a few things."

"I'll be out tomorrow, Bill and see how things are going."

"Thanks Sheriff, I really appreciate your help."

I went out to my truck and drove over to the local grocery store. I bought two boxes of large strong black plastic bags, two bottles of cleaner and a couple of sponges. I bought a small cooler, a twelve pack of Pepsi and a bag of ice. I was heading towards the checkout when I spotted the deli. I bought some roasted chicken and a dozen doughnuts. I had breakfast and supper covered. I paid for my purchases and headed for home and a lot of work. When I parked my truck I went straight to the barn and got the big scoop shovel. There was no need to think of a broom for a while.

When I reached the back door you could smell the rotting food and such even outside the house. I sat the scoop shovel down and unlocked the door. I took a deep breath and opened the door. I went straight through the mess and unlocked and opened the front door. It felt good to stand in the draft of the west Texas breeze that now went through he house. I looked at the mess inside the house and shook my head. I could not understand how a human could live like this. If anyone wanted me to take a drink I'd have no trouble saying "no".

I went back to the porch and picked up the scoop shovel and began raking the mess in the kitchen into the middle of the floor. I had filled eight trash bags and had not, in my opinion, got a good start on the mess. I walked through the empty food boxes some of them only partially emptied, to the door to my bedroom. When I opened the door I was shocked to see everything in the room turned upside down. I assumed my father had been looking for the money I had collected for the horse I had ridden.

I picked up my dresser and began putting the drawers back into it. I put the springs back on the bed and then the mattress. Both needed to be replaced but they would have to wait like a lot of other things. I sorted through what few clothes I had left behind in my bedroom as I picked them up and began putting things away. The things I didn't want I threw into the pile of trash in the kitchen. I began to carry out trash bags and stack them out in the back yard. When I had the last of the filled bags out in the yard I washed up at the hydrant and walked to my truck and decided it was time to eat. The chicken was great and the Pepsi cold. When I finished eating I sat for a few minutes listening to the big trucks going east and west on the Interstate. I began to think of the things I needed to do the next day.

I needed to contact the phone company, gas company and the electric company. As I was searching my mind for anything I had forgotten, I remembered the blanket. The blanket was one mom had hand quilted for me just a short time before she had left. I walked back into the house and went to the closet in my room. I took a chair and looked on the top shelf. The blanket was still there. I had folded it up the day after mom had left. I was afraid my father would tear it up or throw it out. I couldn't help but smile, tonight I would use the blanket when I slept in my truck. There was no way I could sleep in the house tonight.

I took the blanket out to my truck and went to sleep. The sun was just beginning to come up when I woke up. I washed up and ate three doughnuts and drank a Pepsi. Not much of a breakfast for some folks, but it was good enough for me this morning. I walked into the house and again began to scoop clean as I would later call it. I filled four more bags and had just carried them out into the yard when the truck came up the drive.

Two gentlemen got out of the truck and walked to the gate.

"Are you Mr. Patton?"

"I am, sir. How may I help you?"

"We're the Parker brothers. The Sheriff said you needed a barn built."

"I do if we can make a deal."

"How big a barn are you needing built?"

"Thirty six by sixty. I'll need eight, twelve by twelve stalls. Four on each side. I'll need a wash rack and an enclosed tack room. Think you can do that?"

"Yes sir, we heard you plan on putting in a training center here. Is that true?"

"It's true. I'll be building a track and be breaking thoroughbred colts."

"Wait a minute. Are you the Bill Patton who helped train Gray Light?"

"Yes, I am. I'll have his half brother here this fall."

"Mr. Patton, the Boys' Home over east of here makes some really nice metal stalls. We'll get a quote and add it to ours."

"When will you have your quote ready for me to go over?"

"Tomorrow afternoon. Say two o'clock."

"Fine. I've got to leave Friday morning so the sooner the better."

"When would you want us to start?"

"Yesterday would have been good."

"Fine, sir. We'll see you tomorrow afternoon."

I went back to cleaning and an hour later I finally had the kitchen and living room in decent shape. I still needed to do my father's bedroom and the bathroom. My bedroom was in fairly decent shape so I walked to Pa's room and opened the door. The smell was unreal. I quickly opened the two windows and went back into the living room. I was almost sick from the smell. I would have to let the room air for a while. Once again I began carrying out the last of the trash bags. I had just finished stacking the last of the bags when I heard a car coming. I walked to the back gate and saw the Sheriff and another gentleman drive up and park.

"Good Lord, Bill. You trying to fill the landfill by yourself?"

"I didn't really plan on it Sheriff, but I've still got a lot to do before this house can be lived in."

"I know what you mean. A couple of my boys came out here and looked in the windows. They said it was a disaster."

"Bill, this is Sam. He's a friend. He needs to talk to you about breaking a colt for him."

"Mr. Patton, not just broke but very specially broke. My daughter is only eight years old and is partially blind from an auto accident."

"Sam, you don't want a three year old for your daughter to ride. You need an older horse that has seen everything, done everything and learned how to take care of a child."

"Do you know of any horses that will suit my daughter's needs?"

"I know of a couple, sir. But they won't be cheap."

"Sam, didn't I tell you the boy would do right by you?"

"Yes you did Sheriff. Now Bill, find my daughter a horse. Do you by chance know of a place I could stable the horse?"

"I have the small shed over there that I plan on rebuilding. It's sound and solid and is safe. I can take care of the horse here if you want."

"How much a month to keep him?"

"You buy the feed and hay I'll keep him for a dollar a day."

"Mr. Patton"

"Bill, sir."

"Bill, that's not good business."

"It may not be, sir. But there have been a bunch of folks who have helped me these last few months and I think it's time I give something back."

"Can you teach my daughter to ride?"

"Sam, I'm going to be busy trying to beg borrow and steal enough equipment to build a training track. But I have a friend who I know will be glad to teach her. I'm sure Cassie Morgan will be thrilled to help her."

"Cassie Morgan, the jockey for Gray Light?"

"Yes, sir. She will be coming down to help me with the new colts when I get them started."

"Good Lord. Wait until I tell my daughter who will be teaching her to ride. Bill, take this check and buy the horse. The check is signed, just fill in he amount and let me know how much it was. Now, show me where you're going to build your track and barn.

I liked the Sheriff's friend Sam even though he did seem to be a little reserved or stiff. I took him and the Sheriff out to where I figured I'd build my track. I told him about how I planned to borrow the old tractor pulled grader and scrape the grass and a little bit of the top soil off before I began hauling sand up from the dry creek bed. I explained how you needed a good soft cushion on top of the track so that you wouldn't injure the young colts' legs.

"Will you have Gray Light here, Bill?"

"I doubt it, Sam. I'll have his half brother here this fall, however."

I was explaining that at the present time Mr. Davis hadn't figured out exactly what the plans for Gray Light would be. I heard a truck coming up the driveway. I saw a new bright red pickup drive past the parked cars and come across the open pasture towards us.

"Friend of yours, Bill?"

"Not to my knowledge, Sheriff. He sure doesn't care much about his truck, though. He'll sure enough scrape the paint on that fancy truck."

I walked over to where the man stopped his truck.

"Good morning, sir. Can I help you?"

"Good morning, son. I'm Willard Bland. I train running quarter horses. I'm sure you've heard of me. Fellow over at the truck stop told me there was a training center going in over here. I wanted to see when it would be ready. Here, take my card and give it to the owner. He can get in touch with me when he gets a chance."

Now, this gentleman was not from around our area or had just recently moved into our area. I knew one thing. I didn't think too much of him. I reached in my wallet and took out one of my cards and when I took his I gave mine to him. His card, which was a standard black and white business card paled in comparison with mine. I noticed the puzzled look on his face.

"Bill Patton. You're not the Bill Patton who helps train Gray Light are you?"

"Yes sir, I am. I'm Mr. Davis's assistant trainer at the track in Raton. I'll be breaking and training a bunch of colts here this fall. I'm having a new barn built and will begin working on the track when I get back home in August. At this time I'm not planning on this being a public training facility. I've got a year of high school to finish and with the colts Mr. Davis and several other gentlemen are sending I won't have time to take any quarter horses."

"Then you won't have any stalls for rent."

"No, sir. All the stalls in my barn are already spoken for and I've got colts on my waiting list."

"In that case, I wish you luck and I'll see you later, Mr. Patton."

I watched as the gentleman drove his fancy truck out of the pasture and down the drive.

"I'm Willard Bland and I'm sure you've heard of me. By golly, Bill. The feller seems to think he's somebody."

"Bill, let me see his and one of your cards please."

I handed Sam the two cards. Then saw the smile on his face as he showed them to the Sheriff.

"No wonder the fellow didn't hang around. He handed you a hamburger and you handed him a steak. Sheriff, did you notice the look on his face when he read Bill's card? It was priceless. Bill, I think we're going to get along."

I had read Sam's name on the check he had given me. Sam J. Cooper Construction Co. I'd seen his trucks at various jobs all over the city.

"Sam, we'll get along fine, but just remember one thing. When you come through the gate, you're just plain Sam."

"Sounds good to me, Bill. Now finish telling me about this track."

We visited for an hour or so before the Sheriff and Sam left. I went back to work on the house. I'd stopped long enough to finish off the chicken for lunch and had just taken the last bag out of my father's room when another truck came up the drive. This place was becoming a parking lot of sorts. I carried the last two bags out and went to see who was in the truck.

"Hey, are you Bill Patton?"

"Yes I am. How can I help you?"

"Show us what you want done and go do something else. Our baby sister sent us down here to help you get things lined out."

"You're Cassie's brothers?"

"We sure are. We're between jobs for the next couple of days and she said you could use our help. So here we are, ready and willing. You've looked after our baby sister this summer and we want to thank you. Mom sent these cleaning things along and told us to wear them out. You've met our mom and when she speaks we listen."

The boys were twins but didn't look alike. Don was blond and fair. Dale was dark headed and was dark. Both of the boys played football, and I could see why. They were both over six feet and weighed in excess of two hundred pounds. They began to laugh.

"You're wondering how in the world our baby sister can be so small and we got so big?"

"Yes I am."

"That is exactly what we figured. Our mother's dad, our grandpa, is six three and weighs about two fifty. We took after him. All of dad's folks are tiny like sis."

"I don't know how it happened but I'm glad to have you. I've been cleaning with a scoop shovel trying to get the place cleaned up enough so I could sleep in it. I've got most of the stuff carried out but I haven't got the filth scrubbed off things."

"Bill, we'll help you get these bags on your truck. You take them to the dump. We'll start on the scrubbing and such while you're gone. Looks to me as if you've done one heck of a job."

"Fellows, I've never seen anything like the inside of this house. I'm ashamed for you all to see it."

"We help grandpa refurbish rent property Bill. We'll not be shocked."

The boys helped me load the black plastic bags into my truck. It was a full load and the heat outside the house hadn't helped the smell of the things inside the bags. When we finished I asked the boys if they liked pizza.

"You bet, Bill"

"I'll stop on the way back and pick some up. Thin or deep pan."

"Deep pan, extra cheese. Any kind of topping will do except those little fish."

I had to laugh. I waved to them when I drove off to the city land fill. I paid the fee at the landfill and unloaded the bags. I drove to the pizza parlor and ordered three large deep pan pizzas. Extra cheese, one sausage, one Canadian bacon and one supreme. I figured the three would be enough to feed the boys. I picked up a six pack of Coke and headed back to the house.

When I got to the house and walked to the back door I couldn't believe what I saw. The boys had scrubbed everything in the kitchen. The stove, the refrigerator, the table, everything was spotless. One was mopping the floor and the other was scrubbing the walls. It was unreal what a change they had made in such a short time.

"Hey fellows, take a break. Let's eat something."

The boys sat down in the shade on the back porch and began to eat. I'd never seen pizza disappear so quickly. Don and Dale had two cans of pop. The pizza was wiped out in record time. I got what was left of the doughnuts and the boys each had a doughnut. A short time later they were back in the kitchen and were hard at work. I walked into my father's room and took out the top drawer of his dresser. I sat it on the bed and began to sort through things. There was not much of anything of value or anything I wanted to keep. I put the things into a plastic bag and figured I'd have another load before I left. I took out the second drawer and found a cigar box with a string tied around it. I untied the string and opened the box. Inside I found a bundle of letters from my mother begging my father to let me come live with her. There were even checks made out to me. Checks I could have used for school clothes and such. I found a medal my brother had been awarded from the army and a few other minor things. I sat the box aside and went through the rest of the drawer. When I finished I took the box out to my truck and put it in the seat. I carried the bags outside and stacked them like I'd stacked the others. I had found my brother's wrist watch and found that it still worked. I put it on and asked the boys the time. I set the watch and a short time later told the boys to quit. They had done enough, more than enough.

They nodded and finished what they were doing. They walked around and smiled after their inspection of things.

"Sis will be down and look things over. We don't want her thinking we didn't get things done right."

"Boys, I don't know how to thank you."

"Just look after our sis, Bill. You got any carpenter work you need done? We're pretty good hands with a hammer and a saw. Besides we have tomorrow off and you feed good."

I couldn't help but laugh. The boys had done a fantastic job on the house. I'd be able to finish it up before I went back to Raton.

"Boys that little shed over there needs some work. I'll be taking care of a horse for a little blind girl and it needs some repair. You can use any of the lumber from the big barn for the repairs. I'm going to have to burn it down anyway."

"We'll be here first thing tomorrow, Bill. You'll want a run-in shed put on it won't you?"

"If you all have the time it would be nice."

"Who is the little girl, Bill?"

"A Mr. Sam Cooper's daughter."

"The Sam Cooper, of Cooper Construction Company? My goodness, Bill. How did you meet him?"

"He is a friend of the Sheriff and the Sheriff brought him out. I've got to call a friend of mine and see if I can buy his horse. I've got a signed check and all I have to do is fill in the amount of the sale price."

"Bill, tell your friend the check is good. Sam Cooper owns one of the largest construction businesses in the state. He is a very wealthy man."

"He may be, but I liked him. He was a little bit stiff at first but he seemed to relax after a while and enjoyed himself."

I waved to the boys as they drove down the driveway and walked back into the house. I wanted to call Cassie and was surprised to find the phone was still working. I reached her on the second ring. It was great to hear her voice. She had far more questions than I could answer in one phone call. The horses were all doing well and everyone was looking forward to the party Friday night. It seemed that the track management had taken over the party and were paying for it. Spunky and Patty were sort of disappointed but figured we'd have our own party later.

I filled Cassie in on what was going on. I told her that her brothers had been down and what a wonderful job they had done. I told her about meeting Sam and his wanting me to find his daughter a horse. I told Cassie about the girl's sight problem and told her I had sort of volunteered her to give the little girl lessons.

"Bill, you know I'll help her. It will be a challenge to teach someone who can't see. I guess she and I will learn together. Do you have her a horse yet?"

"Not yet, but I'm going to call a friend of mine and see if I can buy his daughter's old horse. He's helped raise my friend's three girls and is just what I think we need. I don't know if I can buy him or not, but I'm going to try. I'll call you tomorrow night and let you know if I get him bought."

"Do that, Bill. I'll be looking forward to your call."

I told Cassie I missed her and hung up the phone.

I dialed my friend's number and got him on the phone. He told me he was happy that I had had so much success in my new job. We visited for a few moments then I asked him about the horse.

"Dusty, do you still have Coalie?"

"Of course I do, Bill. Why?"

"I'm looking for a very special horse for a very special young lady. She only has part of her sight and Cassie Morgan has agreed to teach her how to ride. I'd like to buy Coalie for her if you will sell him."

"Bill, I'd never even thought about selling him. He's almost part of our family. You say the girl is almost blind?"

"That's right, Dusty. She was in a car wreck and only has about ten to twenty percent of her sight. By the way Dusty, I'm not making a thing on the deal. I'll be keeping him here at the house for thirty dollars a month.

"Bill, let me talk to the wife. I wouldn't dare to sell him without talking to the boss first about selling him. I'll call you back in a little while. Are you at home?"

"I am until Friday morning. I have to go back to the track then. I'm trying to get a new barn built and a track laid out for the training center I plan to build this fall."

"Give me a call when you get home and I'll come help you. I'll talk to the wife and call you back."

I hung up the phone and grabbed the mop bucket and went to work on the floor in my father's room. I had just finished my mopping when the phone rang.

"Bill, this is Dusty. The wife and I have talked and we'll let you buy the horse on one condition. If the little girl doesn't get along with him I get to buy him back at the same price."

"Sounds fair to me, Dusty. How much do you want?"

"I'll take twelve hundred for him, Bill. And you know that's cheap."

"It's more than fair, Dusty. I'll bring you the check tomorrow. I'd like to leave him at your place until I come home."

"That's fine with me, Bill. He has his own pasture and seems to like it"

"I'll see you tomorrow Dusty."

I opened my billfold and took out the card Sam had given me. I dialed his number and was surprised by the voice that answered.

"Cooper residence. This is Jen. How may I help you?"

"This is Bill Patton and I'd like to speak to Mr. Cooper, please."

"Are you the gentleman who is getting me a horse? Have you found one yet?"

"Yes and yes to your questions"

"You've found one! What color is he? What is his name?"

"He's black and his name is Coalie. He's raised three little girls already and I'm sure he will be looking forward to meeting you in August."

"Oh, great!. Is it true that the lady jockey will be giving me my riding lessons?"

"Yes, it is true. I talked to her a few moments ago and she is looking forward to meeting you and teaching you to ride."

"Oh, great! Wait until I tell my friends that Cassie Morgan will be teaching me to ride. They will flip. Here's dad, Bill. I'll talk to you later."

"Bill, did my daughter talk you to death?"

"Not at all Sam. She's just excited about getting her new horse."

"What did you get for us Bill?"

"I got you a thirteen year old quarter horse. He's fourteen hands or so tall and has already raised three little girls. He was my first choice and the gentleman who owned him priced him right. He only wants one thing understood, Sam. If Jen doesn't get along with him he gets the horse back at the same price."

"Good enough, Bill. What did you have to give for him?"

"Twelve hundred, Sam. And it's a great price. I told him about Jen's problem and he agreed that Coalie was the horse she needed."

"Sounds like you did a little sales job Bill. I really appreciate your help. The Sheriff was right. You have done the best for me you can. Cassie has said she will teach Jen to ride?"

"She'll be down the first Saturday after we get home to give Jen her first lesson. She is really looking forward to working with Jen, Sam. I think they will get along fine."

"Bill, thanks again for all your help."

"No, thank you Sam. I'm feeling better already. I've been able to help someone like I've been helped these last few months. I'll talk to you when I get home and go get Coalie."

"I'll see you then, Bill."

After I hung up the phone I drove down to the truck stop and had supper. When I got back to the house I went into my room and stretched out on my bed. The soft breeze coming through the window felt great. I pulled the blanket up over me and went to sleep.

As usual I was awake just as the sun was coming up. I got a clean towel from my bag and got myself a shower. I put on clean clothes and went to work on the bathroom. I was just finishing when I heard a large truck engine. It sounded like it was coming up my driveway. I walked outside and saw not only one truck, but three. One hauled a road grader, one a bulldozer and the last a backhoe. The men must have gotten lost and taken a wrong turn. I watched as the first truck pulled up to the gate and stopped.

"Are you Bill Patton?"

"Yes sir, I am. How can I help you?"

"I think it's the other way around. My boss, Mr. Sam Cooper, told me to get this equipment and get my butt out here and do whatever you needed doing. I've worked for Mr. Cooper for twelve years and never heard him say a curse word. So when he told me to get my butt out here, I did. Now what are you planning on building?"

"A track to gallop and train race horses. I'm having a new barn built, too."

"You'll need a pad built for your barn. Let me get this equipment unloaded and then we'll walk things out and you can show me where you want things located."

I stepped aside after opening the gate to the pasture and watched as the big trucks pulled through. The men were experts at what they were doing. They soon had the equipment unloaded and the gentleman who had driven the first truck came walking over.

"Mr. Patton, I'm Ike Johnson and I work for Mr. Cooper. Now where do you plan on building this new barn?"

"I want it right over there on that high spot."

"Good location, it will drain well. We'll build you a pad so it will be even better. Now, where do you want this track built?"

I explained to Ike how I wanted the track built. And how I wanted the sand from the dry creek bed put on track surface. How I wanted the turns large so that the colts wouldn't stress their legs.

"Wait a minute. Are you the Bill Patton who helped train Gray Light?"

"Yes, I'm that Bill Patton."

"Oh boy, wait until my wife hears I'm building a race track for you. She had a bet on Gray Light when he ran in the big state race. She did all right but was so excited during the race. Do you know Cassie Morgan well or does she just ride Gray Light?"

"Cassie is a good friend of mine and will be giving Sam's daughter riding lessons here as soon as the meet ends up at Raton."

"That explains it. Sam wants Jen to have a good place to ride. Let's walk the ground out and I'll place some flags as we go. We'll adjust them later after we've got an idea as to what you want. I'll put a slight bank to the track so it will drain better. You'll need a pond in the middle to hold the runoff. You want it three quarters of a mile?"

"That will work, but I need the turns large like I said."

"Not a problem. I'll shoot everything with a transit. We'll use the dirt from the Pond to build your barn pad. How big will your barn be?"

"It will be thirty six by sixty."

"Good enough. We'll get started. If I have any questions I'll give you a holler."

"I'll be at the house unless I have to run into town for something."

I walked to the house and listened as the big machines were fired up and went to work. I had no idea what it was going to cost me but I'd worry about that later. Right now I had other things to do. I made the calls to the power company, water company and the gas company and got everything lined out. The phone company said I'd have to make a payment within ten days or they would have to shut the phone off. I went to the local convenience store and got money orders for all of the companies. I mailed the money orders and went back to the house. Cassie's brothers were already at work. They had run an extension cord from the old barn and had their saws going when I drove in.

"You boys have a good start."

"We're working on it, Bill. How about pulling some of the boards for us while we nail these in place?"

"You bet I will."

I began pulling the boards off the old barn that the boys needed to rebuild the small shed for Coalie. The boys kept me running the rest of the morning. When I mentioned lunch they said they could eat a burger if I'd go get them and reached for their wallets.

I got in my truck and went to a burger shop that I thought made a good burger and ordered two each for us. I ordered fries to go along with the burgers. When I got back the boys were adding the shed roof to the small barn that was now neat and solid. I'd have to get a gallon of paint and put a coat of paint on it.

We sat down and ate the burgers and fries topped off with the cold drinks from the cooler. We were just finishing when the Parker brothers pulled up. I looked at their quote and found it was several thousand less than I had figured. I asked when they would start and they told me they would be back first thing in the morning. I took out my money and asked for a receipt. I paid them fifty percent of the quote and told me I would pay the rest when the barn was finished. I saw Ike standing near by and walked over to where he stood waiting.

"What do you need, Ike?"

"I think you'd better come take a look for yourself. We've run into a little problem."

I followed Ike out to where he and the boys had been digging the drainage pond. I couldn't believe what I saw. The pond was full.

"Ike, how did that happen?"

"We were digging and hit a little sand. After the last load was taken off, my backhoe man noticed water was beginning to run into the pond. He barely got the backhoe out of the pond before it filled up."

"Is it salty, Ike?"

"Bill, it's sweet as can be. We must have tapped a vein of water from an underground spring or something. All I know is that you've got good water and plenty of it if you want to raise hay or some other crop."

"I'm no farmer, Ike. I'd not have any idea where to start."

"Bill, why don't you call Dan Fowler. He raises a bunch of hay. You've got a good amount of ground here. Put it to work for you. Let Dan raise hay on your place. He'll have all the water he would need to put on the fields when it was needed. I'm sure he could work a deal with you where you would get all the hay you needed for your horses and probably make a little cash to boot."

"Sounds like a good idea. I've ridden horses for Dan and he's always been more than fair with me. I'll go to the house and call him. Thanks, Ike. I really appreciate your help."

"Not a problem, Bill. Just let me bring my wife out sometime to watch you gallop the horses. It would be a big treat for her."

"Bring her out anytime, Ike. I'll have a half brother to Gray Light here."

"She will flip out, Bill. All of her friends will have a fit when she tells them."

Ike and I walked around the freshly graded ground. After making a few adjustments, I went to the house and called Dan Fowler. I told him about the water and said if we could make a deal I'd let him raise hay on the hundred and sixty acres north of the track. He told me he'd come look at things in a couple of hours. I went out of the house and found Cassie's brothers were just finishing up the shed roof. The extension would let a horse be saddled in the shade and at the same time would keep rain from blowing into the shed.

"Boys, you've done a fine job. Now all I've got to do is get some paint and get started."

"It did turn out rather well didn't it? We enjoy doing this sort of thing."

"I want you boys to know if you need any help all you have to do is ask. It would have taken me a week to even get this barn fixed half as nice as you've done it. You boys better head home. You've done a great job, but I know you've got things to do at home."

"We do have a couple of things that need doing for grandpa, Bill. He sort of depends on us to take care of some of the heavy lifting on his jobs."

I thanked the boys again and watched as they drove down the driveway and headed home. I went to my truck and went to the paint store and bought a gallon of white paint, a brush and some cleaner. When I got back, the Sheriff was sitting in his car next to the now neat little barn. He was smiling as I got out of my truck and unloaded the paint.

"Those boys did a heck of a job, Bill. The little barn will look brand new when you get it painted."

"I sure hope so. Those boys are some kind of a hand with a saw and hammer. They kept me busy carrying boards to them from the old barn."

I told the Sheriff about the water in our pond and about Ike's idea of calling Dan Fowler about raising hay on the land north of the track. He seemed to think it would be a fine idea.

"You got the house all cleaned out Bill?"

"All I have to do is finish mopping the bathroom and my bed room. When I have to leave in the morning I'll not be dreading coming back."

"I know what you mean. At least now you've got things going your way."

"I do until I get Sam's bill for all the work Ike and his boys are doing. I'll have to borrow money from Spunky to get him paid."

"Don't worry about it, Bill. Sam has more money than he knows what to do with. He can do about anything he wants except give his daughter her sight back. When you offered to help him it meant a lot to him, especially when you offered to keep the horse for darn near nothing. By the way did you find anything for him?"

"I bought Dusty's little black horse, Coalie."

"My Lord, Bill. How did you get that done? I didn't think anyone could get that horse bought?"

"I guess you could say I did a little hustling. I told Dusty about Jen and he couldn't say no. I did have to promise him that if the girl and the horse didn't get along, he'd get to buy the horse back at the same price he sold him to me for."

"Now that's horse trading. What do you plan on doing with that pipe you have stacked over there?"

"I took that in payment for a horse I rode. I wanted to build a new round pen. Dad had a fit when he found out I had not gotten money and wouldn't let me build the new pen."

"Bill, I've got a couple of boys in lockup that really aren't bad boys. They just got into a bad situation. They are welders and I just might talk to them about them welding up your round pen and working off a bunch of their sentence."

"I don't want to cause you any trouble, Sheriff."

"No trouble at all, Bill. The sooner I get them out of my jail the better. I won't have to feed them and they can get back to work. I'll have a talk with them and see what they have to say."

We were talking about where I would want the round pen built when we saw the truck turn off the highway and come up the drive. It was Dan Fowler here to see about leasing the hay field.

"Go ahead and take care of business, Bill. I'll be here when you're finished."

I met Dan at his truck and took him out to look at the pond. He was impressed with the way the land lay and explained it would take very little effort to get the water to the hay fields below. He explained it would be a year before he could start cutting hay off the fields but would furnish me with enough hay to take care of the horses I would have here this winter. He'd swap me hay for the lease of my land. We'd work out a deal on the hay when the fields began to produce. When I asked him when they would start planting the fields he said a couple of his boys would be over the next day to start plowing the ground and get the place ready for planting. We both were happy with the lease arrangement. When Dan left I saw that the Sheriff had put on a pair of coveralls and was busy painting on the new little barn. It seemed everyone wanted to help.

That afternoon I took Ike and the boys each a cold pop. They seemed to enjoy the short break. I explained to Ike I'd be leaving the next morning about daylight. We saw the Parker boys coming up the drive with a small load of lumber.

"Bill, you have a dollar?"

"Sure I do Ike, you need a dollar?"

"Give me the dollar, Bill."

I handed Ike the dollar.

"Good, you just hired yourself a construction foreman. Those boys told you they would be here this morning early. We hustled around and got the pad built and leveled so we wouldn't hold them up. They may be in business for themselves but they better learn that if you make a man a promise you'd better dang well keep it. You go get things lined out to go back up to the track. I'll keep an eye on things here for you while you're gone. I want to see just how big you can make this place. We'll haul sand and begin to spread it over the track. You wanted six inches or so, right?"

"That's right. I'll disc it in after it has time to settle. Ike, I appreciate your help. Tell Sam I said thanks."

"I'll do that, Bill. You be careful going back."

CHAPTER 16

I had packed my things and drove into the truck stop and filled both of the gas tanks on the truck. I'd stop in Clayton for a break and top off whichever tank I'd been using. I was anxious to get back to the track and tell Spunky what all had been done. I was looking forward to seeing Cassie, too.

The Parker boys were hard at work when I got back. Ike and the boys had left for the day but I could see the track now had a good six inches of sand on it. I was happy. I had picked up a couple of sandwiches at the truck stop and had a cold pop with them. I'd get a sausage and egg sandwich in Dumas at the little diner for breakfast. I planned on being there early in the morning. I heard the power generator shut off just as the sun was setting in the west. The Parker boys had all the poles in the ground and tied together with stringer boards. They stopped at the house long enough to let me know they would really make headway tomorrow. I told them thanks and that Ike would keep me posted on how things were going. The boys left and I did a quick walk through of the house. There was really no need to lock it because there wasn't anything in it anybody would want.

The next morning I left well before daylight. I locked the gate and hung the key on the back of the gate post where I had told everyone it would be. I walked into the small diner in Dumas just as the sun was beginning to peek up over the horizon. I ordered my sausage and egg sandwich to go and a large hot chocolate. I had just sat down at the counter when Cassie's brothers walked in.

"Hey, Bill. Headed back up north?"

"Yes. I've got to take your sister to a supper tonight. She even has me wearing a suit."

"You going to wear a tie?"

"Well, yes I am."

"Dale, you were right. She is serious about him. He must think a lot of her. Otherwise he'd never wear a tie."

"All right, you two. I do think your sister is neat but right now I have my hands full just trying to get things shaped up for fall. They started the barn yesterday and Ike and the boys are going to push the old barn and all the trash into a hole and burn it."

"That Ike feller is a dandy. He works hard but he has a sense of humor that makes a feller want to work for him. He said he'd put us to work anytime we needed a job."

"He will do it, too. He's looking after the barn construction for me while I'm gone."

I paid the waitress for my food and the boys' breakfasts as well. I was out the door before they knew I had done it. Don was shaking his fist at me as I pulled away from the café parking lot and headed north. I knew I'd hear about it later but they had both worked so hard and would not let me pay them. After a quick stop in Clayton I once more headed north, toward Raton. The drive seemed to take a bit longer than usual, but I knew it was because I was anxious to get back. I wanted to see Spunky and tell him everything but I also wanted to see Cassie. Her brothers were right, I cared for her an awful lot.

I got to Raton a little earlier than I had figured on. I stopped at a gas station and called Cassie.

"Where are you, Bill?"

"At a gas station at the edge of town. Have you had lunch yet?"

"No. I was just going to have a sandwich."

"How about a burger and fries? I've just about forgot what good food is all about."

"Get over here you smooth tongued devil. I'm hungry, too."

I hung up the phone and drove over to Cassie's apartment. She came running down the stairs before I got the truck parked. I got a kiss that was great.

"I've sure missed you, Mr. Patton."

"I've missed you too, Cass."

I filled her in on how things were going down at the house and how her brothers had shown up and helped me. I told her I'd never be able to repay them.

"Bill, the two of them called last night and told me you were a fine feller. They even approve of my going with you."

"I'm sure glad. Those two are huge. I don't know how you stayed so small."

"I'm not going to worry about it, Bill. Now feed me."

We had burgers and fries and had a wonderful time together. I took her home and then headed back to the track. I saw Spunky standing at the barn door waiting when I pulled in.

"Bill, I'm sure glad to see you. Come in and sit down. Patty and I have been talking about you."

I went into the barn and got a kiss from Patty. She told me they had just been lost without me. They were glad I was back and would be going to the dinner tonight. They were both sort of upset that the track had taken over the affair but said they could live with it.

"At least you won't have to worry about paying for all the steaks, Spunky. You'll save a bunch of money there."

"That's true, Bill but we don't have any control over who will be there, either. Patty and I have had a bunch of offers for Light and some of the folks seem to think we shouldn't have him. We've been told we can't take him to the places he needs to go."

"Bill, it's been awful to hear someone talk that way. We've both worked so hard to get this horse and now we're hearing we can't do right by him."

"Look folks, maybe some of the folks are not telling all the truth. Spunky, what are your plans for when the meet ends?"

"I figured we'd go home."

"Why not take Light, Slinker and the two year old over to Oklahoma City. The purses are good and they have a couple of nice stakes that you just might win. Slinker has come a long way and I think he may win the stakes race here next week. I'm sure you can pick up a couple of nice horses to train for folks here that would work over there."

"That's what I've told him, Bill. I'm sure we could get stalls and we'd only be a hundred miles or so from home. All we'd need is someone to help with the string."

"Take Donna. She's a good hand and you know she is honest. Her husband just might be able to find work at the track himself. At least she wouldn't be waiting tables this winter."

"You may be right. I'll ask her when we do chores this evening."

"Why don't you let me ask her? You all need to go home and get some rest before the big celebration tonight. I'm sure Donna and I can handle things here. Besides I need to spend some time with Light."

"Go visit Light, Bill. Patty and I are going to get some rest and be fresh for tonight. Don't you and Cassie be late."

"We won't be late, Spunky. I'm even going to wear my new suit. Cassie can hardly wait to see me dressed up."

I waved to them as they left the parking lot. I went to Light's stall and was greeted as an old friend. He had missed his ear rubs while I was gone. Donna showed up an hour or so later and I asked her about going to Oklahoma City with Spunky after the meet ended. She was thrilled to be asked and said she would talk to Spunky in the morning.

I got my things out of the truck and went to the track showers after we finished chores. When I came back to the tack room I quickly changed into my suit pants and white shirt. I put on my new loafers and then began trying to tie the knot in the tie correctly. I finally remembered on the third try. I tucked in my shirt and then took my coat out of the bag and put it on. It felt great. I made a quick check in the small mirror in the tack room and then went out into the barn aisle. Folks began to whistle and point. It was all done in good sport and didn't bother me. I got into my truck and headed over to Cassie's apartment. I parked my truck and saw one of Cassie's roommates looking out the door. I walked up the stairs and was told to come in. Cassie would be out in a minute.

"Bill, you look great. But wait until you see Cassie. She is beautiful."

The roommate was right. When Cassie walked into the room I was speechless. She wore a deep burgundy dress with matching shoes and her sandy red hair had been styled.

"Bill, you can close your mouth now."

"I'm sorry, Cassie. It's just that you're so beautiful."

"You look pretty special, yourself. Now let's go. We don't want to be late for the party."

I followed Cassie to my truck and held the door open for her. When she was seated I closed the door and walked around the truck in a daze. I had always thought Cassie was cute but I had been wrong. She was beautiful. When I got into the truck Cassie was smiling.

"Bill Patton, you look great. Very handsome in fact."

"It will take a lot more than a suit to make me match up to your class."

"Bill Patton, don't you ever say anything like that again. You're handsome, have a great personality and I just happen to think I'm in love with you."

"I think I love you too, Cassie but I don't have anything to offer you. My house is clean now but it's sure nothing special. The furnishings are worn out and the whole place needs to be redone. I've got the center started but it has such a long way to go."

"Bill, I don't care what you've got. All I care about is you. You'll do well and I intend to be there to help you. Now just relax. Things will work out fine."

"You really think we have a chance after graduation, Cassie?"

"Bill, as far as I'm concerned it's a done deal."

CHAPTER 17

❀

When we arrived at the steak house a car was just leaving the parking lot. I pulled into the spot and started to get out of the truck.

"Wait a minute, Bill. I have something for you."

Cassie opened her small purse and handed me a small black box. I opened the box and found it contained the gold racehorse cuff links and tie clasp. I didn't know what to say. Cassie took the tie clasp and put it on my tie. I removed the cuff links from my shirt and put the gold race horses in their place.

"Cassie, I don't know what to say."

"You don't need to say anything, Bill. The look on your face was enough. Now, let's go inside. I want to show you off."

I helped Cassie out of the truck and held her arm as we walked into the steak house. We spotted Patty and Spunky and walked into the room. The whole place became silent. Patty got up and came across the room to us. Cassie got a hug and I got a kiss on the cheek. Patty showed Cassie and me to our seats. I held Cassie's chair and then took my seat. As I quickly looked around the room I didn't know a third of the people that were there. I could tell from the look on Cassie's face that she was thinking the same thing. I didn't see a half dozen of Spunky's friends who I was sure would have been there if they had been invited. I understood why Spunky had been upset.

The President of the track stepped up to the podium and tapped the microphone. He began by thanking Patty and Spunky for bringing all the attention to the track. He told them how proud of them the people of the town and the track were of them and wished them good luck in the future. He introduced the Governor of the state who made a short speech and asked Spunky to come up.

We watched as Spunky, in a suit and tie walked up to where the Governor stood waiting. He was presented with a beautiful trophy for having won the state's largest race. He was asked to say a few words after a bunch of pictures were taken.

"First, I'd like to thank my wife Patty who decided what stud we would breed our mare to in the first place. She has stood by me for years as we dreamed of having a horse like Gray Light. Second, I'd like to thank two kids for all their help. First, Bill Patton my assistant trainer who turned Gray Light from a rogue into a race horse and for suggesting the finest jockey a trainer could ask for, Cassie Morgan. These two kids are more than just employees to Patty and me. They are our kids and we love them. Bill, would you and Cassie stand up so folks can see you?"

Cassie and I stood up and the people applauded. We quickly sat down. Spunky thanked the track and the Governor for the trophy and the dinner tonight. He took his seat and gave me a thumbs up sign which I returned.

Suddenly the room was filled with folks serving salads drinks. We ate our steaks and desert then went over to say thanks to Patty and Spunky. After a short visit I told Spunky that Cassie and I wanted to put a short work on Slinker and Light the next morning when we had enough light to work them. We'd rather a lot of folks wouldn't be around to know we were working him with Light.

"Sounds like a plan, Bill. I'll be there to put the watch on them."

"I'm coming too, Bill. I'd like Spunky to win the stakes race. If we can win another couple of races he can win the trainers' award for the year. I think he deserves it."

"So do I, Patty. We'll give it our best shot. We'll see you in the morning"

Cassie and I left the steak house and instead of going straight to her apartment I drove to the ice cream parlor and got us each a double dip cone. Cassie was laughing about us eating cones while we were "dressed to the nines". It had been a wonderful evening but would have been better if Patty and Spunky's friends had been there. I dropped Cassie at her apartment and, after getting a kiss goodnight, I drove back to the track.

As I undressed I took the tie clasp and started to put it in my suit coat. I felt something rough on the back and looked to see what was there. What I found was "To Bill with love, Cassie". I put the clasp into my suit coat pocket and after hanging everything up went to bed a very happy young man.

The next morning I was up early and had the feeding done some time before either Spunky, Patty or Cassie showed up. I was saddling Light when Spunky and Patty arrived. Spunky helped me finish saddling Light and then we saddled Slinker. Cassie arrived just as we finished and was ready to go to work. No one would believe this small little jockey was the same young woman who was the most beautiful woman at the dinner last night. Her helmet hid her curls and the baggy shirt and faded jeans looked nothing like the girl last night.

The eastern sky was just beginning to lighten when Spunky gave each of us a leg up on the horses. Our plan, if it worked, was to gallop both horses an easy half mile then work the last quarter. We wanted Slinker in front and wanted to see what he would do when Light tried to pass him in the stretch.

Cassie and I rode the horses onto the track and began to warm them up. After we had worked them a slow half, I released my hold on Slinker and let him begin to work as we turned into the stretch.

I could hear Light coming up behind us and felt Slinker suddenly dig down and really begin to try. When we reached the wire Slinker had a nose in front. I began pulling up him up as Light and Cassie went by and finished working another furlong. Both horses felt like they had won.

Spunky was waiting at the gap when we rode back. He showed me the watch. Slinker and Light had worked a very fast quarter.

"Bill, he is as ready as he will ever be. He dug down and didn't quit. We may have ourselves another race horse. A very good one."

The next week we won two races and ran second in another by a head. Spunky was in the race for best trainer of the meet. If Slinker could win the following Saturday he would win the "Best Trainer" award for the first time in twelve years at Raton.

The first part of the week or dark days as they were called was a welcome change for us. We'd been working hard and a couple of the horses had had the last race they would run at the meet. Spunky and Patty took three of the horses to their home in Oklahoma and turned them out. It meant fewer horses to take care of and gave us more time to relax. Spunky had requested stalls at the track in Oklahoma City and had just gotten notice they would be ready when he got there. He had taken three outside horses to add to his string over there. Cassie and I had a chance to go hiking one afternoon in the nearby mountains and had a wonderful afternoon.

I had called the Sheriff and he told me Ike and the boys were still putting the finishing touches on the track. I was surprised because I thought they were finished when I left. I had talked to Spunky about the things I would need when I got home. Buckets, corner feed tubs, muck buckets and such. He had told me to just wait and we'd go to the store down town and get what I needed at the end of the meet. I thought he had forgotten until this morning when he said we were going shopping.

We took my truck and drove to a tack store out at the edge of town. They catered to the track people but I had not had any occasion to go there. When we walked in I found the place had a little bit of everything. Spunky spoke to the owner and when he came over he was smiling.

"Bill, the meet is about over and he wants to get rid of a bunch of this stuff. You can get anything you want for forty percent off the marked price."

"That's great, Spunky. I'll need eight water buckets and corner feeders, a couple of muck buckets and gosh I don't know what else."

Spunky got a big shopping cart and began putting things into it. Things I'd not thought of because Spunky already had them in the tack room to use. When we had everything we could think of we went to the counter and checked out. The gentleman was thrilled with our business and gave me another five percent off. I ended up getting half again as much tack as I had intended and got it for less than I had put back for the purchase.

We put my things in the front of Spunky's trailer so they wouldn't walk off, as Spunky put it. The meet was ending and folks that didn't have any horses in races the last week were moving out. Some were going home. Others were going south. Myself, all I wanted to do was go home and get started on my track. I'd have three weeks before school started and I knew I'd need every minute of the time.

The last of the week we gave Slinker a long controlled gallop. He was in perfect shape and was developing an attitude, as Spunky put it. Light was enjoying his light works and the break. He was kicking up on the walker and felt great. I took over his gallops and let Cassie work Slinker. On Friday afternoon Spunky, Cassie and I had a conference. We discussed what we thought we should do with Slinker. It was Cassie who came up with the idea of how she'd like to ride the race. When she finished I saw Spunky grin.

"Cassie girl, you just might be right. Do it your way and lets see what happens."

The next day I was up early and had the horses all taken care of by the time Spunky and Donna showed up. I walked over to the track kitchen and had a good breakfast. When I got back to the barn Spunky was talking on the phone to someone. Donna told me she and her family were leaving Monday morning for Oklahoma City. Her husband had talked to some folks over at the track and had gotten a job. He'd be helping clock the horses at their morning works. The pay was decent and it could lead to a better job later on. She was happy he had found something. He had been taking accounting classes by mail and if things went right maybe he could go back to school and get his degree. I was happy for her and hoped things worked out.

Spunky came out of the tack room and let out a sigh.

"One more fellow tells me I can't do right by Gray Light and I'm afraid I just might lose my temper. Bill, if you were in my place what would you do?"

"I'd take Light to the City and see if I couldn't win a couple of those nice stakes races over there. Slinker may not be a stakes horse over there but he should be able to run well in the allowance company. I'd give them thirty days rest then get them ready and go to Oaklawn Park in Hot Springs. I'd want to know if Light was as good as I thought. If he does well there then you may look at the big one."

"That's what you would do?"

"That is exactly what I'd do. This may be your only chance at the big time, Spunky. I'd just have to give it a shot. You know a man is a long time dead."

"By dang, Bill. You're right. If Light does well at the City, I'll take him to Oaklawn. Patty has always dreamed of having a horse good enough to run over there just one time."

Spunky went home and changed his clothes. I started getting Slinker ready when he came back. I'd changed while he was gone. I was down on my knees putting the last wrap on Slinker's legs when I heard the voice.

"See, Sam. The boy really does work."

"Sheriff, Sam. How are you? What brings you all up here?"

"We came to see this horse, if he's Slinker. We want to know if he can win the stakes race."

"Well, here is his trainer. Ask his opinion. Spunky Davis, these are my friends Sam Cooper and Sheriff Thomas."

"I'm pleased to meet the two of you. Bill has said some wonderful things about you."

"Thank you, Mr. Davis. Bill here is some sort of a celebrity down our way right now. His idea of building a training center has a lot of folks running through themselves to get a chance to talk to him. We know who and what he is but some folks just can't understand how a young man like him can even think of starting something like that."

"I know what you mean, Sam. And please call me Spunky. All my friends do. Bill here has made this year something special for the wife and me. If

Slinker here wins today I'd be honored if you and your friends would get in the win picture."

"You can bet on it, Spunky. Bill, Ike and the boys are all here today. Their wives said they could stay home or come along. Needless to say they came along."

"Ike and the boys are here! I'll have to look them up before the race. I've never seen a man who can do the things he can with the big equipment. The guys that work with him respect him, too."

"I know. He has worked for me ten years and I've noticed that when I send him on a job it always gets done and I don't have any problems. I made him my foreman last week. I guess I should have done it years ago."

"He'll do you a great job, Sam. He's a good man."

"Sheriff, we'd better get out of these folks way. They have a horse to run."

"Sheriff, Sam, I'll see you boys in the grandstands before the race. Say hello to Ike for me."

"We'll do that, Bill. You all get your horse ready. I want to have my picture taken. I know my daughter will."

I got my lead shank and was ready to take Slinker to the saddling paddock at the second call. I followed Spunky into the saddling paddock and led Slinker around the walking ring. I walked him until Spunky waved to me. I led him into the saddling stall and waited while Spunky got Cassie's saddle set. Cassie walked up just as I led Slinker out of the stall. She was wearing Spunky's black and gray silks. She waved her stick at me as I led Slinker around the walking ring.

The call of "Riders Up" was made and I held Slinker while Spunky gave Cassie a leg up onto Slinker. I led the two of them to the gap and turned Slinker over to the pony rider.

"See you in the winner's circle, Bill."

"I'll be waiting, Cassie. Good luck."

I walked into the grandstands and went looking for Ike and the boys. I found them and their wives busy studying the form sheet. When Ike saw me he jumped up and ran over to where I stood. After shaking hands I was introduced to all the wives and was asked what I thought of Slinker's chances. I told them what I thought and asked Ike if he would make a bet for me.

"What do you want, Bill?"

"Twenty to win and a twenty dollar exacta. Slinker and the three horse."

"I'll take care of it, Bill."

I watched as Ike went to make our bets. The horses were warming up on the back side. I watched as Cassie and Slinker were led behind the gates. I noticed that Cassie didn't have her goggles on. She planned on being in front. The horses were quickly loaded and the track announcer said the horses were all in line.

The gates suddenly flew open and the bell rang. I saw Slinker and Cassie break even with the favorite. I watched as Slinker suddenly dug down and took a length and a half lead. Cassie looked under her arm and guided Slinker across the track and set him just off the rail. Slinker seemed to be going well and it looked as if Cassie had a good hold on him. The race was six furlongs and would only have one turn. Cassie maintained the lead down the backstretch and as she and Slinker started into the turn she sat down on Slinker and shook the reins. She was asking him for his all. Suddenly their lead was five lengths and was getting larger with every stride. The other riders were caught flat-footed. They had expected Cassie to start her run just before she entered the stretch for home. It was wonderful to hear the crowd's reaction to what she had done.

"Caught them boys half asleep. Look at her ride. I'll bet she picked that trick up over at the other track."

The track announcer couldn't believe what had happened. He was caught by surprise, too.

Cassie and Slinker crossed the finish line a good four lengths in front of the favored three horse. The crowd went wild. Cassie was their favorite rider. She seemed to always win for the little people, the two dollar betters who made up most of the folks at the track. I rushed out of the stands and got out onto the track in time to catch Slinker when Cassie brought him back. The clock on the tote board showed he had run just three fifths of a second off Gray Light's new track record. He had just shown he was a race horse.

Cassie hugged his neck and jumped off so Spunky could remove the over-girth. When Spunky put her back on Slinker I led them into the now crowded winner's circle. The picture was taken then Spunky brought a little girl that I figured was Sam's daughter around and set her up in front of Cassie and had another picture made. Cassie had told her to smile and she had. The crowd cheered again as I led Slinker off to the test barn.

Donna met me at the test barn with the water bucket. I gave Slinker a small drink of water and then led him around the lot until the men from the test barn came out and got him.

"I hope you had something on the race, Bill."

"I did Donna. He went off at six to one. I also had the exacta."

"I did, too. This has been a very good year. I've made enough for us to move to the city and have money left just from my bets."

"That's great, Donna. I hope everything works out for you."

The men from the test barn brought Slinker out and turned him over to me. Donna and I led him back to the barn. We had just finished his bath when Spunky and all of the other folks from down home showed up. It almost looked like the day Light had won the big state race. The folks were all in a grand mood. I was standing off to one side when Sam came over and introduced me to his daughter Jen.

"You're Bill, aren't you? Would you bend down so I can see what you look like? I don't have very good eyesight and I'd really like to know what you look like. I've seen Cassie and she's pretty."

"She sure is, Jen."

I squatted down so Jen could see me clearly.

"Bill, you're very handsome. No wonder Cassie likes you."

"Jen!"

"She does, dad. She told me she did. Bill, would you take me down to see Gray Light? I've got his race on a disc and I've watched it a hundred times."

I took Jen's hand and walked with her to Light's stall. I opened the top gate and spoke to him. I picked Jen up in my arms and told her to be still. Light came over to the gate and extended his head over it. He seemed to know there was something wrong with the little girl and gently touched her hand with his nose. Jen giggled.

I took her hand and told her to scratch his ear. She did and Light let out a big sigh. Jen laughed again.

"He's wonderful, Bill. His color is just beautiful."

I put Jen down and closed the top door of Light's stall.

"Bill, the ladies would like to see Gray Light. Would you get his halter and bring him out so they can take some pictures of him?"

"Sure I will, Spunky."

I got the halter and let the ladies take their pictures. Everyone was in a great mood. Spunky called for quiet.

"Folks, Patty and I have had a great year and we'd like to have a party and celebrate. We'd like you all to come with us and have dinner tonight. On us, of course."

"But Mr. Davis, we can't let you do that. There are too many of us."

"Sir, we just won a nice stakes race we never thought we had a chance to win this spring. Please go with us. We'd love to have you."

A short time later Cassie came into the barn and the party seemed to start all over again. She signed programs and it seemed everyone wanted to know what it was like to ride in a race. When we finally had Slinker taken care of and settled for the night we all loaded into our cars and trucks and followed Patty and Spunky to the steak house. This time we knew everyone and had a wonderful time. When Jen began to yawn the party broke up. Spunky and Patty said they were going to sleep in. The season was over for us and they were going to bring the books up to date and write our final checks. There was one more week of racing but we didn't have anything running. Spunky planned on taking everything except Slinker and Light to their home to rest. He'd take them and three more horses he had decided to take for other folks to Oklahoma City.

I was happy and yet sad at the same time. It seemed that the summer had only started. When I thought back on all that happened I began to realize how lucky we had been to not even have had a sore horse. We'd seen horses break down and have to be taken home or, in some cases, be put down. It had indeed been a great year.

Cassie and I sat in my truck and talked for a while when I took her back to her apartment. She had sat next to Jen and the two of them had become great friends. She was looking forward to teaching Jen how to ride.

I got a good night's rest and after feeding everything and cleaning the stalls I went to the track kitchen and ate breakfast. I'd just walked back into the barn when a gentleman came down the barn aisle and asked to speak to Mr. Davis.

"Sir, Mr. Davis won't be here today. He and his wife are taking the day off. We don't have any horses running today and the meet is over today. Could I take your name and number and have him call you, sir?"

"I would appreciate that. I represent a group that would like to make an offer for Gray Light. We think with the right training he just might be good enough to run at Oaklawn Park next spring."

"Sir, I might save you some trouble. Gray Light will be running there next spring. Mr. Davis intends to enter him in a couple of stakes races there. He's going to go to Oklahoma City from here."

"Young man, there is a lot of difference in Oaklawn and Oklahoma City."

"Sir, I'll not argue with you about that. But both Mr. Davis and I think Gray Light can and will run a route of ground. He has wonderful speed and rates great. We've been giving him long works and he seems to love them. Mr. and

Mrs. Davis have decided to take Gray Light and try him against the best. He's set track records, sir and never been touched with a stick. I myself am new to the game of horse racing but that seems to me to be a very good thing. I'll take your card, however. I'll have him give you a call."

I took the man's card and hung it on the tack room door, then went back to cleaning the tack that would have to packed away for the move. Spunky planned on leaving on Friday morning. He had thought about going east out of Clayton but had decided he would go south down past my place and take the interstate highway. It led straight into the city and would be easier on the horses.

Cassie's boss had a couple of horses in races the first part of the week but she would be finished with her job when Spunky and I were ready to pull out. The next morning Spunky found the man's card and called him back. He was laughing when he came out of the tack room after he had finished the call.

"Bill, it's a strange thing. Folks didn't know who I was a few months ago and now everyone is worried about me and my health. They are worried that I may not be able to keep training Light like I should. It's really funny. Patty is going to leave early Friday morning when I head out of here. She's going to ride home with me today and open our house up. We'll be back on Thursday after-noon. You can take down all our stuff from the stalls and begin packing it in the boxes in the tack room. With only Slinker and Light to take care of you should be able to get all the stuff packed by the time I get back."

"Spunky, I'll be able to have everything packed in a day's time."

"That's great, Bill. Maybe you and Cassie can slip off and have a picnic. You all deserve the time off. She is going to follow us home, isn't she?"

"That is the plan. She rides the last horse Thursday afternoon."

"We'll time it so we have her home by six or so."

"That's great. Her folks are planning on having a cookout for us when she gets home. Her father is fixing his famous Mexican food for us."

"Sounds great, Bill. Patty and I will have your checks ready when we get back. I'm going after Patty now. We'll be ready to load the horses I'm taking home as soon as we get back."

"I'll have their halters on them. I'll clean and strip the stalls after you pull out. I'll start taking all our hardware down when I finish."

As his assistant trainer Spunky had promised me a two percent bonus of the string's winnings for the year. I had no idea how much I had coming but I'd need every nickel I could lay my hands on before the place at home was ready.

I put the halters on the horses Spunky was taking home and had them ready when he got back. I had wondered why he had not taken them with him on the first trip but he had explained he had dropped the older mare off at the farm of his friend where she would be bred shortly after the first of the year. Besides, he and Patty had done things this way the last few years.

We hooked up the trailer and loaded the horses. Spunky and Patty waved to me as they pulled out of the parking lot. They planned on being home by sundown. I picked up my muck buckets and began cleaning the stalls. By late afternoon I had the stalls cleaned. I had almost filled the trash container outside the barn. I took care of feeding Slinker and Light then went to the showers and cleaned up. Cassie and I were going to eat at a popular chicken place this evening.

We had a wonderful time and stopped and got our ice cream on the way home. Spunky and Patty would not be back the next day. Cassie and I planned a picnic and the next day had gone to the mountains for the last time. I was going to miss the mountains and the wonderful smells. If things worked out, I'd be coming back next spring but I was going to miss them for sure.

Spunky and Patty arrived the next day. We watched Cassie ride in her last race. Her owner had had to scratch her last ride because the horse had gotten sick. Cassie helped us unhook Spunky and Patty's motor home. Patty said they were going to fix burgers that evening and they would have our checks for us then.

I picked Cassie up later that evening and saw she had already packed her truck. She was ready to head home. We drove over to Spunky's place and had great burgers. When we were finished Patty handed Cassie and I each an envelope.

"Kids, Patty and I have had a wonderful year, most of which we figure is because of you two kids. We decided to give each of you a bonus. Bill, the two percent you were promised is ten percent, and you've earned more. You are getting ten percent of the stakes wins just like Cassie. Without you two kids the summer may have never have happened. We will be looking forward to you all coming to the City. I'm going to be lost for a while without the two of you not being around."

"Spunky, we're going to miss you, too. You and Patty have made me feel almost like a member of your family. I want you to know how much I appreciate it."

Patty got up and gave us both a hug and a kiss on the cheek. She made Cassie promise to call her at least once a week and keep her informed on things. Spunky shook my hand and gave Cassie a hug. Everyone was wiping tears from their eyes when Cassie and I left. On the way back to her apartment we stopped and got a malt. A very thick, very rich malt. Afterwards, I dropped Cassie off at her apartment and returned to the track. I opened my check and was shocked at the amount. I had spent very little of my paychecks and with this added to them the sum was going to enable me to get a lot more done than I had planned on. I took the money I had won at the track from a canvas bag I kept in my pillow and began counting. My paychecks and a part of my betting money had gone into the bank but I had kept the biggest part of my winnings close at hand. When I finished my counting I couldn't help but smile. It had indeed been a grand summer.

The next morning I fed and watered the two horses and began packing my truck. My things from the tack room didn't take up much room inside my truck, but when I began to unload my things from Spunky's trailer, it took me a while. I was just finishing when Spunky drove into the parking lot. I helped him hook up the trailer then we went to eat breakfast. He had had a bagel with Patty before she left but needed some soul food, as he put it. Cassie found us just as we were ordering our breakfast. She and her roommates had had their last breakfast together so she only had a glass of juice.

We took the boxes from the tack room and loaded them into Spunky's truck. We made the rounds and made sure we had everything except what little hardware was on the last two stalls. Cassie took Light and Slinker and hung them on the walker while Spunky and I removed the metal gates from Light's stall and put them on the side of his trailer. When we had everything loaded I quickly cleaned the two stalls. We were ready to start home. For me, it would be a new beginning, one that I was looking forward to.

A short time later we loaded the two horses into the trailer and, after one more walk-through of the barn, were ready. We would follow Spunky to Dumas where he would fill up his tanks and go on to the City. Spunky pulled out of the track parking lot with Cassie close behind. When we reached the highway and headed south I adjusted my radio and settled in for the drive.

I watched as Spunky kept the big rig rolling up and down the rolling high plains desert. We were going down hill all the way from Raton to Clayton. We reached Clayton and went on towards Dumas. We were right on schedule and would reach Dumas about five thirty. When we reached the outskirts of Dumas, Spunky pulled the rig into a truck stop.

Cassie and I parked out of the way of other truckers and went to say good-bye. He figured to be in the City about one or one thirty. The new exercise boy and Donna would be waiting for him. After a handshake for me and a kiss on the cheek for Cassie he got into his truck and pulled out onto the highway. We watched as he and the rig went out of sight. We got back in our trucks and I followed Cassie to her home. Her folks were waiting when we drove into the driveway.

Art and I went to work carrying things into the house. I couldn't help but notice the wonderful smell coming into the house from the cooker outside. Art had things cooking. He had promised Cassie her favorite Mexican meal on her return home. He had taken a day's vacation so that he could get everything done.

"Think you'll be ready to eat, Bill?"

"After smelling the things you have cooking for a while, you bet I will."

"Hey, Bill. We got lucky. My brothers are gone to a football interview at a college. We won't have to compete with them for Dad's feast."

"Sounds good to me, Cassie. I've seen those boys eat."

I had a wonderful visit with Cassie's folks. The meal that Art had cooked was fantastic. I ate way too much and was miserable afterwards. I started to leave but Cassie's mom told me to spend the night. I could sleep in the boys' room and drive home in the morning. I'd have to buy food and things, anyway. Cassie thought it was a great idea. I could take her to her favorite waffle place for breakfast. When I stretched out later that evening I knew I had to get a new bed when I got home. My bed, like everything else in the house, was worn out.

CHAPTER 18

❁

The next morning I awoke to the smell of coffee. I got dressed and found Art sitting in the kitchen having his coffee and reading his paper.

"Morning, Bill. Sleep alright?"

"Sure did, Art. I thought Saturday was your day off."

"It is, but I can't sleep late. Too many years of getting up early."

"I know what you mean. I have trouble sleeping in myself. I've always gotten up early to do chores and it's become a habit."

"I'm glad you're up, Bill. Now you can take me to eat breakfast. I've been thinking about one of the waffles they make at the café here for a week."

"Better take her and feed her, Bill. She gets real testy if she doesn't get her waffles on Saturday morning."

"I'll take care of that right now, Art. I've never seen her upset but I'll bet she can get short with folks."

"Good thinking, Bill. Don't push your luck."

"I'll have her home early this evening, Art. I want to show her the place and get any ideas she might have."

"Enjoy your day, kids. We'll see you this evening."

Cassie kissed her dad goodbye and we went to my truck and headed uptown. Cassie gave me directions to the café where she ordered cherry waffles with whipped cream topping and a cup of hot chocolate. I told the waitress I'd have the same.

Cassie had been right about the waffles. They were wonderful. When we were finished with our meal we got another cup of hot chocolate to go and went out to my truck. As I pulled out onto the highway I told Cassie not to expect too much when she saw my place.

I told Cassie about the new barn and my hopes for the future. The road home seemed to fly by like my dreams.

"Bill, I wish you would relax. I don't care what it looks like. We can fix up what ever needs fixing and go from there. Bill, folks have started with a lot less and done well for themselves."

"I know, Cassie but you've been brought up in a nice home and I have nothing to offer you but a run down house and a dream."

"It's enough, Bill. One of these days we'll have a place like that one."

I looked where Cassie was looking and suddenly pulled my truck over to the shoulder of the road and stared.

"Bill! Bill, what is wrong?"

"Cassie, that is my place!"

I couldn't believe what I was seeing. My new barn was up. The track, which had only been a dirt circle with sand piled on it, was smooth as silk and had white painted rails all around it. There were pipe lots off the barn and a new pipe entryway with an arch across the top with the name Running P across the top. The drive up to the house and barn was freshly mowed and everything was painted. Even the house had been painted.

"I don't know what has happened, Cassie. When I left, the barn was nothing but a bunch of poles sitting in the ground. The track was level but had extra sand stacked on it. The house has even been painted, and where did all the pipe for the pens and fences come from? Cassie, I'll never be able to pay for all this."

"Bill, wait until you find out who has done all this. Who do all the cars and trucks up by the barn belong to?"

"I have no idea, Cass but I guess we'd better go find out."

I pulled back onto the highway and then turned up the driveway. The fresh mowed grass smelled great. I was in shock. I pulled up to the house and parked. I took Cassie's hand and we walked up towards the barn. Just as we got close to the barn Spunky, Patty, Mom, Sam, Jen and the Sheriff all walked out and welcomed us home.

"What do you think, Bill? Did we do it right?"

"Sam, I don't know what to say."

Spunky came over and shook my hand.

"Bill, you don't need to say anything. I felt the same way when I saw the place on the way down. Come on into the barn. A lot of folks have been waiting to see you."

I walked over to Mom and gave her a hug.

"Did you know about this?"

"Of course I knew. Tom called and gave me a report every other day."

"Tom!"

"The Sheriff, Bill. He and I went to school together. Now you and Cassie go on inside and meet the rest of your friends."

Spunky and Patty walked with Mom while Cassie and I followed Sam and Jen into the barn. The barn seemed to be filled with people and all of them were smiling. The stalls were all in place and I could see Slinker and Light munching on their hay nets.

Sam, how in the world did this all get done so quick, and who do I owe the next twenty years of my life to?"

"No one, Bill. My new superintendent got on the phone and informed a bunch of boys who weld for us on jobs year around that if they didn't get out here and help they didn't need to call him for anymore work. The Sheriff had a bunch of boys who wanted to shorten their time in his jail so he let them come out and help. Ike and the rest of the boys have been out here every evening for the last two weeks putting the finishing touches on things."

"How will I ever thank them, Sam?"

"Thank them, Bill. They wanted to do it. We came up to the track and you and your friends treated us like royalty. We had our picture made in the winner's circle and then were taken out for a fine meal. The wives took pictures of Light and Jen had the time of her life. Bill, you and Cassie go shake hands with the folks who want you to be our neighbor for a long time."

I thanked Sam and with Cassie went to thank the folks who had worked so hard for us and told us nothing about it. Ike had tears in his eyes when I saw him and I had to admit I did too. We hugged like brothers and everything was right between us. Cassie was doing the same thing with the women present.

"Bill, how about we give these folks a treat for all the hard work they have done."

"What sort of treat, Spunky?"

"Why don't you and Cassie give Slinker and Gray Light a work over your new track. I've walked over it and it's in fine shape. The work certainly won't hurt them and I think the folks would enjoy watching."

"The exercise saddles in the trailer Spunky?"

"Right where we put them son."

Cassie and I headed to the trailer to get the saddles.

"Bill, my folks and brothers are here."

"Where, Cassie? I've not seen them?"

"Right over there. They are helping the man over at the smoker. He's a neighbor of ours. My brothers help him from time to time when he has a big job. It looks like we were the only two people here that didn't know what was going on down here."

"I think you're right, Cass. I guess we'd better put a good show on for the folks."

When we got back to the barn Spunky had the leg wraps on Slinker and was working on Light. When he finished he put the saddle on Light and gave Cassie a leg up. Ike had watched Spunky and gave me a leg up on Slinker. We took the two out into the sunlight and rode them thru the gap and onto my new track. Spunky was right. The surface was fine. It had enough cushion on top to where the horses' hooves seemed to be muffled as they moved over it.

We backtracked the two horses almost all the way around the track and then turned them together and began to let them work. Both were fresh and well rested. Each one had his nose tucked as we went down the back stretch at a good gallop. As we rounded the turn we loosened our hold and let the horses work up the stretch. Folks were lined up all along the rail and some were taking pictures as we passed them. The folks were clapping and hollering. When we passed the finish line we began pulling them up. When we got them stopped we sat a moment then turned them around and rode back towards the gap.

"Bill, smile pretty. You're on candid camera."

I looked up to see two of the local television stations crews had been filming our work and were interviewing Spunky. As we reached the gap Spunky called to us and waved us over to where he stood.

"These are the two young folks I've been talking about. Cassie Morgan is our jockey who rides the races and Bill Patton is my assistant trainer. Bill worked with Gray Light and with Slinker here and has helped make them into stakes class horses. This center belongs to Bill and he'll be breaking and train-ing colts here this fall for folks from several states."

The gentleman doing the interview came over near me and began asking me questions.

"Mr. Patton, may I ask how old you are?"

"I'm seventeen, sir. I'll be a senior this year."

"You're still in high school and own a center like this? Isn't that a little bit out of the norm?"

"It could be, sir. But the horses that I work don't ask my age."

"Good point. Mr. Davis says you helped with the training of Gray Light. Had you had experience with race horses before?"

"No, sir. Mr. Davis gave me a job at the track. He had a problem with Gray Light that I thought I could fix."

"Did you fix the problem?"

"Yes, sir. I think so. He's undefeated and is the New Mexico State Champion."

"I'd say you did a pretty good job."

"Miss Morgan, you ride the Davis string of horses in all their races, is that correct?"

"Yes, sir. It is."

"How did you become their jockey?"

"Bill here told Mr. Davis he thought I should ride the string for him."

"I take it Mr. Davis respects Mr. Patton's opinions on the horses?"

"Yes, sir. He does. Bill has a knack for solving problems with horses and saw that I had potential to be a good rider. It seems he was right again."

"Miss Morgan are you and Mr. Patton involved?"

"Sir, that is none of your business."

"Excuse me, Miss Morgan. We'll cut that part out."

The gentleman went on talking about how the newly opened training center just north of town was indeed a first class facility and something the local folks should be proud of.

Cassie and I took the horses back to the barn and unsaddled them, unwrapped their legs and gave them a bath. Donna was not here so Cassie and I walked the two horses dry while folks took more pictures.

We put the two horses into their stalls and walked among the folks who were visiting. I saw Ike, Sam and Jen standing off to one side. Cassie and I walked over and Jen asked Cassie if it would be all right for her to scratch Light's ears again. Cassie picked Jen up and they went across the barn talking like a couple of old friends.

"I've heard my girl laugh more in the last three weeks than in the last year and a half. She and Cassie really seem to get along."

"Just wait, Sam. Wait until she starts riding. She'll want to come out here every day."

"We'll come if you don't mind."

"I don't mind at all. It's fun to watch her. She's going to learn to ride. Now, how I don't know, but Cassie seems to have things figured out. I'm just going to stay out of the way and let those two do their own thing."

I noticed a truck coming up the driveway pulling a trailer. It was Dusty. Jen's new horse had arrived. I walked out to meet him and motioned for him to park over near the new little barn.

"Just leave him in the trailer, Dusty. I'll go get his new owner."

I walked into the barn and asked Cassie if she and Jen could help me. They both followed me out of the barn and I nodded to the trailer.

"Jen would you help Cassie unload the horse in the trailer?"

Cassie led Jen around to the back of the trailer and showed her where the latch was located. Jen got her nose up close and then undid the latch. With Cassie's help she opened the gate on the trailer. Cassie asked Coalie to back. The little black gelding backed slowly out of the trailer. Cassie picked up Jen and put the lead rope in her hand. Together they led the little horse over to the small barn that would now be his new home.

"Bill, would you get me a brush please?"

I got her a brush then went back to stand near Sam, Ike and Dusty. Jen began to brush the little horse's neck. We all heard her giggle when the little horse turned his head and touched her hand with his nose.

"Bill, is that the little girl you were telling me about?"

"Yes it is, Dusty. Why?"

Dusty reached into his shirt pocket and took out the check I had given him. He handed it to me.

"Dusty, I can't take the check back now. What will I tell her?"

"Tell her the horse is hers. I'm giving him to her. If my daughters or wife sees this little girl riding Coalie and know that I sold the horse to her I'd have to find a new home."

"Excuse me, sir. Dusty, the little girl belongs to me. Please take the check. Find another horse. Train him like this one and fix some other little girl or boy up with a horse. Please take the check. Donate it to your church if you like."

"I'll find another one and work on him. I may have grandkids one day that will need one just like Coalie. Sir, I'm Dusty Flare.

"Dusty, I'm proud to meet you. I'm Sam Cooper."

I saw the look in Dusty's eyes.

"The Sam Cooper of Cooper Construction?"

"I'm afraid so."

"Cousin of mine has worked for you for several years. He seems to think highly of you sir."

"Dusty, my name is Sam. All my friends call me that."

"Sam it is then. Bill, I brought you some oats to feed him tonight and in the morning. I figured you'd be a little bit busy with everything."

"Dusty, is your wife at home?"

"Yes, she is. She didn't know if she could stand to be here knowing Coalie wasn't going to go home with us."

"Why don't you go get her? We're not going to eat for a while and from the smell of things, it's going to be good. I'm sure you know a bunch of folks here anyway"

"Sam, I think I'll do just that. She was worried about Coalie but when she meets your little girl things will be just fine."

Everyone seemed to be having a good time. I saw Cassie's dad and mom. They were standing next to my mom and were visiting. I walked over to where they stood and said hello.

"I thought you had to work today Mrs. Morgan?"

"Bill, I had to tell you all something so you wouldn't suspect anything."

"Well it worked. I almost wrecked my truck when I first saw the place. Art, you had a hand in this didn't you?"

"Not much, Bill. I just spoke to a couple of folks. When Mr. Cooper got involved things just began to happen. I came by here one morning on my way home and your place looked like a parking lot for welding rigs. I had to stop and see what was going on. I met Ike and he explained the deal to me. When he found out I was Cassie's dad he took me for a tour. I had to promise I'd not say anything to Cassie, though. Ruth and I have been coming down here every other evening just to see what got done."

"Oh, yes. It has all been so exciting."

"I see an old friend of mine over there so I guess I'd better go say hello"

The old friend was Mike Sloan. He had bought and sold horses as a hobby for years. I'd ridden many of them for him at the sale barns. He had always paid me well when he had made a profit on is horses.

"Hello, Mike. Glad you could make the grand opening."

"Wouldn't have missed it for the world, Bill. You've got yourself a real nice place here."

"It wasn't when I went back north a month or so ago. I had no idea what was going on down here until I came down the highway today.'"

"I reckon it was quite a shock. I've been out here off and on just to see what was being done. I brought my brother's tractor over here and worked the track. Ike asked me if I knew what I was doing. He didn't want anything screwed up. When he found out I had been taking care of several tracks in the area for the

Quarter Horse folks for years and was a friend of yours he relaxed. He even asked my advice on several things over the next several weeks. He's a nice feller Bill. He really cared about what was being done."

"Are you working now, Mike?"

"Lord, no. I helped the boys at the little training track just to have something to do. I sold my business two years ago and retired. The track the boys were using sold last month and the boys are in a bind. You had any thoughts about letting folks use your place, Bill?"

"No I haven't, Mike. This thing has all been so overwhelming I've had to catch my breath every now and then."

"You might want to think about it, Bill. You could pick up some nice cash and not spend a dime of your own money."

"Mike, why don't you stop by tomorrow and we'll talk about it. I'm going to need every dollar I can lay my hands on until I'm out of school."

"I'll do that, Bill. I'll be out about ten tomorrow."

I found Cassie with Spunky and Patty. They were laughing as I walked up.

"Bill, what do you think, son?"

"I'm afraid I'll wake up and all this will be gone, Spunky."

"No danger of that, son. It's all real and all yours. I've not seen many that were any finer."

"I don't know about that, Spunky but I know I'm proud of it. It's what I dreamed I'd have in maybe ten years. I don't have any idea as to how I'll pay Sam and the boys."

"Bill, when Spunky and I saw Cassie working with Jen on the little horse we were watching Sam's face. You've paid him ten times over, son. I've never seen a man so proud and yet thankful at the same time."

"I felt pretty good myself, Patty. I saw more than one person wiping tears from their eyes."

"Bill, there wasn't a dry eye in the house."

"Spunky, a friend of mine has an idea where I might make some money. Maybe enough to live on while I'm going to school. He seems to think I could let the Quarter Horse folks work their colts here. They pay to work their colts and have lost their training track over west of here."

"Bill, you only need the track for half a day, so why not do that. Hire someone you trust to take care of the money and go on with it. You won't have anything to work on the track for several months anyway. You can make some money and at the same time your track surface will settle and you will be able to find any trouble spots before you start working the colts this fall."

"Thanks for the advice, Spunky. I'll talk to my friend and see if he'd like to take care of it for me. He'll be out tomorrow morning.

One of Cassie's brothers shouted "Let's Eat!" Folks began to drift over to a huge smoker that sat behind the barn. My grandfather had planted a few trees that now sat on the east side of my barn. Folks began setting their chairs in their shade.

Cassie and I got in one of two lines and had our plates filled. The brisket and ribs were cooked to perfection. The Texas style beans with just a hint of hot peppers were wonderful. Potato salad and cold slaw completed the meal. The cold iced tea just seemed to set the meal off.

"Bill, do you have any idea how many people are here today?"

"None at all, Cassie. I've been too busy to even think about it. There must be a hundred or so, however."

"Mother and Dad tried counting them a while ago. Bill, there are closer to two hundred people here."

"That could be, Cass. The problem is, I think I know almost all of them."

"That's nothing to be ashamed of, Bill. It says a lot about you. Folks are here to see the place. From what I've heard said, they are proud of you. I even heard one woman say she wished you were dating her girl."

"You're kidding, Cass."

"No I'm not, I almost told her she could forget about you, but I was nice. I remembered what my mother said about being a lady."

"I've had folks shaking my hand and wishing me well all day. It's great, but the day was a complete success when you let Jen work with Coalie."

"She's a wonderful little girl, Bill. She tries so hard. I only wish she could see."

"I do too, Cass, but maybe they will be able to fix her eye sight. Sam said they were going to Houston just after the first of the year."

We were visiting when Sam and Jen came over to where we were sitting.

"Kids, Jen and I are heading home. She is give out and I'm about whipped myself. I wanted to thank you all for all the things you've done for us. Bill, I'll call you tomorrow."

"I'll be looking forward to it, Sam. Jen, did you enjoy your day?"

"Oh yes Bill, I think I'll adopt you and Cassie as my big brother and sister."

"We'd be proud to be your brother and sister Jen, does that mean I can ride your horse?"

"Brother Bill, don't push your luck."

Cassie, Sam and I burst out laughing. Jen had got me and good.

CHAPTER 19

❀

After the crowd was gone, Mom, Patty, Spunky, Cassie's folks, the Sheriff, Cassie and I sat visiting. My mother asked for everyone's attention.

"Bill, as you know, I have the deed to this property. As of Monday the property will be in your name. Tom, "the Sheriff" as you call him, will see that it is filed in the courthouse properly. Bill, your grandfather would have been proud of you. He always had a vision of making this place into something special. Now you have done it. Maybe not all by yourself, but with the help of your many friends. I'm proud of you, son and I hope you never change."

I didn't know what to say, this day had just been too much. I got up from my chair and walked over and hugged my mother. I couldn't help but shed a tear and I wasn't the least bit ashamed. My mother waved to Cassie and when she came over my mom hugged her and said she was proud of my choice in a young lady. It was a very emotional moment for all of us.

Tom "the Sheriff" took my mother to her motel even though I asked her to stay with me. She had said she just wasn't ready to walk back into the house. There were too many memories she didn't want to contend with yet.

"I walked Cassie, who was going to ride home with her folks, to their car. Cassie gave me a kiss and said she would call me later. Her folks didn't seem the least bit upset about her show of affection for me. Spunky and Patty had gone to their motor home. I'd told Spunky I'd help him load the two horses in the morning. I walked into the house and sat down in the best chair after turning the television on.

Sometime later I woke up to find the news was on and the piece that had been filmed here this afternoon was coming on. The place looked great on the screen. People were walking to the track and then the camera switched to

Cassie and me on the two horses. It was the first time I'd ever seen myself ride and enjoyed it. The picture then switched to Cassie and me letting the horses work up the stretch. They then switched to the interview with Spunky. He said some wonderful things about the place and about Cassie and me. Then the interview started with me. It was strange to see myself on television. When the interview ended I waited anxiously for the interview with Cassie. When the interview ended my phone rang.

"Bill, did you see it?"

"Yes I did, Cass. You did a wonderful job. I think Spunky did a wonderful job too, even though he gave far too much credit to me for his success this year."

"No he didn't, Bill. You were a major factor in his success this year and he just wanted to give you credit. Besides, I like it when folks say nice things about you."

"Thank you, Cass. That means a lot to me."

We visited a few more minutes and then hung up. The phone continued to ring for the next half hour. When it finally quit ringing I ran a tub of hot water and got myself a hot soaking bath then shut out the lights and went to bed. It had been a very long day.

I awoke the next morning and quickly got dressed. I walked up to the barn and fed Light and Slinker. I had just refilled the water buckets when Spunky walked into the barn.

"Morning, Bill. I see you've taken care of things, as usual. Patty said for you to come to breakfast. She's got things cooking and won't take no for an answer."

"I'll be ready when you are, Spunky. I've mucked their stalls already. Let's get their wraps on and they will be ready to load when we finish breakfast."

"I wrapped Slinker's legs while Spunky took care of Light. When we finished we went to the motor home and had a wonderful breakfast. After a short visit about the television show Spunky and I moved the trailer around to the front of the barn and loaded the water and feed buckets. I led Light into the trailer and connected his trailer tie. I scratched his ears and told him I'd see him soon. I closed the divider panel behind him and took Slinker from Spunky and settled him into his place. Spunky and I closed the rear door of the trailer and I walked up to the truck with him. Patty came around the corner of the barn in the motor home. She stopped long enough to remind me to call at least twice a week. I promised I'd remember and watched as she drove down the drive and turned onto the highway.

I shook Spunky's hand and then watched as he went down the drive and turned onto the highway. He honked his horn and waved. I waved back and then walked through the barn and looked out onto the track. The three people who had been the most important people in my life were gone. Now I had to sit down and make the decisions about where I was going to go from here.

I changed clothes and drove down the lane. I stopped at the gate and after locking it I headed over to my school. I needed to talk to my principal and see if I could get my schedule set up for the fall. Fortunately I had almost all the credits I needed to graduate in the spring. I only needed two credits and hoped to be able to get them the first two hours of the day. As I pulled into the parking lot I saw my principal working on a hinge on the front door.

"Good morning, sir. May I have a moment of your time?"

"Good morning, Bill. Or should I say Mr. Patton?"

"Sir?"

"I saw you on television last night. I thought you'd sold the place after your father's death. How may I help you, Bill?"

I explained my situation and waited for his reaction. He told me he didn't see any problem with my getting the classes like I wanted. I had explained I wanted the accounting class so that I would know how to take care of books. He asked if he could come over and look at my place sometime. I'd told him he was welcome to come over anytime. On my way back to the farm I stopped and bought groceries. It dawned on me that everything I had planned on paying for was done and that all the money I had set aside for them was still in the canvas bag at the house. I needed to open a checking and savings account. I'd do that this afternoon after I talked to Mike.

I had just finished putting everything away when Mike pulled up and parked by the house. I greeted him at the back door.

"Morning, Mike. Come on in. I've just put coffee on."

We sat down and had coffee. Mike outlined what he thought I should do with the track.

"Mike, your idea is good, but I have a problem. I have to go to school in the mornings. I'd have to find someone I could trust to look over the operation. You know anyone I could hire, say on a sharing basis?"

"I might, Bill. What sort of sharing are we talking about?"

"What do you think would be fair?"

"Say ten percent?"

"I was thinking more like fifteen. I want someone who will look after things and knows the boys. I don't want the place trashed up if you know what I mean."

"Fifteen percent? Bill, for fifteen percent I'd be interested in the job."

"It's yours if you want it, Mike. I'd really appreciate your help. Don't you live in a trailer?"

"I sure do. Sold my place and bought a trailer a couple of months ago."

"Why don't you move it out here and set it up in back of the barn? We can fence you in a yard and you'll have the trees for shade."

"What kind of rent are we talking about, Bill?"

"Rent goes with the job Mike. I want your help."

"You just hired yourself a hand, Bill. How are we going to take care of the track?"

"I'm going to have to find a tractor, Mike."

"I know where there is one, Bill. The fellow who had the last track leased had a dandy. He wants to sell it. Probably would make you a good deal on it. He has a disc, nice harrow and a trailer."

"Give him a call and see what he will take. Cash on delivery."

Mike made the call and bartered a little. When I thought the price was right I nodded my head. The deal was made and the tractor would be delivered late that afternoon. I'd just bought a tractor and all the equipment for seven hundred less than I had figured on. It seemed as if everything was going fine.

Mike had a friend who would move his trailer for next to nothing. He had everything he needed to hook it up to the sewer system and the water line. I said we'd have to run a gas line to the trailer from the house.

"Bill, there's a gas line already in the barn. Ike and the boys installed it along with the water line. I can tie into it and run the water line at the same time."

"Get it done, Mike. The sooner the better. I'm going to have to go to the Ccity in a week or so and I'd like to have you here when I'm gone."

I'll get it moved tomorrow, Bill. A friend of mine has a small ditch witch I can use to run the lines. I'll dig the ditches this afternoon and get the lines stubbed up."

"I've got to take care of some business, Mike. If you need any help I should be back by two this afternoon."

Mike left and I picked up the phone and called Sam. He answered on the second ring.

"Bill, what can I do for you?"

"I need to open a checking and savings account Sam. What bank do you think I should use?"

"Panhandle National, Bill. They aren't the largest but they are growing and can do you a lot of good."

"Thanks, Sam. I don't have really that much but I can't leave it laying around the house."

"Good Lord no, Bill. If they want any references you can use my name. You know where the bank is don't you?"

"Yes, sir. I'm going over there now. Thanks a bunch. Is Jen still flying?"

"Oh yes. She wants Cassie to go with her to buy a new bridle and such tomorrow."

"I'll tell Cassie to be ready. I hired a friend of mine to run the quarter horse operation for me. He's a good friend and will take care of things when I'm gone."

"Good, Bill. You're going to need help. I have a feeling that you're going to be a very busy young man. I'll be out tomorrow. It seems Cassie and Jen are going to have a lesson. See you then."

I went to the bank and opened a savings account as well as a checking account. When they asked about a reference I gave them Sam's name and offered to give them his phone number. They didn't seem to need it. My checking account was set up for the training center. The lady told me my checks would be ready in a couple of days and would be mailed to me. I thanked her and walked out of the bank. When I got outside I noticed a store across the parking lot that sold cell phones. I walked across the parking lot and told the clerk I wanted one. There was a problem. I wasn't old enough to buy a cell phone. That was until another clerk came in and saw me standing there.

"You're the young man I saw on television. You own the fancy horse farm just north of town. How can we help you?"

"I wanted a cell phone but the gentleman says I can't buy one because I'm not old enough."

"Mr. Patton, I'm sure we can make an exception for you. The Sheriff has spoken highly of you. Now let me show you our phones."

Fifteen minutes later I left the store with a phone. When I reached my truck I called Cassie.

"Cassie, can you hear me?"

"I hear you fine, Bill. Where are you?"

"I'm standing in the parking lot down town. I just bought a cell phone."

I gave Cassie my cell phone number and was told to be sure and keep it with me. I got in my truck and headed to the feed store. I bought Coalie feed and made a deal with the gentleman for the feed I would need when the outside horses came in. After telling him I would pay cash on delivery I got another discount. I left the feed store and headed home. As I drove up the drive I saw that Mike was already laying pipe around the barn. After I parked the truck I walked up to the barn and found he had just finished. All he had to do was cover the pipe. I got another shovel and in a short time we had the ditch covered.

"My friend is going to move my trailer over here tomorrow morning. He had an off day so I guess we'll get on over to the park and get things unhooked."

"Need any help, Mike?"

"Nope. Won't take me ten minutes, Bill. I figured I'd find me a little piece of ground and set it up there. I didn't plan on staying there very long. I'll see you tomorrow morning, Bill."

"I walked back to the house and was thinking about what I'd fix for my supper when the phone rang. It was Spunky. He was at the track and had the horses settled. He was really impressed with the track and wanted me to have his phone number. I wrote the phone number down and then gave him my cell phone number. I promised I'd pass the number on to Cassie.

I fixed myself a meal and remembered I liked to cook. I washed the dishes and watched a little television. When I went to bed I was happy, happy and full.

I was up and just getting ready to fix my breakfast when my cell phone rang.

"Running P. This is Bill."

"Have you had breakfast yet?"

"No. I was just getting ready to fix it."

"Don't. I'll be there in ten minutes. I'm buying breakfast."

"Alright, Cass. Why?"

"I just got a beautiful trophy from the track in Raton. It turns out I was the leading jockey in money earnings. I also got a nice little check. Breakfast is on me."

"I'll be ready, Miss Money Bags."

"Bill"

"Yes ma'am. I'll be nice.

CHAPTER 20

Cassie showed up early and we went to the truck stop to have breakfast. Cassie was happy she had won the trophy from the track and I was happy for her. We were half way through our breakfast when her cell phone rang.

It was Cassie's mom and she had a phone number for Cassie to call.

"Now who in the world is wanting to talk to me?"

"I guess you'll have to give them a call and find out."

Cassie dialed the number and after a moment began talking. From what I could gather from the conversation someone wanted to do an interview. When she hung up the phone she had a huge smile on her face.

"Bill, Tri State Sports magazine wants to do a feature article on me. On me! Why, I don't know."

"Because you're a girl, pretty and a jockey to boot. You're a celebrity, Cassie. Everyone wants to know how you've accomplished what you've done. I think its great. When do they want to do the article?"

"Next week. They will call and set the time. It will have to be after school."

"I know. School starts Monday. I hope my principal has everything set up for me. If I can take my classes in the morning then everything will be great."

"Let's get going. Sam and Jen will be out in a short while and I need to get changed into my riding things."

We drove out to the farm. Cassie went into the house and changed her clothes. I walked back outside just as a truck came up the drive pulling a tractor on a trailer behind. It looked as if my tractor had arrived.

"Are you Bill Patton?"

"Yes, sir. Let's unload the tractor."

We unloaded the tractor and I checked it over. It was in excellent shape. I checked the oil and fluid levels and found them to be in good shape. The disc was hooked on so I took it for a trial run on the track. Everything worked perfectly. It would be all we would need to maintain the track. I went to the house and got the man his money. He was happy to be paid and told me if I needed anything else to just have Mike give him a call.

Cassie and I were getting things out for Jen's riding lesson when she and Sam drove up. I had borrowed an older gelding from a friend of mine for Cassie to ride. Sam and I watched as the two girls got Coalie ready for his ride. They were laughing and having a wonderful time.

"Bill, we need to talk."

"What do you need, Sam?"

"What do you think about me buying some brood mares and raising some colts?"

"Sam, if you're wanting a race horse I'd advise you to buy yourself a long yearling. You can see what you're getting and the colt can be put in training without having to wait three years."

"That's a good idea, Bill. But where will I find them?"

"Sales, Sam. They have several you could go to and look over the prospects. They are having one in Oklahoma City next week. Spunky was talking about it before he left."

"Think we could get a book to look over what is in the sale?"

"I should think so, but the sale is next Saturday so we don't have much time."

"Do you think Spunky might have one?"

"I can call and find out, but with the mail we won't get it until Wednesday."

"Bill, I have a truck in the city right now. If I can pay Spunky to take the sale book out to the truck stop my driver will have it back here tonight. We could go over the book tomorrow and make a decision."

I called Spunky and yes, he did have a sale book. In fact he had two. He wanted to know where we wanted the book taken. Sam gave the address of the truck stop where his driver would fuel up before heading back. Spunky told us that we were in luck. Donna was at the barn and knew where the truck stop was and would have the book there in twenty minutes. He told me to look at a mare that was in foal to Light's sire. He said she had not made that much but had never had a chance to show her ability. I told him we'd look things over and get back in touch with him.

Sam called his business office and told them to radio the truck driver and for him to be looking for Donna at the truck stop.

"Well, I guess all we can do is wait, Bill."

"I guess you're right, Sam. In the meantime, I think the girls are waiting on us."

I gave Cassie a leg up on the older gelding and then sat Jen up on Coalie. I handed the lead rope to Cassie and waited while she gave instructions to Jen on what she was to do. Sam and I watched as Cassie led Jen and Coalie out onto the track. They walked for a while then went into a trot. Jen began to post as Cassie had taught her before. A short distance later they went into a slow canter. Jen bounced some at first then began to get in tune with her horse's motion. Soon we heard the sounds of laughter as the girls rode the two horses around the track. Jen was having a ball.

"Bill, hearing her laugh is wonderful. I don't know how I'll ever repay you and Cassie."

"For Lord's sake, Sam. Look around you. Four months ago all I had were the clothes on my back and four hundred dollars. Quit worrying about paying us back. Just be our friend and let us enjoy Jen with you."

"By dang, Bill. I think I will."

CHAPTER 21

❀

Sam and Jen left for home and Cassie and I both got a bath and cleaned up. We were going shopping. I had needed furniture but now, it was a we needed furniture. We got in my truck and headed into town. We went to a furniture store where Cassie's mom always bought their furniture. The older gentleman was more than glad to help us. He and his wife were getting ready to retire and were thrilled we had come in. We looked at living room furniture, bedroom sets, kitchen tables and even stoves and refrigerators. Then my future wife went to work. She would have made a lot of my horse trading buddies proud.

When everything was over, she had saved us several thousand dollars. We stopped on the way home and got a couple of take out orders of Bar B Que. The folks from the furniture store would be out in an hour or so to deliver the things we had bought. We had to strip the beds, empty the refrigerator and take all the pots and pans out of the stove.

We went to work and began getting things ready. When the folks showed up they moved the old stuff out then replaced it with the new. I couldn't believe the change it made in the looks of things. The beds we had bought were queen size and looked great in our bedrooms. Cassie laughed when she told me we'd have to buy new sheets and blankets to fit them. Having her as my wife was going to be great but she had a lot of educating to do. One of the gentlemen offered to buy the stove and refrigerator. He made an offer and I accepted. At least we'd have money for some sheets and a blanket.

When the men left we both sat down and laughed. Our first shopping trip together had been a blast. We turned on the television, got a couple of sodas and ate our carry out.

We called Spunky and visited for a short time, then called my mom and told her about the new furniture. She had been thrilled we had gotten the things. She said she'd try and get out in a couple of weeks to visit.

Cassie and I visited the rest of the evening, planning on what we needed to do before winter set in. When we went to bed I was full and happy.

When I walked into the house after feeding the two geldings it was nice to smell the bacon that Cassie had cooking.

"Wash up, Bill. I'll have breakfast ready in a few minutes."

I washed up and found that she had my breakfast sitting on the table when I returned. I sat down and ate. The food was great I found it had a lot less grease than when I cooked them.

The hot chocolate was great. We were just finishing up when my cell phone rang.

"This is Bill."

"Bill, this is Sam. I was hoping you all were up. You were up, weren't you?"

"Sure we're up. In fact we just finished breakfast."

"Good. Mind if we come out? I've got the sale book and I've circled a couple of horses."

"Come on out, Sam. We'll put the coffee pot on."

"See you in a few."

"Sam is so excited. I'll bet he was up half the night."

"He probably was. When he gets started on something there is never anything done halfway."

Cassie washed the dishes and I dried. She put the coffee pot on and made another half pot of hot chocolate for Jen. Everything was ready when Sam and Jen arrived a few minutes later.

"Hey, kids. Ready to pour over this sales—What in the world have you kids done to this place?"

"We bought some new furniture, Sam. Everything in here was worn out or so nasty we couldn't use it. So we went to town and got what we needed."

"Well, you did great. The place looks fantastic."

"It was Cassie's doings, Sam. She has good taste."

"Of course I do. I caught you, Bill. Now let's get coffee and hot chocolate. I want to see what Sam has picked out."

Ten minutes later I was wondering how I was going to tell Sam what I thought of his choices. Cassie came to my rescue.

"Sam, the mares you've picked out are alright, but Bill and I have been talking and we think that you'd be way ahead if you bought coming two year olds.

That way, Bill could start them right after the first of the year and you'd be able to watch them run this summer."

"I'd not considered that. Bill do you think I should buy long yearlings and not brood mares?"

"I do, Sam. With brood mares you've got to buy them, pay a stud fee and wait almost a year before she has a colt. You're gambling the colt will be a good one and then you've got care and feed for two years before you know if the colt is any good. You can buy a long yearling and see if his legs are straight, if he's a well balanced colt and if he looks like you want him to."

"Then let's get to looking at long yearlings."

We began going through the sale book looking for long yearlings. Two hours later we had five circled. Three were colts and two were fillies. I told Sam about the mare and said that if she went cheap enough and I liked her I might just buy her. She was in foal to a good horse. I could afford to take a chance. I'd have all the good hay and wouldn't have that much feed in her.

"Kids, the sale is Saturday. Cassie, can you go?"

"I'm sure I can, Sam. What time do you want to leave?"

"I figure we'll leave at eight."

"Sam, the sale starts at eleven, we can't make it to the City in time to look the colts over. It's a four and a half hour drive."

"Bill, we won't be driving. We'll take my plane. We'll be in the City by nine thirty and we'll have plenty of time to look the colts over. You don't mind flying do you?"

"I don't know. I've never flown before."

"You'll love it Bill. I've flown several times and it's great."

"Then I'm ready to go. Mike will have his trailer here today. He'll be able to look after the two horses and keep an eye on the place. Some of the Quarter Horse people will be here tomorrow morning to work their colts. Cassie and I both have school."

"So do I, and I'm not looking forward to it."

"Jen, things will be fine. Just think of all the things you'll have to tell all your friends."

"I'd not thought of that. Maybe things will be alright."

After Sam and Jen left, Cassie gathered her things and headed home. Mike and his trailer arrived a short time later. I watched as the man set the trailer in place. It was clear he had done this many times before. When the trailer was set in place Mike and the gentleman began leveling the trailer. The two men had done this before and soon had the trailer leveled. I helped Mike hook up the water, gas and septic line.

"Well, Bill. It's all set. I'll start work in the morning. I've passed the word to a bunch of the boys that they could work their colts here. I figure there will be at least thirty or so colts here tomorrow."

"I sure hope so, Mike. The money will get the farm started off on the right foot. You take care of collecting the money, and take out your fifteen per cent every day. That way I won't have to worry about making you out a check each week."

"Fine, Bill. That's what I'll do."

CHAPTER 22

❀

The next morning I got up and got ready for school. Normally I rode the bus but I'd have to drive home after my two classes. When I walked out to go to my truck I saw at least twenty trailers parked around my barn and several horses were galloping on the track. Things were looking up, at least for a while.

My first hour at school was an English class. To my surprise it seemed all anyone wanted to talk about was the farm and how I had spent my summer. The second hour was the accounting class. My instructor said we would be keeping a set of books and could make up our subject. When I asked if I could set up a set of books on my farm she told me it would be fine. She would help me set up a set of books and would be glad to do it.

I left school feeling pretty good about things. My accounting instructor had given me a list of things I would need to set up my books. I went directly to the store she had told me about and bought the supplies I would need. I was really looking forward to the class.

Mike saw me pull in and walked down to the house. He handed me a stack of bills.

"We had forty one horses this morning, Bill. I took out my cut but I think we need to spend a little money to keep the boys happy."

"Such as, Mike?"

"We need a big coffee pot. I'll fix the coffee and put out a coffee jar. I figure the boys will be sure they don't run out of coffee."

I handed Mike some money and told him to get the coffee pot. He told me the boys had loved the track and were thrilled that I'd allowed them to train their colts on it.

I called Spunky and told him about the first day's works and about my school day.

"Good deal, Bill. Keep the boys happy and you'll have a steady income all winter long. We worked the horses over the track today and they seem to like the track. I'm thinking of entering Slinker in an allowance race week after next. You think Cassie and you can come in so she can ride him?"

"I'm sure we can, Spunky. I'll talk to her this evening then give you a ring on your cell phone."

After talking to Spunky I got all of the receipts from the box in the bedroom and began putting them in order by date. I didn't know what things I would need but I wanted everything in order when I entered class tomorrow.

I was awake early the next morning and went to the barn to tell Mike I had to go look at some exercise saddles before I came home.

"No need to be in a hurry, Bill. I've got the coffee on and I see the first trailer turning up this way now. Get the things you need. I'll look after things here."

I thanked Mike and went back to the house to finish getting ready for school. I got through my first class and went to the accounting class. My instructor gave us instructions on how to set up our books and handed out sheets for us to look at. She came by my desk and looked at the receipts.

"Bill, you need to borrow one of my books and study it."

"You're going to need an accountant to do your tax work. You'll need a tax number so you can buy all of your supplies without paying sales tax. Read the book I'm going to give you and I'll look over your work when you have things set up."

She brought me a book as I was leaving class. I thanked her and told her I'd take good care of the book.

I stopped at the local tack shop and went inside. The gentleman who ran the shop had always treated me fairly. He had repaired equipment for me that was worn out and had not charged me near what he should have.

"Morning, Hank. Got any exercise saddles for sale?"

"Sure do, Bill. You need new or used?"

"Good used will work if you have it, but it has to be good."

"Got one good used one, Bill and two new ones. Come on back and see what you think."

Hank had been right. The used exercise saddle was in good condition. I looked at the two new ones and picked the one I felt was the best made. I'd be putting a lot of miles on both after I got the colts started.

Hank had a deal for me. He had bought all the tack from a couple of fellows who thought they wanted to be trainers. According to Hank neither of the young men knew anything about training but their folks had financed them and they had both thrown up their hands and quit. He led me to the back storage room and showed me a pile of tack.

"Look it over, Bill. You want the pile I'll take a hundred for it. I gave ninety for the pile yesterday."

I looked through the pile of tack and found most of the things were like brand new. I could use almost everything in the pile. I went back into the shop and told Hank to add the pile to the cost of the two saddles. I loaded everything into my truck and headed home. Mike was waiting when I pulled into the drive and drove up to the barn.

"Looks like you've been shopping, Bill."

"I needed a couple of exercise saddles and stopped at Hank's place. He had a deal for me on some tack. How about helping me unload the stuff?"

Mike was amazed that I got such a good deal on all the tack. He told me we had had fifty eight colts work over the track this morning and it looked like we'd have more tomorrow. I was amazed at the number of colts using the track and said so.

"Bill, there are a bunch of colts around here. The boys are all getting ready for the big futurity. They have been working at various little training tracks around here but your place is as nice as the track they will be running on. Our coffee was a success. The tip jar had thirty four dollars in it for more coffee. The boys really appreciated the coffee pot. I heard one fellow say it was nice to work on a first class track and have good coffee to boot."

"That's great, Mike. Let's keep them happy. The money they are paying will keep us going when the weather gets cold."

"Bill, the boys will be starting a new set of colts for next year as soon as the big race is over. The big money in Quarter Horses is in two year olds. Not three year olds like your thoroughbred horses. If they do well they will go ahead and run the colts for the rest of the year. If they don't do any good they will simply start a new one. Either way we have them coming to us to condition their colts."

"Well, as long as we keep the track right and the coffee hot I guess the boys will be happy. I've got some studying to do. The bookwork around here is going to be a job I'll have to stay on top of. I'll talk to you later."

The rest of the week seemed to fly by. I worked on my books and began to understand some of the terms that were used. On Friday I took my set of books to school for my teacher to look over. She was impressed with my work and thrilled I had taken such an interest in the project. She pointed out a few things and made a few suggestions. She told me to continue on and she would look at my books again next week.

"I was thrilled with my books as I headed home. It suddenly dawned on me that tomorrow morning we were flying to the city for the horse sale. I was thrilled but scared to death at the same time. I called Cassie at noon hour and told her I was nervous but looking forward to the trip. She said she was ready to go. Jen had called her every night and was having a ball at school. Several of the kids didn't believe she was actually riding a horse so she had invited them out to watch her ride on Sunday afternoon.

"Bill, we need to put on a show for her. The other kids at school have given her a hard time for the last year or so. Do you have any ideas?"

"Let's see, how about we braid Coalie's mane and put red leg wraps on him. Do you have the old set of Spunky's silks?"

"Sure I do. Spunky wasn't going to use them any more, so I asked if I could have them."

"How about you wear your jock pants and silks. That should really get the kids' attention. After all, most of them will know who you are and to have a famous jockey giving her lessons will make her a very special person."

"Oh, Bill. You're wonderful! We can wrap the gelding's legs and I think Jen and I may just give them something to talk about. I love you, Bill Patton. I'll see you about seven. Have breakfast ready."

"Yes ma'am. It will be ready, along with the hot chocolate."

Mike brought the money from the works and I thanked him. He wanted to know what time we were leaving. I told him we were flying to the City.

"Sounds like Sam Cooper, Bill. The man is a gentleman and he sure knows how to go first class."

"He does that, Mike. We may have some horses coming in after the sale tomorrow. Think you could have a couple of stalls clean by tomorrow evening?"

"They will be ready, Bill. Just go and have a good time."

The next morning I had just taken the eggs out of the skillet when Cassie came through the kitchen door. I pointed to her cup of hot chocolate and motioned for her to sit. She ignored me and gave me a kiss instead. I didn't mind at all.

Sam and Jen arrived about seven thirty. We got in his pickup and drove to the private hangar at the airport. The plane was sitting outside fueled up and ready to go. It was a pretty little twin-engine plane. We parked the truck and loaded into the plane. I sat up front with Sam and could see everything. I never heard half of what he was saying. I was too interested in watching him operate all the things it took to get the plane moving. The next thing I knew we were circling the airport and I could see my place north of town. It was amazing.

"You alright, Bill?"

"I'm fine, Sam. This is fun."

"I thought you'd enjoy it, Bill. Now lean back and enjoy the trip. We'll be in the City in a little over an hour."

Sam had been right. We arrived in the city right on schedule and went to the car rental where a car was waiting. We drove to the sale barn and after finding a parking place went to look at the colts. Sam went to the office and established a line of credit. He received a number and met us outside. He had a map that showed which stall each of the colts had been assigned. We went to look at the stud colts first. The first was a nice bred colt but was not what we were looking for. He didn't have enough bone in his legs to suit us. The second had a crooked front ankle that the folks tried to hide but Cassie and I had both noticed right off. The third was not as royal bred but was a good colt. He had a nice shoulder and long hip. We circled his number in the book and went to look at the two fillies.

The first filly was decent but lacked something I couldn't figure out. Cassie had the same thought. The second filly again was not as royal bred as the first but after looking at her a moment I liked everything about her. It was her eye. There was something about her eye. We circled her number, too. I told Sam she was the best of the bunch. Cassie agreed with me.

I wanted to look at the mare Spunky had spoke of and found her at the far end of one of the barns. When I asked the young man standing at the stall door to see her, he took a halter and led the mare out into the alley way. I began going over her legs and didn't find anything wrong. I liked her shoulder and hip and was happy when the young man said she belonged to his father and had never really had a chance to show what she could do. He also told me she was not in foal.

Not in foal, four years old and sound with little earnings on the track. I noticed that Cassie was smiling. I thanked the young man and walked back over to Sam.

"I'm going to buy the mare if she sells cheap. I think she just may make a nice mare if I handle her right."

"Go for it, Bill. You've done all right so far. What do you think I should bid on the filly?"

We discussed what I thought the filly would bring and decided to not sit together at the sale ring. Some folks had already recognized Cassie and if people knew we were together they just might run the price up on the filly. We worked up some signals so that Sam would know what I thought he should bid.

Sam went on up to the sale ring. Cassie and I went up a short time later. We sat where Sam could see us and watched the first horse come into the sale ring. When the first filly came into the ring, I was surprised when she brought eighteen thousand, crooked ankle and all.

Finally, the filly Sam wanted came into the ring. They started her at five thousand and finally got a live bid at twenty five hundred. I waited until the filly was almost sold then gave Sam the signal. He bid twenty seven fifty and in a few moments owned the filly. He signed the sales ticket then went down to the sales office to pay for the filly. Cassie and I watched another dozen or so horses sell before the mare was brought into the sale ring. When it was announced that the mare was not in foal, interest in her went down fast. After getting a five hundred dollar bid the auctioneer worked hard to get seven hundred and fifty dollar bid. I waited and bought the mare for eight hundred dollars. Cassie and I went to the sales office where I paid for the mare and made arrangements with a hauler to deliver the two horses to my place. He told me he would leave as soon as the sale ended and would be at my place early in the morning. They would call when they were an hour from my farm.

I was happy about getting to buy the mare. Now all I had to do was see if I could bring her around and make a race horse out of her. Sam and Jen were happy to have got the filly and were anxious to see her run. I was glad she wasn't a baby and he would have to wait two years before that would happen. Now we could start the filly and bring her along slow and easy. It had been a good day but tomorrow would be even better. Jen had no idea about what Cassie and I had planned.

Sam flew us back home and we were back at the farm by six that evening. I told Mike we would have two horses coming in early in the morning. I told him there was no need for him to get up. He could see the horses at morning chores.

Cassie and I went out and ate at a local café that served great fried chicken. We discussed the mare and what we thought we should do. We finally agreed to work the mare lightly and then make a decision about her.

The two horses arrived at one in the morning. They had both traveled well and seemed to be relaxed in their new stalls. I noticed the mare was busy on the hay Mike had put in the stalls. I gave each of the horses a small amount of grain and then left the barn, leaving one small light on to keep the two horses relaxed.

The next morning after breakfast Cassie and I went to the barn and found the place was buzzing with people. Mike had everything under control and told me he had fed the two horses along with the two geldings. I thanked him and told him about what Cassie and I had planned for Jen's riding lesson. He said he'd have the track worked and standing tall when the folks arrived. Cassie gave him a kiss on the cheek and told him thanks. I think Mike actually blushed.

Cassie and I went to Coalie's barn and began braiding his mane. When we were finished we braided the big gelding Cassie would ride. I would put the leg wraps on just before everyone showed up. We went to the house and got cleaned up. Cassie put on her white riding britches and Spunky's old racing silks. She even had her riding boots. She was going to do her best to impress Jen's friends. Thirty minutes before everyone was to arrive I went to the barn and put leg wraps on the two geldings. Mike helped me and then sprang a surprise on me. He had a portable microphone and sound system. He wanted to do the announcing when Cassie and Jen rode out onto the track. All I could do was smile.

When Jen, Sam and the rest of the folks arrived, Cassie walked out of the barn and greeted them all. Sam had a smile like I had never seen before. When they came into the barn they saw Mike and me holding the two horses. Sam gave Jen a leg up on Coalie and I gave Cassie a leg up on the big gelding.

"They are eating this up, Cass. Jen will be someone special come Monday morning at school."

"I think so, Bill. But just wait until you see what Jen and I have planned for her friends."

I had no idea what Cass was talking about but I figured I'd find out soon enough.

As the girls rode out of the barn Mike began to do his job.

"Next on the track to work are Jen "Ride Hard" Cooper and Cassie "The Whip" Morgan.

He went on to tell about the horses they were riding and then asked the question.

"Are you girls ready?"

"Cassie waved and the two girls who were going at a slow canter began to speed up. They came around the turn and suddenly both girls seemed to get lower on their horses backs. Jen was suddenly in front on the little black gelding and was screaming at him to go faster as they seemed to fly up the stretch. Jen won the race by a length and a half. I watched as Cassie caught Coalie's bridle and slowed him down. The two girls stopped the horses and came back to where Jen's friends were jumping up and down and calling to Jen. Cass had just made Jen a very important person indeed. The race call up the stretch by Mike had been grand. It made the day complete. Sam came over to where Mike and I stood smiling.

"Gentlemen, I don't know what to say except this day is one I'll never forget. Would you all do me the honor of going to supper with Jen and me this evening?"

"Sam, you don't have to do that."

"Bill, I don't have to do anything. It's what I want to do. Mike, do you think you could eat a steak?"

"Why, Mr. Cooper. I think I might just be able to do that."

"Mike, out here at the farm or anywhere else you see me you will call me Sam. After the race call today I swear my list of real friends is growing and I'm enjoying it."

Later the girls and their friends came into the barn with the horses. Mike and I took the horses and went to work. We unwrapped their legs while Cassie explained to them the reason for using them. We gave each horse a bath, and then walked them dry. Cassie was explaining the various use of the equipment that was hung in the tack room to all of Jen's friends. Sometime later one of the parents came up to her and asked if she would come to the school and talk to the other children.

"I'll have to check my school schedule then get back to you. I'll call you as soon as I have checked."

When all of Jen's friends were gone she told us we were the greatest. Her friends were all amazed that she not only could ride but owned a race horse too.

Sam and I got his new filly out of her stall and showed her to Mike. Mike was impressed with what he saw.

"Bill, I'm new to the business but this filly is a nice horse. There's just something about her."

"Look at her eye, Mike."

"That's it, Bill. I couldn't figure it out but now I see it. I can't wait for you to start working her."

"We'll start her ground work tomorrow, Mike. W're going to take this little lady slow and easy."

After Cassie had changed her clothes we loaded up in Sam's truck and went to eat. Mike had relaxed and he and Sam had a grand time visiting about various folks they both knew. Jen was laughing at me because she and Cassie had surprised me with their race. I had to admit they had surprised me but I was happy everything had gone well.

Later, Cassie gathered up her things and prepared to head home. I was looking at my books and planned on making entries and make out a deposit slip to leave at the bank tomorrow. Cassie looked over my shoulder and whistled.

"Bill, you're doing great. You keep this up and you'll be in great shape by the time the outside colts arrive."

"Most of it is because of Mike. It was his idea and it's really paying off. I'm sure glad I've got him here."

"Me, too. What are your plans for your mare?"

"I'm going to ride her in the pasture tomorrow and start getting acquainted with her. I want to get some weight on her. We'll see about giving her a light work Wednesday afternoon. I think the most important thing is to get her mind adjusted. I'm going to talk to Spunky and see what he remembers about her."

"You'll let me know if Spunky gets Slinker into the race next week?"

"Just as soon as I hear I'll call you. When is your interview with the sports magazine?"

"Tomorrow evening. I'm sort of nervous about it but then again I'm really looking forward to it."

I walked Cassie out to her truck and loaded her bag into her truck. After getting a kiss I watched as she drove down the lane and headed north towards her home. I walked back into the house and went to work on my books. When I had the books brought up to date, I put them in my bag and walked up to the barn. I wanted to start getting acquainted with my new mare.

The next morning when I got to school I was shocked to be asked about the horse race we had staged at the farm. When I asked how they had heard about the race I found several folks had heard about it from friends who had been there. It seemed one of the mothers who had been there was sending a picture to the local paper where her husband worked. They said the picture would be in this evening's paper. I'd have to make sure I picked up a copy for Mike and me to read.

After class, I headed home, changed clothes, and went to the barn. I saddled my mare and rode her out of the barn and into the pasture around the hay field. The mare rode out fine but there seemed to be something wrong. She seemed to lack the fire that she would need to become a good racehorse. I had to figure a way to bring the desire back. As it turned out, Mike had the answer. We would begin the mare's rehabilitation program the next day.

I drove into town and picked up three papers, one each for Mike, Cassie and me. It seemed Jen was now quite the celebrity. She was front-page news. The heading read "Local Rider Wins". The story told about how Cassie was giving Jen riding lessons and they had quickly become friends. Or, as Jen had put it, sisters. It was a wonderful article and was sure to keep the name of the farm in folks' minds. I wanted the farm to have a good reputation in the community. I drove back to the farm and gave Mike his copy.

A quick glance put a smile on Mike's face.

"Bill, this is gold, pure gold. This is the sort of thing you need every now and then to keep folks happy about having you as a neighbor. Have you called Cassie yet?"

"Not yet, I plan on doing it in a hurry though. I sure don't want someone else telling her about this first."

I called Cass on my cell phone on the way back to the house. She was thrilled to hear about the article and said much the same thing as Mike. The folks from the sports magazine were due at her folks' place any minute. I told her to settle down and relax. She could handle everything fine.

I got back to the house and called Spunky. I wanted him to know about what we were going to try with the mare. He said it just might work. I had all winter to work with her and if things worked out I'd have my first racehorse. It seemed that the mare was held in a bunch of her races and not allowed to win. After a while she just quit trying. When I asked Spunky why anyone would do that he explained that some folks did it to get the odds up. Then they would bet heavy on the horse and let them run. A man could make some real serious money if everything worked as planned. The problem with the mare was she just didn't try and her owner trainer had lost far more than he could afford.

"Well, I'm going to try and bring her back, Spunky. If she shows some ability I may just keep her as a brood mare. I'd like to breed her to Light if we can work something out."

"Bill, that won't be a problem at all. I'd like to see a colt bred like that myself."

CHAPTER 23

Mike and I went to work on my mare the next afternoon. He rode the gelding that Cassie used for Jen's lessons. We took the two horses out onto the track and walked them half way around then began to gallop. I pushed the mare ahead of the gelding and wouldn't let him go by. Every time the gelding got close I asked the mare for a little more speed. When we pulled them up Mike was smiling.

"Bill, we'll try this for a week and then I'll borrow a new horse. We'll have two horses to work with her on Saturday when Cassie is here. We want her to out work everything we work with her. We should know in a week or so if our idea is going to work."

Cassie arrived on Saturday and after the Quarter Horse folks left we went to the barn and got the horses ready. Mike explained to Cassie how we wanted to work the mare. A short time later we rode out onto the track and warmed the horses up. When we had the horses warm we began to gallop them. We kept the horses side by side as we went down the back side of the track and started around the turn. We loosened our hold on the horses and let them begin to work. I was thrilled when the mare moved slightly ahead of the other horses. When Mike came up close on the inside of the mare she again moved ahead of him. I was thrilled. The mare wanted to be in front. We were making headway.

After the work Cassie and I went back to the house. As we walked in the back door the phone rang.

"Running P. This is Bill."

"Bill, this is Spunky. I've got Slinker in a race next Saturday. Do you think Cassie can ride him?"

"Hold on, Spunky. I'll let you talk to her yourself."

I handed the phone to Cassie and listened as she told Spunky she would be thrilled to ride for him but she would have to get a license over there. After another few minutes it was apparent we were going to be going to Oklahoma City next weekend. When Cassie hung up she was smiling.

"Like to take a trip, Bill?"

I took the phone and called my mother. She said she would have everything ready for us Friday night when we arrived. She was thrilled we were coming. When I hung up the phone I asked Cassie what time she could be down here Friday afternoon.

"I can be out of school at eleven. I'll be here by eleven forty five. Will that be soon enough?"

"That will be fine, Cassie. We should be in the City by five, easy. We can be at the track early and get your license when the office opens."

"That will work, Bill. Spunky is getting me a temporary license so I can give Light a work over the track. It will also give me a chance to get the feel of the track."

A few minutes later Sam and Jen showed up for her riding lesson. Sam had his hands full getting her to the back door. She was dragging him along. Then I saw the paper under her arm.

"Bill, Cassie, did you see the paper? Isn't it great!"

"It's wonderful Jen. I think the picture of you and Coalie was great."

"It's made school so much easier for me. The kids aren't picking on me any-more."

"That's great, Jen. But you have to remember, you did the riding and did a very good job, I might add."

I told Sam about the race the next Saturday and asked if we could do Jen's lesson on Sunday afternoon. He told me it was no problem for them at all.

Jen and Cassie rode their horses and Sam and I visited about his filly. I told him we would saddle her the following week. We'd not ride her but we wanted to get her used to carrying the added weight when I worked her in the round pen. He was pleased with the progress I had made and said he was looking for-ward to next year's racing.

With school, my books and working the two horses, the week seemed to fly by. Thursday night I packed a bag so I would be ready to go when Cassie arrived the next morning.

I was at the barn the next morning visiting with Mike while we cleaned the tack I used on the filly and mare. Mike asked me to make a bet for him. He believed that Spunky's horse just might get a piece of the pie, so to speak. I told him I'd find someone to make the bet and took the money and instructions. I headed down to the house where I picked up my bag and put it in the truck. Both tanks were full and we shouldn't have to stop for fuel.

I saw Cassie's truck turn off the highway and head up the drive. She parked her truck and got two bags out of her truck. I knew the one bag had her boots and riding things she would need in the jock quarters. I put both bags in the truck and held the door open for her. A moment later we were on our way. For me it was an adventure, I'd flown to the City but never driven there. Cassie was surprised when I told her to look on the map and find out where we would get off the interstate and go to my mother's house.

We visited all the way to the city and she told me about the interview with the sports magazine. They had taken pictures of her in her riding clothes. She had no idea why but she would know next week when the next issue came out.

When we reached the City, Cassie began to give me directions. Thirty minutes later we were pulling into my mother's driveway. She met us at the door and took us inside. Her home was neat, two bedrooms a nice living room and kitchen. I would sleep on the couch that made out into a bed. Cassie would have the spare bedroom. Mom asked if meatloaf would suit me for supper.

"Mom, I still remember your meatloaf. It was the best. I can hardly wait."

I called Spunky and told him we were at Mom's. We would see him at five the next morning. He gave me directions to the track and said he would have someone at the gate to meet us and get us onto the track. He said Patty would be there when we arrived.

When Mom and Cassie called me to eat I realized I was hungry and was not disappointed with the meatloaf. I told Mom so.

"Thank Cassie, Bill. She made the meatloaf. We compared our recipes and I asked her to fix hers and it is wonderful."

I told Cassie that I was surprised but I'd never complain in the future if she said she was fixing meatloaf. We all got a good laugh and spent the rest of the evening really getting acquainted so to speak. We went to bed early. Mom had to be at work early, too.

When I awoke, Mom was fixing breakfast. Cassie was sitting at the table drinking hot chocolate. I got up and dressed quickly. We ate breakfast and, after giving Mom a kiss, left for the track. When we reached the back gate we saw the exercise boy waiting for us. We signed in and went to Spunky's barn. He and Patty were waiting for us when we drove up. We said hello and heard Light nicker when he heard our voice. We all laughed but walked to his stall where I began scratching his ears. A short time later Spunky and I wrapped his legs and got him ready to go to the track for a timed work. Spunky and Cassie discussed the work while I finished tacking Light up.

When it was light enough to see, I led Cassie and Light up onto the track. When she was set I turned Light loose and watched as she back tracked him to warm him up.

"I swear, Bill. I think that girl could work that horse without a bridle. He listens to her and does what she wants."

We watched as Cassie stopped Light and waited for an opening on the track. She found an opening and turned Light around and began to let him work in the middle of the track. He seemed to glide over the track. When he and Cassie came by she was talking to him and had him under complete control. We watched as she started around the turn and suddenly moved Light down onto the rail. She released her hold on Light and let him work the last quarter mile. I heard Spunky click his watch. Forty six flat, just what we wanted.

I led Cassie and Light back to the barn. We unsaddled and bathed him then turned him over to a hot walker. Donna had gotten a chance at a great job at a factory and Spunky had told her to take it. Her husband had a job here at the track and they were doing great.

Spunky took Cassie, Patty and me to the track kitchen where we had hot chocolate while we waited for the license office to open. Spunky had a horse for Cassie to ride in the fourth race to get a race over the track. The horse was a mare that the trainer thought should run as well as third. We got our license and went back to Spunky's barn until almost race time. Cassie took my truck and drove over to the Jock quarters. I had been amazed at the size of the grandstands. The front was all glass and, unlike Raton's small stands, it was about two hundred yards long. It was beautiful.

Spunky and I began to get Slinker ready. We didn't have to hurry. He was in the eighth race. We put his leg wraps on and left him to relax. Cassie was in the fourth race on the mare. Spunky and I stood on the backside and watched as they warmed up the horses in front of us. When they loaded the gates we were looking directly into the gates. When the gates opened we watched as Cassie got the mare running and settled her into third place a length off the front running horse.

"Bill, she's stalking them. She has the mare relaxed and is waiting for the turn. She just may catch the boys sleeping and get the jump on them."

It happened just like Spunky said. When they were half way around the turn and the boys got ready to get down on their horses, Cassie was already down on the mare and had her in a full out run for the wire. She passed the two front running horses and opened up a three length lead on them. The late running horses were caught flat footed too by the early move by Cassie. They began to make their move but half way up the stretch it was over. Cassie and the mare had just stolen a race. She won by four lengths to the delight of the crowd. She might have been a girl in her first race at a large track but she had just proved to everyone she was a force to be reckoned with.

Spunky and I were laughing and having a great time. The fact that Spunky had really had to talk to get the man to let Cassie ride his mare was what was so funny to him. He'd not have to beg anymore. We had a soda and then finished getting Slinker ready. I led him over to the holding barn and then up the track to the saddling paddock. The saddling paddock was something unlike I had ever seen. It had a padded brick like walking ring. You couldn't hear the horses walking. I waited for Spunky to wave me over and led Slinker over to the stall. I held him while Spunky and the track man sat Cassie's saddle in place. I led him out of the stall just as Cassie walked up in her racing silks. She and Spunky talked while I led Slinker around the walking ring.

The call for "Jockeys Up" was sounded. I held Slinker while Spunky gave Cassie a leg up. I led the two of them over to the pony rider and turned Slinker over to him.

"Go get their money, Cass. Slinker seems ready to run."

"We'll do our best, Bill. See you in the winner's circle."

Spunky went inside to watch the race on the monitors located all over the down stair area. I stood outside and just looked at things. The track to me was amazing in the fact it was so big. Maybe one day I'd come here to watch one of the colts I'd raised run in a race. At least it was something to look forward to.

I watched as Cassie warmed Slinker up on the backstretch with the other horses. Today we'd find out if Slinker was a true race horse. There were two horses that had been winning most of the allowance races they had been entering. There was no doubt that the quality of the horses here at this track was far and above the ones we'd been running against at the smaller track in New Mexico. Finally, after what seemed to be a lifetime, the horses began to load.

"The horses are all in line." The track announcer said. I watched as the gates flew open releasing the nine horses. The bell rang and I was relieved to see Cassie and Slinker were out clean. I watched as Cassie moved Slinker into the lead and moved him slowly across the track and down onto the rail. She had made the lead easy and seemed to be asking Slinker for nothing as she took him down the back side and into the turn. With a two length lead on the field she let Slinker relax and seemed to almost coast half way around the turn. I saw the time for the half mile and had to smile. Forty six and two, she and Slinker had been coasting. Now we would see if Slinker could withstand the charge that would come from behind in the stretch drive.

Suddenly Cassie got down low on Slinker's back and asked him to run. She again had beaten the boys to the punch and had increased her lead over the other horses. With Slinker in an all out drive the other jockeys went to their whips and were asking their mounts for their all.

Cassie had Slinker flying up the lane towards the finish line while the late runners were beginning to make up ground. As they neared the finish line it looked as though Cassie and Slinker would be overtaken in the last few yards. My heart was in my throat when I saw Cassie shake Slinker's reins and ask him for everything he had. It was wonderful to watch as Slinker managed to dig down and gain a full neck lead as the three horses crossed the finish line. Cassie had ridden a wonderful race and had saved just enough of her horse to get up for the win.

Spunky and Patty would be thrilled, as well as Mike and I. Patty had made the bets for Mike and me. The odds had been good and we had made a nice return on our wagers. I caught Slinker when Cassie brought him back up the track. I could see he was tired but there seemed to be a look in his eye that told you he had won. His attitude, as Spunky had said, was going to get bigger.

"He gave me his all, Bill. He reached down and gave me his all. It was wonderful Bill. He's a race horse. Maybe not a Light, but a race horse."

Spunky came out onto the track and after Cassie jumped to the ground he removed the overgirth from Slinker and then gave Cassie another leg up on Slinker. I led Slinker and Cassie into the winner's circle where I was surprised to see Sam, Jen and Ike all smiling and waiting to get their pictures made. Sam had not said a word about coming to the race but I was glad he had.

After the picture was taken I led Slinker to the test barn where I was surprised to find Donna waiting for me.

"I don't have to work Saturdays, Bill and I wasn't about to miss this race. I already had my license so I figured I'd come watch. The kids are all at a soccer match so I had the afternoon free."

"You like your new job?"

"You bet. I go to work at seven and I'm off at three thirty. It's almost like I'm on vacation. I figure my shoes will last a lot longer too."

We were both laughing when the test barn folks brought Slinker back out of the test barn and gave him to us. We led Slinker back over to the barn and gave him his bath after I had taken his leg wraps and bridle off. When we had finished giving him his bath Donna led a very tired Slinker until he was cooled out and dry. I was putting the leg brace on his legs when I heard Spunky and the others come into the barn.

"That's what I like to see, a man working. Some folks seem to think it's a sin, you know."

"That's what Sam said about you the other day, Ike."

Everyone burst out laughing, even Ike. Things were off to a good start, friends enjoying friends. It seemed Spunky had been held up by a reporter who wanted an interview. He was still interviewing Cassie when they had left. Spunky was thrilled with the way Slinker had run and with Cassie's ride. Cassie and I would have to get a couple of papers before we left town in the morning. Later that evening we all went to a near by steak house and had a good meal. Sam, Jen, and Ike were going to fly back home this evening. We were going to spend the night with Mom and would drive back in the morning. Getting to visit with Patty and Spunky was a real treat. I seemed like it had been months since we had gotten to sit down and visit.

Cassie had been slightly upset at the reporter's interview. It seemed he was not impressed with Light's work and thought he was highly overrated.

"Cassie, it's just what we want them to think. We don't want them to know how good he is. That way we will be able to run the race the way we want and not have to worry about what they may do to keep us from winning. We'll only get one chance at them before they figure out how good he really is, so let's make the most of things."

Spunky was right. Why let them know how good Light really was? Let them find out after the stakes race. Sam thought it was a fine idea. He laughed and said he and Ike would make more money that way.

CHAPTER 24

Cassie had been upset before but was really upset with the write up in the paper the next morning.

The writer, we found out later, didn't approve of girls or women jockeys. It was an insult as Cassie put it the way he had written the article. It made her more determined than ever to want win the stakes race with Light. Then when he wanted an interview, simply say "No comment."

We had enjoyed our visit with Mom and she had promised to come out in a few weeks. I was looking forward to her visit. Cassie and I did a lot of talking about our future together on the way home. We discussed the farm and what we wanted to do to make it pay even better. The track was paying for everything right now but we needed another way to generate income until we had the place operating full time.

We arrived home about one in the afternoon. Mike was waiting when we pulled in. He welcomed us home and congratulated Cassie on her ride. One of the local radio stations had given the results of her race the afternoon of the race. I handed him his money and watched him smile.

"Young lady, as long as they keep thinking you don't know how to ride, I'll be able to retire early and quit this slave driving job I've got now."

"Mike, I know how hard Bill is to work for. I mean it's terrible. You even have to take up a collection so you can have coffee of a morning."

"That's true, but until I get rich or find another job I guess I'll just have to suffer."

We all were laughing when we saw Sam and Jen turn off the highway and start up the lane. Jen was ready to ride. Mike gave me the money for the two days works and smiled.

"We've had over sixty head the last two days Bill. This little operation of yours is beginning to pay off. The boys are thrilled with the track and want you to know it. I saw a feller throw some trash out of his trailer this morning and two of the boys got all over him about it. When they were through talking to him, he looked like a whipped pup. As for the coffee, we've got enough money to buy coffee for the rest of the year.

"That's great, Mike. Cassie and I have been talking about some other ways for us to make money next fall. You and I will get together this week and discuss them. I'd like to have your input on them."

"Be glad to help, Bill. Reckon I'd better get the girl's things out for their riding lessons."

Sam parked truck and he and Jen got out laughing. It seemed that Jen was wondering if there was any market for half blind jockeys. Sam thought it was wonderful that she could laugh about her condition. Sam told me she was a completely different child since she had started riding. Her teachers had noticed the difference and had told Sam about it. We watched as she and Cassie walked up to the barn. Sam and I followed. I made a small pot of coffee and we sat on chairs and watched the girls ride. Mike came and sat with us. Sam told Mike about the way Cassie had stolen the allowance race and how the crowd had loved it.

"Bill, when the stakes race takes place the two dollar bettors are going to bet on her. The folks love to see a little person like Spunky and Cassie upset the big boys."

"I know what you mean. Have you seen the article that the reporter wrote about her and Light?"

"No, what did it say?"

I went to the truck and got the paper. I handed it to Sam and let him read the article.

He handed the article to Mike who began reading.

"By dang, what's wrong with this feller? The gal wins two races on long shots and does it with style and he thinks it's luck. And look at what he says about Gray Light!"

"Spunky thought it was great We'd get better odds and no one would be looking to try and block us. I think he has a plan for the stakes race. It's only six furlongs and I know Light can run a mile. I think he is going to let Cassie take him to the front and let him run. If she does they won't know what happened. It will be fun to watch."

"It will be more fun to get a bet down and watch the big boys cry."

Later that afternoon I helped Cassie load her truck and after a kiss watched as she headed home. I went into the house and went to work on my books. Tomorrow was school and I wanted my books in order for my instructor to look over. Cassie called later to let me know she was home and said she'd call the next evening.

I fixed myself a couple of sandwiches and watched some television until bedtime.

My business instructor looked at my books and asked if she could borrow them for a while. I said "sure" and she left the room for a few minutes. When she came back she informed me the principal wanted to see me and gave me back my books. I went to the principal's office. He told me to have a seat. I sat down and waited for him to finish his phone call.

"Bill, I was just talking to the district school superintendent. Your business class instructor says you are doing a wonderful job and already know almost as much as she does about keeping books. She said you have an accountant who will do all your tax work."

"Yes, sir. I'll be using an accountant that Mr. Cooper has do his books. I'm supposed to meet with him next week."

"Good, now here is what your instructor and I have come up with. She says you're making good money and if you had the time you'd even do better, so you'll only be required to go to your business class once a week. Say, Friday mornings. That will give you more time at home to take care of your business. I wish I could do something about your English class but my hands are tied on that one."

"Sir, this is great. The days will be getting shorter and the extra hour will give me the time I need to get the colts worked. Thank you, sir. Thank you very much."

I left school and headed home. Things were great until I got there. The Sheriff's car was parked at the barn so I drove up to see what kind of problem we had.

"Morning, Bill. You're home early. Not skipping school are you?"

I explained to him why I was home early and how glad I was to have the extra hour to work.

"We have a problem I don't know about Sheriff?"

"We have a problem, Bill. The State seems to think you need a guardian to manage things for you until you're eighteen."

"Sheriff, where were they when my father was beating me? No one seemed to care. Now that I've got the center, they want to tell me how to run it. Somehow this just doesn't seem right."

"It's not right, Bill but my hands are tied. You have a meeting at eleven day after tomorrow. I've called your mom and she will be here tomorrow afternoon. She's sort of upset just like you are."

"Sheriff, why are they targeting me? I've not bothered a soul, asked anyone for anything and I'm making a go of a business. It's stupid. They should be helping kids who need it."

"Bill, calm down. I've talked to Sam and if you need someone to keep an eye on you he's more than willing to help. Fact is, he's more upset than you are. He's called his lawyer and told him to be at the meeting to represent you. He's offered to be your guardian if needed. I would have offered, too but I can't due to my job."

"Sheriff, I know your hands are tied and I appreciate all the help you've given me but I have to admit, this deal does burn me a little. I just don't want some state desk jockey telling me how to run my business. I sure hope Sam's lawyer knows his business."

"I'm sure he does, Bill. I've never known Sam Cooper to ever settle for anything less."

"I'll be ready for the meeting, Sheriff. I guess I'd better wear my new suit. I sure don't want them thinking I'm not doing well."

CHAPTER 25

My mother showed up about one the next afternoon. The Sheriff was right behind her when she pulled up to the house. I carried her bags into the house and put them in the spare bedroom. She, as well as the Sheriff, was impressed with the new furnishings in the house. The Sheriff had pictures of the house before I moved back in and wanted more now. While he went to his car for his camera Mom complimented me on my taste in the furnishings.

"Mom, you and I both know who picked the things out. I think she did a great job."

"Of course, she did. She has good taste. She picked my son whom I'm very proud of. Now William, how well are you doing with this training center?"

I got out my books and showed them to Mom. The Sheriff came in and saw how well I was doing.

"I knew you were doing well, Bill but I had no idea how well. You have to take Mike's salary out of this don't you?"

"Sheriff, Mike has already taken his wages out before he gives me my money. Wait until the first of the month when all the outside colts come in. Then we'll really start to make money. Spunky is sending three. A gentleman from Colorado is sending four. I'll start them and take on others if I have time.

"How much will you make a day when all the colts are here Bill, including the track rent you charge?"

"If we average forty horses a day on the track, and the training fees on the colts I'll be making about three hundred and eighty dollars a day."

"Good Lord, Emma. Did you have any idea how much your son was making?"

"No, Tom I didn't, but I did know he has always been smart and had good common sense. After looking at his books it tells me he is using all of his abilities."

"I should say so. I may end up asking him for a job myself."

"Sheriff, I didn't know you knew my mother."

"William, Tom and I went to school together. He married my best friend. How long has Ruth been gone, Tom?"

"Nine years this October, Em."

"You all never had any children, did you"

"No, we went to every doctor we could find but no one could help us. That was one of the reasons she opened the center in town to take care of abused kids."

"I'm glad she did, Tom. She spoke of the children in her letters to me. The last letter I got from her she mentioned she hadn't been feeling well. I heard she had passed on a few weeks later. I would have come to the funeral if I had have known in time."

"She knew where you were all the time, didn't she?"

"Oh yes, she sort of kept an eye on William for me after his brother was killed."

"Good Lord, she knew where you were all the time. She never said a word. I thought I was smart when I was able to find you."

"Don't feel bad, Tom. I asked her not to tell you. I didn't want you to have to lie to anyone about not knowing where I was. Now, about this business with William. What do I need to do?"

"Show up and explain to them how responsible he is and what a good business man he has become."

"Mom, you can take my books if you think it will help."

"I'll do that, William but I think we may need to have a little leverage on our side."

"We'll have that, Emma. Sam Cooper will be there for sure."

The phone interrupted our conversation.

"Running P. This is Bill."

"Bill, this is Cass. What's going on down there? Jen says her dad is having a running fit."

"The State seems to think I need a guardian to oversee me and my business, Cass."

"Why would they think that, Bill? You're making the place pay, going on with your schooling and not causing anyone any trouble. Why would they even bother giving you any trouble?"

"I'm not sure, Cass. Mom and the Sheriff are here right now and they are making plans for the meeting."

"You're about to have more company, Bill. Sam and Jen are on their way out to your place as we speak. My father is ranting a good deal himself. I've not seen him this mad in years. Call me later and let me know what the bunch comes up with. I'm starting to get mad myself."

"Stay cool, Cass. I guess all we can do is let the Sheriff, Mom and Sam take care of things. I'll call you later and let you know what they come up with."

I hung up the phone and was going to fix coffee when Sam came storming into the house.

"Afternoon, Mrs. Patton. Tom, my attorney will be here in a few moments. We're going to get this mess straightened out once and for all. Afternoon, Bill. You'll have to excuse me but I'm upset. This whole deal smells bad to me and if there is any way we can put a stop to it, we're going too."

I'd never seen Sam so upset. A few minutes later an older gray haired gentleman knocked on the back door and asked to see Sam. It was Sam's attorney Mr. Edward Ballard. I had seen his name in the local paper many times and knew for a fact he was not someone who worked cheap. I sat a cup of coffee in front of him and listened while he laid out a plan for the hearing tomorrow morning.

"Bill, you won't be required to be there so go on to school and do whatever needs doing. I've talked to your school principal and he will be there tomorrow to speak for you. As to the question of why they have come after Bill, I have no idea. I can only assume at this time it's because he is under age and has made this place into a growing concern. Well meaning folks can sometimes stir up more trouble than they intend. Now, Mrs. Patton. It's true you signed this property to Bill?"

"Yes it is. I signed it over to him a couple of weeks ago."

"Bill, you've entered into a contract to let part of the place be put into alfalfa?"

"Yes, sir. I'll get all the quality hay I need for the horses I have and so many cents a bale for all the rest."

"That will make you a tidy sum of money. What sort of income are you making from the folks who are using the track to train on?"

I handed him the books that I had given to Mom to look over. A big smile crossed his face.

"Folks, I'm going to enjoy handling this case. Here we have a seventeen year old boy who, without any help from our fine state, has started a business, is making fine grades in school and making the business pay and pay very well, I might add. I'm amazed that you've been able to do what you've done, Bill but it looks to me as if you have more folks looking after your interest than our fine state can provide. Now, if I may have another cup of that coffee we'll lay out a battle plan for tomorrow."

I had called Cassie and told her what was going on. I informed Mike about everything and he went to the house to see if he could do anything. I worked with Sam's filly and stayed out of the way. An hour or so later everyone came up to the barn and I gave Mr. Ballard a guided tour of the place. I answered his questions and was pleased to see him smiling as he walked to his car later. Sam, Mom and Tom the Sheriff, all sat in the kitchen drinking coffee afterwards and visited.

The next morning Mom was up early and had breakfast on the table when I came back from the barn. It was nice having her home again. Tom, the Sheriff was going to pick her up and take her to the meeting. I got cleaned up and kissed her cheek on my way to school. I was nervous about what would happen but there was nothing I could do.

After class I drove home, changed clothes and went to work. I galloped the mare and worked Sam's filly in the round pen. I'd put the light exercise saddle on her for the first time and things had gone well. The filly was smart and willing to work. If she continued to train well I'd start riding her in another week or so. I wanted her to be ready for the spring meets even though the two year old races would be later than the older horses.

I had just finished putting the filly away when I saw the Sheriff's car turn off the highway and come up the lane to the house. I walked to the house and was ready for the news.

"William, relax dear. Everything is going to be all right."

"That's great, Mom. Now come into the house and tell me what happened."

"Let Tom tell you, son. He'll do a better job than me."

I made a quick pot of coffee and sat down to hear what had happened.

"Bill, the people down at the agency had to move the meeting to a bigger room. They had never seen so many folks upset about one case. Sam's attorney got things off to a roaring start. Your Principal from the school, Jen's teacher, Cassie's dad Art, Spunky and Patty."

"Spunky and Patty were there? How did they know?"

"Sam called them then flew to the City early this morning and picked them up. They said to say "hi" to you and they would see you week after next. Sam is flying them back to the City now."

"Good Lord. I had no idea this thing would be so involved."

"Bill, there were folks there you've ridden horses for and even Dan Fowler showed up. When the folks asked if there was a written contract between you and him he told them no. He didn't need one. Your word was good enough for him. It seemed everyone in the room agreed with him. Then Sam got up and asked to be heard. He told the folks if they need to appoint someone as your guardian he sure enough wanted the job. Art and I also offered but they seemed to think Mr. Sam Cooper was quite capable of taking care of the job after his attorney laid everything out for them. Sam's attorney asked them the question you had asked earlier. "Where were they when you were taking the beatings from your father and going to bed hungry most nights?" He also pointed out that through your efforts you were going to make more this year than any of the folks sitting on the board who were judging you. He pointed out that any attempt on their part to appoint someone other than Mr. Cooper or myself would end up in court. By the time it got to court you'd be eighteen and wouldn't be under their care anyway."

"William, I offered to pay the attorney afterwards and he refused payment. He said he'd not enjoyed working on a case like this in years and he had had a ball. He asked if you'd let him come out and watch some of the horses work sometime."

"I've got his card and I can assure you I'll call him. It's noon hour so I'd better call Cassie and let her know how things went."

"No need, Bill. She was there with Art. That young lady told the folks you were a fine horse trainer and had a good head for business. She told them the two of you planned on getting married after graduation and that she was proud that you had chosen her to share your life with."

"William, I have never seen so many people say so many nice things about someone before. You have many friends and I'm proud of you. Now let's go eat. Art and Cassie should be at the truck stop by now."

We had lunch at the truck stop and I thanked Art for coming down and standing up for me. He shook my hand and said it had been his pleasure. He said it was going to take away some of the fun of telling Cassie he had gone out and found her a boy friend though. Everyone at the table laughed and had a good time. I noticed Mom and Tom sat next to each other and seemed to enjoy each other's company. I told Cass I thought it was great and if they became serious we just might have a Sheriff in the family.

CHAPTER 26

I had called Sam and thanked him for all of his help. He told me he had never had a younger brother but felt he did now. I told him I felt honored and would try and live up to his expectations. I had called Spunky and thanked him and got his new home phone number so I could call Patty. She had said some wonderful things about me and I wanted to thank her, too.

When Patty had answered the phone I said, "Mom, this is your adopted son, Bill." I had to wait for a minute before she could talk. I knew she had cried.

"Bill Patton, you can call me Mom anytime or anyplace and I'll be proud you did. Spunky and I have missed you kids like crazy. The only thing Spunky is dreading next year is that he won't have you with him all summer."

"I know, Patty. But Light deserves the chance to show folks what he can do. Besides, I want to see the look on some people's faces when Spunky kicks their tails. Did you see the article on Cass in the paper the day after the race?"

"Oh yes, I thought Spunky was going to go down to the news paper and hit the reporter."

"Spunky and I have talked and here's what we plan to do in the stakes race." When I had finished Patty began to laugh.

"Bill, he can do it, can't he?"

"I sure think so, Patty. At least we're going to try and see. If it works a lot of folks are going to have to back up and eat their words."

"Bill, I'll see you and Cassie next week. Spunky and I plan on buying you all supper after we win the stakes race."

"I'll be ready Patty. See you then."

The next week and a half went by in a hurry. Mike and I worked the horses every day and were both enjoying watching them progress. The mare was beginning to pull on me and get that competitive edge back. She was wanting to run and was ready. I called Spunky and asked if he had a spot for her. She needed a couple of weeks work over the track but should be ready by then. He told me to bring her when I came for the weekend and he'd have things set up for her.

Mike had come to me and asked for a favor.

"What do you need, Mike?"

"You know Dave Warner don't you, Bill?"

"Sure I do. I've ridden a bunch of horses for him. His youngest son is in my class. Why?"

"Well I've talked to him and he's out here everyday. I asked him if he would take care of things next Saturday morning. Sam said if I wanted to fly to the city with him I was welcome and darn it, Bill. I've never got to see Cassie and Gray Light race.

"Get him lined out, Mike. You'll have a ball."

"Thanks, Bill. I really appreciate it a bunch."

"No, thank you, Mike. By the way, we're going to need another hand to help us when the new bunch of horses arrive. We won't be able to handle them by ourselves. If you know of anyone tell them to come talk to me."

"I may know just the feller we need, Bill. I'll look him up this weekend."

The following week I borrowed a friend's good one horse trailer and got things ready to go to the city on Friday afternoon. Cassie called Thursday night and said she was coming down to spend the night. That way we could get an early start to the city and get the mare settled at the track before we went to Mom's house. I shifted things into high gear and got things ready to go. When Cass arrived I had the truck fueled up and the trailer hooked on and ready to go. I would wrap the mare's legs just before we left. Cassie had brought a couple of dishes she had prepared and we invited Mike to come eat supper with us. The meal was great and afterwards Mike had said he had to get moving. He needed everything lined out for Dave the following morning.

Cassie and I went to bed early. We planned on leaving at five. That would let us be at the track by ten and have time to talk with Spunky and Patty before we went to Mom's for the evening.

The next morning Mike helped me load the mare. We had just finished when Cassie walked up carrying a thermos of hot chocolate and a small bag. She was ready to go, she gave Mike a kiss on the cheek and told him she'd see him in the city. We pulled down the drive and heard an oncoming truck honk, its driver waving to us. Art was on his way home. We honked and waved back then pulled out and headed to the interstate. The trip to the city went quickly, now that we knew where we had to go. We signed in at the back gate after showing our license and the papers for the mare. We drove to Spunky's barn and found him waiting at the door for us.

We unloaded the mare and put her in a stall. She lay down and rolled, happy to be off the trailer. Spunky said she looked great but he would work her on Tuesday and give me his opinion on when he thought she would be ready to run. We were fortunate that the man who had owned her had kept her in training after she had been bred.

Spunky told Cassie there were several trainers who wanted her to ride but his friend had a gelding in the sixth race that he wanted her to ride. He wasn't expected to win but needed the race. He had just come back from a throat surgery and needed to be tested.

Cassie said she would ride him. That would give her a good idea as to how the track conditions were and where she wanted to put Light. We parked the trailer in the race track lot later that afternoon and drove over to mom's place. She was on the phone when we arrived so Cass and I put our things away. It seemed she was talking to Tom who was wondering if we had gotten to the city all right. Cassie and I could only smile.

We had a good visit after a good supper and all went to bed early. I was up at daylight and got the paper from the porch. I wanted to see what the paper said about the race. It seemed that two out of state trainers had brought two possible Derby hopefuls in to try and steal the purse. Spunky and I had discussed them the afternoon before and had figured we only had to out run one of them. The second favored horse of the two would fade at the six furlong pole and the other would be running. It seemed no one was giving Light much chance. His odds, of nine to one really thrilled me.

When mom and Cassie were up I gave the paper to them and relaxed. It was going to be a long day. Cassie and Light ran in the featured tenth race. We relaxed and had a good visit. Mom and a friend of hers were coming to the races. Cassie and I got ready and went to the track about eleven. Spunky went to get a bite to eat and we looked after things. Donna came into the barn with a big smile on her face.

"Have you seen the paper Bill?'

"Read it this morning Donna, I like the odds."

"So do I, how do you want your bet made?"

"I handed her my bet. Put it on Light's nose."

"You don't want anything else?"

"No, there are a couple of horses in the race who just might surprise some folks. I just can't figure out which ones. Besides if Light goes off at good odds I'll have done well.

Cassie left a short time later to go to the jock's room.

We braided Light's mane and made sure he got a good ear scratching. Spunky, Donna and I went up the slope of the track to watch Cassie ride in the sixth race. They were loading the horses for the race when we walked up to where we could see. When we got to our spot the gates opened and the horses came flying out of the gate. When they came by our position Cassie had her gelding sitting in fourth position and was not asking him for a thing. As the horses rounded the turn I saw that the front running horse was coming back to the rest of the horses. Cassie kept the gelding going and when they reached the stretch and for the finish wire she asked the horse to run. The gelding gave her his all and ran a good second by only a length. Spunky said his friend would be very happy. The horse had been stopping at the five eights pole in all of his previous races.

We went back into the barn and put the wraps on Light and finished getting him ready. He was happy and seemed to know this was race day. The announcement came for all the horses in the tenth race to come to the holding barn. We put the bridle on Light and I led him around to the holding barn and walked him around until the call came over the speaker to bring the horses to the saddling paddock. I led Light who was on his toes and was ready. He would be running seven furlongs for the first time but I had all the confidence in the world he could run the distance. I led him off the track and through the tunnel and out onto the walking ring. I was leading him around and watching the other horses. I didn't want to have anything go wrong now. I saw Spunky wave me over and led Light into the saddling stall. The track assistant helped Spunky set the saddle and put the overgirth on. I led Light out onto the walking ring and walked him until the call for "Rrides Up" was announced. I held Light while Spunky gave Cassie a leg up. I led her over to the pony rider and turned Light over to him.

"See you in the winner's circle Bill."

"I'll be there to lead you in Cass, let the big horse run."

I walked out in front of the grandstands and watched the post parade. I was engrossed in looking all the horses over when I heard Mike.

"He sure is a good looking bugger Bill."

"He is, isn't he? He's ready to run Mike. You got a bet down?"

"Sure do Bill, I had to bet on you kids. I'd never flown before but I'll not turn down the chance again if it's offered. That Sam is one nice feller, we had a good time coming out."

"Who all came along?"

"The Sheriff, Ed Ballard, Jen and myself."

"I'm glad the lawyer came Mike, we may see something today that may open a lot of folks eyes if everything goes right."

"What are you talking about Bill?"

"Just wait Mike, they are loading into the gates."

The last horse was loaded into the gates and the announcer said, "The horses are all in line". The bell rang and the gates flew open. Cassie and Gray Light seemed to explode from the gate. They had a length lead twenty yards from the gate. I watched as Cassie moved Light over the track and settled him just off the rail. I saw Light flip his ears and knew Cassie was talking to him. Half way down the back stretch he had a three length lead.

"Mike, you can get ready to cash your ticket. The horse is widening his lead and Cassie has him on cruise control."

"You mean he's not trying, Bill?"

"He's just floating along, Mike. Watch what happens when they reach the turn. He'll really start to roll then."

Just like I said, Cassie and Light reached the turn and suddenly she got lower on his back and shook the reins. It was the most beautiful thing I had ever seen. Light seemed to get lower and his stride began to lengthen. With every stride he seemed to get quicker and seemed to fly up the stretch. He and Cassie now had a four length lead. The other horses were trying to close the distance but it was an impossible thing to do. Cassie hand rode Light past the wire and then stood up in her irons and waved her stick in the air. I left Mike after telling him to get in the picture at the winners circle. I raced through the gate to catch Light when Cassie brought him back.

I watched Cassie patting Light's neck as she jogged back towards me. The smile on her face said it all. She had won and the big boys could go home and look for something else to be their Derby horse. They would not forget this day and what the big gray horse had done to them. A roar went up from the crowd as the time of the race was posted. Light had just set a new track record for seven furlongs. Many of the track folks knew the truth. He hadn't even tried.

I caught Light just as Spunky arrived on the track. He hugged Cassie who had just jumped off Light. Spunky removed the overgirth and gave Cassie a leg back up on Light. I led Cassie and Light into the now crowded winner's circle.

Spunky and Patty were presented a beautiful silver tray and then the picture was taken. Cassie jumped off and kissed my cheek. It was then I saw her folks coming over. Cassie got hugs and I got a handshake from Art. A moment later I led Light to the test barn where Donna stood smiling.

I walked Light until the test folks took Light into the test barn. I walked over to where Donna stood.

"You were right, Bill. The two favorites finished third and fourth. Light went off at eight to one. You will have a nice chunk of money coming to you."

I never seem to have enough of the good stuff, Donna. But this time it means less to me. Just getting to see Light run like he did today was worth all the hours of work that got him here. Now Spunky and Patty are really going to have a decision to make."

"What do you mean, Bill?"

"Spunky and Patty are going to get offers for Light like they have never thought possible. It's going to be both a great and sad day all in one."

"I hope they can figure something out, Bill. I'd hate for them to lose Light.

The test crew brought Light back to me. Donna walked with me back to the barn. Light was feeling great and was playing all the way back to the barn. I took off the leg wraps, bridle and put his halter on. We had finished giving him his bath when Spunky walked into the barn.

"Bill Patton, we did it, son. We got the big boys and did it with style."

"That we did, Spunky. Real style. They will not forget this day for a while.

"They sure won't, son. Wait until you see in the paper what Cassie said to the reporter when he asked for an interview. She really put him in his place, and with everyone standing there, he couldn't say a thing."

"She was a little upset about the last article the gentleman wrote. She has had a while to think about what she was going to say. I'll have to ask her when she gets here."

A short time later Sam, Jen, Mr. Ballard, Tom, Mike and Patty walked into the barn. They were all smiling and were patting Spunky on the back. Patty gave me a hug and a kiss on the cheek and said thanks.

"It has been my pleasure, Patty."

Everyone was talking when Cassie, her folks and my mother came into the barn and asked to join the party.

"You can join the party if you want to have a good time."

Cassie, who was leading the group pumped her fist and said, "Yes".

Needless to say, a good time was had by all. That was until Spunky had to answer the phone in his tack room. A short time later he came out and I saw

Sam talking to him. They went into the tack room while everyone was visiting. I was visiting with Mike and Art when Spunky called Patty, Cassie and me into the tack room. Sam sat in a chair smiling.

"Patty, I called you and the kids in to hear what's going on. Gray Light belongs to you so it will be your decision. I had an offer a few moments ago for Light. A very large amount of money. I didn't know what to do, but Sam here has offered a sum that will let us live like we've always dreamed about for half of Light and we get to keep and train him. It's your decision, Patty and what ever you decide will be fine with me."

"Spunky, darling with what this horse has made us this year we can be comfortable but I'm sure we've just received the first offer. I saw one man who you know is connected to the gentleman in Kentucky and he was watching Bill and Donna bring Light back over here after the race. He was on his cell phone and was telling someone the horse is walking on his toes and playing on the way back to the barn. We'll have more offers but if our Mr. Cooper wants to buy half of Light, I'll be more than happy to have him as a partner. Especially since we get to go ahead and campaign Light next year."

I, for one, breathed a sigh of relief. I hated to see Spunky and Patty lose Light. He was keeping them young and had just assured them of a good life after he quit running if Spunky wanted to retire.

"Bill, Sam and I have talked about it and we'd like you to stand Light at your place when we decide to retire him."

"I'd be honored to stand him, Spunky but for now let's just everyone relax and live for this moment. We all know he'll be here in your barn and we'll all get a chance to watch him grow. I, for one, can't wait until next year. I think he'll be awesome as a three year old."

After Donna had walked Light dry Spunky and I rubbed his legs and put on his stall wraps. He went straight to his feed tub and began eating. I rubbed his ears and left him to finish his feed. We all went to a local steak house and had a fine dinner. Sam was a happy man. He now owned half of a race horse. Half of a very good race horse. He and the rest of my friends left for the airport after our meal. They told me they would see me tomorrow evening.

Mom's friend had left after the race so she rode back to her house with Cassie and me. We had to park on the street because we had the trailer hooked on. We went into mom's house and relaxed. Cassie and I got a bath before we went to bed. Mom made a phone call and the next morning I found six papers on her porch instead of one. We had extra papers to take back to the folks at home.

We had a good breakfast with mom the next morning and after saying good bye we pulled out for home. We made the drive home and on the way I pointed to the paper.

"I've not read your interview, Cass. I wanted to know what you said."

"He asked me how it felt to ride a winning stakes horse. I told him no different than the last time. He didn't understand so I explained to him I'd ridden Light in several stakes wins. I'd been his jockey in all his races and would be riding him next year's racing season. Then I told him I guess it just showed that a girl could ride as well as the boys and sometimes better. He really didn't know what to say. I also told him that Light had just destroyed two Derby hopefuls and who would know, maybe, just maybe he'd be in Kentucky in May. Most important of all, I'd be riding him."

I couldn't help but laugh.

"What did he write?"

"He wrote that I was a brash young rider with lofty dreams. But he did say my rides at the track were impressive."

"At least he did give you some credit. After the first article he wrote he had to try and save some face."

"That was what I wanted to slap, Bill."

CHAPTER 27

❀

Cassie and I dropped the trailer off at my friend's house and discussed buying a trailer for the farm. We would be needing one to take the horses to the track come spring. We had talked about how our lives had changed and how much fun we had since the last spring. It was going to be a change after being at the city and then going back to the track at Raton. I told Cassie I felt almost like a teacher and the horses were my pupils.

"Bill, you are a teacher. You take the babies and teach them their manners. How to load in the gates, gallop at a controlled pace and then run at just the right time. It's a gift you have, Bill. The horses learn to trust you and develop because of it. When do you think Spunky will get a race for your mare?"

"I figure three weeks or so, but she may not be as far along as I think."

"Well at least it will be fun to have your own horse running for a change. She has changed so much over the past weeks. I've watched you build her confidence up and bring her along. She has that gleam in her eye now and knows she can run if she wants."

"I am thrilled with the way she has come around Cass. I hope she can win, but I really bought her to cross on Light. I just have a feeling about her."

"I hope she does well Bill. It will be different riding our own horse in a race. That sounds strange doesn't it Bill?"

"Our horse. Yes it does, Cass. I'm thrilled with the idea though. Cass, I've never asked because I wanted to see if I could make this place pay. But now that things have sort of lined out, will you marry me?"

"Yes I will, Bill. I've just been waiting for you to ask."

"We'll have to wait until after graduation but we'll go to town next Saturday and pick out your ring."

"Fine with me, Bill. I'm more than ready."

Mike met us at the house when we drove in. He was flying high. He'd got to tell the boys about the race and told some of them they had better try and get some of their mares bred to Light if they got the chance. It seemed that the local paper had picked up the news of the race and had run a picture of Light on the front of the sports page.

"Kids, I'm having way too much fun for an old man."

We laughed and unloaded the truck and got ready to give Jen her riding lesson. The phone rang and it was a van hauling horses to California. They had three head that the gentleman from Colorado had shipped and would be in town in another hour or so. They needed directions to the farm. I gave them directions and hung up.

"I'll get the buckets hung and filled while you fill the hay nets, Mike. We'll let them settle today and start in the round pen tomorrow."

"Cass, call your folks and let them know we're back."

Cassie was on the phone when Mike and I went out the door. We hung water buckets and hay nets and made sure we had everything ready. True to their word the huge van pulled in about thirty minutes later. We put the fillies on the west side of the barn and the stud colt on the east side.

I signed the transport slip and watched the van go down the drive. Mike and I were looking at the colts when Cassie walked in.

"Bill, give this gentleman a ring on your cell. He says Sam told him to call you."

She handed me a slip of paper with a phone number on it. I called the number and on the second ring a gentleman answered.

"Sir, this is Bill Patton out at the Running P Training Center. I was told you called."

"Yes Mr. Patton, I'm Fred Paulson. I work at the Panhandle State Bank. We have a problem that Mr. Cooper said he thought you might be able to help us with. We have a note that has three mares listed as security and it is well past due. I was wondering if you could find time to go with me and look the mares over. I'd like you to tell me what you think the mares are worth. That is, if you can find the time."

"Mr. Paulson, where are these mares?"

"They are at a farm about thirty minutes west of your place, sir. I'd come pick you up."

"How about nine thirty in the morning. I'll have a couple of hours I can spare then."

"That will be wonderful, Mr. Patton. The bank will pay you for your time of course."

"I'll see you at nine thirty sir."

"I'm going to look at some mares and tell the bank what I think they are worth. You know of anyone who has three mares that's in trouble, Mike?"

"Sure do, Bill. A couple of young fellers wanted to be trainers and their folks set them up about six months ago. I heard they had gone bust some time back."

"They must be the ones who sold their equipment to the tack shop. You remember all the tack I brought in. I hope the mares are good. I have no idea how much the bank has in them."

"Don't worry about it, Bill. Give the man your honest opinion and go on. I'd think they would want someone at the bank with a little knowledge of horses to look at them before they loaned money on them."

"So do I, Cassie but maybe the folks had enough security to back them up. We'll know tomorrow after I look at them."

We saw Sam and Jen turn up the drive and park just outside the barn.

"Should I call you Mr. Cooper now that you own half of Gray Light?"

"Not if you want to stay friends with me, Bill."

"Come on in the barn, Sam. We just got our first shipment of colts in. They came from a ranch in Colorado."

Mike helped the girls get ready while Sam and I looked the colts over. The stud colt was a nice horse. He had a nice long slender neck, good shoulder, hip and had a kind eye.

The two fillies were of the same quality. They showed someone was trying to raise good colts. Colts that could run and maybe make some money. We looked at Sam's filly who was really doing well. She was putting on weight and developing muscle. I was quite pleased with her. She was riding well in the pasture and I'd start her on the track tomorrow.

"Bill, she looks great. When will you start her on the track?"

"Tomorrow, Sam. She's a long way from being ready but we need to start galloping her and get her started into her training."

"Any idea when we might know something about her?"

"It will be three or four months before I can tell you anything Sam. I sure don't want to cripple her."

"Take your time, Bill. We won't have a chance to run her until this summer so there is no need to hurry her. What do you think of my deal with Spunky on Gray Light?"

"I think you've made a heck of a deal, Sam. You know he's a racehorse. Now all you have to do is find out is just how good is he. Spunky is going to start getting him ready to run a route of ground. By that I mean a mile, mile and an eighth or so. If he can go the mile as easy as he did seven furlongs you will have made a heck of a deal."

"I think so too, Bill. Spunky is a good trainer and he cares about his horses. We talked of sending him to Oaklawn next spring. The purses are great but of course the horses there will be harder to beat"

"I think Light and Slinker will both do fine. Light is going to grow and get stronger. I noticed it at the city this weekend. There is one more stakes for him in about three weeks but it is a mile and a sixteenth. Sam, if he wins that one he'll be worth twice what you paid for him. If he really does great, he'll be worth a whole lot more. You and Spunky will be getting offers from all over from folks wanting to send him to the Derby."

"You really think so, Bill? You think he stands a chance of being that good?"

"I do, Sam. He wiped two good horses out this last week that some folks thought were good enough to go. You'll probably see them again at Oaklawn, but you don't have anything to worry about. Light is far better than either one of them."

We got chairs and watched the two girls ride and work their horses. I was amazed at how Jen could ride and really not see. I only wished she could get her sight back and really get after things. Mike told Sam that he was amazed at how well Jen was riding and that if she ever got her sight she would break him buying good horses for her to ride. Sam told us of how she had changed over the last month of so. Everyone around her saw the difference and they were thrilled for her.

"Boys, I've spent thousands of dollars trying to find help for her but there just hasn't been anyone who seems to know what is wrong. We'll just go along and let her enjoy her life like she is doing. Hearing her laugh and talk about her horse and her big brother and sister is worth more money than I've got."

I told Sam I was going to look at some mares for the bank tomorrow.

"I told Fred Paulson to call you. Give him your honest opinion, Bill. The bank is going to foreclose on the note and they need to know how much to go after. I don't know who loaned the money but I'm going to find out. I'm on the board of directors and I want to know."

I saw Mike raise his eyebrows and had the same thought. Someone had some explaining to do. I was sure glad it wasn't me.

Later, after Sam and Jen had left, I helped Cassie load her things into her truck and watched as she turned north onto the highway. Mike came walking down from the barn and handed me the weekend's take from the track. He told me the trials would be held a week from Saturday. He thought it might be a good idea if we showed up and watched the trial races. I had to agree with him and said we'd go. I'd work the colts early or give them the day off. When Cass called to let me know she was home I told her about the trials and that Mike thought we should go. I asked if she wanted to go with us. She was excited and said she would love to go and we'd make plans when she was back to give Jen her lesson.

Later I got a bath and laid my clothes out for the next day. I'd wear a white shirt, because I wouldn't have time to change before the banker arrived. I got a glass of water and sat down and watched the evening news and weather. When the sports section came on I was surprised to see a short story about Gray Light's win at the city. The strip started showing Cassie and Light coming up the stretch with the crowd screaming as she crossed the finish line alone. A short interview with Spunky followed and when he mentioned that I had helped make Gray Light what he was today I almost quit breathing. I'd not heard or seen anything about this interview. I was shocked. A moment later my phone began to ring. It seemed everyone in the area had seen the piece on television. An hour later I finally got to bed.

The next morning at school I was treated like someone special. My business teacher, like everyone else had seen the clip and was happy I had gotten the attention she felt I deserved.

"Bill, the kids here at school are looking at you and thinking it could have been them. They had a good home, money, and plenty to eat when you were struggling to get along. Some have told me they were ashamed to been seen with you because you were poor and had to work. Now they are ashamed of themselves."

"They shouldn't be ashamed. I was ashamed. I didn't have the proper clothes to wear to school. No one ever gave me any trouble. At least they left me alone."

"But you were never invited to any parties or such were you?"

"No ma'am, it wouldn't have made any difference. I was either riding horses at home or riding horses at a sale or sale barn. My father wouldn't have let me go anyway."

"Bill, is it true you ran away from home and went to the track?"

"Yes ma'am, my father came home drunk just after school was out and began beating on me with a skillet. I'd had enough of his abuse and left when he fell down and passed out. I guess you know the rest."

"Yes I guess I do. I just want you to know I'm proud of you. So many of my students don't care about my class one way or another. It's wonderful to have someone who is mature enough to see what the future has in store for them."

"Thank you ma'am. I appreciate that a lot."

When I got to the house there were still a bunch of boys working their horses. I waved to Mike and took my books into the house. I had just gotten a drink when the gentleman from the bank arrived. I walked out to the car to meet him.

"Mr. Patton?"

"Yes, I'm Bill Patton."

"Mr. Patton, you'll have to excuse me I was expecting someone a little older."

"Don't let it worry you, Mr. Paulson. It happens all the time. Everyone seems to think you have to have gray hair to know much of anything. I've been riding and breaking horses all my life. I've had a crash course in studying race horse pedigrees this summer with Mr. Davis. I think I can give you a honest opinion on what the mares are worth."

"I'm sure you can or Mr. Cooper wouldn't have sent me to see you."

A short time later we arrived at a very nice farm with white pipe fences and a couple of nice run in sheds. I asked Mr. Paulson if the farm was included in the foreclosure.

"I'm not sure. I was asked to step in when my supervisor was asked to step down. I'm not sure what is going on and to be truthful I'm glad I don't."

An older gentleman came out of the house and told us where we could find the mares. We walked back down a lane and found the mares in a small paddock. I asked to see the papers on the mares. Mr. Paulson reached into his case and handed them to me. I looked at the papers and matched the mares to the papers and began to look them over. The first was a brown mare whose sire or dam I didn't recognize. She wasn't anything special. The second mare was a bay mare that did have some horses I had heard about on her papers. But then again she was nothing special. The third was a gray mare who was far above the other two mares in looks. I looked at her papers and found the name of the stud that was also the sire of Sam's filly. On the back of the mare's papers I saw she was an allowance race winner. She now had a large ankle which was probably the reason she stopped racing.

"Mr. Paulson, you want to know my opinion of the mares, right?"

"Yes, sir. That's what I want."

"The brown mare is nothing outstanding. Her papers show she never won a race and I don't recognize her sire or dam either. The bay mare is about the same. The mares are worth maybe twelve hundred each if you find a good sale. The gray mare raced and was a winner. Twenty five hundred to three thousand would be about what she would bring at a sale because of the big ankle she has. Some folks will be afraid it will give her trouble somewhere down the line."

"Mr. Patton, I appreciate your honesty. I'm afraid some of the folks at the bank are going to be very upset. I'll give them your figures and the rest is up to them."

"I understand, sir. I'm sorry"

We drove back to the farm. Mr. Paulson thanked me again and left. I went into the house and changed clothes. I headed to the barn and went to work on the new colts. I took each one to the round pen and let them work off the edge before I began getting control of them. All of the colts were easy to handle and went to work in a short time. I was impressed with the stud colt that moved well and seemed to only want to please. Both fillies were nice to handle and were soon working well. I could tell they had all been worked in the round pen before and from their condition I figured I could start riding them in a week or so.

After bathing and cooling them out on a walker, the Quarter Horse boys had brought out. I got Sam's filly and took her outside for a ride in the pasture. I was pleased with her. She went along fine and seemed to enjoy the outing. On the way back I rode her around the track and let her jog when she wanted to. Tomorrow we'd do the same thing. I wanted her to be happy and looking forward to every day's outing.

Mike had a young Mexican boy standing in the barn aisle when I got back from the work.

"Bill, this is Carlo. He's the young feller I told you about."

"Glad to meet you, Carlo. Mike tells me you may be looking for a job."

"Yes, sir. I am. The stable I worked at closed and I got laid off."

"We need a hand to help with the chores and walking the colts cool. We start early and put in a full day. The colts we'll be working are very expensive and we have to handle them special. You'll have Sunday off unless something comes up. Mike takes care of the folks who come out every morning. You'll be mucking the stalls and doing what ever he needs done. When you're done you'll have a couple of hours off then we'll be working the thoroughbred colts.

It takes about three hours or so to get them taken care of. The hours are long but we try and have a good time. Think you'd be interested?"

"I'd like the job, I've never worked with the thoroughbred horses but I'd like to learn. I've known Mike for some time and I think we can get along."

I told him what I could pay and he quickly accepted. I told him to be here in the morning to go to work. It would take more money from my profits but Mike and I needed help. I had just gone back to the house to have a late lunch when Sam called me on my cell phone.

"Bill, I just saw your figures on what you thought the mares are worth. The folks at the bank and I are a little upset. It seems the two young men have used their friend who worked at the bank to work a scam. Bill, the boys had no intention of making a go of the stable. They set out to rip the bank off and thanks to you we can prove it in court. I want to thank you for your help."

"You're more than welcome, Sam. There is something you should know. The gray mare with the bad ankle could be a sleeper. She ran rather well and is the daughter of a very good horse. Spunky told me about him and believes he may just be a good broodmare sire. If the horses go up for auction she might just be something I'd be interested in if it won't cause a problem."

"I'll check it out, Bill. You think she might cross well on Light?"

"That's what I'm thinking Sam. She had some ability and if she will produce it she just might be a real buy."

I grabbed a bite of lunch and went to work on my books. I added Carlo to my employee list and listed his salary. Owning the center was both fun and exciting but it had to be run like a business and I was going to do that.

The next two weeks seemed to fly by. Thanksgiving was fast approaching. Mom had told me she would come out and cook dinner. I was to invite Sam, Jen, Sheriff Tom and Cassie and her folks. Mike and Carlo were invited, of course. Spunky called and said he was entering Light in the last stakes race he would enter at the track. He was looking at a thirty thousand claiming race for my mare on the same day. He told me she was doing well and thought she was ready. If he got both horses into the races he would call me back later.

My heart began to beat faster. I hoped the mare would get in, but at the same time I was scared she wouldn't do well. I called Cass and told her I'd know this evening if Spunky had the horses entered.

"Let me know Bill. We'll be out of school next week for Thanksgiving and we're not doing a whole lot of work right now. I can come down Thursday night like before and we'll get an early start to the city."

"Sounds good to me, Cass. I'll call you this evening. Are you and your family coming for Thanksgiving?"

"I think so, I'll come down and help your mom with the cooking. My mom wants to know what she can bring. I'll sit down with your mom and get things lined out this weekend. Bill, are we going to go shopping this evening after Jen's lessons?"

"We sure are, Cass. It seems as if every time we've planned on going, something has come up. Today we'll go."

Later that afternoon Sam and Jen came out for her lesson. Cassie had pulled in behind them. The girls went to work on the horses while Sam and I discussed the upcoming race for Light. It seemed four of the seven horses he had outrun in the last race had been entered to run against him again.

"I think they thought his last race was fluke. If things go right, Sam they will find out it wasn't a fluke after all."

"You're not worried about the mile and a sixteenth distance?"

"Not in the least. He'll do it, and do it easy. I figure they will enter a horse or two to try and get him to run himself out early. They don't know we can rate him. It should be a great race to watch."

"Spunky said your mare might get in a race on the same day."

"Yes and I've got butterflies. I'm either going to look smart or stupid."

"She'll do fine, Bill. Spunky says she is coming around fine."

The girls had a good time and Jen was beginning to get excited about Thanksgiving and being with her new family for the first time. Later, when Sam and Jen left, Cassie headed into town. I had a ring to buy.

We found a set of rings that we both liked, and I paid for them. We had decided that I would give Cassie her engagement ring for Christmas but by the time we got back to the farm we had changed our minds. Cassie would keep the ring and wear it. We neither one wanted to wait until Christmas. When we reached the farm, she had to show the ring to Mike who gave her a hug and told her he was happy for us.

My cell phone rang and I listened to Spunky tell me both horses had gotten into their races. He wanted to know when we would be in the City."

"We'll be there Friday afternoon, Spunky. We'll come to the barn when we hit town. We should be there by nine thirty or so."

"Good. Patty and I want to take you kids to lunch."

"Spunky, you can tell Patty that Cassie and I are officially engaged now. I got her ring just a little while ago."

"That's great Bill. I'm very happy for the two of you. Patty will be thrilled, too."

Later, after Cassie left I sat down and couldn't help but think just how lucky I was to have found Cass. I'd told Mike that if Sam asked him to go to the City he should get his friend to look after things again. He'd have Carlo to help with things.

When Friday morning finally arrived I was up and ready to go. Cass had spent the night and we were up and in my truck at five. I saw the lights come on in the barn as we went down the driveway. Mike was on the job as usual. Sam had asked him to come along and he was thrilled to be asked.

Cass and I visited on the way and she told me what her folks had said when she walked in wearing the ring. Her mother and father had hugged her and she said her father actually had tears in his eyes. Her brothers had said it was great. She'd found someone they had approved of.

We arrived at the track a few minutes before ten and got hugs and kisses from Spunky and Patty. Patty had to see Cassie's ring. Spunky and I went to look at Light and my mare. I rubbed Light's ears and then went to look at my mare. She looked like a different horse. She had gained weight and looked great.

"Bill, your mare may just surprise a lot of folks today. She has really come around the last two weeks. I'd like to take her with me when we go to Oaklawn."

"If you think she will work, take her along, Spunky. I took a chance on your word and I'd be foolish to go against it now."

We went to lunch and even went to the track and watched part of the day'i races. We were setting in the grandstands when a gentleman stopped and spoke to us.

"Excuse me, but aren't you the two kids who work with Gray Light?"

"Yes sir, we are."

"Could I get you two to autograph my sports magazine?"

The gentleman had had a copy of the sports magazine with Cassie's interview in it. The cover had a picture of Cassie on the front with a small picture of me in he lower corner. I was shocked. Cass looked at me and grinned. She knew the picture would be on the cover with her. We signed the book and asked where he had gotten his copy. He said his company printed the book each month and it would be out in a week or so. Cass asked if there was a chance of our getting a couple of copies while we were in town.

The gentleman made a call and told us the magazines would be at the front gate in twenty minutes. I reached for my billfold and he shook his head. They were a gift. He had seen Cassie's ring and said to consider it a wedding gift. We went downstairs and waited. A young man parked in front of the track entrance and brought a paper wrapped bundle to us. We thanked him and unwrapped the package. We had six copies, now we had to decide who would get them.

We were happy and relaxed. Mom was happy when she saw and read the article. She said it was wonderful that we could do what we loved and do it together. She welcomed Cassie to the family and said she couldn't be happier. She was going to come to the track tomorrow. Sam had had Sheriff Tom call and invite her to sit with them in his box at the track. She was thrilled to be asked. They were going to pick her up on their way to the track

The next morning we ate breakfast and headed out to the track. Spunky told me he would be heading home the first of the week. He felt his horses needed the rest and some time away from the track. He wanted them fresh when they showed up at Oaklawn. He had hired his exercise boy to go with him to the farm and help out with the daily chores. He would take him with him in the spring.

My mare was in the fourth race so Spunky and I went to work on her when Cassie left for the jock room. I braided her mane while Spunky got her racing bandages put on. When they called for her race to come to the holding barn I was nervous and was working hard to not let it show. Spunky laughed at me and said if I never got nervous before one of my horses raced I should get out of the business.

I walked the mare over to the holding barn and walked her until the call was made to bring the horses to the saddling paddock. The mare was feeling good and was walking lightly as I took her up the track and into the saddling paddock. She seemed to see everything but was easy to handle and when Spunky waved for me to bring her over to her saddling stall my heart rate went up again. I watched as she was saddled and then led her back around the walking ring. Cassie talked to Spunky and got her instructions as to how she was to ride the race. When the call "Riders Up" was called I held the mare while Spunky gave Cassie a leg up.

I led the mare over to the pony rider and waited until he had control of her.

"Bill, relax dear. I'll see you in the winner's circle."

"Have a good trip, Cass."

I waved to Spunky as he started up to his box to watch the race. I walked out front and found Mike waiting for me.

"How do you want your money bet, Bill?"

I looked at the tote board and could not believe what I saw. My mare was thirty five to one. I looked at Mike and smiled. Her previous record showed nothing at the much smaller track. I reached for my billfold and handed Mike my money.

"Mike, I may be crazy but I want you to put fifty dollars to win, place and show. Spunky has the mare ready."

"I'll take care of it, Bill. Be back in a few minutes."

It seemed the warm up of the horses took forever and the loading of the gates was no better. When the gates opened and the bell rang I could hardly breathe. The race was six furlongs so the mare would only run around one turn. I saw Cassie settle the mare in fifth place and seemed content to let her run along with the tightly grouped horses. The horse on the lead began to weaken after setting fast fractions for the first quarter mile. Cassie let the mare continue along in her position. Half way around the turn I saw Cassie get lower on the mare's back and released her hold a little bit. The mare was suddenly third, then second and then first as they came into the stretch. I watched as Cassie shook her reins and got lower on the mare's back. The mare began her stretch run in earnest, her ears were laid back on her neck and she began to gather speed. When she and Cassie crossed the finish line I almost went to my knees. All the work and dreams had just come true. I was on the track before I knew it. Cassie jogged the mare back to where I stood waiting. The smile on her face said it all. The mare was going to be all right.

Spunky walked up as Cassie jumped off the mare and gave me a kiss. Spunky removed the overgirth and gave Cassie a leg back up on the mare. I led my first winner into the winner's circle. I was thrilled to see all my friends there to share the moment with me. After the photo was taken, I took the mare to the test barn and waited. When the folks in the test barn were finished, I led the mare back over to the barn where Spunky was beginning to get Light ready.

I bathed the mare and turned her over to a young man to walk dry. I went to Light's stall and began braiding his mane. Today would be the day he either became a super horse in the making or show us he wasn't what we all thought. As I braided his mane Spunky told me what Cassie had told him. She had let the mare run the race the way she wanted. When Cassie felt her wanting to go she had allowed her to move forward. The mare seemed to realize that Cassie wasn't going to hold her back and was suddenly full of run. Cassie then let her go and was shocked when the mare leveled out and began to run. Cassie had told Spunky that we'd better move her up in class because otherwise someone would claim her.

"What do you think, Spunky?"

"I think we'll run her for fifty next time and see where we are. From the race today to where she will be come spring is what will matter. She found out today what it is like to win and she likes it. She needs the break, too Bill. She's come a long ways in a short time. Your working her with horses she could run past has become a game with her. I think you made a good buy."

"What about the race today, Spunky?"

"What would you do, Bill? How would you have Light run?"

"I think I'd let Cassie set him back off the pace and blow by them in the stretch. The folks think he's nothing but a speed horse. Let's show them he's a race horse. They have two speed horses in today, they plan on burning him out in the first part of the race."

"That is exactly what we plan on doing. Cassie and I have talked and that is the way we have it planned. I told her to keep him out of trouble and not get trapped on the rail. She understands how the boys will try and box her in. She's smart Bill and will keep him out of trouble."

The call to the holding barn came over the barn speaker and I led Light over and walked him around. I scratched his ears and he relaxed until the call came for us to come to the saddling paddock. I knew he was ready to run and did my best to keep him relaxed. When we reached the saddling paddock I led him around the walking ring and noticed that people were pointing to him and talking about how well he looked. When Spunky called me over I led Light into his saddling stall where Spunky and the trackman put Cassie's saddle on Light and got him ready. When they had everything in place I led Light around the walking ring until I saw Cassie walk up to Spunky and the two of them talked and when they heard "Riders Up" they walked to where I held Light. Spunky gave Cassie a leg up on Light and I led them to the pony rider.

"Watch yourself Cassie. These boys are tired of you whipping their tail."

"I'll watch them Bill, See you where we usually meet."

CHAPTER 28

❀

"I waved to Spunky and walked out in front of the stands. Mike stood waiting. Here is your money, Bill. You and a few others knocked a home run on the mare. I don't know, but I'll bet you paid for the mare today."

I counted the money and when I was half way through I smiled. She was paid for, in full.

"What do you want on this race, Bill?"

I looked at the odds of three to five and shook my head.

"Put fifty to win on Light, Mike. The odds aren't that good and I really just want to watch this race and see what happens."

"I know what you mean. I've heard folks talking all day about how he'll never get the distance. What are they talking about, Bill?"

"They think he is a speed horse and can't run a mile and a sixteenth. Put your money on his nose, Mike. Then watch the folks around you when the race is over."

Mike went to make our bets while I watched the horses warm up. He was laughing when he came back out to where I stood.

"What is so funny, Mike?"

"I made our bets and a feller next to me laughed at me. Said I'd just thrown my money away. I told him to come back and see who was cashing their tickets."

The horses were loaded and the announcer said, "The horses were all in line". When the gates broke and the bell rang I saw the horses break and begin to run. Cassie and Gray Light broke in the middle of the pack and seemed to stall there. I watched as she slowly dropped back and seemed to lose ground going around the first turn. Then I saw what she was doing. The other jocks had boxed her in and she had simply backed out of the box. She was further back, but now had a clear view of the whole field in front of her.

I saw her drop a pair of goggles and settle down on Light and ran a steady pace around the turn and down the back stretch. Light's ears were twitching back and forth waiting for her to tell him to run. The two front running speed horses were done and began to come back to the field of horses behind them. At about the three quarter pole, just before they reached the far turn, Cassie took Light to the outside and went flying past the rest of the horses. You could hear people gasp as they saw the move she had made on the other horses. Light had looped the field and was now two lengths in front and had the rail. As they came out of the turn and headed for home. Cassie shook her reins and got down low on Light's back. His stride was like before, long and smooth and seemed to get faster with every stride. The crowd was going wild. Cassie guided Light up the stretch towards the finish line.

Once again, she had caught the other jocks napping and was flying home on the big gray horse with her stick still unused. She rode him home with a hand ride, while the other jocks were using their sticks urging their horses on, trying to win second and third place. Cassie had crossed the finish line six lengths in front. Now everyone, not only in the city but across the country, would know Gray Light was a real race horse.

I ran through the crowd and finally got out onto the track to catch Cassie when she came back. She was patting Light's neck and wiping dirt from her face at the same time. I saw the smile and knew exactly how she felt. I didn't know if anything would ever make me feel this great again. Spunky came out onto he track and the three of us were hugging and crying at the same time. We finally got Light ready for his picture and when I led him into the winner's circle I found it was almost full of friends. I managed a handshake with Sam and Jen got a second picture on Light with as she put it her big sis Cassie. When I got to the test barn Donna was waiting, a big smile on her face. I turned Light over to the test crew and visited with Donna. She and her family were doing well. Her kids loved their school and her husband was thrilled to be working again. She hadn't heard about Spunky and Patty selling half interest in Gray Light. She was thrilled they were going to get to go on with him and still be fixed for their retirement.

When the crew brought Light out of the test barn I took him, and with Donna walking with me, took him back to the barn and gave him his bath. Donna had him almost walked dry before the folks from the winner's circle walked into the barn. It was easy to know they had arrived, you could hear them coming from the parking lot. My mom and Patty both gave me kisses and I got handshakes from Sam, Ike, Sheriff Tom, Mike, and Lawyer Ed.

"Bill, he really did it today didn't he?"

"Yes, Sam. He did. He just became a very valuable horse. It will be fun to read the articles in the paper tomorrow."

"You'll bring a few back with you won't you Bill?"

"We'll be sure to bring an extra half dozen back with us Sam."

"Bill, I've got a boy who wants to learn how to ride. Will you have time to teach him?"

"Ed, you came to my rescue when I needed it. Send your son out and I'll teach him to ride."

I heard a cheer go up from outside the barn. People who kept horses in the barn were cheering for Spunky who had just made it back to the barn. When he walked into the barn he began to cry. Patty was holding him and crying at the same time. There was not a dry eye in the group.

Another cheer went up from outside the barn as Cassie arrived. She was all smiles as she walked into the barn. Everyone cheered her arrival and Spunky told her she had just ridden the finest race he had ever seen. Her ability to rate Gray Light would be talked about for years.

"Few people will ever know that our other kid taught him to rate like he does. Bill, you and Cassie are the greatest pair of kids I've ever seen. With out the two of you, none of this would have been possible. This year is something Patty and I will never forget." We may have lost our son in the war but our two adopted kids have helped us to heal. Patty and I can never thank the two of you enough.

I had no idea what to say.

"Mr. Davis, I too have lost a son in a war and lost my youngest when I had to leave. You took him in and made a fine young man of him. Don't worry about adopting him, I'll be more than glad to share him with you and your wife. In fact I'm honored that you've taken the time to help him. Mr. Cooper, I don't know how I will ever be able to thank you for all the things you've done for my son but if there is ever anything I can do for you I will be honored to do so."

"Mrs. Patton, your son was a man when I met him and all I did was help him a little and also to listen to some of his ideas. I owe him as much if not more than he will ever owe me. I know that Sam here feels the same way. His daughter was blind or nearly so and was a very unhappy little girl. Thanks to your son and Cassie, look at her now. She's always smiling and Sam has enjoyed the last few months more than he ever thought possible. Mrs. Patton, we're all sharing your son. So don't feel like you owe us a thing."

Spunky came over to mom and gave her a hug. Sam did the same thing.

"Now that everything is straightened out, let's all go eat. I'm starved."

Cassie had brought everything back to normal. Everyone had a good laugh. Donna said she would stay and keep an eye on Light until we got back. She said she felt like she owed something to him for getting her and her family to the city and to the life they now had.

Patty gave her a hug and we all went to eat at the same steakhouse we had gone to the last time we'd been here, except this time we were treated special. The owner had several bottles of wine sent over to the table. It seemed he had made a bet on Light and won. He was as thrilled as we were that Light had won. He asked if there was any way he could get a picture of Light to hang up in the steak house. Spunky told him there would be a win picture coming to him in a few days.

We finished our meal and went outside. Mike handed me the money I'd made on the race before he left with Sam and the rest of the boys. He was thrilled to have been a part of the celebration.

We went back to the barn and found Spunky had received four calls. One was from an official at Oaklawn Park. They wanted him to bring Light to their spring meet. One was from a National Sports Paper, they wanted to do an interview. The other two were people who wanted him to call them back. Both numbers were Kentucky numbers. It looked as if the big boys had got the word about the race.

Spunky had smiled and nodded at Patty.

"You were right dear, the offers are just starting to go up. Bill, it's going to be fun telling these folks I've already sold half of Light and that we may see them in May."

"Are you really planning on going to the Derby?"

"I've got a chance and why not take it. I've dreamed of it all my life so why not. Like I've heard you say, "You can't fail unless you try.""

"I hope you make it Spunky. I'd feel like I was there."

"You will be there Bill. If we're lucky enough to get that far you'll have to be there. I'll need someone to keep him calm and keep him happy. Just keep your fingers crossed and we'll see what happens at Oaklawn."

Cass and I took mom home and she called the boy next door and asked for a half dozen extra Sunday newspapers. He was thrilled to have the extra business and to discover his neighbor was the mother of one of the trainers of the famous horse Gray Light.

We visited for a long while then went to bed. I slept hard and when mom woke me it took me a moment to realize where I was. I'd really not slept much the night before we left home and it had caught up with me. I had a cup of coffee and ate breakfast. We all had a copy of the paper and read the write ups. Cassie had made an impression on the local newspaper writer. He took a completely different slant on things. Pointing out the number of wins she had posted the few times she had ridden at the track. We all had to laugh at the way he tried to make up for the way he had written before.

After breakfast mom and Cassie decided what we would have for Thanksgiving dinner. Cassie and I were to invite all of our friends to be there. When we left I was already looking forward to the dinner. I'd not had a Thanksgiving dinner since mom had left home. Cassie and I laughed and talked about the looks on the jocks faces when she and Light had blown by them at the head of the turn. She said some of them had cursed as she and Light went by. One of them came to her after the race and said she was a fantastic jock and her rides at the track had proved it. She told him it was easy to look good if you were riding horses like Light.

When we got back to the farm, Mike was waiting at the yard gate. Cassie gave him the paper we had got for him. He handed her a copy of the local paper which had a picture of her crossing the finish line on Light. The article, was great. It would make Cassie even more of a local celebrity. Cassie gave Mike a copy of the sports magazine we had gotten in the city. He was thrilled and said he just might frame the cover and hang it on the wall of his trailer.

Cassie and I put her things in her truck and she headed home. She told me she would be down Wednesday morning and do our shopping. She would be baking pies for the dinner. I asked if I could do anything to help and she told me to take care of the horses. She would take care of the household chores.

That night I watched the sports to see if there was another piece on Light and Cassie. It seemed there was another interview with Spunky who said Cassie had made a beautiful ride. When she had taken Light back and found room for him to run, it had shown just how smart she was. It was a great interview.

I went to bed and slept, I slept hard until the alarm went off the next morning. I went to the barn and looked at the colts and helped Mike and Carlo feed. I went to the house and got ready for school. Several of the kids at school spoke to me for the first time in years. I was becoming someone it was nice to know.

I'd never been invited to a party but got two invitations before I left school that morning.

I got to the house and went to the barn. Mike told me that the trial races for the quarter horses were held Saturday while we were gone. Of the top ten six of them were colts that had trained on our track. The boys were thrilled with the results and said they were going to continue coming here to get their colts ready. The finals were this coming Saturday and I told Mike we would go. I also told him and Carlo they were to have dinner with the rest of the family. They both said they would be there and felt honored to be there.

We went to work on the colts and were pleased with the way they were coming along. Sam's filly kept impressing me. I took her out onto the track and let her have a long slow gallop. There was something I couldn't put my finger on but would worry about it later. After the gallop I took her out to the pasture and had a nice ride.

When I got back to the barn, Mike and Carlo bathed her and Carlo walked her dry. Mike and I mucked the stalls and when Carlo had the filly cool we fed and watered the colts then turned the night light on and left the barn. Mike handed me the money for the morning works. I took the money and headed to the house. I needed to do my bookwork. I was three days behind.

Cassie drove down on Wednesday morning. I helped her carry sacks filled with food, bowls and such. When we had everything in the house we drove to the super market and bought two nice sized turkeys. She explained they would cook quicker and we would have plenty of turkey. We finished our shopping and stopped at Sam's place to pick up Jen. She was going to help Cass prepare the meal.

When the girls were settled at the house I went to the barn and went to work on the colts. I saddled all of the new colts in their stall and had eased up on them. I moved the colts around in their stall and was happy with their progress. The quarter horse people were helping me and didn't even know it. Their coming and going around the barn got the colts used to all kinds of things. The first few days they were a little skittish but had settled down and were not affected by any of the noise. I took Sam's filly out into the pasture and rode her near the new hay fields. Everything looked good as I rode by. The filly was becoming relaxed and looked forward to our daily rides across the pasture. I took her to the track and galloped her around the track among the other horses. She did well and didn't seem to mind the traffic at all.

"I had just put her away when I saw mom pull up and park at the house. I walked down and helped her and the girls carry everything into the house. The kitchen was covered with food. Jen was chattering like a magpie and having a great time. Cassie had her mixing a cake mix. She had brought her magnifying glass and had it hanging around her neck so she could see how everything was going.

I went outside and called Spunky. He and Patty were home and he told me everything was fine. Light, Slinker, my mare Plunder and the rest of the string were settled in and seemed to be enjoying their short vacation. He and Patty had given their exercise boy a few days off so he could go home to be with his family. He and Patty were going to have dinner at home and relax. He said they would call and visit with everyone the next afternoon. He was going to ship his colts to me on Saturday. One was a half brother to Light and he was rather anxious to see how the colt worked out. He had had several offers for him and was thinking about selling. He and Patty were more interested in their fillies. They could breed them to Light and have a market for their colts every year.

After talking to Spunky I went back to the barn and visited with Mike and Carlo. It was nice to be able to visit with the boys and be able to get their views on things going on here at the farm. Mike had told me we needed a box blade for the tractor. It would help get snow off the track later. We all knew it was just a matter of time before the snow would arrive. He and I got in the truck and went to the farm supply store and bought a good used box blade. Mike said he never bought new when he could buy good used equipment. We stopped at a café on the way back and picked up some burgers for us to eat when we got back to the barn. We had just finished eating when Sam and Ike pulled up to the barn.

"Hey Sam, what brings you out here this time of day?"

"Ike and I sent our crews home for the rest of the week and decided we'd come out here and see how Cassie was handling things."

"Fine, I guess. The women more or less told me to get out of the house."

"No, Bill. I mean how is she handling the folks who want her to advertise for them?"

"Sam, I have no idea what you're talking about."

"Bill, Ike and I just saw Cassie's dad down at the truck stop. He said the phone at their house was ringing off the wall. Folk's are wanting Cassie to do television commercials for them. She's going to make a bundle of money, Bill."

"Lets go down to the house and find out, as far as I know the girls and Mom have been cooking all morning."

When we walked in the back door mom pointed to the living room where Cassie sat on the couch writing on a pad.

"She's been on the phone for the last hour son, it seems everyone wants her to do commercials for them. Some she has already turned down but she is going to talk to some of the other folks. She said she might make enough from the work to buy you all a new horse trailer. Bill, I'm proud of her.'

Cassie got off the phone and walked into the kitchen. She took cups from the counter and poured us a cup of coffee.

"Cass, what's going on?"

"Bill, it seems the sport magazine has hit the stands and everyone wants me to speak at their meetings or do a television commercial. So far I've said I'd do a speaking engagement for underprivileged children, and television commercials for the company who built my truck. It seems they want to furnish me a new truck for the upcoming year. For free Bill, can you imagine?"

"Sure I can., They will put a special paint job on it and sell a lot more trucks. Do you like your truck?"

"I love my truck."

"Then do the commercial. You like their product and can be honest about it Cass."

"Bill's right Cassie. Take them up on the deal. Do whatever ads you want just as long as you're honest with yourself. Turn the ones down that you don't want to do."

"Thank you, Sam. It's been a little hectic around here this morning."

"I'll bet it has. I may even try to hire you myself."

"Sam, you can't hire family. I'll do your ad for free if you want me to but as far as I can see you have more work now than you can take care of."

"I wasn't talking about my construction business, Cassie. I'm thinking of when we stand Light."

"Sam, I'd be honored to do that. I might even have some ideas for the ad."

Sam, Ike and I went back to the barn and looked his filly over. I told him how well she was doing and how much I liked her.

"Sam, there is something about the filly that I don't understand. I don't know what it is and it's driving me crazy. I keep thinking I'll figure it out but so far I've not got a clue."

"You'll figure it out Bill. Just take your time."

Cassie came into the barn and wanted to know what it was I couldn't figure out. I explained to her what had been bothering me.

"Lets put a saddle on her Bill, she's far enough along that I can ride her. I'd like to take her around the track and see if I can figure out what's been bothering you."

I looked at Sam and went to get the bridle for the filly. She didn't have leg wraps on but Cassie wasn't going to work her. We put the exercise saddle on the filly and adjusted the stirrups for Cassie. Matt gave her a leg up on the filly and I led the two of them out onto the track. We watched as Cassie began jogging the filly around the track, after one full round she let the filly increase her speed but kept a tight hold on her. As she came past us I knew what it was about the filly I'd not been able to figure out. I watched as Cassie began to slow the filly down. She brought the filly back to the barn and smiled at me. She knew from the look on my face I had figured out what had been bothering me.

"You know don't you Bill?"

"I sure do Cassie, it was so obvious I just couldn't see what was right before my eyes."

"What are you two kids talking about?"

"Sam, I don't know how your filly is going to turn out but she moves exactly like Light."

"She does, Sam. She just seems to float over the ground. Most of the horses I ride I can feel them digging into the track. With Light it seems as if he floats across the ground. Your filly feels exactly the same way. I know now why Bill has been liking her so much."

"Good Lord, Bill. You don't think there a chance this filly could be another Light do you?"

"Sam, moving like and running like are two very different things. We're a long ways from being able to answer that question. All we can do now is bring her along slow and pray."

Later that evening when I went into the house for supper it smelled wonderful. Pies, cakes and things sat on the kitchen counters.

"Ladies, could I take you all out for a meal at the local Bar B Q joint?"

"That would be a wonderful idea, Bill. Your mom and I had just talked about that in fact. Give us ten minutes and we'll be ready."

CHAPTER 29

I fed Mom, Cass and Jen supper and laughed most of the time. Jen had had a wonderful day. She had made a salad her mother had taught her how to make shortly before their car wreck. She was calling Mom Grandma, and felt totally at ease. We dropped her off at home after we ate and went back to the house. Mom and Cassie each got a bath and settled in to relax for the evening. I caught my bookwork up and was pleased with the results. Cassie looked over my shoulder and whistled.

"Mom, you son is doing well. Extremely well I might add."

"Really, you mean the meal tomorrow won't break him?"

"I think he might even have enough money for us to buy whipping cream. Oh my gosh, that's what we forgot, whipping cream."

Needless to say a few minutes later I was at the super market just before they closed and got the last four bottles of whipping cream. My idea had been to buy some of the canned stuff but neither of he women would hear of it. They had to have the real thing. The girl at the check out counter was a classmate of mine and wished me a happy Thanksgiving.

I thanked her and told her I hoped she had the same.

When I got back to the house Cassie was on the phone again. It looked as if she was going to be a busy young lady for the next few months. Mom had put the cream away and we sat and visited while Cass finished her phone call.

"William, would you be upset if I began to date Tom?"

"Sheriff Tom?"

"Yes, William. Sheriff Tom."

"Mom. I think it would be great. He's a good man. He introduced me to Sam."

"I know. He's so thrilled about how everything has turned out."

"Mom, if he makes you happy then go for it. You deserve to have a good life."

"He is going to talk to you about it tomorrow, William. He's very nervous about it."

"Good, I'll make it hard for him."

"William!"

"Just kidding, Mom. But I still think I should make it tough on him."

That night I slept on our new couch and found it to be quite comfortable. I was up early and helped Mike with chores. We wouldn't have to worry about the quarter horse people this morning. Mike had hung a sign saying the track would be closed today. I would give the colts a day off. Tomorrow I'd have Mike pony me on the three new colts.

When I got back to the house I found Mom and Cass had both the turkeys in the oven and were fixing breakfast. I washed up and ate my breakfast. I had a bath and changed clothes. I had just walked into the kitchen when the phone rang. I answered the phone.

"Running P, this is Bill."

"Sorry to bother you at home Mr. Patton, but I figured it would be my best chance to catch you. I'm Ralph Pimberton, with Pimberton Farms in Lexington, Kentucky. I've been trying to get time to call you for a week now. I understand you were the one who helped Mr. Davis get the horse Gray Light straightened out earlier this year."

"Yes sir, I helped Mr. Davis with Gray Light. What can I do for you?"

"We understand you have a training center now, is that correct?"

"Yes, sir. I do."

"Would you be interested in taking some of our colts next year? We know you are booked up for this year."

"Sir, I'd be honored to have some of your colts but I can't give you an answer right now. If you'll give me your phone number I'll get back with you and let you later."

"That will be fine, Mr. Patton. I'll be looking forward to your call. Buy the way, the way Miss Morgan backed Gray Light out of the trap the other day was the most beautiful thing I've seen in years. How did you train him to rate like that?"

"A little time and love, sir, it does wonders."

"It most surely does Mr. Patton. I'll be looking forward to your call."

I told Cassie about the call and what the man wanted.

"Bill, that's one of the biggest farms in Kentucky. How in the world did they hear about us?"

"I have no idea, but he said you made the most beautiful ride he had seen in a long while."

"Oh, Lord. What next? What has happened to our simple little world?"

"I don't know, Cass. All I know is I'm going to enjoy the day and I'll sort things out later. I'll ask Spunky about this mess when he calls this afternoon."

Later that afternoon when everyone had shown up I told Sam about the call I had gotten from Mr. Pimberton. I told him I had no idea how he had heard of me or gotten my number.

"Maybe he talked to Spunky. He has your number and would give him all the information he needed. Besides, Bill. It is what you want, isn't it?"

"If you mean to train good horses, you bet. I just don't want to cut you or Spunky out."

"I'm not worried about that Bill. Talk to Spunky and see what his plans are. Don't get upset until there is something to get upset about."

Sheriff Tom finally caught me off to myself and struck up a conversation about the meal.

"Tom, you planning on dating my Mom?"

"You knew about us, didn't you?"

"Not until this afternoon. I don't mind at all. She deserves someone who will treat her right."

"Thanks, Bill. I didn't want to upset you."

"Have a good time, Tom. It's going to take some getting used to not calling you Sheriff."

Cassie's folks showed up. Her brothers were at different places with their girl friends. I shook hands with Art and got a hug from Helen, Cassie's mom.

We had our meal after Jen said the blessing. Everyone ate too much and later found a place to sit back and relax. Art told me Cassie's new truck would be ready next week. Just in time to consider it a Christmas present. She had not said anything to me as to when the truck would be ready but later that evening she told me she had to go film a commercial the next day in town. I was thrilled and told her so. She had borrowed Spunky's new silks to wear in the commercial. She told me they would make three one minute commercials. That way folks wouldn't get tired of just one.

I looked forward to seeing the commercials. Jen had one of the early editions of the sports magazine we had given Sam and wanted us to autograph it for her. Cassie signed it "To our little sister Jen, Cassie and Bill." Jen was thrilled to say the least. Spunky called and on the speaker phone wished everyone a happy holiday. He and Patty had gone to a friend's house for dinner and, as Spunky had put it, almost foundered themselves. He asked if I had gotten a call from Kentucky.

"I did and I have been wondering how the gentleman knew about me."

"He and some of his friends made an offer for Light and when I told them they were too late, we visited. Someone from the city had sent him a tape of the race. He couldn't believe how Cassie had backed Light out of the jam and then wiped the field out. I told him how you had taken him as a rogue colt and made him a pussy cat for Cassie to ride. He wanted to know if you would take any outside colts. I told him you had a new training center and he would have to talk to you. Bill, Patty and I have talked it over and this next year may be the last year we travel and train. Everything after this year would be down hill, if you know what I mean."

"Don't make any hasty decisions Spunky. We may have a surprise for you to play with after Light."

"You sure of that Bill?"

"I'll know for sure after the first of the year Spunky but Cassie and I think so."

"Patty and I might reconsider if we ran at the city. It's close to home and I love the track. Which colt are we talking about?"

"Sam's filly, Spunky. She moves just like Light. She has the stride and gathers herself so quickly it scares me."

"Go slow with her Bill, if she has those qualities we sure don't want to get her crippled. Sam, what do you think of our boy now?"

"Spunky, I don't know what to think. He just keeps growing every day and we just set back and watch. We're having a ball, Spunky."

"By dang that's the way it's supposed to be. Cassie, how's my favorite jockey?"

"I'm fine Spunky. Bill keeps finding these horses like Light and keeps me fired up."

"He can do that Cassie. When are you kids going to tie the knot?"

"May seventeenth, Spunky. Are you and Patty going to make it?"

"That's after the Derby isn't it?"

"Oh yes. I have a date with my favorite horse the first Saturday in May."

"We'll be looking forward to giving you a leg up girl. Now you folks get back to your deserts. Patty's fixing me a piece of pecan pie with whipped cream on top."

We all told them good bye and did go to get more pie or cake. Later everyone went home except Tom, Mom and Cassie. I told Mom it was the best Thanksgiving I'd ever had.

Later I walked Cassie out to her truck and kissed her goodbye. I watched as she went down the drive and turned north. After May seventeenth she wouldn't have to drive home, she would be home.

CHAPTER 30

The next morning after the quarter horse works, Mike and I went to work on the three new colts. We saddled them and took them one at a time out onto the track with the pony horse. After a round on the track I mounted the colts and rode them around the track a couple of turns. By the time we had made the second round I was able to turn them right or left as we moved along. We were pleased with their works and when Carlo had things lined out we got Sam's filly out and after wrapping her legs I took her out onto the track and began to let her work. The filly was ready to work after her day off and I had to keep a tight hold on her. I didn't want to let her go any faster than she was ready to go. We went two and a half rounds of the track and she settled down about half way through the second round. I was talking to her and by the time we finished she was beginning to listen to me.

When I rode her off the track she wanted to turn to the pasture. She wanted to see some things. I turned her head and we went to the pasture for a good three mile ride. When I rode her into the barn Mike was shaking his head.

"Bill, you told Spunky the truth. This young lady may just be the next Gray Light. The other colts are good horses but none of them move like this girl. I get goose bumps just watching her."

"You should be on her and feel the fluid power she has and she's not near in shape to run yet. You can feel every muscle move as she gathers more ground. I can't wait until Cassie rides her the next time, but first I've got to get her to listen to me.

Cassie stopped by that afternoon late and told us all about the commercials. She was impressed with all the things that had to be done for a one minute television spot. Later she asked me about the filly.

"You can work her again in two weeks Cass, right now we're working on getting her to listen. She wants to run but she's not ready yet. She's getting in shape though."

I told her about the filly wanting to go to the pasture and ride the trails down along the creek.

"She doesn't get tired Cass, she just seems to be able to go and not get tired. That is why I want to work her and get her to listen. If I can get her to relax and listen we may just be able to hand you another Light."

"When are you going to show her to Spunky?"

"Not for a couple of months, I want her to be ready for a full out work for a quarter mile. I'll watch her works and let you know when she is ready for you to take over the works."

"Let me know when you think she's ready Bill. I don't want anything happening to her because we got in a hurry."

"I know what you mean. The other colts are coming along fine. I'll have them galloping this time next week. If the weather holds we'll have them going well by the end of January."

The next couple of weeks seemed to fly by. Sheriff Tom had gone to Oklahoma City one weekend to see my mother and I found out they had been talking on their cell phones for almost two months. He stopped by late one afternoon and after stumbling around asked if he had my blessing to marry my Mom.

"Have you asked her yet?"

"I'm going to ask her tonight if you don't mind."

"I just wish you luck Tom. Would you all live out here?"

"Well, we have talked about it and she seems to think that is the logical thing to do."

"Then go for it Tom. Let me know what she says."

Later that evening Tom called. Mom had said yes. They wanted to know if they could get married here at the house Christmas Eve. I'd told him "sure, everyone would be here anyway". Their wedding would make it a special Christmas. I called Cassie and told her we were going to have the law on our side in the event we needed it. She was thrilled and told me to watch the news tomorrow evening. The commercials were going to start running then. I told her I'd watch and said goodnight.

The next evening we had everything done and were sitting in front of my television when the six o clock news came on. We all cheered when the commercial with Cassie came on. It started with a short clip of her driving her truck out of her drive way and then showed her riding Light in the last big race at the city. She said she always rode a winner, to and at the track.

The phone rang.

"Did I look stupid Bill?"

"You did great Cassie. Mike, Carlo and I all thought so."

"I'll know tomorrow when I get to school."

"Relax Cassie, it was great. By the way, do you have any ideas about what we should do for Mom and Tom's wedding?"

"I'm working on it Bill. Mom and I are going to come down two days before Christmas and clean everything. We want the house to be perfect for the big day."

"Cassie, the house is clean, or at least I think so."

"Bill, I know the house is in good shape, but Mom and I want to give it a good going over. Now, don't get upset. Just do what you do best. Get the filly ready for me to ride. I can hardly wait until you give me the go ahead."

"I'm working on it Cassie. She's starting to come around. Another two or three weeks and she should be ready."

The time seemed to fly by. The filly continued to train wonderfully and when she was ready I found I hated to give up the works. It was such a thrill to feel the filly work around the track with her long fluid motion. I told Mike she was ready and that I'd let Cassie work her Christmas Eve morning. I couldn't think of a better Christmas present. I had bought Cassie and Jen matching turtle neck sweaters. They were good heavy weight sweaters they could wear when they had their riding lessons.

I'd given Mike and Carlo bonus checks and told them to get what they wanted. Mike had bought himself a new set of insulated coveralls. Carlo thought it was a good idea and had done the same. The cold mornings would not be so bad to take now. I had gone to the local jeweler and asked him to make Sam a money clip with Cooper Racing Stables put on it in gold. I'd thought and thought but didn't have a clue as to what to get Ike or Spunky and Patty. Cassie came to my rescue.

It seemed she had gone to a store in town and ordered jackets for Sam, Jen, Ike and his wife, Mike, Carlo and one for each of us as well. They were black and gray with the Running P emblem on the back. They were really neat jackets.

In the early afternoon the day before Christmas eve Cassie and her mom arrived to clean the house and get things ready for the following afternoon. My mother was at Tom's place getting their things together. She had quit her job in the city and sold her home there. She and Tom would live in his home. I stayed out of the way of Cassie and her mom and left them to do whatever it was they wanted to do in the house.

That evening they had a good supper ready for me and the boys. I asked Cassie if she could come down early tomorrow morning. She told me she could be here by six thirty and I told her it would be fine. The boys and I would have things ready.

"The next morning the boys and I got the filly ready. I braided the filly's mane and worked in the bright colored ribbons Carlo had brought with him. We put new red track wraps on the filly while Mike worked the track. It was barely daylight when Mike finished harrowing the track and said it was ready. We set the saddle on the filly and had her ready to go when we saw Cassie's truck turn up the driveway. I had Carlo wave for her to come up to the barn.

Cassie drove up to the barn and jumped out of her truck.

"Bill, what's wrong?"

"Nothing Cassie. In fact, everything is fine now that you're here. The boys and I have a little present for you."

Carlo led the filly out of her stall so Cassie could see her in her Christmas outfit.

"Get your jock boots on Cassie. I think it time you and the young lady get acquainted."

"Oh, my Lord. Cassie ran out to her truck and quickly put her riding boots on. Carlo held the filly while I gave her a leg up on the filly. Mike waited for her to get her feet set then led her and the filly out onto the track. I'd told her to give the filly a half mile work but not to let her get down and really run.

Carlo and I watched from the rail, as Mike took Cassie and the filly around the track. The filly wanted to work and I could tell that Cassie was talking to her by the way the filly was flipping her ears back and forth. As they came around he track I saw Mike take the lead shank loose and turn the filly over to Cassie.

Cassie eased the filly down close to the rail and eased off on her hold. The filly began to work in earnest. Cassie had a hold on the filly and had the filly under control as she passed us and went down the back stretch. I pressed the stopwatch as Cassie reached the quarter pole and began to let the filly go to work. Cassie lowered herself on the filly's back and released more of her hold on the filly. The filly seemed to shoot forward and went around the large turn getting faster with each stride. She seemed to be floating on top of the ground. Cassie brought her up the stretch and after crossing the finish line stood up in her irons and began slowing the filly down. I was thrilled to see the filly relax and slow down. My work with her was working. I watched as Cassie pulled her up and turned her around. The filly walked back to where we stood by the rail watching.

"Bill, she's wonderful. She feels exactly like Light did at this stage of his training. She has the same fluid move and feels as if she could fly if I had asked her. What was the work time?"

I showed her the watch, and saw the smile I knew would appear.

"She's really that good, isn't she, Bill?"

"Looks that way Cass. She just worked two fifths of a second faster on this training track than Light did on the track at Raton. Cassie, how are we going to keep this quiet from Spunky until I really have her ready?"

"Bill, there are only four people who know what she can do and we're all here. None of us are going to tell anyone about the work today."

"Bill, Carlo and I sure aren't going to say anything. We'll want to make a bet on her this coming spring at the track. Besides it will be way too much fun to see the look on Spunky's face when he gets a chance to see this young lady work."

"Then let's get this young lady to the barn and get taken care of. We've got Christmas dinner and a wedding to look forward to."

CHAPTER 31

Cassie put the turkey in the oven and then began to finish decorating the house. We put the presents under the tree and stepped back to see how things looked. It was fine as far as I was concerned. The tree was beautiful with the blinking multi colored lights. It was the first tree I'd had since Mom had left. It was a first for Cassie and I but I hoped there would be many more.

Cassie's folks showed up a couple of hours later. It took Art and I three trips to carry everything into the house. Her brothers would be down later. They were busy working on something special as Art had put it. Sam and Jen showed up shortly after we had finished chores. Cass and I told Sam about the work. His mouth flew open after I showed him the watch I had set on the counter top.

"Bill, she's really that good."

"She's that good, Sam. She's still forty five days away from a real work but I can tell you she has impressed me the same way Light did."

"Will Spunky take her with him Bill?"

"I don't know, Sam. We'll just wait and see. I'm just the feller who starts them and gets them ready."

"Some folks may believe that, Bill but not me. Spunky has told me you'd make a fantastic trainer if you ever decide to do that. He understands how you feel and told me that you will be very successful with the center because you are a hands on person. Bill, Spunky respects your abilities and you as a person. He knows you could have quit him and gone to work for other trainers last year but you turned them down. Add to that he and Patty have adopted you should tell you something."

"It does, Sam. Spunky is the father I feel I never had. Sort of like you. You're not the only big brother I ever had but that's how I feel about you."

"I'm honored you feel that way, Bill. Jen has adopted you and Cass and is so happy. I've learned to back up so to speak and look at things from a different perspective. I know that I have friends who don't care if I have a dime or a dollar. I've watched Ike take over the everyday problems at work and he has let me relax and see things differently. I can come out here to the barn and talk to Mike and Carlo and see things in a different way. They work hard but it's because they enjoy what they are doing. They treat me no different than they would treat anyone else who comes out here. Ike told me the other day that I had become almost human. You know, Bill. That was a compliment."

Mike and Carlo showed up at the back door carrying gifts. They each had a gift for Jen and were smiling as they put the things under the tree. Cassie's two brothers showed up and began unloading some sort of furniture. It turned out to be a new bed and dresser they had made in their grandfather's shop for Cassie and my bedroom. Cassie and I both were both caught by surprise. She gave each of her brothers a hug and a kiss. I shook their hands and went with them to tear down my bed and put the new on in its place. We had just came out of the bedroom when Mom and Tom drove up.

Everyone welcomed them and was thrilled for them. The preacher arrived a short time later and married them. Cassie and I had stood up with them and signed their license. I paid the preacher who wished us a Merry Christmas and went home to his family. We had turkey, ham and quail along with the usual side dishes. When everyone was finished we found places to sit and Cassie began to hand out presents.

Cassie got the packages out and handed them to everyone. When Jen got her sweater that matched Cassie's she was thrilled. They could wear their sweaters and coats at the same time and really look like sisters. Sam's money clip thrilled him, he kept it in his hands and kept looking at it all evening. Ike and his wife were thrilled with their jackets. His wife said all of her friends would just flip when they saw her wearing it. Mike and Carlo kept their jackets in their laps after they had tried them on. Carlo was thrilled that he was included in the holidays here at the farm. He told Mike he would not have had anywhere to go if he hadn't been invited.

Sam had handed Sheriff (step dad) Tom an envelope. Tom had opened it and had a strange look on his face. Sam, this is too much. He handed the envelope to me, inside were two round trip tickets to Las Vegas. Room reservations for three nights and two days. The tickets were for tomorrow afternoon.

"Tom, you and your wife go have a good time. See the lights and take in a show. I've been planning this for a while. I saw the way you two looked at each other over at the meeting that day and figured it was just a matter of time."

We were all visiting when we heard Mom scream! We rushed into the kitchen to find Jen laying on the floor unconscious.

"Cassie, call 911 quick!"

I checked Jen's pulse and found it steady, then asked Mom what had happened.

"We were cutting pie and cake for everyone and she suddenly grabbed her head and fell to the floor. I don't know what happened."

We heard the ambulance coming from town, I ran outside to show them where to park. The ambulance people came into the house and hooked things to Jen and then we watched as they loaded her into the back of the ambulance. Sam was going to ride to the hospital with her. I told Mike to lock things up when we left and ran out to my truck where Cassie waited. We headed to the hospital along with everyone else.

When we reached the hospital we found Sam, Ike and his wife sitting in the waiting room. Cassie's brothers and folks had come but the waiting room had been too small to hold all of us. They went back to the house to put things away and then go home. They told Cassie to call and let them know when she found out anything. They had Jen in the emergency room and as of yet they didn't know anything. They had a new young doctor working on her.

The waiting was the worst thing I had ever experienced. The not knowing what was wrong was the worst. Cassie sat next to me holding my hand. She was as scared as I was. It was Sam that I was worried about. Jen was his whole world. I had never felt so helpless in my life.

We sat in the waiting room for over two hours when finally the doctor came into the room and asked to speak to Sam. They talked for a moment and then Sam came back into the room.

"They are taking her up to do more tests. They have called in a new doctor who wants these tests done when he gets here. He's new but I was told he is very good at his sort of thing. They said it might be hours before they knew anything. You folks can go home. This looks like it could be a long night."

"Sam, the wife can go and take care of the kids. I'll hang around here."

"Ike, go home and be with your family. I'm going to be leaning on you more than ever now. You'll have to look after everything until this mess is straightened out. Please Ike, go be with your family. I promise you I'll let you know if anything happens."

Ike and his wife left to go get their children from one of the grand parents, home.

"Tom, you and your bride might as well go as well. It's your wedding night and there is nothing you can do here. Bill and Cassie are here and I'm going to send them home in a little while."

Tom and Mom left a short time later.

I went outside and called Spunky and Patty. I told them where we were and why we hadn't called sooner.

"Bill, you and Cassie stay with him. You need anything you let me know. We can be there in about three hours or less."

"Spunky, one of us will be here with him until we find out something. I'll let you know what is going on as soon as we know something."

I went back into the waiting room and found the doctor talking to Sam and Cassie. He was wanting Sam's permission to operate on Jen. I listened to his explanation of Jen's problem. He said they had found or thought they had found something pressing on the optic nerve in Jen's head. From the location he couldn't be positive but he felt sure that whatever it was, it was what had caused Jen to pass out.

Sam signed the release form and told him to get started. He told Sam they would have to wait until five the next morning because Jen had had a full meal only a few hours before. They would move her up to the intensive care unit and get her prepped for the surgery the next morning. He explained to Sam that she was stable and not in any danger. He told us we could follow him up to the waiting room and he would tell us when they had her moved and settled into her new room.

"Besides, Mr. Cooper, I'd like to get a good night's rest before the surgery. I do have one question, though. How long has your daughter been blind?"

"Two a half years doctor. Ever since the car accident. Her mother was killed in the accident."

"That could explain what I've been thinking ever since I looked over her test and x-rays. Her passing out and falling to the floor may have been a blessing. It may have dislodged the bone fragment just enough for us to find it. I'm not promising anything but if we can get it out, you daughter may regain her sight."

"Why didn't the other doctors find it? I've had her to every specialist I could find over these last two years."

"Maybe because of the location of the fragment. Like I said, we may have gotten lucky."

"Doctor, go home and get some rest. I want you fresh as a daisy tomorrow morning."

After the doctor left we sat and waited until a nurse came in and told Sam which room Jen was in. He could go see her if he wanted but she had been given a sleeping pill and was resting.

"Kids, you might as well go home. I'm going to check on Jen and go home myself. I might even get a nights rest after hearing what the doctor had to say."

"Sam, call Ike and let him know what is going on."

"I'll do that Bill, thanks for reminding me."

"We'll see you in the morning Sam. If you need anything we'll be at the house."

"I'll get in touch with you. Now get out of here and get some rest."

CHAPTER 32

Cassie and I drove back out to the farm. She went to call her folks while I told Mike we would be gone to the hospital the next morning and filled him in on what the doctor had told us. He told me he'd say a prayer for Jen and to not worry about things here at the farm. He and Carlo would look after things until I got back.

I went to the house and sat down. Suddenly I was hungry. I was making a ham sandwich when Cassie came out of the bathroom and saw me.

"I'll bet you're making that for me."

"It's yours if you want it. I don't know why but I'm starved."

"I know what you mean, Bill. We had a big meal, but I'm starved too. I think the stress and nerves burned up everything we ate."

"We each had a sandwich and a piece of pie. My alarm was set for four thirty so when we went to bed I didn't have to reset it. When it went off the next morning I had everything laid out and was dressed and ready to go in a few moments. Cassie and I had talked the night before and planned on taking a few sausage and biscuits to the hospital with us. We figured Sam would not remember to eat and we could be sure he did. Cassie came out of her room and pitched me my new Running P jacket. We were going to wear them.

We stopped and picked up a dozen sausage biscuits and went on to the hospital. Sam was sitting in the waiting room when we got there. Ike was there too. When we walked in Cassie asked if either of the men had eaten and each shook his head no. They each had coffee so Cassie handed each of them a couple of biscuits. They seemed to have no trouble eating them.

Sam told us they had taken Jen up just before we arrived. Now all we could do was wait and pray. Cass and I tried to keep everything light and positive.

Sam was nervous and had the money clip I had given him and was still rolling it in his fingers. Ike had to leave and go check on the various jobs the company had going. We promised we'd call him the minute we found anything out. The waiting was the hardest thing I'd ever done in my life. Jen may have adopted Cassie and I but we'd done the same with her.

Shortly after one that afternoon the doctor came into the waiting room with a smile on his face. I breathed a sigh of relief.

"Mr. Cooper, everything went fine. Your daughter will be back in her room in another hour or so. She'll be out most of the day and night. We don't want her moving much for the first twelve hours. We managed to remove the fragment and relieve the pressure on her optic nerve. I'm thinking her sight will return, not completely at first but will get better with time."

"Doctor, what can I ever do to repay you?"

"Tell me when this young lady is going to ride again and get me one of those jackets. I'd be the envy of all of the young doctors and nurses in the operating room. We're all fans of yours, Miss Morgan."

"Doctor, Give me your first and last name and you'll have your jacket. How many folks helped with the operation?"

"There were six including the nurses, why?"

"Get me their names, they will all get jackets. My little sister is very important to me."

"But Miss Morgan I didn't mean for you…."

"Doctor, hush! You have to understand. My daughter and Cassie are sisters in every sense of the word. Cassie had taught her to ride and Bill, her big brother bought, her a very special horse. We're a family doctor and we appreciate your help."

"Cassie will you all wait here until I call Ike and some other folks?"

"Go make your calls, Sam. We'll be here."

Cassie and I sat and waited. An hour or so later the doctor came back and told Sam everything with Jen looked fine."

"She's going to sleep the rest of the day and will be awake in the morning."

"You folks might as well go home and get some rest. We won't know anything for a day or so but if there are any problems we'll call. Please go get some rest, I don't need any more patients right now."

"Thank you, doctor. We'll go get something to eat then get some rest. Bill, you need to work the colts. Lets go get them worked and then we'll go get something to eat."

We left the hospital and went out to the farm. We worked the colts and after putting them up we went to eat. Cassie had called Patty and told her what was going on while Mike and I had saddled the colts. With Cassie riding a colt with me we finished in half the time and were more than ready to eat.

Sam called the hospital and found that Jen was resting and was doing fine. The doctor had checked her just a few moments before when he had gone home for the day.

"Kids, I'm liking that doctor more all the time. Cassie we've got time, lets get those jackets ordered."

"We stopped at the small sports supply shop and ordered the jackets. The folks there had just gotten a new stock of jackets in and said they would be ready the next evening. Sam asked what it would cost to get them ready by the next morning. The young man looked at Sam and then went to the back of the store. An older women came to the counter and asked if Sam really wanted the jackets the next morning.

"Yes ma'am, I'm willing to pay what ever to get them done. Do you think they can be done?"

"We will have them ready, sir. My girls will be more than glad to get the overtime. They will be ready by eight in the morning."

Sam reached in his jacket pocket and took out a roll of bills. He paid the lady and added a little something extra.

"Your girls will need something to eat if they are going to work late."

"Thank you sir. They will appreciate that. Excuse me, but aren't you the young lady I see on television?"

"Yes ma'am, the jackets are for the doctor and staff who have worked on my little sister at the hospital."

"We'll have the jackets ready by eight. You all are becoming one of our best customers, besides if you all wear our jackets a lot of other folks are going to want to wear them."

"We drove to a small café that Sam knew about and had a great chicken fried steak dinner. Kids, I've not felt this way in almost three years. If the doctor is right about Jen's eyesight my life is going to get to be a lot better.

"You're going to spend a lot more money Sam. Your daughter is going to cost you dearly. You're going to have to get a trailer because she owns one of the best little barrel horses in the country. She is going to want to go and compete."

"Bill, I'll be thrilled to take her."

Sam took Cassie and me back to the house where we had coffee and cake. We each got a bath and made what calls we needed to make. Sam had called my new stepfather and told him and mom to take the plane to Vegas. He told Tom what the doctor had said and wanted them to go on and have their honeymoon. Tom had tried to argue but lost out.

Cassie and I relaxed and sat on the couch and watched some television. Her folks had called and gotten an update on how Jen was doing. Cass had called them earlier in the day and told them what was going on after the surgery. Art had asked how Sam was holding up and was thrilled to hear we'd gone to eat with him.

Later I got a call from the gentleman in Colorado and gave him a report on how his colts were progressing. He was thrilled to hear I was riding them on the track and about my opinion of each. He had been worried about the stud colt because his half brother had been a tough sort of horse and was just now starting to gallop on the training track at their ranch. He said snow was hampering them in their day to day operation.

Once again I srt the alarm and Cassie and I went to bed. I was up before daylight and helped Mike and Carlo with chores. When I went back to the house Cassie had breakfast ready for me to eat.

"You know I could get used to having you around like this."

"I know what you mean. I've got everything located in the drawers where I want them. When we're married it won't be any adjustment at all for me. You've let me pick out the furniture and it's sort of like my home already. Bill, I really feel comfortable here."

"Good, it's important to me that you do. It's not a new home but its comfortable now that you're here."

I got a kiss on the cheek and ate my breakfast. We drove to the hospital and checked on Jen's progress. Sam was talking to Ike when we walked in. The doctor was in with Jen and would be out with his report in a few moments.

I noticed that Sam had a large box sitting next to his chair. The jackets were done and ready to be delivered. Thirty minutes later the doctor walked into the waiting room and told Sam that everything looked fine. The patient was unhappy about all the bandages but was thrilled to hear she might regain her sight. She had asked where her father, sister and brother were. When the doctor told her they were in the waiting room she seemed to be happy.

"Mr. Cooper, you may go in and visit with her for a short while if you'd like. Just don't stay too long, we don't want to tire her out."

"Cass, would you and Bill take care of the things in the box for me. I'm going to see our girl."

I sat the box out for Cass who opened it up and found the jacket with the doctor's name on it. He tried the jacket on and was thrilled.

"Wait until the rest of my crew see this, they will have a fit."

"No they won't doctor. Take these to the rest of your crew. Mr. Cooper had them made special for all of you."

"Oh my lord, I'll take them to my crew right now. Tell Mr. Cooper I said thanks."

A short while later Sam came back and told Cassie that Jen wanted to talk to her.

Cassie went down to Jen's room. Sam sat down and sighed.

"She's feeling pretty good. She said she has a head ache but her main complaint is they won't give her something to eat yet."

"She'll be fine, Sam. Like I've said she's tough."

"I know Bill, I just want her to be able to see. Not twenty twenty, but well enough to lead a normal life."

"Sam, look at it this way. Day before yesterday you didn't know if you had a chance, now you do."

"You're right Bill, I should be thankful. If that what ever it was had moved the wrong way my girl may have died."

Cassie came back down the hall laughing.

"I have my instructions. I'm to give Coalie his apples and most important. "I'm supposed to bring her a hamburger. They brought her some food while I was there and I fed her. She was not impressed. I really couldn't blame her it didn't look that good at all."

"Cassie, do whatever you want. I'll back you to the hilt."

"Bill, she had instructions for you, too. She wants you to ride Coalie and keep him in shape. She said if this operation works she plans on doing a lot more riding. She wants to be a jockey, Sam. I'm trying to talk her out of that idea. It works for me but then I'm a little different."

"Cassie, I'll back her in anything she wants but I'll try and keep her in line. One of the nurses said they would probably move her down stairs late this evening or early tomorrow. I'm waiting to see what the doctor has to say about when the bandages can come off. You kids might as well go home and do what you have to do. I'll call you as soon as I hear anything."

Cass and I went back to the house. She got some things and took off for her folks' home. She had some errands to run and needed to get some fresh clothes. I worked the colts and Sam's filly. Spunky called and said he was shipping his colts on Monday. I was just off the phone from him when Mike reminded me the finals for the Quarter Horse folks were tomorrow afternoon.

"What time should we leave, Mike?"

"I think we should leave about noon Bill."

"I'll call Cassie and let he know, she may want to bring some extra clothes. Do you think Carlo will want to go?"

"I'm not sure Bill. He has a lady friend and may not. I'll check and see what he wants to do."

I called Cassie on my cell phone on the way back to the house and reminded her about the trials. She was glad I had called. She would load her snuggy underwear as she called them. It would be cool out at the track. She said she would be back in an hour or so and we'd have to stop and get Jen a hamburger.

I told her to be careful and I'd see her in a little while. I had to catch up on my book work. I figured we'd call Tom and Mom tonight and see if they were having a good time.

I went to work on my books and finally got them up to date. I was pleased with my balance and remembered when I had been worried about having enough money to buy feed and hay for the winter. Thanks to Mike, I'd done well and with the outside horses I was doing even better. The center was doing well, and with Spunky's colts coming it was only going to get better. If I decided to stay home and run it after this next spring I had some ideas that I thought would even bring in more money. I'd talk to Cassie about them tonight and see what she thought.

Cassie arrived a short time later with a cake her mom had sent down for us to take to Jen when she was able to have it. Cassie had stopped at a store and bought a plastic box to put a piece of cake in. It was small enough to fit into her jacket pocket. She had another for the hamburger we had to buy. We stopped on the way to the hospital and got the cheeseburger. Cassie put the burger into the plastic container and put it in her other pocket.

"Bill, I feel like a smuggler."

"We both laughed as we walked into the hospital door. We were told Jen had been moved out of the intensive care unit and had a private room. We went to her floor and found Sam sitting with a lady wearing one of the jackets he had bought. He told us Jen was awake and wanted to see Cassie as soon as she arrived. Cassie went down the hall and into Jen's room. The nurse was one of the team who had worked on Jen. She explained to Sam that the new doctor was one of the best she had ever seen. She said she really expected Jen to make a full recovery.

Sam was elated. He was crying and I didn't blame him. After a moment he thanked the nurse and asked me about his filly.

"You own horses Mr. Cooper?"

"Yes I do, why."

"Oh I'm just surprised, I thought you only were involved with your construction business. I know who Mr. Patton is, a good friend of mine works for him."

"Excuse me ma'am but who is your friend?"

"Mike Sloan, he's been a friend of mine for years. He used to live next door to my folks for years until his wife died. He used to help me with my barrel racing horses. He was like a second father to me when I was growing up."

"Good Lord, Bill. Who would have thought we'd have a friend of Mike's working on my girl?"

"I doubt he even knows, Mr. Cooper. I've not really got to talk to Mike in a while."

"Well I'll sure enough tell him tomorrow. Brenda is it?"

"Sam, we'll be at the Quarter Horse races tomorrow. There are five of the colts that trained out at our track in the finals and Mike suggested we go to the finals. Cassie, Mike and I are going to the finals right after lunch tomorrow. We'll tell Mike about Brenda here helping fix Jen. I'm sure he will be thrilled."

"Tell him I'd love to come out and see the center sometime."

"Brenda, you are welcome to come out anytime. I'm sure Mike will be glad to see you. By the way we will be glad, too."

Brenda said she had to get to work and said goodbye. Sam and I were visiting when Cass came back into the room.

"Bill, Jen wants to talk to you,"

"How did the cheeseburger go?"

"What cheeseburger?"

"The one Bill and I smuggled into our little sister's room a short time ago, Sam."

"What am I going to do with you two?"

"Nothing Sam, she'd do the same for us."

I knew Jen's room number and walked down the hall. I had not seen her and was glad she could not see the shock on my face when I saw her for the first time.

"Hey Jen, did the care package work for you?"

"It sure did Bill and it was delicious. You and Cass are the best. I need you to do me a favor."

"Name it Jen. Tell me what you want?"

A young nurse came into the room to take Jen's blood pressure and temperature.

"Sir, you'll have to leave. Only family members are allowed in here."

"Hey wait a minute, Bill is my big brother. You can't run him out."

"Oh, I'm sorry I didn't know you had a big brother."

"I have a big brother and sister."

As soon as the nurse left I looked at Cassie and smiled.

"So I told a little fib. I needed to talk to you and you are my brother anyway. Now about that favor. Take dad to the trials tomorrow. He needs a break and until all these bandages come off day after tomorrow there is nothing he can do here. Besides, he makes me feel like he's walking on eggs. Bill, I know this may not fix my eyes but at least we can hope. Dad's worried about me and needs to take a break. Please, get him to go with you."

"I'll do my best Jen but you know your dad. Folks just don't lead him around."

"I know Bill, but do your best. Please.

I promised Jen I would try and left her room. I didn't have a clue on how to get Sam to go with us but I'd give it my best shot.

Sam and Cassie were sitting and talking when I got back. It seemed I was not the only one Jen had talked to. Cass was trying to get Sam to go with us to the races.

"Sam why don't you come along, Jen said she wished you'd go. She said we'd not know anything for a day or so anyway.

"She said for me to go Bill?"

"Yes, Sam. She did. She can't see or do anything and she said you needed to take a break. I have to agree with her Sam. The folks here all say she's doing great."

"Alright, I'll go. What time are you all leaving?"

"We figured to leave about noon Sam. It should be a good race."

"I'll be at your place at noon. Maybe I do need to get away for an afternoon. Besides, I've never seen a Quarter Horse race."

"That makes us even, Sam. I haven't either."

"Good then I'll not feel bad. What's on tomorrow nights menu for our girl, Cassie?"

"Meatloaf and scalloped potatoes Sam. Want to come out later and eat?"

"Sam, she makes a killer meatloaf."

"You bet I'll come. It's been a long time since I've had a good meatloaf dinner. If my daughter can con you into making her a meatloaf dinner the least I can do is come and eat it."

CHAPTER 33

Cassie, Mike and I were waiting on Sam when he drove up to the house a couple of hours later. I noticed he had a ball cap on with the lettering on it saying Running P Training center.

"Neat cap, Sam. I guess I'll have to have some made like it."

"No you won't, Bill. There's a box in the back of my truck full of them. You all get one. We'll give the others to the boys who train out at the track. Matt, you know who they are so you will be in charge of handing them out. Folks will take and wear a ball cap for a long while. They are great advertising gimmicks, Bill. Besides it will let the boys know you appreciate their business."

We each got a cap and rolled the brim to suit us. Cassie put her pony tale through the back of hers and settled it in place. She looked neat in her heavy turtle neck sweater and her Running P jacket and cap.

"Cassie, you look like a cute little billboard."

"It's business, Mr. Patton, and I'm sure not ashamed to be a part of the Running P Training Center. Just wait until Mike starts handing out the caps, you'll see them all over everywhere."

"She's right Bill, we'll get a million dollars worth of advertising out of these caps. We won't have near enough but these will do for now.

"Lets hit the road, folks. I want to watch some horses run."

"You heard the man Bill. Lets get rolling. I want to check out the young jocks. We may be needing help and I'd like to know what sort of talent we have in the area. Besides you're going to need an exercise rider soon. You're to heavy to be working the colts in their long works every day. I can do the speed works twice a week if needed but for the everyday works you need a jock."

"I guess I do Cassie, but it will be hard to turn the colts over to a stranger."

"Sort of like Ike and I, Bill. You may find out that you will like it Bill. You'll have more time to study the colts in action. It could turn out to be a big asset."

"It might but I think I'm going to miss feeling the colts under me. Like your filly Sam."

We arrived at the small track and watched several races. The Quarter Horses were like the dragsters I'd watched on television. Blast from the starting line and hit full speed in two jumps outside the gates. Mike handed out caps and ran out in the first ten minutes. We saw the caps all over the small track before the day was over.

Cassie had watched the local riders and had sorted out the ones she was interested in. I'd not asked her what she thought I just left her alone and let her take care of her end of things. Just before the big race she told me to watch the number three horse. I watched as the gates broke and saw the jockey on the three get his horse out of the gates and have him running straight. The colt he was riding hit his stride and flew towards the finish line. It was impossible for me to tell which horse was in the lead but when they neared the finish line I saw the three was in the lead by a good neck. The three won by a head in a photo finish.

"Come on Bill, I want to talk to the jock."

Cassie and I walked around to the back of the stands and waited for the jocks to come back to the jock room. When they came around Cassie called to the jock"

"Freddie, do you have a minute?"

"I can spare a minute, I don't have a horse in the next race."

"Do you have an agent?"

"No, I've not got near that important yet. I know who you are though. You're Cassie Morgan and your friend here is Bill Patton. He owns the Running P north of town."

"That's true Freddie. We'd like to talk to you this evening. That is if you have time."

"Miss Morgan, what time do you want me there?"

"Say seven thirty, that should give you time to have some fun after winning the race today."

"Miss Morgan, it won't take near that long, I'll get my money and go home. My mother has milking to do and I need to give her a hand."

"Your mom runs a dairy?"

"She does. Since my father passed away she and I run the dairy. I ride horses to make us extra income. The few cows we have do all right for us but there just seems never to be enough money to go around. I'll be there at seven thirty."

I looked at Cassie and smiled. I liked the young man and had a lot of respect for him. Cassie and I went back out front and watched one more race before heading back out to the farm. Cassie had to get the meatloaf put together and in the oven. Mike, Sam and I went to the barn and discussed how I'd work his filly and what schedule I'd put her on. We wanted her fresh but almost ready to run when we shipped her.

Bill, you're in charge. If she were a building I could tell you within a week of when she would be ready but she's not. You know what we have so do it the way you think is right, Mike and I are just here to help.

"Sam, Mike here is far more than hired help. He's my Ike, if you know what I mean. He is my eyes and ears here at the farm, and keeps things running smooth. I put him and Spunky in the same category. If we stand Light here like you've talked about I think we should fix Mike here up with a small home. We can use his small trailer for Carlo to live in. I'm going to be leaning on Mike a bunch when we get things set up and all the mares come in. I'm going to have to hire some folks to help during the breeding season and I can't be everywhere at once."

"Mike, I think Bill here has just given you a compliment."

"Sort of looks that way, Sam. I don't know what I'd do if I wasn't out here watching the kids build this place up. I've had more fun these last few months than I've had in years."

"Sam, did you tell Mike about the lady at the hospital?"

"No I didn't, Bill. Mike, an old friend of yours said to tell you hello. Brenda Wise."

"Brenda, I wondered what happened to her. She was a neighbor of mine for years. I used to help her when she was running barrels at all the local rodeos. She went off to nursing school and afterwards got married. Her husband was killed in an accident about five years ago. I didn't know she was back."

"I told her to come out and see you anytime she felt like it. She said she had seen things here on television and heard you were helping me run the place."

"She's a fine lady Sam. Her folks and my wife and I were great friends until my wife passed on. I sold out and haven't seen them but a few times since."

Sam told Mike how Brenda had helped the doctor in Jens operation. All Mike could do was shake his head.

"Sounds like her alright. She used to work with a local vet when she was in school. She wanted to be a vet but her folks couldn't afford to send her. Damn shame she would have made a dandy. She was always sewing up some kid's horse that got in the wire and such. Seemed to always be looking out for the little folks."

I saw the look in Sam's eyes. He was thinking and I had an idea about what he was thinking. I enjoyed being around Sam, it seemed he was always looking out for the little fellow too.

We smuggled Jen her meatloaf and scalloped potatoes in to her. Cassie started to feed her when the doctor came in and caught her.

"Now I understand why she hasn't been griping about the food. I only wish you'd brought enough for two."

"When does your shift end doctor?"

"I'm making my final rounds now Miss Morgan, why?"

"If you can be out at the Training Center in a hour or so you can eat your fill. We're going to eat about then and I know we have more than enough to feed you if you're there."

"Miss Morgan, I'll be there. My Lord that meat loaf smells great."

We were all laughing when the doctor left the room. Cassie and I visited with Jen then left for the farm. We had guests coming to supper.

"Sam showed up just before the doctor arrived and the two visited while I set the table and Cassie prepared the meal. The two men ate like hungry men can. They thanked Cassie for the meal before they both left for the hospital. Cassie sent a small piece of pie with Sam for Jen.

They had not been gone but a few minutes when Freddie Long drove up in an older one ton truck, I met him at the back door."

"Come on in Freddie. Cassie has just finished a pot of hot chocolate."

"I could go for a cup of that, sir."

Cassie poured us all a cup of hot chocolate and sat down.

"Freddie how many rides do you get a week?"

"Twelve, maybe fifteen ma'am."

"You get what, five dollars a ride?"

"Yes that's right, may I ask why?"

"We're looking for an exercise rider, one we can train to ride the colts here. These colts are a lot different than the ones you've been riding. Bill here starts the colts and you will find they are well broke. The problem we have is that Bill weighs a little too much to put the works on the colts now that he has them going.

"I come down on Wednesday afternoons and Saturdays for the real works. I think we could offer you a job if you want one that could lead to some better things, that is if you are interested."

"You mean you'd like me to work here?"

"If you are interested."

"What would the hours be?"

"Bill has school of a morning and gets back here at about nine thirty. He'd want to work the colts about eleven every morning."

"That would work out great, I need to help my mom of a morning. We are done by nine every morning. Miss Morgan did you say Mr. Patton got home from school. Mr. Patton are you going to college?"

"No Freddie, I'm a senior in high school this year. I have two hours of classes and have them scheduled for the first two hours of the day."

"Miss Morgan said you broke the colts."

"I do Freddie, I have four colts in the barn now and will have four more Monday afternoon. Have you ever ridden a Thoroughbred before?"

"No sir I haven't but I'm willing to learn."

"In that case I'm willing to teach you. We work six days a week and let the colts rest on Sunday."

"You work the colts every day?"

"Yes we do. We're building the colts up. We go slow and try and keep the colts from breaking down. Most of them will only have a few starts this coming year. The big money is in their three year old year. I like to have the colts worked and put away by three in the afternoon. Would that work for you?"

"Yes sir, it would, that would let me be home to help my mother."

"Freddie, I can pay you a hundred fifty a week to start. If you work out I'll give you a raise and guarantee you'll only ride broke horses."

Mr. Patton, you just hired yourself an exercise rider. When do I start?"

"Monday morning at ten. One other thing, out here at the farm my name is Bill."

"Yes sir, Bill I'll try and remember that."

We visited for another hour and answered Freddie's questions. He had heard about Cassie and Gray Light. He'd heard about me from folks around the area but like so many others thought I'd sold the farm when Sam's boys had gone to work on it. Before the evening was over I found myself liking Freddie more all the time. I began to look forward to Monday morning.

When Freddie left I looked at Cassie. She was smiling.

"He will work Cass. He's going to have to readjust his thinking but I think he'll be alright once we get him lined out."

"He will be fine Bill, he may end up being a fine jock."

"Cassie went home the next afternoon after visiting with Jen. The doctor said they would take her bandages off in four days. Like everyone else, I was a nervous wreck. I spent New Years Eve afternoon with Cassie and her folks. We went to an early church service and then I drove home to avoid the drinking drivers.

Mike and I did chores and spent the rest of the day relaxing. I told him about Freddie and he thought it would be a good idea to have him working the colts. I fixed myself breakfast later and called Spunky and brought him up to date on Jen and everything else here at the farm. He and Patty had leased a house in Hot Springs for the upcoming meet. They were looking forward to moving down in a couple of weeks.

I watched some football and napped in my chair before going to the hospital to see Jen. I was surprised to find Brenda sitting with Jen. They were laughing when I walked into the room.

"I guess I'll go back home. Looks to me as if you're doing fine, sis."

"Bill, did you stay up until the New Year came in?"

"No I didn't Jen. I had to give Coalie his apple and peppermints early so I crashed after the news and weather. Don't tell me you stayed up."

"No but no one would have known if I had with all these bandages on. I'm sick of these things Bill.

"I know Jen but you've only got a couple of days to go."

"I know Bill, that's what Brenda keeps telling me."

"Just get tough, sis. Look at it this way. Your whole life may change in a few days."

"I know Bill, but I'm tired of being stuck with needles and eating this crummy food."

"I might see if I can bring something tomorrow, Jen."

"Bill, don't worry. Brenda brought me a sausage and egg wrap this morning. I know dad will bring me something this evening."

"Jen, if you keep eating like that Coalie will groan when you get on him for your next ride."

We were all laughing when Sam walked into the room. We visited with Jen for a while then I left and went back to the farm. I helped Mike with the evening chores and got my things ready for school. My books were ready for my teacher to check. I was anxious for her to see them. I called Cassie and told her about Brenda checking on Jen.

"Good for her, I'm sure the two of them can talk horses and the time will pass quicker for Jen. Are you going to be at the hospital when they unwrap Jen's eyes?"

"I will if they don't do it before I get out of school. I only have the one hour of class so maybe I can make it. I'll check with Sam and find out what time they are going to take the bandages off. I'll call and let you know what and when things are going to be done.

I watched the commercial with Cassie and went to bed. My school day was short, but my accounting teacher told me I needed to get myself an accountant and not get in any tax problems. I would ask Sam for a suggestion when I saw him next. I headed to the farm. I had a new employee to break in.

Freddie showed up right on time and had brought his race saddle with him. We put it in the tack room and went to work. Mike and I had saddled the two fillies and wrapped their legs before Freddie had arrived. Mike gave us a leg up on the fillies and we rode them out onto the track. Freddie liked the exercise saddle and was amazed at how well the filly he was riding was broke. We back tracked the two fillies and after stopping them for a moment we put them to work. I had told Freddie how I wanted him to ride the filly. When we turned them together Freddie got up in his irons and kept a firm but tight hold on the filly until she relaxed then eased off on her head. Just like I wanted him too.

We did two rounds of the track and let the fillies work at three quarters speed for the last quarter mile. The work was exactly what I wanted for the two. It was exactly what they needed. We took them to the barn where Mike and Carlo took them and began to bathe and walk them. I could see the questions in Freddie's eyes.

"Freddie, we bathe and walk dry all of the colts. We brace their legs with lineament and put stall wraps on them after a work like this morning. It takes almost six months to get one of these colts ready and we sure don't want to cripple them. The filly you rode this morning is by a million dollar winner and out of a mare who made a little over two hundred thousand at the track. The reason I'm telling you this is to let you know the value of the colts you'll be riding. Now lets get the stud colt ready for you."

We put the race bridle on the stud and while Freddie held him I wrapped his legs and then put the exercise saddle on him.

"I want the same kind of work on the colt we just gave the fillies. Take him out on the track and go to work."

I walked to the track rail and watched Freddie back track the stud and then put him to work. He handled the stud exactly like the filly before and I was pleased, so pleased I put the bridle on Sam's filly and then put the leg wraps on. I'd get Freddie's attention in a hurry.

I helped Freddie unsaddle and bathe the stud. Carlo took him and to walk him dry. I told Freddie we had one more to work and he would be through for the day. I noticed Mike looked at me in a strange way. We saddled the filly and I gave Freddie a leg up. I gave Freddie his instructions on how I wanted the filly worked.

"Freddie, don't let her get away from you. This filly is something special and we're handling her with kid gloves. If you think anything is wrong or feel like something is not right, stop her as quick as possible."

"I understand Mr. Patton, I'll watch her."

I watched as Freddie rode the filly out onto the track and put her to work. It seemed strange to watch someone besides Cassie or myself ride her. I watched her long fluid stride take him around the track and watched closer as I saw her relax and go to work in earnest. The last quarter mile was wonderful to watch. When Freddie released a little of the hold he had on her the filly seemed to shift gears and really get into her stride. I thought I saw Freddie shift a little in his saddle then get low and regain his hold on her. I had to smile. She'd not catch him napping again. The young man had just gotten his lesson on a colt that could just be something special. Special and to be a part of her career. Something that few folks ever would get the opportunity to be a part of.

"Mr. Patton, this filly is something else. When she broke into her stride she almost lost me. She'll not get that chance again. Lord, she is something else."

"I know, Freddie. But there is a thing you have to do. You can't talk about this filly. We don't want anyone to know how good she is."

"That won't be a problem Mr. Patton. You've given me a chance to ride good horses, maybe a great horse. They are broke and I'm not used to that. Some of the horses I've been getting on are not anywhere near broke and I've got my mom to think of. You tell me how you want them ridden and I'll ride them just that way."

I saw Mike shake his head. I knew then that I had made a good decision.

"Bill, that boy will make a hand. He sort of reminds me of you. He's not got much and looks at this place as a chance to become something. I know where he and his mom live and they don't live fancy. I think you and Cassie may have hit pay dirt."

"I think so Mike. He's willing to listen and from now on when I tell him something he'll be looking for whatever it is I told him.

Our works for the day were down a little but that was to be expected. The new colts would be starting in a week or so. Everyone knew that colts that had trained here for the big Quarter Horse race had finished first, second and fourth. A pretty good start for a first year training center. The boys who had shown up this morning had told Mike we should have the big race here the next year.

I called Sam's cell phone and asked him who I should use as an accountant. He told me he would have a gentleman call me later today. The doctor had told him they would take the bandages off Jen's eyes day after tomorrow. He didn't know what time but would let me know. I heard a big truck and had to tell Sam I'd call him back later, Spunky's colts had just arrived.

I walked quickly to the barn and helped unload the colts. Light's half brother was nothing like his big brother. He was a streak faced chestnut small in size and looked more like a Quarter Horse. He was heavy muscled and from the looks I figured he'd be a sprinter. The other three were all nice looking horses. The gelding was a tall brown horse that I liked. He was a well balanced colt that had a pretty head and an intelligent eye. The two fillies were both brown, they were well balanced and I could see that Patty and Spunky's breeding program had moved to the next level. The colts were all very nice looking horses. I'd let them rest tomorrow and start them in the round pen the day after.

I stood in the doorway of my barn and admired the scene. All of the stalls were full. Full of good looking horses. I was happy.

"Bill, it's starting to look like you've got a business. It makes a man feel good to see his barn full of good looking horses. The bunch Spunky sent this morning are a fine set of youngsters. It's going to be fun watching you start them."

"Thank goodness I've got you, Carlo and Freddie to help. We're going to have our hands full in a couple of weeks. It's going to take some time to get them all rode every day. We'll be pushed for a while but after we get them accustomed to their routine things will line out."

"What do you think of Light's half brother, Bill?"

"It's too early to tell Mike. He sure doesn't look like his brother, though. He looks like a sprinter."

The next morning after class I started on Spunky's colts. The fillies and the gelding went great. Light's little brother was a different sort altogether. After a few rounds in the round pen I figured he, like his big brother, had gotten his toughness from his mother. He was a strong willed colt and it took me an extra hour before he finally gave in to me. I figured it was only the first day but knew he would take some special attention. After he was walked dry I put him in his stall and before I turned him loose I scratched his ears. He was more like his brother than I thought. He seemed to melt when his ears were scratched. I knew I had made headway with the colt and it was only a matter of time before I had him going.

The morning Jen was to have her bandages removed I went straight from school to the hospital. I'd promised I'd be there. When I pulled into the parking lot I was surprised to see Cassie's truck already parked there. When I got to Jen's room the doctor was coming down the hall. The unveiling was about to begin.

I stood next to Cassie while the doctor explained to Jen what he was going to do and what to expect. He told her that if the operation had been a success things might be blurred at first so don't be upset. The blurred vision would go away in a day or so. She might have to wear glasses for a while but that it would not be a problem.

"Doctor, just get these bandages off and if I can't see I'm no worse off than I was before. I'll still be able to ride so it's no big deal."

The doctor began to cut the bandages away. Finally all that remained were two patches over Jen's eyes. Brenda, who was assisting, dimmed the lights in the room and partly closed the blinds on the window.

"Ready Jen?"

"You bet doctor, get these things off."

We watched as the doctor removed the patches from Jen's eyes. Jen began to blink and the doctor gave her a tissue to wipe her eyes which were watering. She dried her eyes and smiled.

"Cassie, you're beautiful."

Everyone in the room breathed a sigh of relief. The operation had been a success, our little sister could see.

"Bill, what are you doing here. You've got colts to work."

"I figured they could wait a while sis. I sure didn't want to miss this."

"Well I'm fine and I'm hungry. Cassie did you bring me some breakfast?"

Cassie opened her shoulder bag and took out a sausage and egg wrap. She handed it to Jen who took a big bite and sighed. Everyone in the room was thrilled. Sam was wiping tear from his eyes and hugging everyone. His dream for his daughter had come true and he was a very happy man.

I couldn't help but notice Brenda was wiping tears, too.

I told everyone I had to get back to work and gave Jen a kiss. Cassie gave Jen a kiss and laughed as she followed me out the door.

"What was so funny Cass?"

"My little sister just said you were a real hunk."

I had to laugh. My little sister was something else.

I called mom and told her what had happened and told her Jen was doing great. She told me Tom was tied up in court with a case he and his men had brought to trial. She was worried he was working too hard.

"He'll be fine mom, he knows how to back off when needed."

She told me he would be calling home soon and that she would tell him how Jen was doing. She invited me to supper later in the week.

Freddie had the colts worked and was waiting with Mike when I drove up.

"Everything is worked and the new ones are ready to go Bill. How's Jen?"

"She's fine Mike. She can see."

"Thank God."

"Mike, I'll start with the fillies first"

. I took one of the fillies to the round pen and let her go to work and work the edge off. When she settled down I put her to work. When she gave in to me I turned her over to Carlo and took the next from Mike who waited just outside the pen.

Everything went smoothly. Even the stud colt worked great. I scratched his ears as I took him back to the barn. He was relaxed and I figured to work him and the others with a saddle the next day. My cell phone rang just as I was turning the colt over to Carlo.

"Running P, this is Bill.

"Bill, this Phil Ludley. How are my horses doing?"

"They are doing great Mr. Ludley. We're galloping them and have even given them a couple of quarter mile works at three quarter speed. They are coming around nicely."

"I have to fly to Dallas later this week. Would it be alright to drop by and see them?"

"If you'll let me know when you'll be here you can watch them work sir. I've hired an exercise boy to help me and we can work the colts in pairs. That way you can see them for yourself and judge where they are in their training."

"Bill, that would be great, I'll call you from Dallas the day before I head your way."

"Fine sir, we'll be looking forward to your coming.

CHAPTER 34

Everything went great. Mr. Ludley had called like he said and had shown up at ten on Friday morning. Freddie and I had worked the colts over the track and given them their first light three eighths work. Mr. Ludley was more than pleased. He wanted to send four more and would pick these colts up and send them to his trainer in Florida. They were so much further along than he had expected. He had called his trainer in Florida and then passed the phone to me. I visited with the trainer and gave him my thoughts on where the colts were in their training and my opinion as to how the colts would work. He thanked me and said he was looking forward to getting the colts and would let me know how they worked out.

After Mr. Ludley left, Mike, Freddie and I sat down to talk.

"Mike, what do you think about this deal?"

"Bill, I think the man wanted to send you seven colts, you took three. Now he's sending you four more, looks like he's getting his way."

"Could be, but we're going to stay busy however you look at it. The money will keep coming in and everyone will get paid. If our Mr. Ludley wants them shipped to Florida, there isn't anything we can do about it. However, next year we may be too busy to take any of his colts. I don't like to be used."

"If Sam's filly stays sound and runs like we think, you'll have your pick of the outside horses you want anyway. We may have to add some stalls."

"We're going to add stalls. I'll have them put in when they add onto the barn this fall."

"We are going to add onto the barn? How much Bill?"

"Enough for eight more stalls Mike. I won't have school to contend with and we'll have both Cassie and Freddie to help with the riding. That is if Freddie here wants to stay with us."

"Mr.—Bill, I don't want to go anywhere. This place is like a dream to me. I heard Mike here say he was having way too much fun and now I know what he means. I can't even imagine what it's like when Miss Morgan is around."

"There is a lot more class around here for one thing. Now that Jen has her eyesight back there is no telling what will be going on."

"That is a fact Mike, Coalie's days of rest and relaxation are over. He's going to have to go to work."

"Mr. Patt … Bill, Mike here says you'll be leaving in April for the track in New Mexico. Any chance of my going along?"

"I thought you had to be here with your mom?"

"I did until yesterday. My father was killed in an accident three years ago. We got notice yesterday that the case had finally been settled out of court and my mom has a nice settlement check coming. She told me she was going to sell the cows, the place and move into town and take life easy. After the last three years I think she has it coming to her. She said if you could use me I should go along.

"I'm going to need an exercise boy at the track Freddie, but I think with your weight and experience maybe we can get you enough rides that you can make yourself a good living.

Cassie will be doing most of the riding for me but we can get you more than enough rides to get the experience you need to move up and make a good living this summer.

"I'll be ready when you are. I think I might really like this thoroughbred business. You know I won't pull a horse or do anything illegal."

"That's why I said we'd take you along, Freddie. If I thought otherwise you'd not be working here."

I heard from Spunky that night. He and Patty were leaving for Oaklawn Park at Hot Springs Arkansas the next morning. The folks who were going to haul the horses for them would leave the next morning. The exercise boy Spunky had hired would be traveling with them.

I had wished him luck and told him about Freddie. He said to watch and let Cassie help him. If he worked out I was to let him know. I promised him I would keep him informed. He told me he'd let me know when he and Patty were settled and would give me the phone numbers.

The weather changed and I lost two days training. Snow was not our problem. The problem was ice. A good inch of clear Ice hung on everything. What trees there were around the farm were ice covered, the limbs almost touching the ground. Trucks on the Interstate Highway ceased to run. Nothing moved for a full day and then only in an emergency. I talked to Cassie every day and she told me Art was at home and fussing up a storm. Suddenly as it had come a wind came up during the night from the south and the ice began to melt. First it was ice then mud. Every trainer hated this kind of weather but you had to learn to live with it. The sand we had hauled in and put on the track was a life saver. It drained quickly and we could work the colts. I'd had Freddie spend the night to keep him from driving on the ice slick roads. Mike had put Carlo up with him so everyone was cozy even during the cold nights.

Jen was home and having a fit. She wanted to see Coalie and ride but the weather had put things on hold. Sam's filly had just gotten better and better. She had grown and began to fill out. Her muscles were beginning to stand out and she looked wonderful, even with her winter hair. I knew Sam would be pleased when he saw her.

Two days later the new colts arrived from Colorado, and the three I had been working left for Florida. I looked at the four and didn't like what I saw. Three of the colts had faults that would never allow them to become race horses. The fourth was a stud colt that was a real mess. It took two of the men to get him off the van and into a stall. I looked at Mike who shook his head.

"I'll be back in a little while Mike, I've got a phone call to make."

I went to the house and looked up Mr. Ludley's home number. When he answered I told him who I was.

"Bill, did the colts arrive?"

"Some colts arrived sir."

"What did you think of the gray filly?"

"What gray filly? I got three bay fillies and one dark brown stud colt."

"You got what? Are the fillies crooked legged and the stud is a nut case."

"That's what I got sir."

"Bill, I'll have my man here at the farm bring a trailer and pick them up. Now I've got to find out where my good fillies and the two geldings are. Bill I'll call you and tell you what I find out. Bill, I'm sorry about this mess. I hope you didn't think I was sending you all my trash, especially after the fine job you did for me on the first bunch. My trainer in Florida is going to be thrilled with the colts. I'll get back to you in a while".

I hung up the phone and went to the barn. I told Mike what had happened. We talked about the mess and went on with our day. I told the boys I'd take care of the stud. He would charge the stall door and wasn't fooling around about being bad. He would kick, strike with his front feet and would bite if he got the chance. I put up with his bad habits that evening but I had a different plan for him the next day. I fed him that morning and then went to school. The boys were waiting when I got home. I helped Freddie get Sam's filly worked then went to the tack room and picked out what equipment I would need. I walked back to the studs stall and roped him around the neck. Like his owner had said he went crazy. I simply stepped back out of the stall and let him have his fit. Mike who stood next to me could only shake his head.

"Bill, that colt will kill someone."

"Maybe Mike, I want to see how he reacts to different things. I can't believe he was born this way. Someone has spoiled him."

When the colt finally settled down I opened the door of the stall and managed to pick up the end of the rope. I shook the rope and the colt blew all over again. He was soaking wet with sweat when he finally quit. Again I shook the rope and he jumped but didn't throw a fit like before. I stepped into the stall and shook the rope again. The colt looked at me as if frozen in place.

"Mike hand me the old shirt there by the door. I reached behind me and took the shirt when Mike handed it to me. I loosely tied one sleeve onto the rope and then raised the end of the rope over my head. By lightly shaking the rope I managed to slide the shirt towards the colt. At first he looked at the shirt then grabbed the shirt in his teeth and shook it. With the loose end of the rope I coiled in my hand I slung it at the colt. He dropped the shirt and backed into the corner in the stall. I picked the rope up and again shook the rope. This time the colt stood still and didn't attack the shirt. When I finally managed to get the shirt to touch the colt's neck he cringed but stood still. I dropped down low and managed to get the shirt to slide back to me. I pulled on the rope and the colt took a step towards me.

"Watch him, Bill. He's likely to make a dive at you."

I took the rope and flipped it like my grandfather had taught me years before. Before the colt knew it I had a semblance of a halter on him. I handed the rope to Mike and told him to dally the end around the stall post. When Mike had the dally made I took hold of the rope and asked the colt to come forward.

"Mike, if he makes a dive at me take up all the slack you can get and do it in a hurry."

I watched Mike from the corner of my eye as he backed up and was ready if need be.

Again I asked the colt to come forward. He did. He made the dive I was expecting. I stepped forward and to the left as Mike and Freddie pulled on the rope. The colt was suddenly jerked sideways and his head was tied close to the stall corner post with me safely behind him.

"Carlo, bring me the other rope, quick!"

Carlo went into the empty stall next to me and handed me the rope. The rope was soft lay cotton and was used to lead mares when they were being bred. I fashioned a loop and threw it down and around the colts hind legs. I got the results I was looking for. The colt kicked violently. I quickly drew up the slack and had both hind feet in the loop. I threw the loose end of the rope through the bars of the stall and told Carlo to hang on. I crawled up and over the stall wall and helped Carlo hold the rope.

"Mike, we're going to pull the colt's legs out from under him. When he starts to go down let off on his head."

"Carlo and I began pulling and slowly but surely the colt became over balanced and fell to the stall floor. Mike and Freddie had released enough hold on the colt so as not to choke him. I took the rope and made a quick tie on one of the stall bars. Then walked around to the stall door. The colt lay on his side and was trying to figure out how we had captured him.

"Now what, Bill?"

"I'm going in and pet him, Mike. So far we've not whipped him and not done a thing to hurt him. Right now he's confused and trying to figure things out. I'd like him to stay that way. You boys hold what you've got."

I walked through the stall door and stayed away from the colts front feet. I stepped over his body and began to pet his neck. The colt was scared to death, I continued to pet and talk to him. When he seemed to relax I began rubbing him all over his body. Finally I rubbed his ears. He seemed to relax and quit trembling. I had Carlo hand me another small rope, which I attached to the rope around the colt's hind legs. It would enable me to get slack in the rope and remove it without being in the stall and getting struck or kicked.

I went outside the stall and after untying the heel rope so to speak I began to pull on the small rope and managed to get enough slack in the cotton rope to free the colt's hind legs. I walked around to the stall door and stepped inside.

"Mike, release the rope, slow and easy. I want the colt to get to his feet."

Mike and Freddie released their hold on the rope and the colt lay still. I took a step towards him and waved my cap slowly towards his head. The colt quickly got to his feet. I didn't need to say anything to Mike, I knew he was ready to take up slack if need be. The colt stood up and shook himself, when he finished I put out my hand and patted his shoulder. The colt didn't tremble at my touch, in fact he lowered his head and relaxed.

I slowly took the rope off his head and patted his neck. I backed out of his stall and closed the door. Then I took a deep sigh.

"Bill, that's something I've never seen before. The way you flipped that rope and put a halter on the colt was wonderful to see. Where in the world did you learn to do that?"

"My grandfather taught me how to do that Mike. I worked on it for a week and had a pony who was sure enough glad when I got it down. I've used it a lot with a bunch of the horses folks used to bring me. A bunch of them were not halter broke and I had to catch them."

"Bill, it's a wonder you ever survived those years."

"I've got a few scars Mike. Things didn't always work out like I figured. You do what you have to do to eat. You've bought a meal or two for me when I rode a horse at the sale for you. A couple of times Mike I'd not had anything to eat all day and the meal you bought me was a welcome thing."

"Why didn't you say anything Bill? We'd have got a hold of your dad and straightened him out."

"Then I'd have gotten beat again as soon as you all left. It was a matter of self survival Mike."

"What's next with the colt Bill?"

"Let's see if we can get a halter on him now."

"I picked up a halter and walked back to the colt's stall. I opened the stall door and stepped in slowly. The colt walked towards me. I held out the halter and let him smell it then slowly put on him. I patted his neck and then rubbed his ears. I removed the halter and left him alone.

"I saw it but I still don't believe it. Mr.—Bill, that was wonderful."

"Thanks Freddie. Now I guess I'll go to the house and find out how well this colt is bred. Then I just might make an offer for him."

"Bill, you think you could make a race horse out of him?"

"I just might Mike. It will take time but he just might."

I went to the house and called Mr. Ludley. I asked how the stud was bred and found out he was by a nice horse and his dam had also made a good amount of money. The mare and colt had been missed in the fall gather and not been found until the following spring. The colt had been a half starved woolly little thing and had pretty much been written off as a loss. No one had bothered to work with him and when they finally did he like to have killed a ranch hand. As far as Mr. Ludley knew he had never been haltered.

"What will you take for the colt sir?"

"Bill, after the job you've done for me and the mess up with the colts I'll give him to you if you want him. He won't be of any use to me."

"I'll take him sir. I'd like to see what I can do with him. He is a little bit flighty.

"Bill, you're being kind, he was going to be sent to the local horse sale. I have his papers here at the house. I'll mail them to you in the morning. By the way the colts are on their way to you. They were sent to the wrong trainer, or so I've been told. I'm not convinced that it was a mistake. But I'll find out."

I thanked him and told him I'd have stalls ready when the colts got here.

I called Cassie who had just gotten home and told her about the stud.

"Cassie, I believe the colt will make a grass horse, both sire and dam ran on the grass and made a good deal of money. He has heart and if I handle him right he just might make us some money."

"Go with your heart Bill. It's always worked before. I'll be down tomorrow for Jen's first lesson. She said she didn't care how cold it was she was going to ride."

"I'm looking forward to you coming down. I'll put a roast in the crock pot and we'll eat after you and Jen get through riding."

"That will be great Bill. I'm sure we'll be more than ready to eat something."

I told her I'd talked to Spunky and that he and Patty were in Hot Springs. I told her they had sounded like a couple of kids going to their first party.

"Bill, they are finally living their dream. Patty has told me she is having so much fun. Spunky is being accepted as a good trainer and he is loving it."

"They deserve it Cassie. I'll see you tomorrow. I'll put the roast on and see what I can come up with for a dessert."

The next morning I went to the barn and fed my stud colt. He was still unsure about most things but wasn't striking or pawing at things. All in all I was happy with his progress. Mike had the coffee on and was looking forward to the day. The Quarter Horse folks were starting a new crop of colts and according to Mike things were real entertaining sometimes when the colts were saddled and put on the track. He and Carlo were laughing about some of the boys and their new colts.

I left for school after putting the roast in the pot. I'd put the vegetables in the pot after I worked with the colt. Mike, Carlo and Freddie had Spunky's colts going well. I rode with Freddie and we got the colts done in half the time it would take if I was doing things by myself. When I got back from school, I found the new colts from Colorado had arrived. They were truly a nice group of colts. Mike said the boys who delivered the colts were sure glad to get them delivered. They said their boss was more than a little upset that the colts had been switched. They figured that someone was going to be looking for a job soon. They were thrilled that they didn't have to pick up the stud.

Mike had laughed and said he was a different horse now than he was when they had dropped him off. He didn't tell them I planned on making a race horse out of him.

I got everything lined out for the next morning and was just finished when I saw Sam's truck turn off the highway and drive up to the barn.

"Hey Sam, I was about to say you and Jen were early but I see she's not with you."

"Bill, she's in school and can't wait for this evening. I've got my girl back and it's wonderful. How's the filly coming along?"

"Wonderful Sam, she's almost ready to do a full work. I wish Spunky were here to give me his idea as to how good she really is"

I took Sam down to the stall and got his filly out for him to look over. He'd not been out in a while and the look on his face said it all.

"My lord Bill, she's grown and filled out. She's beautiful. You've done a wonderful job on her."

"I've had help Sam. I've been putting Freddie on her and been able to watch her work. She seems to be getting stronger and is maturing a lot. She has everyone in the barn giving her attention and loves it."

"Do you think she's good enough to go with Spunky?"

"Sam they don't run two year olds at Hot Springs. I don't have any idea where Spunky will go after the meet ends but I'd like to get him to watch the filly work too."

"I can't hardly wait to see her run. Just think Bill, a few months ago we went to the city and bought her. It's hard to believe this is the same filly."

"Well it is Sam. She has really done well. When you and Jen come out this evening Cassie and I are having a roast beef dinner. You and Jen are invited."

"I'll bring my appetite Bill. It seems my daughter can't get enough to eat lately. She just can't seem to get filled up. She and Brenda have become great friends and visit almost every evening. They plan on getting together with Cassie and going for a ride. A real girl's day out, if you know what I mean."

"Brenda is a nice person Sam, I'm glad she and Jen have become friends. It will make it a lot easier on Jen when Cassie and I leave for the summer."

"I'd not thought of that but you're right, you kids will be going north and she will need someone to ride with. Is Mikes going to stay here and look after thing while you're gone?"

"Yes, he'll be looking after the day to day business while I'm gone. The boys come out to work their colts and Mike seems to enjoy it. I'm pleased with the way things are going Sam. The farm is paying its way and making my life a lot easier. Have you found me an accountant?"

"Yes, I have. He should be here anytime now. He wanted to come out and look the place over. He wants to learn how to ride, Bill. If you have the time to teach him he'll take the lessons off your accounting bill."

"Sounds good to me. That must be his Jeep coming up the drive."

When the used Jeep pulled up and stopped I was shocked at the gentleman who got out. He was tall, real tall, six foot six or so. He had a big smile on his face and after saying hello to Sam stuck out his hand to shake.

"You must be, Bill. I'm Tom Stephens. Sam says you are in need of an accountant."

"Yes, sir. I am."

"Bill, the name is Tom. I want to learn how to ride. Not anything along the lines of you folks but enough I feel comfortable and can go for rides to get away from the office. I'll be wanting to find a horse that's right for me and Sam says you're the man to find one for me."

"Tom, I can teach you how to ride and can probably find you a horse. You can come out here on Wednesday evenings when Sam and Jen are here. They also come out on Saturday afternoons. We'll work out a schedule when we get started. Have you ever ridden before?"

"Only a couple of times at some dude camps."

"That's great. We'll be able to teach you right the first time and won't have to correct any bad habits. You should be riding in no time. We've got a horse here you can ride until you decide if you really want a horse of your own."

"That sounds great. I can start this coming Saturday if that will be alright."

"We'll be looking for you Saturday morning Tom, say one o'clock."

"That will be great, Bill. Can I get a tour of the place now?"

"Sam here can give you a tour, Tom. I've got to get supper started for this evening."

"I left Sam to show Tom around while I got supper in the pot. I called Cass and found she was on her way down. We visited while she drove and I cut up veggies. It was fun to get to laugh and have fun with her. She said Jen was wound up something terrible. The doctor had finally cleared he to ride if she wore a hard hat. Cassie was bringing hers along so that she would feel better.

"Bill, she's going to really see Coalie for the first time."

"I know, Sam said this morning she is really wound up. He found me an accountant. He wants to learn how to ride. He'll keep my books in order for riding lessons."

"Sounds good to me Bill, you'd probably give him the lessons for free because he was a friend of Sam's."

"Well, I do feel like I owe him Cass."

"Of course you do but I'm proud of the way you've got the center paying. How are Spunky's colts doing?"

"All of them but Light's little brother are doing fine. He just can't seem to get it together. He has the speed and is getting into shape but he's always getting himself in a mess. I'm going to put blinkers on him and see if that will help."

"He must be a mess if you're going to use blinkers. I know you don't like them."

"I don't, but he seems to see things that aren't there. I've been riding him myself the last couple of days because you never know what he's going to do. I've had the vet check his eyes and they are fine so tomorrow we go to the blinkers."

"Let's give them a try this evening Bill. I'll be there in fifteen minutes and we'll have time before Jen and Sam arrive."

"I'll go get him tacked up Cassie. See you in a few minutes."

I ran to the barn and told Mike what was up, he tacked up the gelding while I got the young stud ready. I had just finished when Cassie pulled up in front of the barn. She was wearing her riding clothes so all she needed was a leg up on the gelding. She led the stud colt out to the track where Mike and I fitted the colt with the blinkers. The blinkers with their half cups would let him see what was ahead but not what was to his left or right. Cass led me and the colt onto the track and began to gallop. The colt didn't know what was going on at first but soon got into his work. For the first time in a week or so the colt had his mind on his business. We might take the blinkers off later in his training but for now they were part of his equipment.

We had just finished walking the colt when Sam and Jen pulled in. We waved to them from the barn and they drove up and parked. Sam had barely stopped when Jen seemed to explode out of the truck. She had seen Coalie and run to his pen. She was through the boards of the pen and was hugging Coalie and talking to him all at the same time. He's beautiful, just beautiful. Thank you Bill. Thank you for finding him for me. Cassie, can we ride now?"

"You want to saddle the horses or ride them bareback Jen?"

"Let's ride them bareback Cass. I've never got to do that but once."

Sam and I got the bridle for Coalie and I took the saddle off the gelding for Cassie. Sam and I watched as the girls rode off across the pasture laughing and talking. A moment later a pickup with a one horse trailer pulled up the driveway. It was Brenda, the nurse from the hospital.

"Where are the girls?"

"They went that way, riding bareback last time we saw them."

"Good, I won't have to saddle up."

Brenda unloaded her horse and slipped the bridle on him. We pointed in the direction the girls had ridden off and watched as she swung up on her horse and took off in a canter. She sat her horse nice and was soon out of sight over the rise in back of the barn.

Looks like she's done that before, Sam."

"It does for a fact, Bill. I'll bet the truck and trailer belong to her."

"I'm sure it does. Look at the saddle, Champion Barrel Racer. The lady knows how to ride."

Sam and I walked into the barn and found there were still a couple of cups of coffee left. I was surprised it wasn't strong. Mike had explained it was the third pot he'd made that morning. The boys who worked their colts liked their coffee, especially when it was as cold as it was of the morning. We drank our coffee and had time to visit. Sam had gone back to work and he and Ike had been working on a couple of really big jobs. One of the jobs Sam had wanted to get Ike said no. He explained to Sam that they had done a small job not far away from the site and the ground had been extremely unstable. It had taken a lot more concrete and gravel than had been figured for the job. Sam had ordered a crew to go out and take a core sample and found that Ike had been right. They had not bid on the job but three other companies had. The winning company had begun work and had been in trouble right from the start. When the ice and light snow came along they had quit on the job and walked off. The folks who owned the property had come to Sam and asked him to finish the job. He and Ike had taken the job on a cost plus basis. There was no way they could lose money. Sam said Ike was working with the folks and explaining to them why the job was taking so much longer to do. The owners were thrilled to be informed of the reasons and felt like they were being included in the job.

"Sounds like to me Ike is becoming a very important part of your business."

"He sure is Bill. I'm going to promote him to Vice President of my company and have him pick out his replacement for the field work. He knows the boys in the field better than I so it will be his decision.

We heard laughter and saw the girls coming back. Their hands were moving and you could tell that Jen was the center of attention and enjoying every minute of it. They were all laughing when they rode into the barn.

"Don't tell me there isn't any coffee left."

"Got plenty Brenda. I'll get you a cup."

I looked at Mike as he grinned and looked up towards the ceiling. He and I had the same idea. Maybe Sam was seeing something he'd been needing. I later invited Brenda to eat with us. I told her Mike was going to come so she should feel right at home. She accepted and that evening we had a lot of fun.

Mike was telling stories about Brenda and how much fun he had had watching her grow up. Cassie and Jen were wiping tears during some of the stories. Sam and I were laughing too but we tried to be more reserved about it. Before the evening was over Brenda had invited us over to her place for a Mexican dinner the following week. We were all looking forward to the dinner.

We went to the barn and got Brenda's horse from the stall Mike had put him in and watched as she loaded him into the trailer. We waved as she pulled out of the driveway. Jen and Sam left a short time later. Cass called home and told her folks she was heading home. I walked her out to her truck and got my kiss goodbye. She would be down Saturday but the time was now beginning to go slow. I was getting tired of seeing Cassie drive down the driveway to go home.

CHAPTER 35

The next several weeks brought real cold and one big snow. Mike had scraped the snow off the track and we had managed to miss only one day's training. I had all the outside colts riding and even letting them begin to work on the track. Spunky's colts were working well and would be ready to go when spring arrived. I'd backed off of Sam's filly and was only giving her long steady controlled works. I'd go to work on her a couple of weeks before we shipped to New Mexico.

We had gone to Brenda's place for dinner and had had a wonderful meal. Jen was in the kitchen learning all sorts of things about cooking. Now that she could see she wanted to learn everything. The three girls as Jen called them were hard to get anything over on. Jen even threatened me one night.

"Mr. Bill Patton, if you don't shape up I'll call grandma and tell her how you're acting."

I had begged for mercy and was forgiven. Sam told Cassie he and Jen were taking Brenda to supper this coming Saturday night. Cassie and I were happy to hear that things seemed to be going well for them. Jen really needed a mother but not just anyone. She needed someone who could talk about her interests and guide her without her realizing it.

The next few weeks, things were a little bit hectic. We had a cold rain that was followed by a eighth inch snow. The wind had blown all night and the drifts were blown up on everything in the way of the storm. For the first day we shoveled and scraped snow away from everything that needed clearing. The second day Mike plowed the track and the driveway from the highway. He managed to get the track worked and that afternoon we got to work the colts.

Sam's filly was pulling hard and wanted to work. We'd been giving her long gallops and she was ready but not on the surface frozen like it was now. I talked to Sam who told me the weather was due to change the next few days and suggested we call Spunky and have him come take a look at the filly.

I told him fine but how did he plan on getting Spunky out here and back in time for him to work his string at the track?

He told me it would not be a problem, he would take a friend's jet. He'd leave early and pick Spunky up right after his works. They would be back here before noon and after the work he'd take spunky back. He would spend the night with Spunky and Patty then fly back the next day.

I told him to let me know what he was going to do and went back to work. I called Cass and asked if I could take her to dinner. She would be down day after tomorrow but I was lonesome and needed to get out of the house. There were several patches of ice on the road but I didn't mind. I got to have supper with Cassie and enjoyed every minute. I told her about Sam's idea of letting Spunky tell us what he thought about the filly.

"You will let me know, Bill. I can make arrangements and be there to work her. I know you've been working her yourself but I can talk her around the track."

"I'll call you, Cass. I know Sam will want you to ride her when Spunky looks her over.

I visited with Cassie's folks and her two brothers then left for home. I drove a lot slower in the dark than I had driven up. When I got to the house I found I had two messages. The trainer from Florida had called and had said he had told his boss to hire, bribe or do what ever but get me to break all his colts. The colts that I considered three quarters finished were so far ahead of all the other colts he had gotten in he had to call and say thanks. Their two year old season started a little earlier than the rest of the country and the colts I had sent him would be ready to go.

The second was from Sam and he said he would have Spunky at my place Wednesday about noon. He said he would talk to me later. I called Cassie and told her when Spunky would be here.

"I'll make arrangements and be there by eleven Bill. I'll bring my saddle."

The next morning when I helped the boys with chores I told Mike that Spunky would be here the next day. We're going to give the filly her first real work."

"I'll have the track ready Bill, I'll make sure the cushion is just right."

"Thanks Mike, We'll want it just right."

After working the colts I went to the house and fixed a sandwich. I went to work on my books and was just finishing when I heard a car come up the road. I walked to the window and saw it was Brenda. I walked to the back door and saw it was not only Brenda, but Jen was with her.

"Come on in. I was just getting ready to fix some hot chocolate."

"See I told you Brenda. He always has hot chocolate either on or is just fixing it."

"That you did Jen. I guess your big brother likes the hot chocolate almost as well as you do."

"Jen's spending the night with me. Sam is leaving early in the morning for Hot Springs and I only live a short distance from her school."

"Sounds good to me, draw up a chair and sit down. I'll have the chocolate ready in a moment. Jen, you get the cups."

"Boy, ever since I get my sight back all people want me to do is work!"

Brenda and I both burst out laughing. Jen was laughing with us. Jen had wanted to come out and give Coalie an apple, so the two girls as Jen referred to them had driven out.

"I've got some smoked ribs one of the boys brought out this morning. Mike and Carlo took what they wanted and told me to freeze the rest. I've not put them in the freezer yet so why don't we heat them up and have ourselves a good supper. That is if you all like ribs."

"Light the oven Bill. It won't take Jen and me but a moment to give Coalie his apple. I'll bet I know the feller who cooked he ribs. Ray Lablonk.

"That's the feller. He trains out here and placed his colt second in the big race a while back. Said he'd never have had a chance without the use of our track."

"Ray's a nice fellow, he used to drink a good deal until he got married. His wife got him off the booze and he went to cooking. Best decision he ever made. He cooks smoked meat for all kinds of functions and has built himself quite a business."

"Jen, let's get Coalie his apple. I'm ready for some ribs."

I but the ribs in the oven and sliced some onion. I opened some beans and began to heat them. It wasn't much but when you had ribs nothing much else mattered.

The girls returned and we sat down to eat. Jen had a cup of hot chocolate while Brenda and I had tea. Sometime later a large pile of rib bones were piled on a plate in the middle of the table. Everyone seemed to be full.

"Anyone for ice cream?"

"Ice cream. Bill are you trying to get us fat? Here Brenda is laying a trap for my dad and you're trying to make us fat."

"Jen! Where did that come from?"

"Well it's true, I've seen the way you look at dad and the way he looks at you. I think it's great. My dad needs someone and I like you, too."

"Brenda, "Out of the mouth of babes."

"Bill, I don't know what to say."

"Nothing to be ashamed of Brenda, we've all been wondering when Sam was going to say something. Sort of figured it would be soon. Cass and I were talking about the other night."

"Good lord what next?"

"I think daddy will give you a ring and we'll be a family pretty soon."

All Brenda and I could do was laugh.

CHAPTER 36

Mike, Carlo and I had everything done up in the barn and were ready for Sam and Spunky to show up. I noticed that the boys had made sure everything in the barn exactly where it should be. I was proud of them to say the least. Freddie had never met Spunky and was looking forward to the meeting.

We saw Cassie's truck coming down the highway and turn into our drive. She drove up to the barn and got out.

"Morning boys. Think you all can help me get rid of these doughnuts?"

"Cassie, its no wonder we love you. Want a cup of coffee?"

"Thanks, Mike. But I had mine on the way down. You boys dig in."

While the boys ate their doughnuts Cassie and I went to look at the filly. I had already put her leg wraps on and had her bridle hanging on the front of her stall.

"Bill, she looks great. It seems she just gets better every time I see her. Spunky is going to be impressed."

"I sure hope so Cass. I've done everything I can do to get her ready."

"Relax Bill. She couldn't be in any better shape. I understand you had a fun evening last night?"

"I sure did. It looks like Sam and Brenda are becoming a pair. Jen is all for their relationship. She caught both Brenda and me by surprise last night. It's great to see how far Jen has come in the last month or so. Brenda has been a big help to her."

"I know, she calls and talks to me every night. It seems Sam and Brenda have been talking a good deal every evening. I hope it works out for them Bill. They really are two very nice people."

"Well, we'll have to just wait and see."

A short time later we saw Sam's truck turn off the highway and head up to the barn. We met him and Spunky when they got out of the truck.

"Morning, Sam. Spunky, how does it feel to be a member of the jet set?"

"Different, Bill. It's a long ways from Raton."

"I'll bet that's right. How's Patty?"

"Fine Bill, she sends her love."

"Well, let's get the filly ready. I can't wait for Spunky to see her."

"Relax Sam. She's ready to go to the track."

We took the filly out of her stall and I put her bridle on. Mike had the gelding saddled and waited until I handed him the lead shank. Spunky gave Cassie a leg up and we followed the two of them out to the track rail.

"Bill, the filly looks great. You've done a fine job on her."

"I've just done what I've been taught, Spunky. She's a delight to train she just wants to please. She's a lot like Light in that she wants to be a racehorse. I'm like Sam, I want your idea on just how good she may be."

"I've never seen Sam so excited Bill. He thinks she may be the next Light"

"Spunky, I do too."

"We watched as Mike ponied the filly around the track. I watched as Cassie stayed high in her stirrups letting the filly begin to settle into her work. I saw the filly flip her ears and knew she was beginning to listen to Cass as the started to go around the track for the second time. Mike turned the filly loose and Cassie moved her over near the rail. We watched as she went down the back side. As they neared the half mile pole I saw Cassie get lower on the filly back and released her hold.

The filly seemed to float forward as if not touching the ground. Cassie was lower on her back as they started around the turn. When they entered the stretch I saw Cassie shake the reins and ask the filly to run. It was beautiful to watch. The filly and Cassie coming up the stretch seemed as one. When they passed where we stood I heard Spunky click his stop watch. I saw him check the time and smile.

"Bill, let's get her to the barn and take care of her."

I caught the filly when Cassie came back.

"How did she do Bill? My lord it felt like I was riding Light again."

"I'm not sure Cassie. I saw Spunky smile when he looked at his watch but I don't know anything more than that."

I led the filly and Cassie back to the barn where everyone was waiting. Cassie jumped off the filly and I began unsaddling her. Spunky had her leg wraps off and was feeling her legs when I was through.

"Mike, give this young lady a bath and let's get her walked dry."

"I'll do it Spunky. This little lady worked a little today."

"Alright kids, you and Sam are wondering what you've got on your hands. Your filly, Sam. Just worked a half mile two fifths of a second slower than Light did up at Raton. She did it on a good but not fast track and it was her first half mile work. Sam, Bill here has done a wonderful job on the filly and you should be thrilled with her."

"I am thrilled Spunky. I've watched the kids bring her along with kid gloves and try their best not to get my hopes up. My lord, two fifths slower than Light. I can't believe it."

"You can believe it. She is something special Sam. Handled right she should make you a bundle this fall. Don't forget she's an Oklahoma bred and is eligible for the big race for two year old fillies this fall."

"I'd forgotten all about that Spunky. Do you think she has a chance?"

"Sam, if we can keep her happy and healthy during the summer I think she will have a real good chance. We'll talk about it later Sam. Lets get her legs rubbed and wraps put on her.

Spunky watched as I rubbed the filly's legs with lineament and then put the wrap on her. Matt brought a light stable sheet to put on the filly. Carlo brought her a fresh hay net full of sweet hay and tied it up for her. When we left the barn the filly was eating her hay and looked happy. I told Freddie we'd holler at him in a little while.

We walked down to the house and had coffee.

"Alright folks, we've seen what the filly can do and I'm impressed. Now we need to make a plan for her."

"You want me to ship her to Oaklawn, Spunky?"

"No Sam, they don't run two year olds down there. I think you should let Bill take her to Raton and give her a couple of easy races. We know how good she is but no one else does. With Cassie riding her we can win and never ask her to really run. The filly race they have towards the end of the meet pays really well. You can ship her to me at the city. Sam, every horse has so many good races before something goes wrong. We've been lucky with Light. He's stayed sound and is looking forward to his next race. Now part of his success is because Bill here figured out how to keep him happy. I swear he shouldn't have any hair on his ears. If Patty's not scratching him I am."

We all laughed about Light's scratching.

"Bill, I want you and Cassie to be on the lookout for a good exercise boy. Mine has put on to much weight and has found another job at the track. He doesn't have to get up so early."

I looked at Cassie. She smiled back. It looked as if I was going to be doing a lot more riding the next couple of months. I went to the barn and got Freddie. He was just getting ready to move up in he world and do it in a hurry.

I introduced Freddie to Spunky and told him Spunky needed a good exercise boy if he was interested.

"But Mr. Patton, what are you going to do?"

"Go back to work Freddie. Just the way I was doing before you got here. Everything is riding well and will be leaving in the next month or so. Spunkys colts along with mine will be going to Raton with Cassie and me. Go with Spunky Freddie. Listen to him and learn. You've got a chance to get a million dollars worth of education.

"May I use your phone?"

"Help yourself Freddie,"

I explained about Freddie needing to talk to his mom about the job. I told Spunky that if he went along with him he could trust him to do a good job.

"That's all I need to know Bill. If he's already ridden in some races I'll give him a chance to ride some of my string. If he does a good job for me I'm sure he can get a bunch more rides. He should be able to make some nice money.

"Mr. Davis, when do you plan on leaving sir?"

"In about two hours Freddie, think you can be ready?"

"I'll be back in an hour or so. What kind of clothes do I need?"

"Something warm, we've had snow and ice there too."

"I'll be back in a little while."

"Well Cassie, there goes my help. I guess I'll have to get back in riding shape."

"Bill, you've been riding with Freddie every day. Besides you love to ride the colts yourself anyway."

"Bill, how do you plan on taking the string to the track this year?"

"I'm going to have to get a trailer ordered."

"Bill, do you like my trailer?"

"You bet I do Spunky, I don't need an eight horse but a six horse would be perfect."

"I think I can get you a real deal on a trailer like mine. I've sold several trailers for the boy down there and he wants to breed a mare to Light. I'll call him and see what I can get done. What color do you want?"

"Black and silver Spunky, that is if you don't mind us using your colors."

"Don't mind at all son. In fact it makes me proud you'd want to use them."

Just a short time past an hour Freddie showed up with a duffel bag and was ready to go. He had a release signed by his mom saying he could go to work for Spunky. Spunky explained to him it wouldn't be needed due to the fact he was over eighteen.

Cassie got a hug from Spunky when they were ready to leave. Sam said he'd be back by noon and would be out as soon as he got back. I took Cassie to town and bought lunch. We discussed the upcoming spring, our wedding and the things we'd have to do to get ready for our summer in Raton. Cassie was going to get online and see what sort of housing was available for the summer. She wanted everything done before the last minute. I told her to take care of the housing problem. I'd have my hands full getting the horses and all of the tack ready to go.

After Cassie left for home I walked up to the barn and told Mike about Freddie going with Spunky. He was happy for Freddie and said it was time I went back to work. We laughed and spent the afternoon going over our equipment. We repaired what needed to be repaired and cleaned and oiled the rest. We drove down to the truck stop and had supper later. Mike was laughing about Sam and his relationship with Brenda. I told him about Jen's statement and we both had a good laugh.

The rest of the week passed quickly. I rode the colts and was pleased with their progress. My stud colt was coming along great. He was smaller than the rest but just seemed to have the mind set he was the biggest thing in the barn. He had become a big puppy so to speak. He loved his attention and was more than ready to go to work every morning. The four colts from Colorado were all doing well and would be leaving in another three weeks or so. It seemed their owner was happy to have them broke and training well. He wanted his trainer to finish their training at their track. It worked well for me and I didn't have a problem with his thinking.

Mom and Tom were doing fine, they were like a couple of kids. They had painted and redone most of Toms place and seemed to be having a ball doing it. Tom had been involved with the Federal boys on a big drug ring that was passing through our area. Due to his experience and knowledge of some of the folks in our area they had been able to stop the boys and all got long prison terms. His picture had been in the paper and everyone had been proud of his work. It looked as if he'd be reelected with no problem this spring. Cassie and I had had supper at their place a couple of times during the winter and she and mom had become best friends.

Sam showed up the next afternoon and told me Spunky was more than happy with Freddie. They had discussed all of the horses in Spunky's string on the way back and everything seemed to be going well. We discussed how I would bring the filly along and not get in any hurry. Finally Sam brought up Brenda and their relationship.

"Bill, I've not felt like this but once in my life. She is becoming a very important person in Jen's and my life."

"Sam, I don't see that you have a problem. You like her, Jen likes her so why worry. If everything keeps going along like it is now just relax and go along. If things work out then you and Jen will be a family again. Sam, Jen is going to need a mother and you need a wife. Just think how much fun it will be to share all the things that may happen this summer with her. Jen thinks she's cool and if she's happy then I guess everything is fine."

"You sound like Ike. He thinks it's funny seeing me run around and try to make things just right."

"Sam, I don't think everything being just right means a whole lot to Brenda. She, like you, has lost a partner and has had time to heal. You threw yourself into your work after your wife was killed and she did much the same when she lost her husband. She went back to school and made the most of what she had. She's an honest caring person Sam, and if I were you I'd be thanking my lucky stars I'd found her."

"I am thankful Bill. That's why I bought this."

Sam took a small box from his pocket and opened it. Inside was a beautiful ring, he planned on giving it to her this evening when he picked her up from work.

"I wish you luck, Sam. Let me know what she says. I'll be waiting to hear."

"I'll call you, Bill. I sure don't want to make a fool of myself."

After Sam left I went to the house and brought my books up to date. The accountant Sam had recommended to me was going to come out this weekend and take his first lesson. He would look over my books and tell me what needs to be done. I found I was looking forward to graduation, my grades were fine and I was proud I'd been fortunate enough to go back to school. Cassie called to tell me she had been in touch with a real estate women in Raton and we'd have to make a trip up there to look things over in a couple of weeks. She explained she didn't want us living in some dump. We'd go look, make a deposit and everything would be ready when we pulled in.

I told her about Sam and Brenda. She was happy and hoped that things would work out. I was supposed to call her and let her know how Sam came out.

I had just finished my dishes when Sam called.

"Bill, she said yes!"

"Great Sam, when are you all going to make it official?"

"I'm not sure, we'll have to get Jen to come back down to earth first. Bill, she is so happy."

"Do me a favor Sam. Have Brenda call Cass and give her the news."

"I'll do that Bill. We'll be out tomorrow some time. It's Brenda's weekend off, and she and Jen want to go riding. Bill, that brings up another problem I need to talk to you about. I'll see you tomorrow."

After the phone call I began to wonder what sort of problem Sam could have. I guess I'd find out tomorrow. I was just getting ready for bed when the phone rang. It was Spunky.

"Bill, I just got the new book for the races, there are two races I'm interested in. One is an allowance going six furlongs that I think will fit Slinker perfect. He's about to come out of his skin. The other is an allowance going a mile and a sixteenth that should fit Light."

"Spunky, when are these races?"

"Next weekend Bill, you think Cassie can make arrangements to come ride them?"

"I'll check and let you know Spunky. Have you talked to Sam?"

"No, I figured I'd let you do that for me."

"I'm sure he will want to come Spunky. I'll call him right now and then call you back."

I hung the phone up and called Sam.

"Sam, I just talked to Spunky. He's entering Slinker and Light in races for next weekend. He wanted to know if you would be there."

"You bet we will. You and Cassie will go with us won't you?"

"We'll go if you have room."

"Not a problem Bill. Call Spunky back and tell him we'll be there. When do you think we should leave?"

"We probably should leave Friday if we can. Cassie and I will have to get our license."

"How about eleven Friday morning? That will get us there by three and you all should be able to get your license before they close the track offices."

"I'll call Cassie and then call Spunky. See you tomorrow Sam, tell everyone hi."

I called Cassie and told her about the races. She was thrilled and said she would make arrangements at her school and would be down Thursday night."

I called Spunky and told him we'd be there on Friday afternoon and get our license. He was thrilled and told me Cassie and I were welcomed to stay with him and Patty. I told him about Sam and Brenda, he was thrilled Sam had found someone Jen approved of.

I went to bed and lay there thinking about all the things that had happened the last year. It was like a dream that I didn't want to wake up from. I'd gone from a wired together facility to a fine farm. I'd seen new places and things I'd never dreamed of seeing. I went to sleep wondering what Oaklawn would look like.

When Saturday morning rolled around I was looking forward to Cassie coming down. Sam's filly needed a gallop and I needed to work my stud colt. I'd been giving him long gallops and he had begun to pull hard and want to run. It had taken me two weeks to get him to relax and do what I wanted. I planned on giving him a three eighths work and figured we could work him against another of the colts who was needing a work. I had everything ready when Cassie showed up and we began working colts. She took Sam's filly out and gave her a good long gallop. The filly was becoming a pro at her works and listened to Cassie who talked to her all around the track. I was pleased with the work. I caught the filly and started leading her back to the barn when I saw Sam, Brenda and Jen watching from the barn door.

"She looks great Bill, the work the other day doesn't seem to have bothered her at all."

"No bother at all Sam. She's ready to go but we just want her relaxed and ready when we ask her. Morning Brenda. Jen good to see you."

"Morning Bill, do you and Cassie have plans for this evening?"

"None that I know of Brenda. I usually have to take her out to supper why?"

"Sam and I would like to take you all out to supper. As you well know he gave me this."

"I seem to recall seeing something like that somewhere. Congratulations to the three of you. That includes you little sis."

"Thank you Bill, I'm so happy."

"Have you shown Mike yet?"

"No I haven't, where is he?"

"He went to his trailer to get another coat, the one he was wearing was too heavy."

Mike as if on cue came striding through the barn door. Brenda showed him the ring and got a big hug. He told Sam he was getting a fine girl. Brenda asked him if he would give her away at their wedding. Her father had passed away earlier and Mike was like her second father. He was all smiles and said he'd be proud to do that.

"Where and when do you plan on getting married?"

"You know Sam, Bill. He's not one to put things off. He wants to get married Monday evening at the hospital chapel. All my friends who work there want to help out and it was where we met after all."

"Cassie, we've been upstaged again."

"Don't worry Bill, our time will come. What time Sam?"

"Six that evening if you can make it Cassie."

"Oh I'll be there. I wouldn't miss this for the world. I'll spend the night at Bill's and my little sis and I can have a hen party. I can take her to school on my way. My first class is not until ten anyway."

"Can I dad, please?"

"Yes you can spend the night with Bill and Cassie. Now what else do you have to work, Bill."

"My stud. Cassie has never ridden him and I want to give him a three eighths work for the first time."

I had planned on working the stud with another horse but decided to let Cassie work him and give me her ideas about his abilities. We tacked the stud up and Mike led him and Cassie out onto the track. The stud wanted to work but soon responded to Cassie's voice. They made a full turn around the track and Mike turned the stud and Cassie loose. The colt was more than willing to go to work. His neck was bowed and he wanted Cassie to release her hold. As they neared the three eighths pole she did release her hold and got down on the little horse. His neck suddenly stretched forward and he began to run. I was amazed at what I saw. He seemed to accelerate with every jump and was flat out in three jumps. Cassie was low on his back but still had a hold on him. When they crossed the finish line Cassie raised up in her irons and whooped like an Indian. I knew she was pleased with the colt. I looked at the watch in my pocket and was pleased myself. My little rescued colt was a racehorse. He might just be a six furlong horse but there were plenty of races for horses at six furlongs. Cassie was all smiles when she brought the little horse back.

"Bill, he's fantastic. When I asked him to go he just seemed to explode. At first I thought he might just be a sprinter but now I'm not sure. He's a handful and seemed to have all sorts of energy left. Bill, he just might go a mile."

"We'll find out Cassie, I was worried about him at first but he has just seemed to take to the training and loves it. Up until today I wasn't sure how good he was but now I know. Cassie we're going to make some money with this colt. He will love the track at Raton."

As it turned out I wasn't the only one who had a watch on the colt. Sam was smiling, too.

"Bill, I'd say you had a nice colt there. It looked as if he was just getting ready to roll when he hit the wire."

"It will all depend on how far he can go Sam. I'll not be disappointed if he is a sprinter but Cassie seems to think he may be able to go on out. His dam ran a distance on the grass so we'll try him both ways. If he likes the grass we may just have something special."

We took care of the stud and went to the house. Sam had borrowed his friend's jet again but this time his friend was going along with us. I could tell Brenda was excited.

"Sort of mind numbing isn't it Brenda?"

"Yes it is Bill, this is going to take some getting used too. Until today I'd never seen a thoroughbred worked. I know how Cassie felt when she turned the colt loose. It's the greatest feeling in the world to feel them when they unwind. I've had the experience once or twice myself when I had a really good barrel horse. At the time I couldn't afford to keep them because I was going to school and needed the money.

"I've been there Brenda, you find a good one and someone comes along and you need the money. You sell and cry after the bills are paid."

"That's exactly what I did Bill."

"Brenda, we'll go horse looking this spring, I'm sure Jen is going to want to learn how to run barrels and we'll get the two of you a horse."

"Sam dear, she already has one of the best in the country. Coalie is a real seasoned barrel horse. He has won about everything in the area. The local girls were thrilled when his last rider went off to school and got married. I've got a real fine prospect but I've not had the time or the place to train him."

"Which leads me to why we came out here. Bill how much land lays on the other side of the creek to the north?"

"About forty acres Sam why?"

"I'd like to buy it. I'd like to build a house, barn and an arena if you'll sell.

"Sam, I could never sell it to you but I'll give it to you as a wedding gift. At least I'll be able to get partly even with you for all the things you've done for me."

"Bill, that's not good business."

"Look around you Sam, was it good business to build all this and not even know if a boy could make it pay?"

"That was different Bill."

"No it wasn't Sam, you did this for Bill, now let him do something for you."

"Sam, do as Bill wants, I've been in his shoes and we little folks like to pay our debts. It's a mater of pride."

"You don't think your mother would mind Bill?"

"Sam, it won't be any problem at all. When do you plan on starting?"

"I may have Ike come out and look things over tomorrow."

"Why don't we drive over and look at it now? We've got plenty of light."

"Sounds like a good idea Bill let's go look it over."

We got in our trucks and drove down to the northwest corner of my place. We walked out the piece of ground and Sam, Brenda and Jen were thrilled with the location. Jen was thrilled because she would be able to take care of Coalie herself. They began discussing where they would put their house and barn. As Cassie said later it was great to watch them begin to plan their life together. Later we went back to the house and had coffee. Sam said he would have a man come out and survey the property then have his attorney draw up the deed.

A short time later Mike came down to tell me he and Carlo would handle the evening chores. I told him thanks and that I would be up later to check on the stud. I wanted to check his legs. Cassie called her folks and told them she would be a little late and gave them the news about Sam and Brenda's wedding. We followed Sam and Brenda to the Mexican café that we had eaten at many times before. There was a table waiting when we walked in. I was shocked to see Mom and Tom sitting at the table waiting on us.

We were told Tom was going to stand up with Sam at the wedding. The meal was great and we had a great visit. I told mom about Sam wanting to buy the forty acres across the creek and she suggested I give it to him. We both laughed when I told her I had. I got a hug and a kiss. She told me she was proud of me.

Later Cassie and I drove back to the house and went to the barn. I checked the colt's front legs and made sure he had plenty of water and hay. I had to pet on him and give him some attention before leaving the stall. Even Cassie gave him some attention. When I turned the regular lights out Cassie was laughing.

"What is so funny Cass?"

"Bill, folks are going to feel sorry for you when you show up with this year's string. They are going to be shocked when the racing starts. You stand a chance of winning their big races with the stud and the filly. The colts Spunky has sent you are nice but I do have a question for you."

"What sort of question."

"What about Light's little brother?"

"He's a nice colt Cass, but he hasn't shown me anything at all like his brother. I've tried several things and right now he's training well but I'll just have to wait and see."

"Spunky and I talked the other day and I told him what you had done with him and he was pleased. Like he said the two horses do have different daddies and that makes a difference. It will be fun to watch and see if he comes around. It would be something to see him and your colt in the same race."

"That is what we're going to do Wednesday when you come down. I want to work the two of them together."

"Let them work against each other. Bill that might just work."

I walked Cassie to her truck and got my kiss. She said she'd be here about four thirty. I told her I was going to wear my suit. She was pleased with my decision and said she would dress up too.

The next day after school I was headed home when my cell phone rang. It was Ike and he wanted to know when I would be home.

"I'll be home in about five minutes Ike why?"

"I'm supposed to look over the piece of ground Sam is buying. I'm not sure what I'm supposed to be looking at. I figured you knew so I called."

"Come on out Ike, I know where they want the house and barn."

"I'll be right there Bill, the boss man is just not himself this morning. I think he has something else on his mind."

"I think you're right Ike, I'll be at the house when you get there. The quarter horse folks won't be gone for another hour or so."

Twenty minutes after I got home Ike pulled up in his truck. I had him drive back down the drive and head north on the highway. He'd get a good idea what they would have to do for a driveway into the property. I had him pull off the highway and pointed out the corner of the property. We went through the fence and I showed him where Sam and Brenda had talked about putting their new home. We walked on further and I showed him where they wanted the barn.

"Well now I know what I'll need out here to get the pads built and a road into the place. Sam called and said to come out and get things started he was late for an appointment. Bill, I didn't even know he had bought the land."

"It was a sudden thing late yesterday afternoon Ike. Sam is in love so don't be too hard on him."

"Bill, I'm thrilled for him but even after all these years I can't read his mind. I figured if anyone would know what was going on it would be you. I'll get some equipment out here and go to work. Knowing Sam like I do he'll want this thing done in a day or two. It will take a week but he'll want it done in half that."

"You know Sam. When he gets the bit in his teeth he's hard to stop. He'll settle down when Brenda gets hold of him. She's good people Ike. She understands what it means to work."

"I know Bill. I knew her husband before they got married. He and I had worked on a few jobs together when we were still in high school. She'll be good for Sam and better yet for Jen. She'll teach Jen how to be a real people and work for things."

"That will be great Ike, now that she has her eyesight back things have began to change. She wants to get Coalie down here and take care of him herself. She needs to learn how to do those things. She is a pretty tough little girl and with Brenda's help I think she will be fine."

I went back to the house and changed clothes. I went to the barn and went to work. I finished up with the colts and was just heading back to the house when I saw several of Sams trucks go by following Ike's truck. Things were under way. I laid out my clothes and made sure I had everything ready. I planned on doing things early so I would have time to get ready when Cassie showed up.

Mike and I fed the colts while Carlo worked the track for the next morning's works. Mike was going to the wedding so as soon as we finished he headed to his trailer to get ready. I was walking to the house when I saw Cass turn off the highway and start up to the house. I waited until she parked then helped her carry her things in. It seemed every time she came she brought another box or two of her things. She planned on being moved in by the time we got married.

I got a bath and began to dress. Cass was in the bathroom when I went to the kitchen for a drink. The phone rang and I saw it was Spunky.

"Spunky, how are you?"

"Fine Bill, I called to let you know both horses are in for next Saturday. Slinker is in a six furlong sprint and Light is in a seven and a half furlong race. Slinker is in a fifty thousand dollar claimer and Light is in an allowance race."

"You don't think anyone will claim Slinker?"

"Not really, but if they do we'll not be sorry. It takes a while to make fifty thousand, Bill. Besides, he is running against a bunch of horses that were running allowance company, he'll have to fight for the win if he wants it. If we should get lucky and win then we'll only run him in allowance races."

"I'll tell Sam and we'll see you Friday in time to get our licenses."

"I'll be looking forward to seeing you all Bill. Tell everyone hello."

When Cassie came into the kitchen all I could do was stare. She wore a light blue blouse with a dark blue shirt. Her hair was styled and I couldn't believe that this beautiful girl was soon going to be my wife.

"Bill, you're staring."

"Yes ma'am I am. I'm just thinking how lucky I am to have you."

"Well Mr. Patton, you're pretty special yourself. Folks haven't seen you in a suit and I'm going to stay real close to you. I don't want some young nurse trying to stake a claim on you."

"No danger in that Cass but I'm sure going to keep an eye on you."

We saw Mike go down the driveway and went out to my truck and headed to the hospital. When we pulled into the parking lot we saw Jen standing at a side door waiting for us. She had a small bag, which she brought out with her to my truck. I got out to take the bag and put it in my truck.

"Holy cow, Bill is that you?"

"Pretty spiffy looking isn't he Jen?"

"He sure is Cass, wait until everyone else gets a look at him. Cass, he's almost pretty."

"Hey you two, be nice."

We were laughing after I loaded Jen's bag in the truck and locked up. When we reached the door of the chapel Sam and Ike stood outside.

"Ike, is that Bill?"

"I'm not sure Sam, it could be but it looks more like some high powered lawyer."

"It's me you two roughnecks. Now get off my case."

"Cassie, Brenda is in back. She said for you to come back. Jen can show you the way."

"I guess Mike is going to walk her down the isle. You'd have to fight him to keep him from it, Bill."

"I saw you got things started this morning Ike."

"You bet we did, we'll have the pad finished for the house and barn by tomorrow morning. I'll get the driveway laid out and packed by the evening. Brenda told me she wanted a turn around in front of the barn."

"That's a good idea, Ike. It will come in handy."

The preacher arrived and I went inside the chapel and took a seat. A short time later Ike's wife and Cassie came into the chapel and sat down with me. There were several nurses and other folks I assumed worked with Brenda.

We waited and watched as Sam and Ike came into the chapel and took their place down front. The wedding march began playing and Mike and Brenda appeared at the doorway and slowly walked down the isle. Brenda looked wonderful in an off white suit. Mike looked great too. I'd never seen him in a suit before.

A short time later the service ended and Sam kissed his bride. Everyone in the chapel cheered and then wished the couple well. Cassie and I rounded up Jen and left the chapel. I drove straight to our local pizza parlor. Jen, Cassie and I raced to the front door.

Later that evening we played cards until it was Jen's bedtime. When she was in bed Cassie and sat down on the couch and talked about going up to Raton to look at a house to rent for the summer. She had brought several pictures of homes she had gotten from a real estate person. We sorted through the pictures and settled on three that we would look at when we went up there. We decided to go up on a Saturday three weeks from this coming weekend. We wanted to get things settled before everyone else had taken their pick.

"School will be out in another six weeks. I can't believe the winter has passed so quickly. I remember thinking it would never be over. Now it's almost gone and we're going house hunting. Things have sure changed since I walked away from here almost a year ago. I had no idea where I was headed or what I would do when I got there. Now look at what's happened. We'll be flying to Hot Springs Saturday in a private jet. We'll be going to the track in May with our own string of race horses. Cassie, if I'm dreaming don't wake me up."

"Bill, you're not dreaming. I wake up every so often and think how lucky we've been. All I know is that I love you Bill Patton and I'd have loved you even if you didn't have this training center. Now we'd better get to bed and get some rest."

I got up early and with Mikes help got the chores done in a hurry. I had breakfast started when the girls got up. Jen sat down at the table and ate her eggs, bacon and toast. She drank the rich hot chocolate I had made and smiled at me.

"Bill Patton, you're a keeper for sure. My sis is a lucky woman."

"I sure am, Jen. He cooks a mean breakfast doesn't he?"

"You bet he does. I'm stuffed and ready for the day."

We visited until it was time for everyone to head to school. Cassie said she would be down Wednesday and we'd work the colts. I watched as the girls drove down the driveway then headed to school myself.

School was near an end and everything was beginning to work around graduation. My grades were good and I'd have no problem in getting my diploma. All I wanted was out. I was ready to head to Raton and get to work.

Cass showed up Wednesday and we worked the two stud colts together. It seemed to work. Spunky's colt wanted to compete and showed a lot more than I had expected. He would be happy to hear about how he was progressing.

Friday evening Cassie arrived just before chores. Sam had called and said he, Brenda and Jen would pick us up at eight thirty the next morning. We ate supper watched a little television and went to bed. I was up early and helped Mike with chores. When I got back to the house Cassie was setting breakfast on the table. We ate a quick breakfast and finished getting ready to go. We each had a small bag sitting by the back door when Sam and his family drove up.

The flight to Hot Springs was a lot of fun. We talked about what Sam and Brenda planned for a house and how they wanted the barn built. It seemed Brenda and Jen had everything lined out and Sam was to take care of it. When we reached the Hot Springs airport we got a rental car and drove over to the track. We got our licenses and went to find Spunky and Patty. We were all looking forward to seeing Light.

Spunky and Patty were waiting when we drove up and parked. Gray Light saw Cassie and began to holler. When I walked over to where I could see him he began rearing up and kicked his stall wall.

"Bill, go scratch his ears before he cripples himself."

I scratched Light's ears until he was half asleep and happy. It was nice to be missed.

We discussed the upcoming races and how Spunky thought they would be run. Cassie asked a few questions while I went to Slinkers stall and gave him some attention, too. He had grown and matured since I'd last seen him and was a good looking horse. He like Light, enjoyed his attention and nudged me to let me know I was doing things right. I'd be proud to lead him into the saddling paddock tomorrow.

Spunky told me about the saddling paddock, it was unlike any other I had ever seen. It was under the grandstands in what seemed like a pit. Folks stood up above you and looked down on the horses. For horses not used to the pit it sometimes caused some interesting things. Things would get festive as Spunky called it.

We waved to Sam and his family who had a room at a local motel. After Spunky and I finished feeding we went to their small home and relaxed while Patty and Cassie cooked our supper.

I spent another night on the couch and was up early and went to the track with Spunky for morning chores and to watch the other horses in his string work. Freddie was waiting when we arrived and helped with chores. He told me he was happy and was learning a bunch while working with Spunky. He said he just might get a ride in a day or so and was looking forward to watching Cassie ride today.

After chores and works, Spunky and I went back to his house and changed clothes. When we went back to the track, Sam and his family were waiting. He and Spunky visited about the race. He had a box up in the grandstands for his family. When the races were about ready to start Spunky and I went to work. Cassie had a mount on a friend of Spunky's horse in the second race so she would get a race over the track and know where to put Slinker and Light. Spunky and I stood on the backside and watched as they loaded the horses into the gate. Spunky told me the mare Cassie was riding had one run and it had to be saved till the last minute. The owner said she needed a race, and would be thrilled if she ran as good as third in today's race.

The gates opened and the race began. Cassie settled the mare in mid pack and got her settled. The race was a mile and a sixteenth and she had all kinds of time to get the mare ready to fire. Two of the front runners began to fall back as they approached the final turn. Cassie and the pack began to gather them up as they started around the turn. Spunky had explained to Cassie about the long stretch. It was one of the longest I had ever seen and a jockey would have to rate his horse and move at the right time.

We watched as Cassie suddenly moved the mare to the outside and began the run up the middle of the track. Cassie had gambled the mare would have enough bottom to make the run to the wire. She was down low on the mare's back and helping her every way she could. They ran a good second beaten only by a head. Spunky had smiled and said his friend would be very happy.

We went back to the barn and began putting the finishing touches on Slinker. When the call came I led him over across the track to the saddling paddock. I led him around and was glad when Spunky waved me over to the saddling stall. The area was too confined for my taste. With the track man's help Spunky got Cassie's saddle set in place and got the over girth put in place. Cassie arrived at the stall and visited with Spunky while I took Slinker around the walking area. When the call "Riders up" came I held Slinker while Spunky gave Cassie a leg up. I led the two of them out and turned them over to the pony rider.

"Go get them Cassie, he's ready."

"Let's get our picture taken Bill. I think he's ready, too."

I stood out front of the stands and watched the horses as they were led in front of the grandstand. I always enjoyed this part of the race. Every horse was ready to run and you could feel them getting themselves ready. Slinker was on his toes but Cassie was talking to him, and he was settled down before they reached the back side to where they would warm up. When they were led in back of the gates my heart rate began to quicken. I watched as the horses were led into the gates. Cassie and Slinker were in gate four. I watched as he was led in and settled. Finally the gates were full and the track announcer said "The horses are all in line."

The gates opened and I saw Cassie get Slinker settled in behind the front running horse. By the quarter mile pole Cassie and Slinker were a half length off the leading front running horse. Cassie was up high on Slinker and was letting him roll along at the speed he wanted. As they entered the turn the front running horse began to falter and dropped back. Cassie suddenly had Slinker on the lead and was sitting perfectly still not asking him for anything. She and Slinker had a good five-length lead. Just as they began to come into the long straight away, Cassie got down on Slinker and asked him to run.

He ran and actually managed to put another length between himself and the rest of the horses. Cassie had timed it perfectly and had given Slinker every chance to win if he had the desire and ability to do it. Slinker showed Spunky he was ready to move up to allowance company and won by two full lengths. Being a long shot the crowd roared and cheered. Cassie had ridden a beautiful race. She had set her horse exactly where he needed to be and let him run when the time was right.

I caught Slinker when Cassie brought him back at a trot. She was smiling big time.

"Hi Bill, didn't he do great?" He sat there just like we wanted then when we got the lead he waited until I asked him to run then gave me his all. He's become a real professional Bill and you helped make him one."

"He sure did Cassie girl. Now hop off and let's get our picture made."

Cassie jumped off Slinker and Spunky removed the over girth then gave Cassie a leg back up on Slinker. I led them into the winner's circle where our picture was taken. Sam, Brenda and Jen were all smiles. Sam was flying so to speak. He and Spunky were smiling and talking like magpies when I followed the track steward to the test barn. I walked Slinker around the test barn area until one of the crew came out and took him inside. I waited a few minutes, then they brought Slinker back out to me.

I took Slinker back to the barn and turned him over to a man Spunky had hired to bathe and walk his horses cool. Spunky was already working on Light. He had the wraps on his front legs and was putting rundown bandages on his hind legs because of the heavy sand in the track. He had just finished when the first call to the paddock was called for Light's race.

I put Light's racing bridle on and then his halter over it. I put the lead shank on him and led him out of his stall and started for the saddling paddock. When we got there I led him around and talked to him. I even scratched his ears as I led him and he seemed to relax. When Spunky waved to me I held him while he and the track man put Cassie's saddle in place. I led him out of the saddling stall and and walked him while Cassie visited with Spunky. I had no idea how they were going to work out how she would ride this race.

The track man called "Riders up."

I held Light as Spunky gave Cassie a leg up. As I led her to the pony horse I wished her luck.

"There are some horses in here who are million dollar winners Bill. To'day they are going to go home and tell mamma they saw a real race horse. See you in the winners circle."

I watched the post parade and saw that Light was not wasting any energy. His ears kept flipping back and forth as he listened to Cassie talk to him. Freddie walked up beside me.

"Boy he looks great. I've never seen him flip his ears that way before."

"Cassie is talking to him Freddie. He listens to her and will run only when she tells him to. We worked with him last year and he's not forgotten. Spunky says she could ride him without a bridle."

"She rode a beautiful race on Slinker. She made that move before I would have but it caught everyone else flat footed."

"She has that ability to do that Freddie. She just seems to know when the other jocks are going to push the go button and simply beats them to the punch."

"Is she going to rate Light like she did Slinker?"

"I have no idea. She and Spunky make that decision just before the race. I was walking Light, so I don't know. We'll just have to wait and see what happens."

The horses were loading into the gates. Light had drawn the ten gate on the outside of all the rest. He'd have a tough time getting the rail from that position unless he got a fantastic start. The track announcer said "The horses are all in line."

The gates opened and the bell rang. The horses broke from the gates and I saw Cassie let Light run straight ahead then moved him over and settled him into about sixth place. I overheard a gentleman say Light was out of his class and never should have been entered in this race. I was watching Cassie and knew she had Light exactly where she wanted him. As they went down the back side Light and Cassie moved up two more spots. They were now fourth. As they started into the final turn I saw the favorite who was running third start his run. It was what Cassie and Light had been waiting for. Suddenly she was down on Light and he seemed to be flying. Suddenly he was even with the favorite and was a good half length in front before the other jockey realized he had made his move and been caught. Cassie got lower on Light and they pulled away from the favorite with ease. Light won by two lengths and had never been touched with the whip. The papers the next day would question just how good Light really was.

It made no difference to me because I felt I knew. Besides I'd given Sam my money and had done well for the day. I'd won on Slinker's race, too. I ran out onto the track and caught Light when Cass galloped him back. He wasn't even breathing hard. He'd waited for Cassie to tell him to run and had not worked that hard. Cassie jumped off and Spunky removed the over girth and then gave Cassie a leg back up on Light. I led them into the winner's circle and had our picture made. I got a kiss from Cassie before she went to be weighed out. I led Light to the test barn and again waited until he was brought back out and turned over to me.

When I got back to the barn I gave him his bath before turning him over to the hot walker. I was cleaning his stall when Freddie showed up and began to help me.

"Sorry to be late, Bill. But a couple of reporters caught me and wanted to know just how good Light was."

"What did you tell them?"

"I told them I was only his exercise rider and had never let him down to run so I had no idea how good he was."

"That's good. You didn't have to lie and I'm sure you don't know how good he is but you're beginning to form an opinion."

"Yes I am. I saw him when he came off the track, and he wasn't breathing hard. I've ridden enough horses to know when a horse has worked. Gray Light didn't have to work hard to win his race."

"You're right, Freddie. But we won't talk about it. Let folks form their own ideas. You'll be getting a lot less sleep before the meet is over. When the big stakes start and Light is entered, you'll be sitting outside his stall all night. Reading a book or whatever you like to do. I did it last year and you'll have to do it down here. I like to think everyone is honest, but I'd sure enough not trust them with the amount of money involved."

"Bill, I know what you mean. I'll tell Mr. Davis I'll be honored to sit up with Light when the time comes."

"Just be sure to scratch his ears. He loves it and it seems to keep him relaxed and happy. That's how we want to keep him."

"I'll do my best to keep him happy."

We had Light's stall ready for him when he was cooled. Freddie was holding him while I rubbed his legs with liniment, when Sam and his family showed up.

"How is he, Bill?"

"He's great, Sam. He thinks he just had a work."

"God, he was beautiful when Cassie asked him to go. Brenda was afraid he was going to get beat when Cassie sat him in sixth place. She began to get excited when they moved to fourth and then saw what we all knew Cassie was doing. She was toying with the favorite."

"She rode two great races today, Sam. The race with Slinker was great."

"I agree with yo,u Bill. We've got a great jockey. Oh yes, I have your money."

He handed me my money. Slinker had gone off at twelve to one and Light had gone off at eight to one. I'd indeed done well for the day.

Spunky, Patty and Cassie all showed up and were smiling.

"Got him wrapped up, Bill?"

"Sure do, Spunky. I bathed him myself and rubbed his legs, before I put his stall wraps on."

"Sorry we're late but we got cornered by the press and they were hard to get away from. They seemed to be impressed with our jockey."

"Why not, Spunky. She's sure enough the prettiest jockey here."

"That is a fact Brenda. I watched her ride Light and watched Bill down on the apron. He rode every jump with her. It was fun to watch. Bill, what do you think we should do next?"

"I'd not run Slinker for claim again, unless you want to lose him. He's become a pro, Spunky and is getting better. With Light I'd look for a stakes race and if there is not one in the book I'd run him in an allowance going a mile or better. He's shown everyone he can win short, now let the big boys know he can go long. I think if you ask, the track condition man might just write you a race that will fit him.

"You're thinking the same way I am, Bill. I think it's time we wake some folks up about how good he really is right now. I think there is a fifty thousand dollar stakes race going a mile and seventy yards in about three weeks. He should be ready to run by then."

"He'll be more than ready. You want to remember there are three big stakes races at the end of the meet. You'll want him fresh for all three of them."

"He needed the race today, and in three weeks he should be on go again. That should give us three weeks before the big boys show up for the first of the big stakes races."

"Sounds like a plan, Spunky. What do you think Sam?"

"Bill, I know construction. Planning what to do with the horses is your and Spunky's job. What ever you all think is right suits me. Everyone involved in this operation is doing a wonderful job. I know there will be setbacks but they won't be because some one didn't care."

"Sam, the offers are going to start coming again you know."

"Well Spunky, we're in this deal for the long haul. I think my wife is having a ball on her first trip to the track."

"Gentlemen, I'm the new comer to this group but I do know horses. The ones I've seen you all run today are good horses. You all are having a ball and don't need the money folks are going to offer you. I've had good horses before and had to sell. I'd like to keep these and see what its like to watch them grow. Spunky, you've worked your whole life to have a horse like this and I think it's time to reap the harvest and enjoy the ride."

"That is why I sold Sam half interest in the horses. We can both enjoy the ride. Bill is getting our next string ready and I think he's excited about a couple of them. Now when Bill gets excited I pay attention. He's proved to me he knows what to get excited about. I think we have a great team. Patty and I are having the time of our lives."

"Bill, we'd better get to the airport before that front moves in."

"I'm ready when you are Sam. If we hurry we'll be home before dark."

We said our goodbyes and headed to the airport. Patty said she would mail us copies of the local paper. Cassie told us about the interview she had given the reporter. It seems he had done some research and knew she was a high school senior and only rode for Mr. Davis. She said the man was a gentleman and had asked some questions no one had ever asked before. Like what was she going to do after high school? What her family thought about her riding horses and what were her dreams for the future. I was anxious to get the papers and read the article.

We landed at home an hour before sunset and went to the farm. While Sam went with me to do chores. The women ran into town and did some quick grocery shopping.

Mike was thrilled to hear both Slinker and Light had won their races. Sam told him about how Brenda had really gotten into the racing game.

"I'll bet she did. She's had her hands full for a while. I'm glad to see she's having a good time."

The women came back from town and we were put to work. We carried everything into the house and watched as they went to work. They fixed sandwiches, had two types of salads and a couple of deserts. Brenda was loading Sam's plate with vegetables. He frowned but smiled when she told him to eat. She said she wanted him around for a long while.

The early evening news came on and one of the first things shown was Cassie and Light winning today's race. They said they would have more coverage later in the sports section. Needless to say everyone grabbed their plates and moved into the living room. Jen turned up the sound when the sports section came on. The sports section had film clips of all three races Cassie had ridden in that day. The featured clip was when Light made his move and seemed to blow by the front running horse. I had not gotten to see any video replay of the race and was amazed at how easy he had taken the lead. Everyone in the living room cheered when Cassie and Light crossed the finish wire.

The phone began to ring and we were kept busy for the next hour or so. Cassie's folks called and gave her a couple of numbers to call. It seemed she was becoming a local celebrity. It seemed everyone wanted her to do a commercial. Sam was busy talking to a gentleman. He had talked to Spunky and thought maybe he could buy Sam's share of Gray Light. Sam had laughed and said no thanks.

"What are people thinking? They see a horse that just might be good enough to run in the Derby and they think just because they have never heard of us they can buy us out."

"They are folks with money, Brenda. They want the prestige of having a horse in the Derby on Derby day. It's something that is important to them and a tax write off at the end of the year. Like our trip today, Sam can write it off on his taxes. He took us to the races but it was an expense, he could deduct."

"Sam darling, I'm liking this racing business more all the time. It's been a wonderful day but I think we should get home. Jen's had a big day and I for one want a good hot bath and a good night's sleep."

"I know what you mean, Brenda. I need a hot soaking bath myself. Bill, we'll see you and Cassie later."

I had enough stuff left over to feed me lunch for a week. Cassie ran herself a bath while I got out my money and counted my winnings. I put most of the money in a small fireproof box I'd bought a few weeks before. I'd been putting money back for a while and thought I just might have enough to pay the lease for the place up at Raton for the upcoming summer. I'd have to make a trip to the bank tomorrow and make a deposit. I'd write a check for the lease and turn the receipt over to my accountant. He had really helped me learn how to run the business end of the farm.

The next morning I'd bought Cassie breakfast. We had driven up to look at the new building site. Ike and the boys had been working hard and it showed. The home Sam and Brenda were building was not going to be a monster. It would have three bedrooms, a modest living and dining room. They would have a large family room with a kitchen area which would overlook the barn and pasture area. They planned on having tile floors because of their coming and going from the outside and barn area.

Sam had turned the house project over to Brenda and Jen. The two of them had taken over and were enjoying the planning. A large fireplace was being planned that would have a nice insert that would not waste wood. It would keep things toasty and warm on the cold winter days. Sam had only requested one item. He wanted a pool where he could swim and try and stay in shape. He was studying how to cover the pool and use it year round.

Spunky called every other day. He had entered several races over the next two weeks only to have the other horses scratch and the race be canceled. The big boys were playing games.

After three scratched races Spunky decided he'd change Light's training schedule. He planned to let Freddie and an exercise boy work Light against

Slinker and bring Light up to the next race, the same way we had done at Raton. I had agreed with him. Let the big boys play their game. We'd play our rules.

The first of the three big races were two weeks away. He'd work Light with Slinker and be ready in spite of the big boys.

I continued working the colts and was more than pleased with their progress. It seemed Mike was always smiling. He and Carlo kept the barn spotless. They seemed to take a lot of pride in it being just right.

Mike had told me how much fun they were having just watching the young horses come along and develop.

Our little track was still making good money. The number of folks using it each morning was increasing. Mike was laughing one morning when I got back from school. It seemed several of the boys asked why he didn't have doughnuts for them to buy each morning. He started with three dozen and his sales had gone up to five. I told him the money from the doughnut sales was his. He had smiled and said thanks.

Cassie came down on Wednesday and worked Sam's filly. She was doing great. Now all I had to do was decide when to enter her when they started writing the filly races at Raton. I wanted two races in her before the filly stakes race was run. She would need the experience.

When we were finished working the colts we drove up to Sam and Brenda's new house site. We wanted to see what they had done since moving into their new home.

We saw Brenda coming up from the barn. She and Jen had their horses settled into their new home. They rode every day and the progress Jen had made was wonderful. She was becoming a real cowgirl. Coalie and Brenda had given her a crash course in barrel racing and she had survived. It was amazing how far she had come in such a short time. Brenda was really pleased and proud of the way she had progressed.

The house was nearing completion and Brenda was excited. She wanted to show us everything. It was great to see her so happy. She took us to see Jen's room, which she had decorated herself.

There was a picture of her and Cassie racing up the track the day her class had come out to the center. Another was of me working her father's filly and a large picture of Cassie, Jen and me hung on another wall. A brass plaque at the bottom read "My Big Brother, Sister and Me." It caused tears to come to my eyes. I noticed Cassie had the same problem.

The following week Spunky called. The first of the "Big Three" races was at seven and a half furlongs. The race had drawn only six entries. It seemed the big boys had figured Light was too tough at that distance and would wait for the longer races to run against him.

Everyone was ready for the first race of the series. Sam had his friend's jet ready to go to Hot Springs. The day before the first race I had just finished breakfast when Cassie arrived. Sam and Brenda pulled in right behind her. I picked up my bag and went out the door. I for one was more than ready.

I was surprised to see Jen but happy she was going to get to go along. When we arrived at the airport we found our plane was fueled up and ready. The flight down was a lot of fun. Jen, Cassie, Brenda and I had a big Hearts game. When we landed we got our rental car and drove to the track. Spunky was waiting for us when we pulled in.

"Morning, partners. It's good to see you."

"Morning, Spunky. How's Light?"

"He's fine, Bill. He'll be better after you and Cassie let him know you're here."

I saw Freddie get up from a bale of hay and wave to me. He had a new Western in his hand and was ready for a long night.

"Bill, this kept me awake last night. I figured it would help you tonight."

"Thanks Freddie, I have a couple of new ones myself. I figured we might need them."

I walked to Light's stall and gave him some attention. He rubbed his head on my shoulder and nickered softly. He was glad to see me. I scratched his ears and in a few moments he was relaxed and seemed to be ready for a nap.

Cassie left for the jock room and Spunky went home to change. Sam, Brenda and Jen came for a look at Light then walked over to the grandstand. They would have lunch before the races started.

Spunky had Cassie a mount in the third race. A friend of his had a horse entered and was thrilled to get Cassie to ride him. It looked to be a tough race and he wanted every advantage he could get.

I got the grooming box out of the tack room without disturbing Freddie who was sound asleep. I braided Light's mane and had him shining when Spunky and Patty came back. It was strange to see Spunky in a suit and tie. I some how wished he was wearing his flannel shirt, jeans and boots.

I got a kiss from Patty who was going over to join Sam and the bunch in the clubhouse. A couple of her friends were going to give her a ride. Spunky looked at Light and smiled.

"Keep him happy, that's the secret to a good racehorse. Bill, Patty said to tell you you'd need to take your suit to the Derby. She really thinks we're going to get to go."

"I had it cleaned last week, Spunky. I think we have a very good chance of going, myself. We have three tough races but I think Light can win them all. The big boys won't like it but at this point their money doesn't make their horses run any faster."

Freddie came out of the tack room just as Spunky finished putting the bandages on Light's legs. He was going to go get a sandwich and would be back so Spunky and I could go over to the track kitchen and watch the third race. A short time later he came back and Spunky and I walked over to the kitchen to watch the closed circuit T.V.

The third race had just come on the track when we walked in. We found a booth and ordered coffee and pie. The race turned out to be as tough as Spunky and I thought it would be. Cassie and the horse she was riding battled two others up the long stretch. At the finish wire she had finished third by a neck. Later I would find out she had ordered a picture to put in our scrapbook.

Spunky and I walked back over to the barn and finished getting Light ready for his upcoming race. When the call to the paddock came I was more than thrilled that the time had come. I put the lead shank on light and with Freddie carrying all the things we would need in a bucket followed Spunky over to the track.

Light was on his toes and I noticed for the first time was the favorite in the race. A late scratch left only five horses in the race. I led Light around until it was time to saddle. It seemed to take forever, but when he was ready I led him around while Spunky and Cassie decided how they would run the race. "Jockeys Up" came over the loud speaker. Spunky gave Cassie a leg up on Light and I wished her luck.

"See you in the winner's circle, Bill. Today is Light's time to shine."

Freddie and I went outside to watch the horses warm up. We found a place high up in the outside bleachers where we could see the entire track. After warming up on the track backside, the horses were led to the gate and began to load.

"The horses are all in line" The bell rang and the gates flew open. Thirty yards from the gate Cassie had Light out in front and down on the rail. They suddenly had a three length lead on the field. I watched and knew Cassie had Light on cruise. She was not asking him for a thing. As they entered the far turn I knew the race was as good as over. Cassie got a little lower on Lights back and released a little of her hold on him. Suddenly they had a five length advantage. She still had not asked him to run.

They rounded the final turn and maintained their lead. I saw Cassie get down on Light and let him run the last three eighths of a mile. He seemed to explode and won by many lengths over the other horses. Suddenly the lights on the infield tote board began to flash. Light had just equaled the existing track record and everyone knew he'd not even tried.

Freddie and I rushed out of the grandstands and made our way out onto the track. I watched Cassie turn Light and bring him back around the track at a slow pace. The crowd was cheering him as I snapped the lead shank onto his bridle. Cassie was grinning and got a hug from Spunky when she jumped off Light. Spunky quickly took the overgirth off Light and gave Cassie a leg back up on our winner.

The winner's circle was full of folks. Most of them I didn't know. But I didn't care. Light had won and that was all that mattered. A trophy was presented to Spunky and Patty then our picture was taken. I got a kiss from Cassie as she was leaving to go get weighed out. Jen came over and wanted to scratch Light's ears. I quickly lifted her up and to her delight Light nickered softly and rubbed his head against her. We knew someone took a picture but later saw it on the front page of the local newspaper. Several papers had picked up the picture. Suddenly Jen was a very important part of the team.

I let Light to the test barn where Freddie and I gave him a small drink of water. When the test folks took him into the test barn we discussed how easy he had won the race. When the folks brought Light out of the test barn we led him back to the barn. Folks were waving to us and telling us what a great race Light had run. They were all wishing us luck in the next one.

When we arrived at the barn, I took the track bandages of light while Freddie took the race bridle off and put his halter on. Freddie held Light while I gave him a warm bath. Freddie had him walked better than half dry when Spunky and Patty finally made it back to the barn. Patty was flying to say the least.

"Bill, Spunky said you had your suit cleaned. Keep it ready son, you're going to need it."

"One down, two to go Patty. The boys will try and beat us any way they can, but I'm not worried. We know our horse and I think he's the best."

"I agree with you Bill, he didn't even know he had a race today. He was just out for a work with his favorite jockey and was enjoying himself.

Spunky had apologized for being late getting back to the barn. He and Patty had had to talk to the reporters. Sam and Cassie were still being interviewed when they had left. Cassie and I spent the night with Spunky and Patty. Sam had had a bunch of old college friends show up and had taken them to supper. He wanted them to meet his family.

Cassie and I discussed how we thought the next big race would go. The big boys were in trouble and would enter a horse they knew couldn't win just to try and tire Light out on the first part of the race. We talked late into the evening.

The next morning after breakfast we went to the track. Sam, Brenda and Jen were waiting for us. Jen had to show us the picture of her and Light on the front page.

We visited for a moment then said our goodbyes. We went to the airport and took off for home. I had colts to work and couldn't afford to miss many days if I wanted to have them ready.

Sam told us about his friends and about how a couple of them wanted to buy in on his filly. He'd told them he already had a couple of partners and didn't think he needed anymore. Both Brenda and Jen smiled.

We arrived home and everything went back to normal for me. Sam and Cassie had their hands full. Several newspapers interviewed Sam. Cassie was busy filming commercials for several of the local merchants. Mike and I sat back and watched the fun. Brenda rode over one afternoon to visit just as we were finishing works. It seemed Sam had had a couple of offers for his half of Light. It was really bothering Brenda.

"Brenda, don't worry about it. Sam has no intention of selling his share in Light. He's in this business for the long haul and having way too much fun to quit. You think its bad now, wait until we let his filly go to work. It will really get busy then.

"Bill, I'm like you and Mike here. I've never had much and this is all sort of overwhelming to me. Sam said something the other night about he had liked some dip I had made one evening when we were dating. I told him the fruit for the dip was sky high right now and as soon as the price dropped I make him a batch. Bill, he looked at me and grinned. The next evening, he brought home a whole sack of the fruit and told me we could afford it. That man is taking some getting used to."

"Well, it's eight more days to the next race. He'll begin to wind up shortly. That will keep him busy just getting ready."

"Bill, it's all Jen and I can do to just keep his feet on the ground now. Jen told him the other night to settle down and relax. He was acting like he had ants in his pants."

After Brenda had left Mike and I had gotten a good laugh. It seemed we were the only ones who were relaxed and enjoying this situation.

The time seemed to fly by. Sam and his family had moved into their new home and were happy. Cassie and I had been thinking about a new house and making some sketches as we went along. When the time came for us to go back to the track I was ready. Spunky and I had talked at least once a day and sometimes twice. I was very thankful for my cell phone.

Cassie came down the day before we were to leave for Hot Springs and worked both Sam and Spunky's colts. They had both worked great. We had gone to supper and just got back when Sam had called. It seemed Jen had made the honor roll at school. When he told her he was proud of her she had said "It's easy when you can see."

We were ready and waiting when Sam and his family pulled up in their truck. We were going a day early and I figured Freddie and I would split the night watch outside Light's stall. We'd come too far to do something stupid now.

"We had left at four thirty and watched the sunrise as we traveled east. When we reached the airport we got in the rental car and quickly made our way out to the track. We had noticed a lot more jets at the field when we landed and figured there would be a lot more people at the track to watch the second of the big races.

Spunky was waiting on us when we showed up. He and Freddie were working on Light when we pulled in.

"Cassie, want to take him for a long slow gallop? Just to work the kinks out so to speak."

"Let me get my boots on, Spunky. I won't be but a minute."

Cassie came out a few moments later with her riding boots and crash helmet on. She was ready to take her buddy, as she called him, around the track. Spunky gave her a leg up and we all followed them to the edge of the track to watch Light go for a light gallop.

We watched as Cassie backtracked Light a hundred yards or so before she found an opening on the track and put Light to work. Light was something to see. His neck was bowed and he seemed to float around the track. His ears were flipping as he listened to Cassie. When she was in the stretch she moved to the center of the track and let him work a little faster. Just the way Spunky wanted it done. After Light had been bathed and put back in his stall I went to the trunk of the car and got my bag. I'd hang my clothes that I would wear the next day in the tack room. I'd brought a new pair of slacks, sport coat and shoes for the big race. I didn't plan on looking like a hick when race day arrived.

Spunky had already worked the string and was ready to head home. I got a kiss from Cassie and took my place outside Light's stall. Freddie brought me a burger and fries then went into the tack room to get a nap. We had a long night coming up and wanted to be ready.

Later that afternoon Spunky came back and checked on everything. We fed the string and made sure everything was ready for the night. I went to the track kitchen and ate a good meal then came back and told Freddie to do the same. I'd take the first watch and wake him shortly after midnight. I picked a western book from a stack in the tack room and settled in for the evening. I had one of Spunky's sodas near at hand.

I woke Freddie at one and lay down on his still warm cot and went to sleep. I woke up when Spunky showed up at four thirty to do the feeding. It was race day and we were ready.

CHAPTER 37

Cassie and Patty showed up a few minutes later with coffee and doughnuts. While I drank my coffee and ate a couple of doughnuts Cassie gave Light some attention. Slinker had nickered at her and wanted some attention, too.

Spunky and I discussed the race. There were only two horses that had any early speed and they had nothing like Light. All the rest were come from off the pace late running horses. I told Spunky that if Cassie and Light got out good they should be able to open a lead and never look back. The race was ours for the taking.

"Bill, I agree with you. We'll have to wait and see how things go, but I believe you're right."

Spunky and Patty went home to change. Sam and his family showed up and visited with us for a while. He told us they had overheard two trainers talking at the hotel last evening while they were eating supper. The trainers were discussing our race. If they sent their horse after Light early they wouldn't have anything left for the stretch drive. If they waited they didn't know just how far Light could carry his speed.

"But we know, don't we, Sam?"

"You bet we do, Bill. I'm really looking forward to the race today. I think the world may suddenly discover we have a racehorse. The television folks are all here and it will be on national television this afternoon."

"I know. Mike and Carlo have plans for some of the boys to come out to the barn and watch the race today. One of the big stores downtown is going to bring out a big screen T.V. for them to watch. One of the boys is bringing out his smoker and they are going to have burgers and such. With Cassie doing all the ads our place has become a gathering spot for every little horseman in the country."

"I know what you mean. We'd better leave now. I sure enough don't want someone getting our table upstairs."

Finally it was race time. I had changed clothes and even had a tie on. Patty had been very proud of me. When the call to the paddock came I led Light over and led him around the saddling stalls. I led him into his stall to be saddled and waited for the track steward and Spunky to get Cassie's saddle set in place. I led him out of the stall and talked to him. The call came for "Riders Up." I held him while Spunky gave Cassie a leg up and then led Light over to the lead horse.

"See you in the winner's circle, Bill."

"I'll be there with the lead shank, Cass. You have a good trip."

Freddie and I again found a spot high up in the outside grandstands. We watched the horses warm up and start towards the gate. The race today was a mile and a sixteenth. It was the start of a test for Light. Not for us but for the rest of the folks across the country who had never seen him run. If he won the race today, tomorrow he'd be a household name. My heart picked up its beat as the horses were loaded into the gates. I watched as Light and Cassie were led into the gates and waited for the rest of the field to be loaded. "The horses are all in line."

The bell rang and the horses broke from the gates. The jockeys' bright colored silks shone in the afternoon sunlight. As the horses passed the grandstand for the first time it was wonderful to see Light well out in front and moving down towards the rail. He seemed to float around the first turn and seemed to be floating across the track. He and Cassie had a good four length lead and were increasing it with every stride. Light's ears were flipping back and forth waiting for Cassie to tell him to go. There was no need for him to run any harder. The distance between him and the second place horse was now six lengths and widening. As he and Cassie started around the final turn the jockeys on the late running horses went to their whips. They had to make their move now or they would never be able to catch Light.

I saw Cassie look back under her arm and see the late runners begin to close the gap between them. She got lower on Lights back and released a little more of her hold. The closing horses seemed to suddenly stand still as the distance between them and Light widened again. Cassie and Light came around the turn and still she did not ask for him to run. Then at the three-eighths pole she got down lower on his back and shook the reins. She let him go. I would remember it the rest of my life. A gentleman standing next to me said it all. "My God. What a horse."

Cassie and Light crossed the finish wire as Freddie and I fought our way through the crowd to get to the track opening. When we reached the track it was impossible to hear each other talk unless we shouted. People pressed together all around the winners circle. They all wanted to get a better look at Light.

Cassie brought Light back and waved her stick in the air. Again the crowd went crazy. I snapped a lead shank on Light as Cassie jumped off. Spunky quickly removed the overgirth and gave Cassie a leg back up on Light. I saw that he had tears in his eyes. I led Light into the now crowded winners circle and had to wait for the folks to move back. Spunky and Patty received another trophy and after a short speech by one of the track officers we had our picture made.

Cassie gave me a quick kiss then rushed of to the scales to weigh out. Freddie and I followed the track steward to the test barn and after giving Light a drink waited for the test folks to bring him back to us.

"Bill, do you think we'll ever see another like him?"

"That's something I don't know. Spunky has waited a lifetime to have one like him and others have retired and never had anything like him. It seems as if about every thirty years or so a horse like Light comes along but to this point only a handful of little folks have owned them.

The test barn folks brought Light back out and turned him over to us. We started for the barn but when we arrived there was a bunch of folks waiting. I had to ask them to move back so we could take care of Light.

I removed the racing bandages and replaced his bridle with his halter. Folks kept crowding forward but backed up when I turned the water hose on. I saw Freddie smile and I had to admit I had to smile, myself. When we were finished with Light's bath I had Freddie start walking him dry. Most of the folks turned out to be reporters from small papers who wanted something different for their readers. I answered their questions as best I could but was thrilled when Sam and his family showed up. I introduced Sam to the folks, then went into the tack room. Brenda followed me into the tack room and we both got a good laugh. Sam owned half the horse and should do the interviews. A few minutes later, Spunky, Patty and Cassie showed up. That was when Sam came hunting me. When he saw Brenda, Jen and me all smiling, he couldn't help but laugh too.

Suddenly Sam's cell phone rang. It was the airport, there was a fast moving front headed our way. If we wanted to get home we were going to have to leave as soon as possible. I waved to Cassie and told her what was going on. She said all her things were in the back of Spunky's car and she was ready. Sam went to Spunky and told him about the storm front. We got handshakes, hugs and kisses and were on our way to the airport.

It took us a little longer to get home because we had to circle to the south to get around the front. When we got home we had time to fix some sandwiches and hot chocolate before the news and sports and weather came on. We were all sitting in the living room when the news came on.

The news started with a short film clip of Cassie and Light crossing the finish wire. They said a more detailed report would be forth coming on the sports section. I got up and brought more hot chocolate while Jen handed out more sandwiches to those who wanted them. Finally the sports came on and the sportscaster had a clip of the race starting at the last turn and then we all got to see the move Light had made at the three-eighths pole. Even after seeing it again it was hard to believe.

"Bill, I've owned horses all my life and never seen such a move as he put on today."

"I know, Brenda. It was just unreal. Now folks, two down and one to go."

Sam and his family made the short drive to their new home a short time later. Cassie called he folks and told them we were back home and she was going to spend the night. She told them we were going to work on our house plans and she would be home early. She had to go talk to her grandpa."

We went into the kitchen and went to work on the plans. An hour later we were satisfied with what we had accomplished. We both got a hot bath and went to bed. It had been a long day.

I got a report from Mike the next morning. The crowd the day before had been even bigger than the one before. Two of the boys had left their big smokers because they knew there would be another party in two weeks. He told me folks had had a wonderful time and had thanked us for allowing them to come out to our place and share the fun.

We did chores and when I went back to the house I found Cassie already dressed and waiting.

"Get cleaned up, Bill. Sam and Brenda have invited us over for breakfast."

Needless to say I got cleaned up in a hurry. When we got to Sam's place Jen met us at the door. Sam was grilling small breakfast steaks while Brenda and Jen were fixing eggs and toast. I went out onto the covered patio and visited with Sam until the steaks were done. Jen said the blessing and we ate a great breakfast. We were having another cup of coffee when Sam told us what the breakfast was for.

"Kids, the breakfast this morning is our way of saying thanks for all you've done for us."

"Sam, we haven't done that much."

"Yes you have, Bill. You and Cassie have worked your tails off. You've got your school work done so you could be gone to help Spunky with Light."

"Sam, we get paid for doing that."

"Not near enough. Spunky and I have discussed it. We've made some pretty good money in the last few weeks and we want to share. We've decided to give you kids another five percent of the purse. Now that will give you twenty five percent and you should be able to get your new house built."

"Sam, Bill and I will take it. I have to admit, I really want the new house. It will be ours. Besides I have a feeling we're going to be having some important folks out here soon and you know how some folks like to be impressed."

Sam's front doorbell rang and Jen rushed off to answer it. She returned carrying a bunch of newspapers.

"Mr. Brandon said he'd see you in the morning at the pancake house."

"Frank and I have coffee at the pancake house every Monday morning. We're on the board of directors for Save our Children."

"I'm speaking at their meeting this Thursday night."

"I know, Cassie. I didn't want to ask you so I had a friend of mine do it. We're really looking forward to having you. By the way we're planning on giving you a little something special. Our way of saying thanks."

As Cassie and I left, we were wondering what in the world they were going to give her. We didn't have a clue. Cassie left a short time later for her folks' place. She never referred to it as her home. It was her folks' home. As she had said "Her place was here with me." I was more than ready to get married and have her here.

Cassie stopped on her way to the meeting. She was looking forward to finding out what in the world they had gotten her. She left a short time later and said she would stop on her way back. I had brought my books up to date after Mike had brought me the daily figures. We were having coffee when Cassie came back.

"Boys, come on into the living room. You've got to see this."

We followed Cassie into the living room where she turned the machine on and inserted a DVD into the machine. As it turned out, the DVD was about

Cassie and Light. Every race Light had run was on the disk. They had even put the race where Jen and Cassie had raced up the stretch at the farm. The interview with Spunky and even the interview with me were there. It had been put together and had music to go with every race. It was a wonderful thing. Someone had gone to a lot of work and trouble to put this disc together. I had a feeling I knew who was responsible. Sam.

"It's wonderful Cassie, I figure I know who was responsible for putting this together."

"I do too. I hugged Sam's neck and told him thanks "Big Brother." Bill, Sam had to wipe tears from his eyes."

"I can believe that, were Brenda and Jen there?"

"Oh yes, my little sis was really styling. Since Brenda has moved in, our little sis has really become quite a young lady. She has changed so much. All for the good, I might add."

Cassie left a short time later so that her folks could see the DVD before they went to bed. Mike and I discussed what he would do while I was gone for the last race. The phone rang and it was one of Mike's friends. He'd tried Mike's number and when he couldn't get him he had called me. I handed the phone to Mike and went to get us another cup of coffee. When I came back Mike was hanging up the phone and was laughing.

"Alright, Mike. What's so funny."

"It seems we've run out of room for all the folks who want to come out to watch the next race. The boys have contacted a feller down south and he's bringing up a big tent he carries around with him to the fairs. They want to set it up just outside the barn. The folks down town will bring another big screen T.V. Oh it seems someone has chartered a big plane and sold the seats to anyone who wants to go to Hot Springs and watch the last big race. The seats were all sold in twenty minutes. The folks in charge are thinking about chartering another."

"Good Lord. That's wonderful. There is no telling how big this thing can become. Cassie has done a dozen commercials and has been asked to do that many more."

It seemed everyone wanted to get his or her name in front of the television cameras. In the next few days things were donated to the party. It was going to be some kind of party.

The next few days Mike was running all day long. The boys who worked their horses helped out when they could. Folks from town actually sent some of their employees out to help set things up.

Sam stopped by to see how things were going and couldn't believe what had happened in such a short time. He told me we would be using a different plane for our trip down to Hot Springs. His friend was going to go to the race himself. Sam had called one of the local airlines and leased a large plane. We'd be able to fly us and our friends down to the race. Cassie's folks, my folks, Ike and his wife and some folks I didn't know could all go together. We would leave Friday morning and Sam had even made hotel reservations for those who wanted them.

This was becoming a major production. Sam explained he had gotten a huge discount from the airline because they wanted the good public relations too.

When Thursday evening finally arrived, Cassie drove down and was ready to go. We took Mike and Carlo to town and fed them supper. They had a big weekend coming up and we wanted them to know we appreciated their help.

When Sam and his family showed up the next morning we were standing outside waiting. Sam was really wound up and ready to go. When we got to the airport the plane was ready and waiting for us. They even had banners tied over the gateway door saying "Go Gray Light."

When everyone was on the plane the tune "Call to the Post" came over the P.A. system. Two of the airline stewardess came out of the back of the plane and were dressed as jockeys. Needless to say the trip down to Hot Springs was something to behold.

When we reached Hot Springs, we got our car and headed out to the track. Spunky and Patty were waiting when we drove up. They had a newspaper for us to read. It had a story that said a rumor was going around that Gray Light might not run in the race because of lameness.

Cassie and I began to laugh. Spunky and his smelly leg brace had struck again. When Sam realized what had happened he had to sit down because he was laughing so hard. Brenda didn't know what was going on so Spunky explained to her how he and Freddie had given Light a good work at daylight one morning. They had come back and put heavy bandages on him. Spunky had used his special leg brace and that is how the rumor got started. They had walked Light the next morning and everyone suddenly believed he was crippled.

"It's been a lot quieter around here. Freddie and I have looked sad for so long we'd almost forgotten how to laugh. Bill, will you and Cassie go let Light know you're here? I'm sure he will glad to see you.

Light was glad to see us. For the next twenty minutes he really got spoiled. Cassie scratched his ears while I brushed him and then gave him a back rub. He loved to have the muscles along his backbone massaged. He got the full treatment and loved every minute of it. When we left his stall he was standing in a corner of his stall asleep. Light was a happy horse. I again put my clothes in the tack room.

Cassie went to see if her and my folks were settled into their rooms. They had all planned on going to races today. I was happy that my folks were able to come and maybe be a part of one of the most important days of my life.

Spunky and I discussed the upcoming race and what we thought might happen. It was something we had neither experienced before so our nerves were on end so to speak.

Freddie and I took over things while Spunky went home for lunch and an afternoon nap. I sent Freddie over to the track kitchen to get us something to eat. I got a brush and gave Slinker a good brushing. I was working on him when a gentleman walked up and asked to see Spunky.

"Sir, Mr. Davis is at home eating lunch. He'll be back in a couple of hours. Is there anything I can help you with?"

"I don't think so, young man. I'll come back by later."

Freddie and I ate our late lunch and both settled down to do some reading. When Spunky came back I told him about the gentleman who had asked for him. A few minutes later I saw the gentleman walk up to the tack room and begin to visit with Spunky. I went on reading my book outside Light's stall until Spunky called me.

"This is my assistant trainer Bill Patton. Bill breaks and starts all my colts at his training center in Texas. Bill is the one who took Gray Light as a green broke colt and has helped make him into what he is today."

"But Mr. Davis, when I was here earlier today he was grooming a horse."

"We're a small stable and are a hands on group of folks. We like to know how our horses are doing and not rely on some one else to tell us. We've gone the whole year and not crippled a horse in the string."

"Bill, this gentleman is from Kentucky. He is wanting to know if Light wins tomorrow will we be coming to the Derby."

"I don't see why not. Light is on top of his game and deserves the shot. I think it would be a crime not to give him his chance."

"That's what I think, too. Sir, if we're lucky enough to win tomorrow. We'll be in Kentucky for the big dance."

Spunky and the gentleman shook hands and the deal was settled. I grinned at Spunky and began getting the evening feed measured up. We wanted everything happy and ready to run when their time came.

Later that evening Freddie went into the tack room and went to sleep. I would wake him like always before and get a short nap myself. We had half the string fed when Spunky showed up the next morning. His alarm had not gone off and he was upset. I'd told him to relax. He probably needed a new clock anyway.

Sam came into the barn area with coffee for everyone. Spunky sent Freddie and me to get some breakfast. We went to the track kitchen where everyone was talking about today's big race. We listened and enjoyed the talk. When we got back to the barn Spunky was being interviewed by a reporter for a big racing publication. He introduced me to the gentleman and had said some very nice things about me.

As noon hour approached Cassie came by on her way to the jock room. She had a horse to ride in the fourth race and was ready for the big race.

"Bill, I'm not even nervous. For some reason I'm relaxed and slept like a log last night."

"That's great Cassie. If you're relaxed Light will be, too. Now go give him some attention. He's got his head out of his stall and seems to think you should come say hello."

Cassie went over and talked to Light. He was rubbing his head on her shoulder as she rubbed his head and neck. He was happy with his jockey and so were we.

Spunky went home to get ready for the race. Sam and all the folks from home were already up in the grandstands. Sam and some of his friends had been up since daylight. Jen and Brenda had gone shopping the afternoon before and would be ready for the race. Jen wanted to look nice for the win picture. My little sis was something else.

I went to Light's stall and began to braid his mane. I wanted to be finished when Spunky got back. I talked to him as I worked and enjoyed having him rub on me. When Spunky got back I had all the things ready for him to put the racing bandages on Light. I went over to the track showers and cleaned up. Today I would wear my suit and try not to look out of place. Freddie left for the shower when I returned and came back wearing a nice set of slacks and a sport coat. We were both making an attempt to look nice. We both had ties on for the occasion.

Cassie's horse in the fourth race was scratched. The horse had come down with a fever and couldn't run. She would just have to watch the races on the monitor and see how the track was playing out.

Spunky and I went to Light's stall and put on his bandages. We had his race bridle ready and when our race was called we were ready. The horses would be saddled in the track infield where everyone could see. I knew Light would like being out in the sunshine and out of the hole as I called it. I followed Spunky up to the track and then into the infield. Numbers had been placed in the grass where we were supposed to saddle. I led Light around until the track steward showed up with Cassie's saddle. I led Light over and held him while the saddle was set in place. When they were finished I led Light, until I saw the jockeys walk across the track and come into the infield. A short time later I held Light while Spunky gave Cassie a leg up.

"Bill, when we go to the winner's circle. You're going to have lipstick on your face."

"Looking forward to it, Cass. Now go show them a race horse."

I led Light over to the lead horse and watched as they were paraded in front of the stands. We quickly crossed the track and went to the outside grandstands where we could see the entire track. The race today would determine if our work for the year was a success or failure, and it all depended on Light.

I watched as Cassie warmed Light up. He seemed to be relaxed and was moving in his usual flowing way. The starting gates were set just to the left of the grandstands. The horses would pass the grand stand twice in today's race of a mile and one eighth. I watched carefully as the horses were brought back past the grandstands. Now my nerves set in. We were racing today against some of the finest horses in the country. The big stables from Kentucky had all the money and fancy things it was supposed to take to win the big races. We, on the other hand, just had a horse that could run and loved doing it.

I noticed Cassie had several pair of goggles on her helmet today. She was taking no chances of letting anything go wrong. The gate crew began loading the horses. I watched as Light and Cassie were led into the starting gate. I saw Cassie pull down a set of goggles and get set. "The horses are all in line."

The bell rang and the gates flew open. It was a good, clean start. Cassie and Light had the lead for the first fifty yards. Then two speed horses went by her and Light. The speed horses would never be close at the finish but their job was to draw Light into a speed duel and burn himself out. It was a good plan and would work most of the time. This was not one of those times. Cassie set Light four lengths back and got him on the rail. The two speed horses were going at an insane speed. The first quarter time was almost like a Quarter horse race.

Cassie kept Light tucked in on the rail as they went down the backstretch. She was content to sit just off the leaders and out of trouble. Just before the three quarter pole Cassie and Light began to make up ground on the front running horses. As they started around the far turn I saw the horse on the rail begin to move out from the rail. This caused the horse on his outside to move out too. It was what Cassie and Light had been waiting for. Cassie got down on Light and seemed to suddenly fly through the opening on the rail. Light had carried Cassie to the lead. They now had three lengths on the front running horses, and more on the rest of the field. A gasp had gone up from the crowd when Cassie had moved Light through the space on the rail.

I saw Light flipping his ears just waiting for Cassie to tell him to run as they came around the turn and headed for home. Cassie looked back under both arms and settled down on Lights back. She shook the reins and let him run. The late running horses who had been making up ground were left in his dust as he seemed to get lower to the ground a get faster with every stride. His lead increased and the crowd went wild. The big gray horse and his girl jockey were going to upset the apple cart again. When Cassie and Light crossed the finish line Freddie and I were already down out of the stands and fighting our way through the crowd. The place was a mad house. It had been loud before but nothing like this.

When I reached the track I saw Cassie had just got Light pulled up and had both of her arms around his neck hugging him. She turned him around and started back towards the winner's circle. Several of the jockeys gave her high fives when they went past her and Light. I could see Cassie had been crying when she brought Light back to where Freddie and I stood waiting. She waved her stick in the air and jumped off when I snapped the lead shank on Light. Spunky and Patty were both there and it seemed everyone was crying. I got a hug from both Spunky and Patty, but the kiss I got from Cassie was the best.

Spunky got the overgirth off Light and gave Cassie a leg back up on Light. We needed to get our picture taken. As I started into the winner's circle it was indeed a strange sight. The people standing there had tears in their eyes but were laughing at the same time. I saw Cassie's and my folks standing together and my mother blew me a kiss. Sam, Brenda and Jen were all laughing and having a great time. Once more a trophy was presented and our picture was taken. As I waited for Cassie to dismount I saw Jen come running. I handed Freddie the reins and lifted Jen up onto Light's back in front of her big sis, fancy dress and all. Another picture was taken, then I helped Jen down. Cassie jumped off Light and went to weigh out. I got a kiss from Jen, then took the lead rope from Freddie and followed the track steward to the test barn.

We gave Light a drink and then I walked him until the test barn folks came out and got him. Freddie was jumping up and down. He and I both hollered and gave each other high fives.

The walk back to the barn was great. Everyone was wishing us luck. A few said they would see us in Kentucky. It was becoming a very good day. Once again there were folks all around the barn area. Freddie and I managed to get to the barn and get the wraps off Light. We removed his race bridle and put on his halter. We quickly gave him a bath and got him cleaned up. Freddie began to walk him dry. I went to the tack room and began answering the phone and answering questions from some of the folks who were wanting to get an interview. Sam and our families showed up. How he got them all back here I didn't know, but it made no difference. I was thrilled to see them.

"Bill, we did it. We're going to the Derby."

"We sure are, and we can do it in style. It looked as if half the town was here today. I almost couldn't get into the winners circle."

Shortly after Sam and I had talked Spunky, Patty and Cassie showed up. It seemed the party started all over again.

Patty called for everyone's attention.

"Folks, or should I say friends. We're going to go out and eat. If I can get a count I'll call the steak house so the folks can be ready for us when we show up. Hands were raised and Patty got her count. A few minutes later two security guards showed up. Spunky had hired them for the evening. As he put it "The whole team was going to go eat together."

We were on our way to the steak house when I took my cell phone and called Mike. When he answered it sounded as if a party was going on. When I said so, he laughed and said the local T.V. stations were filming the shindig. He would have a copy for us to look at when we got home.

"Bill, there must be close to a thousand people out here. There are folks here from towns a hundred miles away. I'm sure the folks down town heard the crowd cheer, when Cassie guided Light through the hole on the rail. Bill, I'm proud of you kids. I couldn't be there but somehow it doesn't matter. The folks here at home have really felt like they have been a part of this deal. It's just been unreal."

"Mike we'll see you tomorrow just after lunch. Our plane leaves at nine thirty. We'll be out at the ranch just as soon as we can. You'll miss out on your evening with your lady friend tonight."

"No I won't, she's out here helping me and having a ball. You kids enjoy your evening and we'll see you when you all get home."

Our steaks were wonderful. Spunky thanked everyone for coming and said Patty wanted to say a few words.

"Friends, I'm not that much of a speaker but this is a very special occasion. A few years ago Spunky and I lost our only child. But this spring we adopted two very special kids. Bill Patton and Cassie Morgan showed up at our barn and things took a very dramatic change. First, Bill managed to get Light on the right track and made the suggestion we use Cassie as our jockey for him. Bill, you're our behind the scenes man and don't get near the attention you deserve. Spunky and I both want to thank you. Cassie, what can we say, you've become a fine jockey. Bill had faith in you and you again proved him right. We're going to the Derby and, as Spunky said to one of the reporters today, we're going with our two kids. They have worked hard and gotten us this far so there is no need to change now. We just wanted the two of you to know how proud of you we are."

"Patty, I know I can speak for Cassie's mother when I say we're honored that you all consider our kids yours, too. My son has become a fine young man with a wonderful future in front of him. Thanks to your and Spunky's help, he has become a kind and caring person. I only hope he and Cassie will be as happy together as you and Spunky are."

Cassie uttered "Amen."

We spent the night with Spunky and Patty. We made plans as to when Spunky would ship to Kentucky. We made our plans and planned on being in Kentucky the weekend before the Derby. Cassie would need a couple of trips around the track before the big race. There were also many functions Cassie would need to attend.

The next morning the trip home was one of the finest times I'd ever had. Everyone on the flight was in a great mood. We sang songs, laughed and had a wonderful time. When we reached home several of the local papers were there and wanted interviews. Brenda, Jen and I stood back and waited patiently while Sam and Cassie did their interviews.

All we could do was smile. Smile and look forward to the next race, the race everyone had dreamed of.

CHAPTER 38

✾

The next couple of weeks were crazy. It seemed Cassie was running here and there talking to various civic groups. Our schools had both been more than understanding with us. We had received our assignments and already turned them in. We were free to go to Kentucky this coming Saturday morning. Sam had leased a Lear Jet from a company in town and had it checked out and ready to go.

I had talked to Spunky every day since the last race. He had called me when they had arrived at the track in Kentucky. He had been shocked when he arrived. They had been given stalls that overlooked the track from the backside. He had been offered a stall in the stakes barn but had said he'd rather keep Light around his other horses. Besides he figured it would be much quieter.

He and Patty had located an apartment close to the track and had moved in for a month. They didn't figure to use it even that long. Freddie was staying in the tack room so he could keep an eye on things.

Finally it was time to go. Mike and his lady friend Lynne, were beginning to make plans for the upcoming celebration. They had had calls from all over the surrounding area. Mike was flying, so to speak. His phone was ringing all day long. Folks were wanting to know what was needed for race day. The television folks were already planning on different camera locations. This was going to be one of the biggest events of the year. It was a chance for folks to get their names and products before the public. It was turning out to be more like a fair than a horse race.

We left home at four in the morning. The plane Sam had leased was very nice. I would have asked Sam how much it cost but figured it was none of my business. When we were approaching Kentucky, Sam said that he actually owned half of the plane we were using. The gentleman who owned the other half had been out of the country for a while on oil business.

We landed at the airfield and found our rental car waiting. There was a map of the city on the front seat. We looked for the track and with Sam driving and me reading the map we found the track a short time later. Spunky met us at the gate and took us to the office where we could get our license. Spunky introduced us to several of the trainers he knew.

One of the track officials welcomed us to the track and told us they were happy we were here. A gentleman came over and asked to speak to Cassie. He was a reporter for a local newspaper and he wanted to get her view on the upcoming race.

She explained to him she really hadn't had time to study any of the forms of the other horses so she didn't have any opinion like that. She was happy to be here and was ready to go to work. She really looked forward to her first work over the track with Light.

When she had finished her interview we went to the backside where we found Patty and Freddie waiting on us. After hugs and handshakes we went to Light's stall and let him know we were here. He was glad to get the attention and seemed to be in good shape. Spunky wanted Cassie to work him around the track the next morning. Then he dropped a surprise on me. My mare and Slinker were both in a race on Thursday. Now I was going to be nervous.

Patty brought out a schedule and explained to Sam there were several functions that he and Brenda were expected to attend with her and Spunky. It seemed that Cassie had a full schedule too. All of the jockeys were expected to attend the same functions that the owners were to attend. I told Jen that we would have a Hearts game while the owners played high rollers. She was happy with my idea.

I stayed with Freddie and we looked after Light and the string. The next morning we had everything almost done up when Spunky and Cassie arrived. Cassie was staying with Spunky and Patty at their apartment. Cassie came over to where I was standing and explained to me she hadn't known about all the parties and didn't have the proper clothes. I reached into my boot top and came out with some money. I handed her half and asked if was enough.

"My Lord. I should think so, Bill. Just how much have you got there?"

"Enough to make my bets on my mare and Slinker. This is the money I've made on previous races so don't worry. I've got more in my billfold."

"Bill, we're going to have to sit down and have a talk. I thought your money was all in the bank."

"Not all of it Cassie, I always have a little in case money with me."

We got the horses ready for Cassie and Freddie to work. I led Cassie and Slinker to the track while Spunky took my mare. I was thrilled with the way she looked. She had put on weight and her overall condition looked great. After we turned the two horses loose to work Spunky told me the mare had really come on and had become a lot more aggressive on the track. The race she was in was a forty thousand dollar claim and she should go off at great odds. He thought she had a chance to win.

Slinker was on his toes and it took Cassie a couple of hundred yards to get him to relax and start listening to her. Once he settled down he went to work and had a fine workout. My mare on the other hand was trying to pull Freddie's arms off. Spunky was right. She was ready to run.

"Bill, I have a favor to ask."

"Ask away, Spunky."

"Would it be alright if I named Freddie to ride your mare. They seem to get along and with her being as aggressive as she is, I think it just might work out best."

"Name him on the mare Spunky. I trust him completely and I'm sure it would be a big deal for him to have ridden a race over this track."

The stage was set, Freddie would ride Plunder in the fifth race and Cassie would ride Slinker in the eighth race. We would have time to get everything done if we hurried.

"Cassie and Brenda went shopping. They neither had the type clothes they would need for the two dinners they were to attend. Cassie had my betting money and Sam handed Brenda his credit card. Patty said she wanted to go along and just might find something she needed as well. Both Spunky and Sam had groaned.

Jen and Sam hung around the barn with us. Jen and my mare seemed to get along. Jen had given her a peppermint candy and made a friend for life. Sam and Spunky had been going over the condition book and then got out the form sheets on the horses in the Derby. There were two colts in the race that, like Light, had not been outrun. One was a colt from California, who had never been a mile and an eighth before. He would be a question mark on the program as to where he could get the distance. The other was a New Jersey bred that was a real speedster for a mile. He was expected to set all the fractions, but wasn't expected to win.

I listened to the conversation and mapped out a plan in my head as to how Cassie should ride the race.

"Bill, what's your opinion on the race?"

"I'd have Cassie set Light a couple of lengths back and when the rail opened up go after them. No one knows if the California colt can get the distance, because of his pedigree. But one never knows, look at Light. I'd sure enough not let them get to large a lead on me."

"I agree with you, Bill. That is exactly what I've been thinking. We'll let Cassie get Light out and set just off their hips. They neither one have had many races and it just may make them nervous and expend too much energy.

"The women showed up and had their dresses. Cassie had two great looking dresses. She had used all my money and part of hers. I gave her some money out of my billfold and laughed. I could see my wife was going to be something in the years to come. The little girl who could stretch a dollar a mile was not going to be ashamed at the dinners. I knew I wouldn't. I wanted folks to eat their hearts out.

"Cassie worked Light the next day and he seemed to love the track. As a couple of the trainers standing at the gap had said, "He just seems to float across the track." When Cassie brought him back she was all smiles.

"He's ready Bill. The work today just got all the kinks out."

We went along for the next few days watching things get more intense. It was Derby week and already two horses had dropped out of the race. The race was now down to fourteen horses. The draw for post position would be held Friday morning. Both Spunky and Sam would have to be there. The first of the parties was to be held tonight. I knew that Cassie was nervous but when she came by with Spunky and Patty on their way to the party I was shocked to say the least. Her hair had been styled and she looked fantastic.

She did a quick turnaround for me. To say I approved would have been an understatement. I knew I would have the best-looking girl there for sure. The smile on my face must have said it all. I got a kiss and was told she loved me. I was a happy feller and planned on besting Jen at Hearts. I didn't, but I had planned on it. When the grown ups returned Jen was sound asleep on the cot in the tack room. Sam picked her up and they had left for their hotel. I'd find out how things had gone tomorrow morning. Right now I had to get back to my western. I had a fellow in a real mess and wanted to get him out of it before I woke Freddie for his turn as night watchmen.

"When Spunky and Cassie showed up the next morning I got all the news about the night before. Cassie had been interviewed on television and no one could believe she was Light's jockey. She had suddenly become the darling of the Derby. One of the nation's top jockeys said she not only was pretty but she could ride too. We worked the string and things settled down. That was until Freddie got sick. He'd eaten breakfast and an hour or so later was deathly sick. Spunky had taken him to the hospital and found out he had a case of food poisoning. They had pumped his stomach and had kept him over night. Tomorrow was my mare's race and my jock was in the hospital. Spunky asked Cassie if she would ride the mare.

"Of course I'll ride her. I've ridden her at Bill's place."

"Cassie, she's a different horse now. She's got more aggressive and is hard to hold."

"I'll hang my feet in the dash board if I have to, Spunky. I'll get her to settle down."

I sent Spunky home to change early. I had the mare's mane braided and had her racing wraps on when Spunky got back. When the call came over the barn speaker for the mare's race we were ready. The mare was running a seven and a half furlong sprint and the race looked to be tough. The mare's racing record was awful when you looked at it on paper and I saw she was fifty to one on the tote board. When I saw Sam I asked him to make a bet for me. Fifty to win and fifty to place. He'd taken my money and went off to make the bet. The mare was a handful but before she was saddled I had her settled down some and was more than ready to see her out on the track.

I held the mare while Spunky put Cassie's saddle in place. Later when Spunky gave Cassie a leg up on the mare I saw Cassie smile.

"Relax, Mr. Owner. I'll bring you back a winner."

"I'll be waiting for you lady. Have a good trip."

It was strange not having Freddie standing outside the grandstands with me. I watched the mares parade past the grandstands on their way to the backside to warm up. My heart began to pound. This was a whole different ball game. The mare belonged to me. I watched as Cassie warmed the mare up and was led to the gates.

"The Horses are all in line"

The bell rang and the mare seemed to explode from the gates. Cassie managed to slow her just enough to settle her in third place down on the rail. The race was short so position was everything. The mares started into the turn and the front two were battling head and head. Half way around the turn the mare on the outside began to falter and drop back. Cassie now had my mare in second place right behind the front running mare. Just as the front running mare rounded the turn and headed into the straightaway, the jockey shifted his reins and got down on the mare. It was just what Cassie was waiting on. When the jockey went to shift she had the mare running and had her running full out before the other jock realized what had happened.

Cassie and my mare seemed to fly by the front running mare and had a two-length lead. She maintained the lead and won by two lengths. My first race-horse and my first win. Cassie had just ridden a beautiful race. The other jock had said something to Cassie when he had ridden by her on their way back towards the winners circle. I'd have to ask Cassie about it when she got back.

I caught the mare and held her while Spunky took the overgirth off the mare. I got a quick kiss from Cassie then watched as Spunky gave her a leg up on the mare.

"Bill, I'll lead the mare in. You're the owner. Stand next to Patty and smile."

I walked into the winner's circle and stood next to Patty. Needless to say, I smiled.

I took the mare to the test barn and gave her a drink. The test folks took her inside and a short time later brought her back. I led her back to the barn so I could help Spunky get Slinker ready. I was shocked to see Sam helping Spunky when I arrived. I got the mare's leg wraps off and replaced her bridle with her halter. I gave her a bath in record time. I turned her over to a hot walker. Just then Freddie walked into the barn. He was pale, but said could keep an eye on things until we got back from the track.

When the call came for Cassie and Slinker's race, we were ready. Sam would walk over with us. I led Slinker over to the saddling paddock and was wondering what my bet on the mare had paid. I'd been too busy to look. Spunky saddled Slinker and I had held him while he had given Cassie a leg up. I led Slinker over to the lead horse rider and wished her luck.

"See you in the winner's circle, Bill."

I again watched the post parade and then watched as Cassie and Slinker warmed up on the backside. Slinker was ready to run. He might not win but I knew he would be trying his best.

"The horses are all in line."

I watched as the bell rang and the gates flew open. I saw that Cassie and Slinker were out clean. Suddenly the horse next to Slinker broke to the left and went down. The jockey was thrown over his head and right in front of Cassie and Slinker. I saw Cassie's reaction as she suddenly jerked Slinker's head sideways and saw him jump the jockey and the downed horse. The race was six and a half furlongs and for all practical purposes the race was over for the two of them.

I saw that Cassie had her legs down around Slinker. She was attempting to get her feet back in her stirrups as Slinker began to run. When Cassie regained her stirrups I saw her try and slow Slinker down. Slinker was not going to quit. Cassie got down on his back and let him run. No one could believe how he was soon up to the late running horses and continued his run. He was fourth, third and then second. When the horses crossed the finish line no one knew who had won. I, like everyone else, had never seen a horse make a run like Slinker had made.

When the photo had been read Slinker had lost by a nose but no one would ever forget the run and the heart he had shown in doing it. When we took him back to the barn we had treated him as if he had won. I think he actually felt he had won the race.

"Bill, when he gets too old to run allowance races, I'm going to take him home. I'll turn him out. He won't ever have to do another thing. My Lord, what a horse he has become. I'm really going to have to look at his little sister."

When Cassie came to the barn later, she told us the jockey who had gone down was fine. He was bruised up but would be riding in the Derby. He had come to her and told her he would be honored to ride against her in the Derby. She had been accepted by all the other jockeys and was a happy camper.

Friday morning we gave Light a good work and after putting him away we sat down and again went over the upcoming race. We had our plan but as Spunky put it. "The way it would be run would be up to Cassie and Light."

Sam showed up and was ready to go to the draw. Spunky quickly changed clothes in the tack room. Sam, Spunky and Cassie all left together. Cassie and the other jockeys who would ride in the Derby were to have their picture made just after the post position draw.

Freddie and I were busy cleaning and getting things ready for the next morning works. That was when the first of the television folks arrived. It seemed they had already filmed all of the other horses and only had Light to do. I put his halter on and led him outside. I took him to a spot where there was a little bit of grass and let him graze. When the folks had all the film they needed they wanted to ask me some questions.

Freddie took Light and put him in his stall. The gentlemen wanted to know if we really thought Light had a chance of winning the Derby.

"Well gentlemen, there are five horses in the race we have outrun already. We have yet to be outrun and yes, I think we have a chance."

"But he's not a Classic bred horse. In the past, these sort of horses have not fared well in the Derby."

"Well, he may not be a Classic bred horse. But we're certainly not going to tell him. We plan on keeping him happy and letting him do what he does best. Run."

"Is it true that you and Miss Morgan are going to get married soon?"

"Just as soon as we graduate school. We will go to a small track for the summer and start a bunch of colts for Mr. Davis and Mr. Cooper."

"What college are you attending, sir?"

"None sir, we will both graduate High School later this month."

"High school? But we were told you have a new training center."

"Sir, I do have a new training center and am quite proud of it. Cassie and I have a bunch of outside colts coming to us this fall from all over. Even some from here in Kentucky."

"Mr. Patton, would you tell us how you managed to get a training center built at your age?"

"Friends, sir. Very good friends who believe in me. Mr. Davis was kind enough to give me a job and teach me the business. I can't thank him enough."

"Thank you, Mr. Patton."

The men left and were going to do another interview with Cassie. They now had a new slant to the storybook story of Gray Light and his young lady jockey.

Some time later Sam, Spunky and Cassie came back to the barn.

"What gate did we draw?"

"Number five, Bill. The two speed horses drew the eight and nine gates."

"That's great. They will have to play catch up to Cassie and Light."

"That's what I told Sam. They will have to hustle to catch us. That may be a good thing. I don't think either of the two have ever had to come from behind. We may just take the heart out of them."

"Bill, did you do an interview while we were gone?"

"Yes I did. Some folks from the television station came by and wanted some footage of Light. I took him outside and then answered a few of their questions, why?"

"They caught me after the picture was taken of all of the jockeys and asked a bunch of questions. It seems they may have not believed you when you told them we were both still in high school. They asked my permission to use a photograph taken of me at the dinner the other night."

"Did you give them permission to use the picture?"

"I didn't see why not."

Later that afternoon we saw the picture in the local paper. A picture of all of the jockeys in their silks with Cassie sitting with them dressed in her ball gown.

The caption below the picture read "The Darling of the Jock World." We later found out it was the idea of all of the jockeys. We all thought it was a great idea.

Freddie and I would entertain Jen again tonight while the grown ups went to the last party before the race. We didn't mind at all, it made the evening go much quicker. We had a good time but when I saw Jen start to yawn I told her to hit the hay. Tomorrow was going to be a big day and she would want to look her best.

Freddie and Jen were asleep when Sam, Spunky and the ladies all came back from the party. It seemed someone was always taking pictures of Cassie. She had told all the jockeys she would get even for the joke they had pulled on her. Everyone had had a wonderful time. I got a kiss goodnight from Cassie and watched them drive off. I got a soda, my western book and sat down. I was ready for the evening.

I let Freddie have an extra hour's sleep then went to bed. I'd finished the book and was tired.

The next morning we hit the ground running. Freddie hand walked Light, while I cleaned his stall. I washed and filled his water bucket. We'd taken his hay bag out last night. Spunky put his feed in his stall and watched as we gave him a bath. We wanted him to look good this afternoon.

One of the major trainers came by to wish Spunky luck. He had just scratched one of his two entries in the race. The horse had developed a bad quarter crack in his hoof and wouldn't be able to run. He didn't seem to be to upset about things. After years of training he said a person had to learn to roll with punches.

Spunky went to change and eat lunch. Freddie and I changed in the tack room after I had braided Light's mane. I had scratched his ears and rubbed his back. When I had left his stall he was relaxed and sleeping.

Sam and his family had come by and were taking Cassie over to the jock room. They were going to eat in the clubhouse dining room. It seemed all Jen, who looked like a little doll in her fancy dress and hat, wanted was a hamburger and fries. Like the old saying, "You can take the girl out of the country but you can't take the country out of the girl."

I gave Cassie kiss and wished her luck. This would be one of the biggest days of her life.

"Bill, I was nervous these last few days but not now. I'm really looking forward to the race. I think we can win it."

"So do I Cassie, now go give Light some attention, he's looking for you."

After Cassie left we had several folks come by wanting to talk to Spunky. I'd taken their names and told them he'd call them tomorrow. We were going to be busy today. When Spunky and Patty showed up, everything was ready except wrapping Light's legs. We waited until after the fifth race and went to work. Patty had taken the truck over to the grandstands and would be there to watch us walk over to the saddling paddock.

"Bill, how in the world can you be so cool. I'm scared to death."

"I'm not sure, Spunky. I guess I just believe Light is going to win. He's in great shape, happy and loves his jockey. We may not win today, but we'll all know we gave it our best. Besides Spunky, we're not supposed to be here any way. Let's face it, this sure isn't New Mexico."

Spunky began to laugh.

"Bill, you're right. We would have never dreamed our problem child would ever have gotten this far. I still remember you walking into the café in Clayton where I hired you. Bill, let's get this horse over to the track. I'm ready to watch the Derby and not to have to watch it on television."

The walk over was something else. The whole infield of the track was filled with people. Some had been there since the gates had opened just after daylight. The grandstand was filled to overflowing. It was something we would never forget. When we reached the saddling paddock I led Light around the ring talking to him. I saw Jen and waved to her and Brenda. Light was on his toes and ready to run. When Spunky waved to me I led Light into the saddling stall and waited until he was saddled. I took him back out onto the walking ring. I saw Cassie and the rest of the jockeys come to the paddock. They were all getting their instructions from the trainers. Sam was standing with Spunky listening to the race plan.

"Riders Up"

I held Light while Spunky gave Cassie a leg up.

"Go get them, Cassie girl."

"We'll try Spunky. Bill, we'll see you in the winner's circle."

"Have a good trip Cassie, just guide him around."

I led Light over towards the track and through the shaded tunnel. When we reached I turned Light over to the pony rider. I had done all I could do. The rest was up to Cassie and Light. I found Sam waiting on me. He had my money from the mare's race.

"I've been a little busy but figured you want something on this race."

I looked at the tote board and saw Light was eight to one. I gave Sam three hundred and told him to put it on Light's nose.

I stood next to Freddie and listened to "My Old Kentucky Home." It made my knees get weak. Freddie looked to be as nervous as I was. We were standing next to the winner's circle and would have to watch the start of the race on a nearby monitor. The waiting was terrible.

I watched Cassie warm Light up and he seemed to be moving great. He was ready and as they lead the horses to the gates my heart rate just seemed to double. We watched the monitor as the horses began to load. We saw Cassie pull down a set of goggles and get ready for the break from the gate.

Finally all the horses were in the gate.

"The horses are all in line."

The bell rang, the gates flew open and the horses and their brightly colored jockeys exploded onto the track. The Jockeys were all low on their horses' backs, trying to get a good position. No one wanted to get hung up on the outside when they reached the first turn.

Cassie and Light seemed to fly away from the gates. I watched as they moved over onto the rail and had a two-length lead. I watched as the two speed horses who were outside Cassie and Light came across the track and pulled even with Light just as they reached the first turn. Cassie would let them have the lead but they were going to have to work for it. She had Light on cruise and had no intention of pulling him up.

As the horses rounded the first turn and entered the backstretch the three horses looked as one. The main group of horses was a good four or five lengths behind. The two favorites in the race were another three lengths behind them.

As the horses continued down the back stretch I saw the jockeys begin to move their horses and try to get into position for the run up the stretch. One of the speed horses began to drop back just before the final turn. Cassie had Light going well and still had the rail. With the second speed horse just outside, Cassie sat still on Light asking him for nothing. Suddenly I saw the other front runner's head come up and knew he was done. Cassie and Light had the lead as they entered the straight stretch.

I saw the two late running horses begin to close the distance on Light and Cassie. Cassie looked back under both of her arms and suddenly got lower on Light's back. She shook her reins and everyone watching saw his stride suddenly lengthen and with every stride he pulled away from the other horses. Light seemed to fly up the stretch. When Cassie and Light reached the finish wire I took a breath and watched the second and third place horses. They were four lengths behind Cassie and Light and battled to a photo finish.

The dream had ended. The dream every horseman dreams of at one time or another. We'd just won the big one.

I rushed out onto the track and watched Cassie as she pulled Light to a stop. The outrider caught Light and a television reporter mounted on a horse was interviewing Cassie as they were led back towards the cheering grandstand.

Suddenly, Spunky had his arm around me.

"We did it Bill. We did it."

"We sure did Spunky. We did it and did it in style."

I snapped the lead shank on Light when the outrider brought him up.

Sam and Spunky were watching as Cassie jumped off of Light and into Spunky's arms. They were both crying and laughing at the same time. Cassie came over to me and gave me a kiss in front of everyone. Spunky managed to get the overgirth off Light and gave Cassie a leg back up on Light. We had a very special picture to be taken. A blanket of roses was put across Light's neck before the picture was taken. Patty was hugging me and telling me how much she and Spunky thought of Cassie and me.

I was shocked to see our parents standing in back of the winner's circle. Both our mothers gave us hugs and kisses. I finally got back to where Freddie held Light and we followed the track steward to the test barn. At the test barn I was still in shock. It just hadn't settled in. When the test barn folks brought Light back out of the test barn Freddie and I headed back to the barn.

A large group of folks were waiting when we got back. I took the leg wraps off Light while Freddie put his halter on. I put the wraps in the tack room. When I went back outside folks were asking me questions faster than I could answer them. I told them they would have to wait until we got Light bathed.

We got Light bathed and Freddie began walking him dry. I walked back to where the folks waited and began answering questions again. I was thrilled when Sam and his family showed up. I began answering the telephone, which was ringing. A short time later I turned the phone over to Brenda. My cell phone had rung twice and I needed to answer it.

I called Mike at the farm and he answered it on the first ring. It sounded as if a real party was going on back home. He told me there were over fifteen hundred folks there and they were all having a party. They had had their first day of racing that morning and had finished just before the big race came on. He wanted me to tell Spunky he was proud of him and to tell our girl she had ridden a great race. I thanked him and told him I'd be home by noon. I told him I was shipping my mare home. She would be there tomorrow evening. He told me he'd have a stall ready and waiting. I hung up my phone and went to check on Light.

Sam came over and handed me a roll of bills. He was smiling and showed me a roll he had in his front pocket. Light had ended up going off at six to one and we had both done well.

Spunky and our folks showed up with Cassie a few minutes later. Cassie had had a national television company ask her to fly to New York and be on their television show on Monday morning. They would put her up for the weekend and fly her home after the show. I told her to go for it. I'd tape the show Monday morning. She told me she had asked for a copy of the race, as well as the two races she had ridden Thursday. The T.V. folks told her they would be delivered by nine the next morning to our barn. The television folks were waiting for Cassie's answer and when she told them yes they all loaded into a large car and left for Spunky's place so she could get her bag.

The party at the barn went on for a while. Sam and Brenda went out and came back with all sorts of sandwiches and deserts. Some of the big barns would have had a black tie dinner. We had a picnic, and it was enjoyed by everyone. Folks from all of the barns showed up and wished Spunky and Sam good luck on the upcoming races. It was wonderful to see Spunky having such a good time. I only hoped that someday I might be as lucky.

When things finally began to settle down, I got to see the cup that had been presented to Spunky and Sam for winning the race. Sam was going to have another made to go in his and Brenda's new home. That was when Brenda let everyone know it would go right next to the baby bottles. She and Sam were going to have a baby. Jen was jumping up and down. She was thrilled at the idea of having a new brother or sister.

Sam was proud of his wife and daughter. It had indeed been a perfect day. When all the folks finally left, Spunky and Patty and I sat down and had a talk.

"Bill, if Light seems okay day after tomorrow, I'm going to take him to the next race in the series."

"Spunky, that would be the thing to do. It's a shorter race and he didn't hurt himself any today. I think you may have a horse that can win all three of the races. It would be the first time that's been done in a while. Spunky, he would be worth more money than you have ever dreamed of having. You and Patty could fix your place, just the way you wanted it done."

"I know Bill, but if anything goes wrong with him I won't run him. I just couldn't do that to him. I owe him too much."

Spunky had hired two security guards for the next three nights. Freddie and I each would get a good night's sleep. We were up and had the morning chores done when Spunky arrived. We'd bathed Light, and Freddie was walking him when Spunky arrived.

We had coffee and doughnuts that he had picked up on the way in. He and Patty had watched the news and had seen the rerun of the race and the trophy presentation.

Cassie called me from New York and was very excited. She was in a huge fancy room in some huge hotel and was being treated great. The television folks were going to send someone over and give her a tour of the city. I told her to buy a camera and take plenty of pictures. She said she would and to be sure and watch the show on Monday. I handed the phone to Spunky and listened while he and Cassie talked. Our life was good and only looked to get better. Maybe not as exciting, but good.

The disc of the races arrived just before Sam and his family arrived. I told Spunky and Freddie goodbye and we left for the airport. I hated to leave, but yet I was ready to go home.

CHAPTER 39

When we arrived home a couple of reporters was waiting. Brenda and I waited while Sam handled the interviews. She and I were both smiling when he finally got loose from the reporters.

"Folks, let's go home. I'm tired."

When they dropped me off at the house I sat my bag down on the porch and walked up to the barn. Mike met me at the door. Everything seemed to be in order except for the big tent he said would be gone this afternoon. He said he had been taking the colts out every day with our pony horse and they seemed to be doing fine. I told him to come down to the house and I'd show him the disc with all three of the races on it.

He was tickled that my mare had won. After he saw Slinker's race he was really impressed. Of course he had seen the Derby race, but had missed a bunch of the extra things because he had been so busy. He handed me the receipts for the weekend and I was shocked to say the least. He explained they had charged a dollar a car and a four dollar entry fee for the races. Everyone who came just to see the big race had got in free. We also got a dollar from every win picture and ten percent of the concessions his friend ran at the races. Mike was doing all right for us.

Mike said I should get some rest, he and Carlo who would be back shortly would do the evening chores. I did just that. I got a hot bath and stretched out on the bed. I woke up in time for the news, weather and sports. I watched the interview with Sam from the airport. Sam was really quite good at the interviews. A short clip let everyone know Cassie would be on the major morning show at seven the next morning.

I got up and went to bed. Chores would come early.

In the morning, I helped the boys finish chores and then rushed back to the house. I sure didn't want to miss the interview with Cassie. When the program came on I had a big cup of hot chocolate and was ready.

The host of the show said that he had a very special guest. He introduced Cassie as the Darling of the Derby and the picture that had appeared in the local Kentucky paper appeared on the screen. Cassie was blushing when the camera panned onto her.

The interview continued.

"My guest today is Miss Cassie Morgan. For those of you who don't know Miss Morgan was the jockey who rode Gray Light to the win Saturday in the Derby. We were fortunate enough to have her as a guest today to hear her unique story. Miss Morgan, how does it feel to ride a horse in one of or the biggest horse race of the year, and win?"

"Ray, it feels wonderful. Just to have a mount in the race is something I'll never forget."

"But to win the race, how did that feel?"

"It was the most wonderful thing in the world. To be my age and to come from nowhere, so to speak. It makes it even more special. There are jockeys who have been riding for years who never get a chance to ride in the Derby. Not because they are not good enough, but because the folks they work for never have a horse of Light's quality. Mr. and Mrs. Davis, who bred Grey Light have been in the business for years and never had anything like him."

"How did you become his jockey?"

"When Mr. Davis brought Gray Light to the track he was somewhat of a problem child. Mr. Davis hired Bill Patton as his assistant trainer and Bill took over the breaking of Gray Light. In a couple of weeks Bill had Gray Light eating out of his hand so to speak."

"Bill was too heavy to ride Gray Light in any of his races and suggested to Mr. Davis that he let me ride him. The rest is history."

"This Mr. Patton sounds like someone sort of special."

"Oh he is, Ray. He's one of the finest hands with a young horse I've ever seen. He has a new training center back in Texas and will have colts from all over the country to break and condition this fall. Even a bunch from Kentucky will be there."

"I seem to get the feeling, there might be something between you and this Mr. Patton."

"We're engaged and will be married just as soon as school is out."

"What college do you all attend?"

"Ray, we're not in college. We'll graduate from high school in a few weeks."

"High school? Good Lord, Miss Morgan. How old are you?"

"Seventeen, Ray. I'll be eighteen in two weeks."

"Excuse me Miss Morgan, but this is a bit unreal. A couple of teenagers, from a small town. A horse no one had ever heard of, come to the Derby and upset all the big boys. It's unheard of."

"We know it is, Ray. But you have to understand. It happens more than you realize. When Gray Light began to show signs of being something special Mr. Davis began to get offers to buy him. Every time he won another race there were more offers and they kept going up. Mr. Cooper, who is like family to us, bought half interest in Light so Mr. Davis could keep Gray Light and go on with him. A little trainer can't afford to keep a horse of Gray Light's quality because you never know when they will break down and be worth nothing. They simply can't afford to keep them. The folks with money buy them and the little man is never heard of again."

"I'd never thought of it like that, but I can see what you mean. What do you think Gray Light's chances are in the next two races?"

"Well Ray, he's not been outrun yet. Mr. Davis will have him ready and Mr. Patton will keep him happy for me. I'm looking forward to the next two races."

The interview ended and I took the disc out of the machine. I ran out the back door and got into my truck. I didn't want to be late for school. When I arrived, I thought they must be having a fire drill. Everyone was outside.

Then two of the students, raised a banner saying "Congrats Bill."

It was wonderful. I told everyone thanks, and then went to my class. Three weeks from tonight and I would graduate. I was ready to get it over with. Besides, if Light were to win again I'd want to be in New York with Spunky the week before the race.

When I got back to the farm I asked Mike if he knew of a boy we could hire to help me with the horses the fall.

"There is one, Bill. He's new out here and is having to ride the colts the other boys don't want. He seems to be a pretty good hand. That's him out there now trying to get on that half broke colt."

I watched as the young man tried to get on the colt. The owner had his hands full just trying to hold onto the rank colt. Some how the young man managed to get on the colt I have no idea. When he was suddenly on the colt, the colt bolted towards the trainer who was knocked down and turned the colt loose. The next few moments were something to see. The colt dropped his head and began to buck.

The young man clamped his legs and attempted to get the colts head up. I grabbed the reins of our pony horse and swung into the saddle. The colt began to slow down in his bucking and took off across the pasture. I was right behind the colt and had the gelding running full out. Before the colt could reach his stride, I grabbed the near side rein and began to pull the colt into a circle.

The colt was still full of himself and tried to get away. I got enough of the rein to take a turn around the saddle horn. When I finally got control of the colt the young man thanked me.

"Let's get this colt back to his owner. I'd like to talk to you about a job riding broke horses."

"You're Mr. Patton, aren't you?"

"I'm Bill Patton, and I still want to talk to you about a job."

"Mr. Patton, I'll sure enough listen. These green broke colts make a feller think about how he wants to make a living."

We returned the colt to his owner. The young man hopped off and began to remove his saddle. The trainer still wanted him to gallop his colt.

I thought he had. Half way across my pasture.

The trainer didn't want to pay the young man for his efforts but due to the fact I was there, he paid. I started back to the barn with the young man walking beside me. I found his name was Jim Slaton and he had been raised a hundred miles or so south. His father had been a ranch foreman for a small spread down there and he had been breaking the colts for the ranch for a couple of years. He figured he could make a lot more money, riding colts at the track than he could working on the ranch. Lately he was beginning to question his decision. He found it was a tough job getting rides from trainers who already had a jock they used regularly.

I told him what I could pay to start and if he worked out what I would pay him. He was more than willing to go to work for me. I was happy to have him, that afternoon he got his first ride on a broke thoroughbred.

To say he was happy would be an understatement. I worked a colt by him and coached him as we went along. He listened and took my directions well. He had good hands and stayed off the colt's head once he settled down and went to work. We worked the rest of the colts and by the time we were finished he was doing a great job.

"Jim, you just got yourself a raise. We work the colts every day after the other folks leave. But I expect you to be here earlier and learn everything you can from Mike and Carlo. I'll be taking the colts north to Raton in another few weeks and if you continue to improve I'll want you to go along."

"Mr. Patton, I'd be thrilled to go along with you."

"I'll get you a license and you may be able to pick up a few rides on the side. As you probably know Cassie Morgan will be riding most of my colts."

"Oh, I understand. I'll be thrilled to work with her. I'm sure I can learn a lot from her."

"I'm sure you can. She's a great jock. She just seems to have the ability to know when to let her horses run. Study everything she does and ask her questions if you don't understand something. She'll be more than glad to help you."

We finished working the colts and I went to work on my books. I was playing catch up after all the time I'd been gone. I'd just finished an hour or so later when my cell phone rang. Cassie was in Dallas and would be home in another two hours. I told her I'd be at the airport to meet her.

I cleaned up and took her truck to the truck stop and filled her tanks with fuel. I drove out to the airport and began to wait. I was twenty minutes early but it didn't matter. I just wanted to see Cassie.

When I walked into the airport terminal I was shocked to see a banner hanging across the gate entrance. "Welcome Home Cassie." There were two reporters waiting for Cassie to return. When her plane landed I stood back and watched as a television crew began filming her arrival. The interviews were finally done and Cassie came running to me. The kiss I got was what I'd been waiting for. My future wife was home and I was thrilled.

I carried Cassie's bags outside and listened while she told me all about her trip to New York. When we got to the house Cassie called her folks and told them she would be home soon. She had presents for Mike, Carlo and me. The boys were thrilled just to have her home. I told her about hiring Jim and was going to call the brothers to come out and extend the barn.

We discussed our new home and how folks had reacted to Light winning the Derby. Cassie had a couple of interesting stories about the people in New York. They were thrilled that someone other than a Kentucky bred had won the Derby. They were looking forward to seeing him come to New York for the final race of the series.

I kissed Cassie goodbye and watched as she went down the driveway for one of the last times. We'd be married in three more weeks and I was more than ready. We had another race before she would become my wife.

I had no idea how or what the future held for us but together we'd be together and that was all that mattered. The little man had won. I'd not been the man but it had been my second father and Cassie and I had been a part of it. We'd go north with a new string and pray maybe in our lifetime we'd have a Gray Light, too.

THE END

978-0-595-48537
0-595-48537-5

Printed in the United States
201484BV00002B/193-222/P